Jameson Hotel

The Dark Suite Series
Parts Four, Five & Six

Aven Jayce

Mirror Call Press

Jameson Hotel

SECOND EDITION, MAY 2016

A&M Michigan Editing
Cover Image © Andrey Ushakov /Dollar Photo Club
Cover and Book Design by Triple J Marketing
Published by Mirror Call Press

Published and printed in the United States
ISBN 978-0990498582

www.facebook.com/AvenJayceAuthor

Welcome back to the JAMESON. Please remember, this HOTEL contains strong language, explicit sexual content, violence, drugs, and murder...

... plus a touch of humor.

PART FOUR

STARTING OVER

"Talk to me, Jack. What can I do to help?"

I catch sight of my son's pale face and tear-stained cheeks. I haven't seen him eat in three days, and I doubt he's slept much since his mother committed suicide. She'd been fighting an aggressive form of cancer for a year and the last three months have been hell, for her and my son.

People will likely say she took the easy way out, that she gave up and didn't finish the fight, but that's fucking bullshit. Her body and mind were dog-tired and she wasn't going to last much longer. I knew it was over when she called two weeks ago to discuss arrangements for our son. Years of accusations, calling each other bitch and cocksucker ended with that call. I flew out to Philly immediately.

Fuck, she was only thirty-eight, but looked more like eighty when I arrived. It was the right thing for her to do. She wanted to end her life before the cancer finished eating her alive, but nothing is going to comfort my kid. Nothing.

"Your things will arrive in a few days. I'll help you get settled and take you to register in a school. I heard the local high school's decent, but I'm fine paying for a private school. Of course, that's your choice. Either way, it will be good for you to get into a routine once you unpack. The longer you sit around and do nothing, the harder it'll be to get out of your depression... psychologists are an option too, if you think you need one."

He stares out the window of my Tacoma, gazing at the mountainous landscape as we drive from the airport to the hotel. This is a massive change for him, not just losing his mother, but the environment as well.

He grew up in Vegas and was still getting acclimated to Philadelphia when this shit happened. Now, he has to be uprooted for a second time from his friends, familiar places, and my ex-wife's family—moving out of a large city and into my isolated hotel in the woods. He could've stayed close to Philly and lived with his grandparents, and I'm still surprised by his decision to move here. Then again, he knows his grandparents would want him home each night by six, in bed by nine, and up bright and early every Sunday morning for church. That's no life for a sixteen-year-old. I'd choose a bastard father over that lifestyle any goddamn day.

"The holidays are upon us and I just had a thirty-foot tree and lighted garland installed in the lobby. White lights line the exterior paths and drive, plus there's—"

"Shut the fuck up."

At least he finally opened his mouth. "I know you're hurting more than you ever have, but—"

"Do you *not* understand what 'shut the fuck up' means?" He flashes a repulsed look; his face red and fists

2

clenched, sitting close to me in the truck, yet so detached from my life.

I absorb his words, nod, and try to stay calm while he puts on his headphones. What the fuck am I gonna do with this kid? Shit, what the fuck are Jules and I going to do with him in my suite, within earshot of our bedroom?

"Jack." I pull the damn headphones off his head. "We need to talk, or I'll talk and you listen, but snubbing me when you're two feet away isn't going to happen, not anymore. You're in my life now, and we should—"

"Not for long."

"What the fuck do you mean, *not for long?* You need to finish school before you get any ideas in your head about taking off somewhere on your own."

"I don't have to do shit."

An exaggerated sigh escapes my mouth. I know he's hoping for a shitload from his mother's estate, but insurance companies aren't going to pay out a fucking dime after the coroner writes 'suicide' as the cause of death. The house and other belongings go to her parents, not my son. He's unaware of that for now. I'll tell him after his things arrive so he has some form of comfort within arm's reach, something to reassure him that all is not lost.

He'll get his college tuition paid for, the basics that he needs, but not a large sum of cash. My ex was smart in setting that up with her family. She knew he'd take off the moment he had enough money to live on his own... he still will, but I don't expect that to happen for some time, maybe years. He's only got three grand in his bank account, not enough for a kid his age to survive for long. And he knows my motto when it comes to money. *What goes out must come back in.* You can't keep spending without replenishing the pot.

"I'll get you a ski pass for the rest of the winter. My friends own one of the resorts in town. Good guys. I'll ask them what days kids your age hang out on the slopes."

"I don't need my dad making friends for me."

He turns up his music, filling the truck with a bass so loud I can hear every beat coming from the device around his neck.

"You're old enough to get your driving permit in California, but don't expect a license for another year and a half unless you take driver's ed. I'm fine with you getting the permit, *only* if you get a work permit too... if you're gonna drive, you're gonna work. You can shadow my pool boys a few days a week... and don't fucking roll your eyes at me either. I'm being a good guy here so don't... what... what the fuck is that look for?"

"A good guy? Are you in denial?"

"I want you to be happy," I say, raising my voice.

"Then let me do my thing and leave me the fuck alone until I can figure out how the hell to get out of this mountain shithole. You and mom had no right to call my friends' parents and insist they not take me in. That should've been *my* choice, not yours, or hers. It was a complete stab in the back as far as I'm concerned. I could've lived in my friend Dave's basement for years, but then his parents changed their minds. What the fuck? What did you say to them? And I'm given a choice between your hotel and grandpa's fucking cow farm? Jesus. That's not a choice. I got screwed."

"You did, I'm not denying it. Life sucks. Now, you can either put one foot forward and make the best of it or be a miserable fucker and see where it gets you."

"Yeah, that's right, I might end up owning a hotel in the middle of Bumfuck, California, sticking it to some fourteen-year-old, while living off my daddy's porn money."

My nostrils flare as I turn onto the hotel drive and slam on the brakes. "Not another fucking word about my life or my fiancé! Show some respect to every person here, and that goes for my guests and employees too. This is a place of business, not some freakin' carnival!"

He responds with a harsh laugh.

"I mean it, or you'll find yourself at a boarding school."

"Is that a threat, fuckwad?"

I wish he'd flinch at my raised hand. Damn, this kid. In all honesty, a good smack is exactly what the little bastard needs.

"I can't wait for my sword collection to get here. You won't say shit like that to me once it arrives."

"It's not coming. Your grandparents will send it out when you turn eighteen."

"Fuck you!" He opens his door and kicks my truck before heading toward the woods.

"Get back here!" I shout. My dress shoes sink into the deep snow as I follow him into the pines. He's quick, but I know my property well, and he doesn't stand a chance of getting away from me in this forest. "I'm right behind you." I pant, close to reaching his coat. "Running away is what little kids do. Stop and talk to me like a man."

"I *am* a man!" He turns and plants a harsh kick into my abdomen, only to have his foot grabbed and his body flipped. He lands on his stomach in a gasp.

"Okay, tough guy." My hand grips the belt loop of his jeans and he's lifted like a piece of luggage. His arms and legs swinging in a continuous thrashing motion as we walk back to the truck. "Enough!" I set him down and open the passenger side door.

"One morning you'll wake up and I'll be gone!" His high-pitched voice echoes throughout my property. "I need to figure out where... who..." His words sound like a warped record, rising, falling, fast, then slow until the anguish is too much for him to bear.

My son just turned sixteen and is at odds with himself, trying to act like a man, physically starting to look like one, but emotionally still a boy attempting to comprehend death. That's one of life's greatest disappointments at any age. And now his hatred over his living situation is replaced with extreme sorrow. "I don't have any... my friends are gone! My mom..."

His lower lip trembles as he punches my chest in a sobbing rage. "I can't believe you didn't go to the funeral! You stood outside in the fucking parking lot! You bastard!"

"I couldn't," I whisper, pulling him into a tight embrace. "I went earlier when no one was around, but your mom's family wouldn't appreciate—"

"I saw you standing by your rental car smoking dope. Everyone saw you, Dad." His words are muffled against my chest as he fights to escape my arms.

"Shh, I'm not letting you go, buddy. You can swear and beat the hell out of me all you want, but my way of doing things is always the right way. You should know that by now. I paid my respects in private, spoke to your grandparents in private, and that was all I could do. But from this point forward, I'm going to make sure you have a decent life."

"Fucker."

There's a loud click, he exhales a grunt, and I feel a sharp burning sensation in my side.

"What the fuck did you just do?" I step back and touch the warm blood under my coat. His face turns pale and his trembling hand drops the bloodstained blade, painting the snow a deep red.

"First time?" I ask with a fake smirk, about to go ballistic on his ass. "Get in the fucking truck!" I force him inside, slam the passenger side door, and pick up the knife. It's one of mine; he must've found it in my glove box when I was putting the luggage in the back.

He keeps his head low while we continue down the drive to the garage—his hands still a shaky mess, his breathing quick, and his chest trying to tame his sporadic, heaving sobs.

I'm torn whether I should follow a societal norm and have him put away, someplace where he can get professional help, or praise him for stabbing me.

He mumbles a half-assed apology while taking his bag from the truck and heading for the stairwell, leaving me to carry three bags with a gash in my side.

"An apology means nothing to a man who's been stabbed," I say, following close behind. "And remember, if you weren't my son, you'd already be dead... stop rolling your eyes at me, damn it! I'm pissed, Jack."

"Mark!"

"Hey, princess." I drop the luggage, watching Jules race down from the bedroom and into my arms. She's wearing shorts in the dead of winter, on purpose, showing off her clean-shaven, tanning-bed bronzed legs. "Nice outfit." I bite her lip and tug her closer for a warm kiss before slipping my hand under her shirt. Her tits brush against my chest and her pussy rubs into my dick. "You look fuckable," I say in my softest voice, not wanting my son to hear. "But I'm in the middle of something... give me five minutes."

Jack groans as he takes a Coke from the fridge. "What room am I in?"

Jules joins him in the kitchen, giving him a hug and offering words of comfort for his loss. He's only met her once, last fall, and I'm surprised when he doesn't back away... I guess it really is just me.

"This situation is far from over. Get your ass

upstairs."

"What?" He acts like nothing happened.

I take off my coat in haste, pitching it across the room before gripping the back of his neck.

"What's going on? And why are you bleeding? Did you get yourself into another *situation*?" she asks.

He's pulled upstairs, through my bedroom, and into the bath with Jules close behind. She's confused, but not surprised. I take out a small medical kit, keeping him confined in the process.

"Stop struggling. This is serious."

"What are you gonna do to me?"

I hold a small needle between my teeth and unbutton my shirt to examine the wound. "You fucking did this, now you're gonna fix it." He winces when I open the gash, wanting to see how deep and wide it is. "About four stitches," I say, threading the needle.

"Hell no, I won't."

"You did, and you are. If you're man enough to stab a guy, then you're man enough to do a stitch job. Learn a skill, son."

"Dad," he whines like a toddler, regressing thirteen years in order to get his way, only that shit never works with me.

"Mark, don't make this worse than it actually is. I'll stitch it for you," she says.

"No. This is about consequences for his actions. Besides, I could stitch it myself if I wanted to." With her hand on her waist, I can sense she's about to call me a hypocrite. "Don't," I caution. "He's doing this." She takes the needle and heats the end with the lighter from my dresser as I clean the wound, using a washcloth, soap, and water. I hold the wet cloth over the cut until she's finished and my son's ready. "Pinch the skin, only a little... and gently... stick the needle in vertically. Don't drive it straight inside, do it at an angle. Not too deep, but deep enough so the flesh doesn't tear when I move. I don't want the stitches to come undone. You understand? Are you ready?"

Jules warns, "Be nice. Don't leave him with such a horrible memory."

"Excuse me?" I remove the washcloth and motion toward the gash. "*This* is a horrible memory. He needs to see it and repair it so he feels compassion for his victim. That way the ghastly image in his head will be replaced with pretty fucking butterflies."

"Oh, I get it. You've made the decision to stop the succession of the Jameson family? You believe what he did was wrong? I say boo-fucking-hoo. If he stabbed you, then you slipped up, not him."

Jack makes a quick turn, shocked by her words.

"This is one of those moments we've discussed. Are you going to be proud of him for being like you? Or punish him and hope he turns out to be different? Forcing someone to change never works, remember?"

A drop of water from the washcloth hits the ceramic floor every few seconds. *Pat... pat... pat.* Jack looks at the two of us, his head turning back and forth to see who's going to speak next. We stand in silence, my cock wanting to slap her face, but my brain surrendering like a pussy. Everything always comes down to cock and pussy.

"Look into my eyes," I demand, peering over my son's head and at her face. "You wanna get bitch-slapped?" I say, half-jokingly.

"Do you wanna get bitch-slapped, knocked out, and wake up with a soda can shoved up your ass?" She crosses her arms, apparently *not* joking, but her words are too comical for me not to crack a smile. "First, stitch your own stab wound. What the fuck did you say to piss him off anyway?"

"Dang." He raises a brow.

"And we're not hiding our love for one another from him, or anything else for that matter. It's unhealthy. This is who we are, how we speak to one another, and yes, Jack." She looks down at him. "The circumstances that led you here suck, and I'm sorry you lost your mom, but we're thrilled to have you in the hotel. I mean that... although you're going to have to deal with some badass shit that Mark better be open about. Living at the Jameson isn't going to be easy, not at first, but it will be worse if we walk around on eggshells trying to please you... change you..." She points her finger at my wound. "Or act like we're a couple of virgin unicorn fairies who don't appreciate a good stabbing."

"What the fuck?" He turns to me. "Dad?"

I'm trying not to get an erection from her words. Leave it to Jules to make me fully understand that at this moment, Jack's either in my life one hundred percent, or not at all. Fuck, she's the best.

"Fine." I exhale. "I'll try a different tactic. What she means is I shouldn't be upset by your actions, considering the things I've done in my past. Whether you like it or not, a part of me is inside you... cool it... put an end to the rolling eyes and unpleasant faces. Pay attention. You were timid and wussed out when you felt the blade cut into my flesh. You wanted to stab me, but backed off before any serious damage was done. You either have to kill or be killed."

"Ugh," she objects. "You're really bad at this."

"Well what the fuck? Then you talk, little Miss Hotshot." I turn to my son. "And you stitch."

His hands continue to shake as he pierces my skin, following my directions to the best of his ability. He looks up for approval and I toss a hand gesture his way to hurry things along.

"Mark, if you want some parenting advice," she says. "Do the opposite of what your dad would've done in this situation and you'll get it right."

"Tie a knot and clip the end," I command while ignoring her comment. "That's good. Perfect. How do you feel?"

There's a long pause, a forceful swallow, and a quivering hand setting the needle on the counter before he speaks.

"Lonely," he whispers.

I stare at our reflections in the mirror. His medium-length, blond hair is greasy from not showering for three days and dark circles outline his blue eyes. Add a foot to his height and another sixty pounds and I'd be looking at my clone. "Jack." I lift his chin. "I'm here for you, in spite of all the shit you've thrown my way, and besides the fact you were a dumbass last year and took off with a bundle of cash... no matter what you do and how much you hate me, I'll be here for you. But I have to say, loving you would be a hell of a lot easier if you didn't jab me with a knife. Got it?"

Jules rubs antibiotic ointment over the stitched flesh as I continue holding his chin, waiting for an answer. She positions her head between us, looking closely at the sutures before covering them with a bandage.

"Good as new. Next time we'll use duct tape."

He smiles at her playfulness; the first I've seen his face light up in ages. And she seems comfortable with kids, the type of stepparent who's bold and in charge, but considerate of everyone's feelings. Her behavior might be a pleasant change for him compared to the usual frustration and anger he experiences with me. She'll end up being the good cop while I continue being bad. Good, bad, badass, whatever... "*all is well in my hotel as long as I'm bringing in money and can retain an exquisite pussy to fuck.*"

"What are you mumbling? Did you say *exquisite pussy*? Mark, put your shirt back on and stop daydreaming. Let's get him set up so we can relax. I haven't seen you in forever."

Jack hauls out of the room like a peregrine falcon,

performing a stairwell dive to clutch his prey... and to a sixteen-year-old, that's his can of Coke and whatever other scraps he can find in my fridge. "I'm not staying in this suite while the two of you fuck," he says.

His back is turned when I reach the bottom of the stairs and I feel like I'm talking to a wall. "And I'm not discussing my sex life with you. Nothing's going to happen when you're around anyway... and if you're hungry, you can eat in the restaurant or order room service. I don't have much besides crackers and bread in here."

"What room am I in?"

"Your room is right up those stairs." I point to the second floor guest bedroom, comprehending his request, but worried about placing him in his own suite.

"You have like two hundred rooms." His high-pitched voice is back. "It's no different than if you owned a mansion and my bedroom was on the opposite end of the house from yours."

"It's completely different."

"No, it's not," Jules says, joining us on the main floor. "He doesn't know anyone in this town, he has no car, no friends to sneak out with..." She opens a drawer in the kitchen and hands him a key card. "And if he was going to run away he'd already be gone, besides, it's obvious he's in love with money as much as you are. He won't disappear until he saves up enough cash, but hopefully by then we'll have won him over. Right, Jack?" She bumps his arm and he nods in approval, flashing a *listen to your girl* grin my way.

"Dad, if I can stay home alone, I sure as fuck can stay in a hotel room by myself. Pretend I'm in my bedroom, which will be the truth."

I rub my forehead, wishing I could eradicate the last week of arguments and events from my mind. This is bullshit. Total fucking bullshit. "I don't think you're stable enough to be alone."

"Oh, screw you." He grabs his bag and walks out.

"Jack, wait!"

I scowl at the sound of the slamming door. My kid's gonna swipe that card in every reader until he sees a green light and hears a click.

"What the fuck... now what?" I take a pile of mail from the kitchen counter and toss it into my office doorway. The envelopes scatter along the floor and Jules gives me a pissy look.

"At his age he needs a little freedom. Trusting him will bring him closer to you."

"That's crazy."

"Calm the fuck down and stop pacing. What are you so furious about anyway?" She pours me a shot of bourbon and I toss it back then hold out the glass for a second.

"He stabbed me, remember?"

"Yes, Mark, I remember," she says in a condescending tone. "It's possible you deserved it." Her fingers do a provocative waltz down my chest, tumbling to my zipper where I watch her hand disappear inside my jeans. "Not hard for me yet?"

"Jumping right in? No conversation, no nothing? You just wanna fuck? Is that all I'm good for?"

She finger fucks her mouth with an expression of lust. Very amusing. I've missed her, especially moments such as this when I know there's no turning back from a hard and sweaty fuck.

She licks her hand and coats my shaft, bringing it toward her in short jerks. It only takes a few seconds to get erect, pre-cum and all... and watching her mouth open ever so slightly... mmm, what a tease.

"I'm not going to give you some pansy-ass 'I love you' sensual bullshit fuck, like the one before I left on my trip. It's been over a week since I filled your pussy with my cum and—"

"Dad?" Jack opens the door, waving the key card.

"Fuck." I pull back and zip. "What?"

"Ah, fuck! That's sickening!" He emits an exaggerated gag and turns swiftly around. "Hurry up and tell me what room I'm in before I pass out in horror. Fuck, that was nastiest thing I've ever..."

"Sorry," she mouths to me.

"... and I'll never, ever, ever, be the same! The suite... tell me what suite! Hurry, so I can get outta here!"

"It's the one directly on the opposite end of the hotel," she says.

"The big one?" He turns back in higher spirits. "Hell, yeah." The slamming door is repeated as he rushes out.

"You gave him the dark suite?"

"Why do you call it that? If anything, you're living in

a dark suite. That one's pretty. I had housekeeping get it ready for him and it's packed with food—teenage boy food. I also left an iPad on the counter. Let him shower and relax for the night. If he's anything like the rest of your family, he's desperate for some time away from you... Mark, stop pacing. You always wanted him here."

"Yeah, for a weekend."

"You sought custody at one point."

"Only because I didn't want my ex to win. It was a lot different when I could send him back to Philly."

"Oh, so you're one of those?"

"No, I'm *not* one of those. You know I love him, but his spoiled brat act needs to stop."

She laughs with a quick tilt of her head toward the ceiling. "What? Who's the spoiled brat around here?"

"Don't start with me, I've had a miserable time away from my hotel, my knives, and my woman."

She crosses her arms. "Really, in that order?"

"Yep, my weed too. Good thing I was able to connect with an old friend from high school who's a pothead. I never would've made it through the week without—"

"Stop pacing!"

"You're right. We need to fuck."

She laughs as her body's lifted over my shoulder.

"God, I'm glad I went on the pill. Hey, careful you don't trip carrying me up these stairs... Mark! Slow down! The last thing either one of us needs is a broken neck... ouch, watch my foot on the doorframe."

"Strip, spread 'em, and call out 'Mark' in your

sluttiest voice so I know you're enjoying my brutish attack."

"I do enjoy your—"

"Not fast enough." A baby powder perfume fills the air as I yank open her shirt, sending the buttons of her blouse bouncing onto the hardwood floor. They mimic the cascading snow outside my windows, covering the ground in frozen white dots. "Don't waste time with a response, just do it."

"Okay, Mr. Prick." Her shorts, underwear, and bra drop to the floor and she struts to the bed in a drama queen runway walk, her ass deliberately taunting me before positioning herself for play.

"Nice. You looking for a bitch fuck?" She's on all fours with her ass held high. "Are you giving me a choice between the high road or the low?"

She tries to nod, but one hand's already wrapped around her hair while the other's unzipping my jeans. "Fuck yeah, I'm free from solitary confinement. Welcome back, big boy."

"Already with your dumbass comments?"

"Quiet. I'm excited. We haven't been apart from one another since we first got together last fall, and my time away has left me craving you even more. I've missed being able to admire your face and pussy each day. And heads-up, I didn't beat off while I was in Philly. I've been saving a big cum shot all for you."

"Because?" She laughs.

I release her hair so she can relax.

"Because." My eyes close, hearing her pleasurable sigh as I possess her pussy. "Because." I take a slow ride in and clench my jaw, feeling a heavy compression around my cock.

"Say it," she speaks affectionately. "Pleasure me with kind words before we fuck."

My weight shifts and she's pinned to the bed, my chest against her back and my arms next to her head. This position's her favorite—I can give her light kisses along her shoulder blades, ending with a tender tug on her neck.

"Whisper sweet words into my ear," she pleads. "Make me cum from your soft voice before you fuck me hard."

I sneak in a few ass-tightening thrusts, unable to control my need for her flesh.

"Pleassse," she repeats with a hiss. "Hold out for me."

My cock glides forward. I keep the position with curled toes and my arms wrapped around her chest. "You're adored." I kiss her ear. "I'm aware of everything you desire. I know when your nipples beg to be kissed, can sense when your body craves a slow tongue fuck, and can predict when you want my dick to glisten from your wet pussy."

She moans as I work my hips back and forth, her hand creeping underneath and resting over her clit.

"Move your fingers if it'll help."

"No," she whispers. "I simply want the pressure there... keep talking."

I bite her shoulder and hold her waist as she tries to

push against me.

"I bet you've been thinking about this all day. You daydreamed about my erect cock, caressed it in your hand, and lowered to your knees to suck me off. You love my dick in your mouth as much as it loves being there."

Another sweet moan fills my ears.

"But you love it even more when my cock is in your pussy." I place my hand behind her head and nudge forward, burrowing further inside. "I'm in charge, and I demand you follow my lead. Understand?"

"Yes," she says in a compliant voice, turning her head for a kiss. Our lips join briefly and I exhale, gliding faster as I begin...

"How many men did you imagine fucking while I was gone?"

She entertains me with a clever response, "Twenty-two... and they all looked exactly like you, only bigger."

I grin, kissing her upper arm as we fuck. "Did you make them... did you make *me* lick your pussy? Did my tongue swirl around your clit until your lips quivered and you could no longer breathe?"

"Yes." Her body tightens as I gift her a satisfying visual of getting eaten out. "I love to lick and suck every inch of you, rub your tits, and ride you until you cum." I replace her finger with my own, massaging her flesh as I speak. "I bet I fucked you hard in your fantasies. Did you picture me dragging my tongue along your sensitive clit and flicking your soft pussy lips?" My dick comes out and a finger goes in. "You feel me down there? I love you,

Jules. I want more."

The slow start is over. She gets flipped on her back, her legs pulled up, and my dick's rapidly inside.

"You okay to do this?" She touches the bandage covering my stitches.

"As long as my heart continues to beat, we'll continue to fuck. A couple of measly stitches won't keep my cock out of your pussy."

She smiles as I lean in, her lips wet on mine and tasting like strawberries, one of her favorite desserts... it's something I've missed, both the comfort of her lips and their taste.

Jules isn't flashy and she's not the type who needs to be the center of attention. Her natural beauty and confidence, along with the fresh scent of her skin will cause any man's head to turn. You can't help but marvel at her, and lucky me, I get to look, touch, and stick.

Her tongue swipes her lips as she peers at my dick. "You wanna lick it, don't you?" She nods, opens wide, and I dive in. "Yeah." I exhale. "Damn, sometimes I wish I had two dicks so I could enjoy your mouth and your pussy at the same time."

I can feel her smile as she sucks me off. Her mouth tight, head bobbing... and she loves to watch. Her eyes stalk my length as it glides in, then she looks at my chest and abs when I ride back. "You're such a good fuck, beautiful."

I'm serious when I say that. It's the biggest turn on when a woman, *my* woman, is open to anything and everything. And she lets me home my dick wherever I... fuck, I better stop before I cum.

"Wait... uh, slow." I slide out as her sly tongue maneuvers start, but she grabs my nuts and drags me back in. "Fuck, I'm close. Let me finish getting you off first."

She doesn't. Damn her, I'm gonna cum.

"Jules... not yet."

She turns her head with a smirk and I'm freed.

"Five more seconds and you would've had a mouthful."

"I like my fantasy men better. They'd cum then be up and ready to fuck a minute later."

"Silence." I pin her wrists by her side and storm over her. My groin rubs rhythmically against her clit as we continue to fuck.

"God, that feels amazing," she says. Her cheeks are flush... she's close... head's back... neck fully exposed... I feel it. She's cumming. "Mark." My hair's gripped tightly. "Yes!"

"Shit." My fingernails dig into her ass while my entire body begins a pursuit, causing the headboard to hit the wall. *Thwack. Thwack.* "Shit," I repeat in a heavy pant. "I'm..." *Thwack.* "Fuck!"

She cries out as her pussy spasms around my cock. *Thwack.* The headboard sounds like it's splitting in two. *Thwack.*

"Uh, Jules!" I call out.

Her hands streak down my back searching for something to grasp. She locks onto my shoulder then hauls me closer, needing my mouth to entomb her final screams. Damn, this is a good one.

Thwack. Thw-thwack.

The bed quiets, my lips part, and I whisper while I cum... "Good pussy brings you back to life after being responsible for death."

"What?" She sets her hands on my chest, trying to slow me down.

Did I say that out loud? Shit, I can't stop now. "Fuck." I draw out, watching the cum seep from her pussy and my cock. "Jules." I smile, opening her wide to watch more flow out. "That's superb."

"Don't," she says, closing her legs and sliding away. "I can't believe you just said that. Thanks for ruining our post-orgasm embrace, asshole."

She's angry. I always fuck up my words during my orgasms and now she doesn't know what to think.

"I say stupid things when I cum. That's not what happened."

"For fuck's sake, then why say it? Especially when we're in our best moment."

"I just told you..."

"Oh, I forgot, because you become a blithering idiot when all of your brains spurt out your dick. I get it." She dresses and stomps out of the room, annoyed by my... by what?

"What the fuck's your problem?" I call out after her.

I hear a bottle open and a glass slam on the counter after she tosses back a shot. She rushes upstairs and stands next to the bed, her arms crossed, foot tapping, brows furrowed like an evil witch.

"What?" I grin, lying back on the bed. "I only watched. She wanted to make sure no one found her before she was dead. She said her parents and Jack would've called 911 and her friends would've never agreed to stay by her side while she died."

"And she trusted you?"

"Yeah. That's one thing my ex trusted me with—death."

"Are you sure that's all you did?"

"What does it matter?"

"It matters if the person examining the body finds something else."

"They won't."

"No?"

I grab her legs and pull her to the bed, needing to smack her ass.

"Ouch! Stop it!" She lets out a yelp, kicking her legs like a frenzied cat held over water. "I want to make sure nothing bad will come of this."

"Thanks, but I'm invincible. Besides, I'm telling you the truth. I took the situation very seriously. She called to ask if I knew anything about assisted suicide, but got an earful for mentioning it over the phone. Her next call said she needed me to come out to help her with a few end-of-life decisions. I knew what she was asking based on the previous conversation. All I did was help her pick the right pills then stayed around until it was over. Nothing more."

"Who found her?"

"It doesn't matter."

"Let me guess, you left and let your son come across the body? Jesus, Mark. That's low, even for you. You certainly don't treat him well."

"Hey, I wasn't going to stick around and call it in, that's too suspicious."

"And Jack doesn't know you were there?"

"Of course not. And just so you know, I helped her die in a humane way and with dignity, no pain, that's it. It was her decision... if you had seen the state she was in, you'd understand. I'm sorry I ever mentioned it. Maybe it upset me more than I realized... just forget about it. It's over."

"I think we need to discuss things like this."

"Fucking let it go."

"You're impossible sometimes." She stands and opens our closet door, bringing out her tightest black dress and a pair of heels.

"Where are you going?"

"I told you two weeks ago I have a birthday celebration tonight."

"But I just got home." I scratch my nuts and sigh. "With Angie and Michelle?"

"Yep."

"Can I go?"

"Nope, ladies night."

"Can I be your stalker?"

She frowns, aware that I'm not kidding. "Don't

embarrass me like last time. Why don't you find some friends to hang out with? You could watch porn with them, or football, or something."

"Oh, that sounds like a good idea... no, really guys, that's not me fucking on that porn site."

She laughs and slips into the dress, pulls her hair back, and rolls on some deodorant. "I hope I don't smell like sex."

"Going to Miller's Pub again?"

"Don't follow me, Mark. I'm serious."

"I won't." *I sure as fuck will.*

She heads for the bathroom to put on a fresh coat of makeup, something I'll never understand. If I'm not invited, why does she have to look so damn hot? I'm sure Angie and Michelle won't be disappointed if she shows up without the mascara and lipstick.

"Why don't you throw on a sweater over that dress?"

I'm ignored.

"It's cold and snowy, I suggest you wear those heavy duty ski pants and some snow boots."

Still ignored.

"You sure I can't tag along?"

"You're pathetic." She exits the bathroom and walks over to the bed, planting a kiss on my cheek. My hand drifts under her dress, making sure she's wearing... fuck, she put on a thong.

"See ya, hot stuff."

"Remember, I own you!" I shout, watching her leave the room. "I'm Mark Jame—"

"I know, I know. I've heard it a million fucking times. I'm Mark Jameson, welcome to my hotel," she mocks. "You're an arrogant control freak, Mark. But I love you!"

"Don't steal my line!" I yell, left alone to gaze into the mirrored ceiling with my hands behind my head, a smirk on my face, and a bead of cum lingering on the tip of my dick.

"*I'm* Mark Jameson, and yeah, I love you to death, Jules... don't you ever fucking forget it."

LURKING

I can be good... sometimes.

In all honesty, no, no I can't.

The last girls' night out was a disaster. Jules had just moved into my suite, things were great... then I made the mistake of following her to the bar and sitting at the table directly behind her and her friends. They don't know me and she wants to keep it that way—says she's embarrassed by the age difference. Fuck, at least she wasn't serious. And it's not like I look old or anything, I still have the young, handsome face of a twenty-five- year-old.

Anyway, she noticed I was there and by her tight lips, damn, I knew she was going to beat my ass when she got home. Only she didn't... instead she packed her things and went back to her own suite. Took me an entire month to convince her to move back in.

I guess it didn't help much when I flirted with one of her friends at the bar—just as a joke—nothing would've happened. I'd be a fool to cheat on such an ideal woman. I was only trying to blend in with all the other assholes in the place, make it seem like Jules and I had never met, but I ended up pissing her off even more.

So here I sit, in my truck, in the lot behind the bar, waiting for a glimpse of my princess.

"Fweeeee. Phweeeep-phweep." I whistle, tapping the steering wheel. "Fuuuiit, fwee... uh, this is so fucking boring." I take out my cell in need of company, having a love-hate relationship with myself when I'm alone. I tap the screen, lean back, and wait...

"I'm busy, Mark. This better be important," Cove answers.

"Appease me just once by saying hello instead of 'I'm busy.'"

"Oh, did that piss you off?" he says sarcastically and hangs up.

"That won't do, Mr. Everton." I call him back.

"Fine. I'm listening. You've got one minute before Sophia hauls my ass out of the office and to the bar to greet our customers." He mumbles something about getting his number changed.

"I have a terribly important question."

"What?"

"I'm wondering why so many children's books are crude and disturbing?"

"Is there a reference to you in that remark?" he asks.

"Yep, knew you were going to say that. But seriously, think about *Watership Down* and *Billy Goats Gruff*."

"Speed it along. I'm at work."

"Another favorite of mine is about a dog trying to seduce a pussy. I can remember bits and pieces of the story from my childhood and how erotic it sounded."

"And this just happened to pop into your head, why?"

"I'm thinking about using a line from the story on Jules... tell me what you think."

"What? Are you seriously wasting my time with this shit?"

"Listen..."

In my bed sits Pussy Cat Puss, sunning herself today.
I'm the Gingerbread Doggy who comes prancing along. And with my Pussy I want to play.

The line deadens. I wonder if he hung up or just put down his cell.

Pussy says, "No, please go away," and slides further up on the bed.
I bark and I bite then lick my sweet Puss, saying, "Spread your twat for my big head to slay."

There's laughter from my end, but a feminine moan from the other.

"What are you talking about, Mark?" Sophia questions.

"Hey, sis. Children's books."

"A children's book would never be so vulgar. Spread your twat? Pussy? I don't believe it."

"Well, I made the last line up, but the rest is real."

"Cove's busy tonight, we have two private parties.

You want to talk to me instead? Is Jack okay?"

"Ja..." Oh, shit. I forgot my son's at the hotel. "Yeah, he's fine. He's settling into the guest suite, but the little prick knifed me."

"You probably deserved it."

"Why does everyone keep saying that?" I look up and see Jules' friend, Angie, taking a piss behind the bar. Snow lands on her head and a single light over the back door illuminates her face.

The lines for the women's restroom are always long at this place, and it's the norm for the bladder bursting, drunk chicks to end up behind the bar. Squatting in a parking lot, even on a cold, wintery night, is better than pissing oneself while waiting in line. And here she comes... my girl. Why must women piss in pairs? And how can they talk to one another when they're in full stream? It's so bizarre, something I can't help but watch.

"You there?"

"Sorry, yeah. All is well. You guys okay?"

"Well, Daxton fell off his bunk bed yesterday and..."

Most people would say, yes, we're good, but not my sister. She has to break into some drawn out story recounting every hour since we last spoke.

Angie fixes her skirt and rubs her crotch in an attempt to soak up the remaining urine dribbles before she kicks through the snow on her way back inside. I notice Jules copies the same maneuver after her friend disappears. Trying to keep her balance through the white, powdery drifts.

31

"... and Cove bought me a fantastic new dinnerware set for the holidays. You should see it. Oh my God, the plates are scarlet red and our names are inlaid in gold lettering..."

"Fuck."

"That's what I said. Fuck, it's dazzling..."

The dinnerware set has nothing to do with my vulgarity. It's the scene behind the bar. A full-bodied brute, twice Jules' size, is blocking the door. I can tell by her body language that she's not only uncomfortable, but also irritated. The fool better watch out, she can pack a punch.

"... and you should see our Christmas tree this year. The boys picked it out from a tree farm and they helped cut it down and decorate it. I have photos. I'll send..."

"Shit."

"... yep, holy shit, right? It's so pretty, Mark! Just wait 'til you..."

I toss my cell and race out of my truck as Jules arm is grabbed. She's hauled away from the door and into the darkness, losing a heel along the way.

"What the fuck?" I cradle my blade as my heart pumps wildly.

The icy pavement under the snow makes it impossible to attain a solid foothold and I can't run without falling on my ass. Damn. Damn. Slow and steady. Don't slip, keep the pace, you'll get to her.

I don't see her.

Must find her. Protect her. I'm gonna kill him.

"Jules!"

I hear a muffled noise then, "Bitch, you're dead," before a low distressing bellow. That wasn't her. Sounded like... like a monstrous end to a shithead's foul life.

Only the fucker's not dead. I follow the groans and find him in the snow, holding his dick and pining for help with a soprano wail. There's blood on his hands from an obvious stab wound and his pants are partway down. Asshole was getting ready to attack her.

"Help," he yelps like a seal. "Help me."

A gust of wind swirls the snow, dispersing our footprints. She's gone, and with the snow tumbling down and the moon blocked by thick clouds, there's no-way to tell which direction she took.

"Please, help me."

"Crap, buddy, what happened? Can you get up?"

"No." He pants. "Call... help."

"Hold tight. I'll get my truck and take you to the hospital."

I pretend to hurry away, slowing down once I'm out of view. I rub my hands, excited for a kill. Get the bastard into my truck; take him home, and play.

Jules made a critical mistake by leaving him alive, and we'll have to discuss that later, but I'll also thank her for making my night. I think I'll even be able to fuck again after I witness some well-deserved suffering. That's a sure erection-producing scene.

I drive down the alley, stopping a few feet from his curled up body.

"See if you can step up." I lift him toward the passenger side, guiding him into the seat. He flops forward, resting his head on his knees. "That's good, buddy, stay down. Get comfortable. You'll be feeling better in no time." I shut the door and smirk, taking a shovel out of the truck bed to remove the bloody snow off the ground. I pile it in the back then drive to the spot where Angie and Jules took a piss, hauling the yellow snow into the bed along with the heel that she lost. No evidence. No fluids. My father taught me that. Never leave behind any fluids that can be traced back to yourself or the victim.

A CR-V pulls into the lot and drives down the alley, replacing my truck tracks with its own. Perfect. Finished just in time. And when the bar closes and people pile out, there'll be no sign of my tire tracks over the numerous cars and footprints in the snow. If this is the last place this guy was seen, it will be a jumbled mess for the cops.

I start to drive toward the hotel with the guy falling in and out of consciousness. When he's awake, he repeats over and over how he's going to *kill the bitch*, and when he's passed out, I'm able to call Jules. She doesn't pick up, forcing me to leave a message.

"Hey. You didn't finish what you started. What gives? You okay? Bet you're angry I was there, but I'm taking care of your mess, so I better be rewarded. Get your ass home so we can talk."

Then I text her multiple times...

Worried. You okay?
Where are you?
Everything's good. Heading home.
Got your shoe.
Don't be scared.

I wonder if she freaked out. This is the first time she's used her blade, and when she felt the puncture or saw the blood, she may have been panic-stricken, just like my son. It doesn't come naturally to everyone, only the best of us.

"There yet? Pain. Help." The bastard moans.

"What's your name, buddy?"

"Lucky."

How ironic. I try not to laugh, but shit, Lucky? "I'm going to take good care of you, *Lucky*." I hit the remote for the garage and see Jules standing next to my workbench. With crossed arms, she embraces herself. It's been over a year since I've seen such a glum face on my woman. I recall this same expression of sadness when she told me the story of being attacked by that piece-of-shit, Roland.

She waits for the truck to come to a complete stop before walking cautiously to the passenger side. Our eyes meet through the window and I notice a tear on her cheek. Fuck, this has really affected her, probably stirred up a bunch of bad memories. I've only seen her cry twice in the past year.

Now I'm pissed. Men like this guy are the scum of the earth and should have a catheter shoved up their dicks, gasoline injected inside, and their junk set on fire.

I nod toward the moron bent over in the front seat, but she refuses to look. The downhearted stare... I can't stand to see her like this. I rush out, set to kill. Fuck this asshole for doing this to her.

Dragging the wounded hulk out of the truck and to the ground by his hair, I push his face into the concrete, flick open my blade, then pierce the back of his neck in a forceful drive. He swings one arm back, striking my abdomen, while his other hand claws at the concrete. A deep red appears and unites with his brown hair... brilliant. And I love it when they squirm.

I swear, a man who wastes his money taking a woman out for a fancy dinner doesn't know shit. This is free. It's stimulating. Sometimes it makes you laugh. And killing a man who fucked with your woman will get you laid faster than buying the lobster special at Sea Food Chalet.

"Scream like a baby." I spit and grin, watching him strain frantically for the back of his neck. A second later he feels his mutilated groin and sets his bloody hands back over his dick.

"Stop!"

And so it begins. My pal Lucky enters the great land of 'piss and panic.' I imagine urine flowing through a sliced cock can't be very pleasant, but I don't feel bad for the guy, after all, this *is* a torture session. Let's see... how much pain do I feel like inflicting before he takes his last breath?

I turn to Jules for my answer. When she emerges

from gloom and smiles again, I'll know it's enough.

Whoa, hello.

Her blade is clasped between her front teeth as she frantically wiggles her arms free from her winter coat. It's off, in a heap on the ground, and she's pushing me out of the way, moving in for an attack. The blade flickers in the fluorescent light as she impales his ass. Deliberately, she stabs the guy in the ass.

"Bitch!" He tries to roll, but it's too late. She's on his back, sending deep piercing thrusts into his flesh. Plunge in—pull out. Plunge in—pull out. "No! Oww!"

Hell, yeah. Give him a good knife fucking, but slow down.

"Take your time," I urge, wanting her to enjoy her first kill for as long as possible.

Five stabs, six... the bloodstains take on the pattern of the Big Dipper. Seven, eight... she's gone mad. I've never heard such carnal noises bursting from her mouth, not even when I'm eating her pussy. It's far more than a typical grunt and groan.

"Fucking cocksucker!" she shouts. "Aargh. Uh. Uh. Fuck. I hate you. I hate your fucking guts."

Bloody guts, I think, taking a step closer to admire the scene.

Eleven stabs... twelve. Damn.

"Calm and steady. You've got him, now enjoy it." She's not listening. "Jules, you could stab him fifty times and still have to wait for the pinhead to bleed to death. Remember what we've discussed, there're specific kill zones on the body. You have to—"

"Shut." *Stab.* "The fuck." *Stab.* "Up."

Is she talking to me, or the sack of shit?

"Back off," I mutter, bending down to finish the job with a quick slice of his jugular. He grabs his neck and kicks her off, spurting blood onto the floor. "This is a fucking mess."

I toss her a rag from my workbench so she can clean her blade. "I was doing just fine on my own." She sniffs, brushing the back of her hand across her wet cheeks. A smudge of blood is left behind, matching her smeared mascara.

"No, you became too emotional. And you fucked up by leaving him alive behind the bar. If he survived, he could've given your description to the cops. What the hell happened? Do you know him?" I'm drawn away from her as the guy starts to make the usual end of life gurgling sounds.

"I took off when I heard someone coming, and no, I don't fucking know him."

"Hush, I like this part. Let me listen."

His mouth opens, searching for a breath that never comes. The throaty noise reminds me of a garden hose when it's first turned on; a quick spurt of water juts out, there's a loud gush of air, a second spurt, the hose thrashes, then it goes limp and a steady stream of water flows.

"That someone was *me*. I was the person coming toward you, and this was all too fast," I criticize. "I didn't even have a chance to sing my troll song."

"Sing the damn song now." She puts her hands on her hips, aggravated that I'm more concerned about my ritualistic killing song than her.

I shake my head in disappointment. "I can't sing it now, it'd be like singing Happy Birthday after someone blows out the candles—the moment's over."

"Well, should I go out and find another guy to attack me?"

"Funny." I turn, taking her shoe out of the truck bed and tossing it by her feet. "I wanted your first time to be special, better than this, that's all. And we're supposed to fuck afterward, but I didn't get erect like I normally do."

Her head tilts, still holding her blade in her hand. "We can fuck when you're ready. Now, sing your song. You'll lose sleep if you don't."

With a deep exhale I watch the pool of blood growing in size. "*I'm a troll, fol-de-rol,*" I sing quietly, searching for his wallet. There's nothing of substance inside—just a license, a small amount of cash, a few credit cards, the norm. "Are you hurt?" I ask.

"No. I stabbed his dick before he had a chance to use it."

I nod and hum my song, stopping every so often to inquire about the night. "*I'm a troll...* you sure you don't know him?"

"No."

"Was he with anyone at the bar?"

"Another guy, around his age, but he wasn't there

when I went inside to say goodbye to my friends."

"You said goodbye with a missing shoe?"

"I said I lost it in a snowdrift, and I felt sick and needed to head home. They understood."

"You drunk?"

"Maybe."

I can smell the alcohol on her breath so she better fess up. She'll get spanked if she was driving drunk, but will get an even harsher ass smack if I catch her in a lie.

"Yes. I had a few drinks. But I'm not wasted."

I continue to stroll, circle, and hum, observing her emotional state while inspecting the lifeless body. The humming changes to a slow whistle before words float freely from my mouth.

"And I'll eat... you... for supper."

I raise an arm, offering an apologetic embrace. She hurries by my side, better now that it's over. "I'm sorry you had to go through something like this again," I say, kissing the top of her head.

"It sucks. What are the odds?"

"High, actually. It happens all too often. I used to witness it almost daily in my dad's company; both physical and verbal assaults were common." I lift her chin to view her face. "Are you upset that I followed you?"

She shakes her head. "Not this time."

"Why didn't you and Angie stick together?"

"Mark..."

"If you thought I was a possessive and controlling ass before, just wait. I'm not letting you out of my sight again.

You and me, every damn place we go, side-by-side, hand-in-hand, cock in pussy."

She finally cracks a smile.

"You laugh, but I'm serious. I'll even make arrangements for you to be handcuffed to my body and put in my coffin when I die. Next time you're itching for a girls' night out, they're coming here. The three of you can hang out at *my* bar, swim in *my* pool, and get a bite to eat in *my* restaurant. Everything you need's right here, including me. You're not leaving the Jameson."

"The Jameson? Are you referring to your hotel or yourself?"

"Both."

"I was only alone for two minutes and this isn't my fault," she says, indicating I'm once again taking things to an extreme. "If you didn't notice, the guy's twice my size and I still managed to protect myself *and* take him down."

Her head's held in the palm of my hands, unable to turn or look away. "You're *not* leaving the Jameson unless I'm by your side. I told you when we started this relationship about my past and you can't be out on your own. Once you step inside my life, you're here for good."

"You know what, Mark? That's fine, considering you refuse to meet my parents and I'm having dinner with them in a few days. It will be so nice to have you *by my side* for that one. Sounds great to me."

She's so clever. "You always win."

"That I do," she says triumphantly.

I scratch the side of my face and squint. My biggest

fear is losing her to a guy like myself, someone who will slice her open and leave her for dead, a former business partner, employee, or porn star seeking revenge. Shit, maybe even my own son. "We'll discuss this another time. For now, I need to know you're okay." I caress her earlobe, getting semi-erect when she leans into my hand. Her teeth nibble at my wrist, wanting to play. She feels it—the rush, the arousal from a blade possessing a body, mirroring a dick being coated in thick, slippery, fluid as it powers inside flesh.

"I'm proud of you. You know that, right?" She nods, enjoying the attention and engrossed in a post-kill buzz. "Your face is glowing the same way it did the first time we fucked. I take it you're satisfied with the way things played out?"

This time her hand moves over my dick, in sync with her nod. I want her to speak, to tell me how she feels, that this moment is the best she's ever experienced, but my head's rapidly changing to thoughts of tits, pussy, and a warm mouth.

I'm unzipped, she drops down, my cock's out, and my hands are on her head. She sucks, I spread my legs. She sucks, I gaze at the ceiling. Suck. "Oh fuck." A suck, and my mouth tightens... suck. "Slow, beautiful." Suck and gulp. "You could ask for anything right now and I'd give it to you."

Christ, she has so much power over me. Her mouth and tongue are secure and steady, nipping, pulling, and sliding the flesh of my shaft without a single pause.

"You're gonna get a facial if you don't slow down. Slow. Uh." My hands clutch her head, forcing her to stop. I think she's still crazed from the kill.

Yeah, she's visibly lost in a rush.

I laugh, being pushed to the wall like I'm her plaything. Her arm is across my chest, holding me in place while she whacks me off. Frenzied, hard, tugs on my cock—sometimes painful, yet sensational. I'm told not to speak, just to watch and enjoy, that she can't wait to taste my cum.

"Dear fuck, that's good."

"Cover my hand in it. I want it to come out so I can use it as lube."

I pant, bringing her closer for a kiss, but she pushes me away with determination to get me off faster than ever before. "Do it, Mark. You know I love your cum."

"I'm almost there." My head drops to her shoulder, looking down at her jackhammering hand. I'm at the point where I want it fast *and* slow, in her mouth *and* in her pussy. I want my cum to cover and drip from her lips. I want it all. "Damn it, damn it." My eyes shut. "Uh, fuck!"

She playfully cuffs my mouth and the room is filled with, "mmph, mmm, mmm," while I'm detained.

"Look down," she commands. "The reward you wanted for cleaning up my mess is here."

I don't need to watch when I can feel the semen all over my cock. Her hand does such a flawless job spreading it over my flesh as it shoots out then drips down my shaft.

"Mmmph... mmmph." It's so fucking intense when she won't allow me to speak.

"Good boy, now look. Open your eyes, Mark. Do it." She drops her hand and I gasp for air.

"Oh shit." I exhale. "Fuck." I stare dizzily, in disbelief that she was able to get me off that fast, especially since I just came four hours ago. I'm still a young stud, whether she wants to admit it or not.

"You're a goddess," I say with blurred vision.

"A princess," she insists. "And this wasn't my first kill."

DISCIPLINE

"Don't." I jerk away from her while trying to slide into my sport coat and oxfords. "I'm in no mood to talk to you. Start cleaning the mess in the garage and give me some time alone before you find yourself drowning in a tub full of water." I dash out of our bedroom and down the stairs.

"It's eleven o'clock," Jules protests. "You can't go to work this late. Besides, we need to talk."

"This is my hotel and I'll go to work whenever the fuck I want, just like you seem to do whatever the fuck you want without telling me, right?" I slam the door and stride down the corridor to the opposite end of the hotel, needing to make sure my son is okay before I escape to the main office for the night.

The lights seem dimmer than usual, the walls darker, carpet duller, and as I approach the door of his suite, my usual tranquil second floor has been transformed into what sounds like a heavy metal concert. I doubt the little shit can even hear me knocking.

"Jack, open the door."

I give him plenty of opportunity to let me in on his

own, but after multiple fist pounds, I have to resort to using my master key card. Thank fuck Jules didn't give him the option of using a code with the keypad; otherwise my card would be useless. I knock one last time, then for the sake of my guests, swipe and enter.

Fuck his privacy.

"Hey!" I shout. He's in the dining room with a room service cart by his side. I shut off the sound system and notice right away that he's settled in just fine. A wet towel hangs off the arm of the sofa and the television's on with no sound. He has the window shades closed and the heat turned up to eighty. Jesus. And Jules didn't clear out the liquor cabinet. I thought she had this suite set up for him, but the cabinets are full... and there's a space on the shelf where a bottle's missing.

Jack's talking to one of his friends online and my presence isn't acknowledged. I'm completely appalled by all of this. Not the music or being ignored, but the fact that he's sitting at the table buck-naked. And not only that... no, not only is he video chatting online in the nude, but he's acting like a king—having ordered a steak dinner, a slice of chocolate cake, and nursing a bottle of vodka. No glass, just the bottle. He takes a sip and frowns at the interruption, waving his knife for me to have a seat.

"Say goodbye to your friend." I place my hands in my pockets, keeping them away from his scrawny teenage neck. "Now!" My voice is stern, yet has no effect on him whatsoever.

Leaning back, he positions his arm over the top of the

chair and sticks out his chest to signal he's in control. What a little shit. I sure as fuck wouldn't want to be him right now.

Keep calm. Stay in control. Treat him like he's a human being. "Trust me, buddy. You don't want to do this."

I'm always talking about being a better father, wanting to establish some type of father-son bond with the kid and, at the same time, I don't want to have anything to do with him. I know nothing about parenting and I'm full of contradictions when it comes to our relationship. What I want and what I'm actually capable of when it comes to being a father are two different things. One minute I regret everything, craving to give him what he wants and needs, and the next minute I want to toss him out the window. And the window is in the front-running right about now.

"Get off the fucking iPad and put on some clothes."

"Is that your dad?"

"Nope," Jack responds to the voice with a smirk. "Just some guy pretending to be."

The iPad's closed the minute I take my first step forward. This is about to go one of two ways. Either he gets forced into a pair of pants like when he was two, and gets dragged kicking and screaming to my suite, or I sit at the table and try to have a grown-up conversation with...

"What the fuck is that?" I grab his upper arm and pull him away from the chair to view his back. It's inked. He's got a huge tat. "Jesus Christ, who the fuck did that to you?"

He bolts to the opposite side of the table and slicks his wet, blond hair with his fingers, aggravated that I had the nerve to touch him.

My jaw and hands both clench. "Oh, I'm sorry. Did I fuck up your hair? Get the damn towel, cover yourself, and sit back down!"

I'm given a dirty look in protest, but he follows orders.

"When was this? Who did it? And what does it mean?"

The gold Jameson Hotel lettering on the black towel is folded down at his waist when he returns. I grab the vodka from his hand before he can take another swig and point for him to sit.

"I need a drink a hell of a lot more than you do." I take a swig and slam the bottle down. "Talk."

"Last year." He slumps into the chair and clutches the steak knife, rubbing the blade along his jawline. "When I was fifteen and fucking that girl, Maria. Her older brother has his own tattoo parlor... well, he works out of his parent's garage, but he's good."

"Put the knife down. You have no idea the position you're putting me in and what I could do to you. Put it down!"

He sets it next to his plate and laughs. "Better, Daddy?"

A strand of blond hair dangles freely, white teeth appear behind split, dehydrated lips, and he starts to crack his knuckles. I should go easy on him, right? His mom died so his attitude's excusable? Whoever thinks that way is fucked in the head. Jack's been like this for years and his guilt about stabbing me lasted only a second, now he's back to being a prick. I've been saying for years that I'm not gonna lay a hand on a child, but he's long past that stage in his life. Even the kindest, most patient, easy-going soul would snap at this moment, and since I'm none of those things, he's in for more than a *snap*.

"You wanna act like a man?" I shout with a sudden and firm grip of his precious hair. The table gets cleared with a quick swipe before the side of his face smacks against the wood. He shouts that I'm dead, swinging his arms in anger while my blade flicks open.

"Getting tats, drinking booze, fucking women, and stabbing your father?" His lips draw back in a snarl as he watches my silver blade spin and twirl through the air. "You wanna act like a tough guy, like you're in a gang? If that's the case, then it's time to experience getting your ass kicked, because that's what happens when you disrespect another gang member. And let me tell you something, *son*, you're not the boss around here, I am."

"Fuck! Dad!" My blade pierces his earlobe. It's a wound that will heal quickly, but hurts like a son of a bitch. "Dad!" he screams in pain, kicking his feet under the table and flailing his arms. I grab his neck and push him into the back of the chair, glide my ass onto the table directly in front of him, and set my feet to either side of his legs, confining him in place. Those years of karate lessons were clearly a waste of time. He's helpless and weak against me.

"You're fucked," I say.

Blood trickles down his neck while his chest heaves, fighting to absorb a deep breath. I hold my blade in front of his eyes and grin.

"Why is there so much blood on that thing? Did you cut off my ear?"

"Nope. Not yet." I wipe the blade on his shoulder. He's hurt, angry, and still fighting to regain power. "Don't worry, the blood's not all yours."

"You're crazy! I can't believe you did this to me! I'm gonna cut your throat tonight when you sleep!"

"Great, I'll be happy to show you the best way to go about that. I have a guy in my garage we can practice on." I push my wrist into his neck, demanding silence. "It's time, Jack. You were born a Jameson and there's no easy way to explain what that means except to throw you in the deep end to see if you sink, swim, or if you're gonna be a pussy and call someone for help."

He continues to whine while struggling to escape. "What the fuck? You're not listening to me. You tried to kill me!"

"If that's the case then why don't you call the cops?" I slam my hand into his chest, knocking the wind out of him. "I wouldn't mind explaining to them that you stabbed me and the measly scratch on your ear was in self-defense. I can take my stitches out and make my wound look brand spanking new, like it just happened. And, by the way, the cops aren't going to believe some sixteen-year-old over a prominent business owner."

"What the hell... what's wrong with you?" He finally abandons his superiority complex.

"And if the cops, for some odd reason, *don't* believe me, then lucky you, you'll either get sent to your granddad's farm where he'll drag you out of bed at four each morning to shovel shit, or child services will come and haul you away. Who knows where the fuck you'll end up then. Maybe a nice religious family will take you in and buy you a bible then enroll you in Catholic school... an all-boys Catholic school."

That got him. My alpha boy is getting a taste of my world, breaking down with tears forming and about to pour out.

"So go ahead, Jack, either cut my throat or call the cops, your choice."

He insists on turning away, humiliated that he might cry from my words. Fuck, I hope he does. I grip his jaw, dig my nails into his flesh, and force his glossy eyes to mine. He's me, twenty years ago, finally getting a taste of who I am and what his future holds. I had no power when he was miles away in Philly and our arguments happened over the phone. Now, I'm not backing down. It's all or nothing at this moment.

My blade sinks into the leather chair next to his chest, nicking his flesh and causing him to jump in fear. He panics with quivering lips and a trembling voice, pleading for freedom.

"I'm not finished asking you questions. I want the story behind that skull and roses tat on your back and if you've gotten yourself into something you may not be able to get out of."

Damn, my fucking cell. It distracts him from coughing up an answer. No need to look, it'll be Jules.

"Mark, please don't hang up," she says. "I get it, you don't want to discuss my first kill until you're ready— that's fine. I was just wondering if you want me to wait, or if I should cut up the thing in the garage and burn the parts myself? Would that be a good enough punishment?"

What the hell is she talking about? "Not on my cell. You know better... fuck, just meet me in my son's suite and bring an empty box along." I end the call and repeat my question about the tat.

"It's... it's just something I... it's my life and I don't have to tell you anything."

He's stuttering and still refuses to look me in the eye. "Don't make me ask twenty questions. Just speak."

After a minute of silence, he says the tat represents his future and he wants to join a club. "My dream is to get a bike and just ride. No rules, no fucking school or people telling me what to do, like you. Your lifestyle sucks and I don't want it, but I have a feeling if I stay here long enough that you'll get me what I need."

"Like a bike and my money?" I hold his neck and lean closer to his face. The kid watches way too much television and I think he's confusing the Hollywood glorification of those motorcycle clubs with reality. He has no idea what he's saying.

"Yeah, Dad, I want a decent bike and my freedom, not all of this!" he yells, raising a hand to motion at the contents in the room. "Some cash and a tight cunt to pop would be nice too, but I don't need much else. And I can predict what you're going to say... a kid like me won't last a day on the road, let alone in some biker gang... well fuck you! And my ear is killing me! You had no right to hurt me!"

I squeeze tighter until he turns red and can no longer get a word out.

"Son, I've tried giving you my love since the day you were born, but that hasn't seemed to work. You appear to be incapable of any emotional response other than hatred. Well, let me tell you something, little one, I've also had days where I hated you to the point that you're lucky you're still on this earth, only that hatred hasn't taken our relationship anywhere but into a deep hole." I release my hold so he can catch a breath before clutching again. "I've tried my best to support your so-called *dreams* to this point, from baseball and karate, to that damn ninja association. I've gifted you a quality education and trips with your class to Europe, and all you ever do is spend your time bitching at me to buy you every new hot commodity that comes on the market. Now, you're saying you don't need any of that shit? Just the open road? No job? No security?"

He's allowed another breath, only this time my wrists are gripped while he pleads for me to stop.

"I don't believe I can do that." I shake my head. "You think you've had enough?"

His body's motionless and there's no response. Blood continues to drip down his neck in slow trickles as his expression deadens, finally indicating defeat.

I slide off the table and walk behind him to massage his shoulders. The kid hasn't looked this magnificent since the day he was born—all bloody and teary-eyed, weak, and unable to speak.

He remains silent. His body's tense and I imagine his nose is scrunched in revulsion. I lean over and confirm that I'm correct, not feeling an ounce of guilt for my actions. For once, my shitty parenting skills have paid off. When in doubt, when nothing's getting through to your teen, just slice 'em and dice 'em.

He touches his ear, jerks from the pain, and stares at the blood on his thumb and forefinger, rubbing it between the two.

"As I was saying," I speak in a slow and direct tone while clutching his jaw. "You're about to be thrown into the deep blue sea, and since you're my son, I know you'll swim and hunt like a shark. You'll make the right choices from here on out." I take hold of his other lobe and twirl my blade.

"Don't," he says nervously.

"And before you try to worm your way into some fucking biker club, you'll need to learn how to survive in mine."

"Dad." He shudders. "Please don't."

"I can teach you to be street smart, top dog, and pass along the survival skills you'll need to stay alive on the treacherous road you're headed down, then when you're older, finished with school, and have worked your ass off to save some money, you can live in your fantasy world. But trust me, tough guy; you've got a lot to learn about respect, brotherhood, and *family*. Especially if you don't want to end up in a ditch with a bullet through your head." The tip of my blade punctures his other lobe and blood drips to his shoulder. Finally, he apologizes like he genuinely means it, and a powerless young man in tears emerges. "That's a pussy wound, Jack. If you can't handle it, you won't be able to handle a fist in the face or someone sticking a blade in your gut."

I walk next to him and untuck my shirt to flash my stitches, then turn and show off a few other scars from my past. "No hard feelings, right?" I smirk. "It's good to have scars, but best to have the ones that are seen, not the ones that damage your soul. Either way, wear them with pride, son." I lower my shirt and close my blade as Jules enters the suite.

"I'll never forgive you." He wipes his eyes before looking up into mine.

I pat his shoulder and laugh. "Lesson one. Never expose your neck to a man with a blade."

He slowly lowers his head, keeping quiet when Jules walks into the room with the cardboard box I requested.

"Jesus. Now what? Are you piercing his ears?"

"We're just having a friendly discussion about his

55

birthright." I take her by the arm and lead her to the living room. "You see anything wrong in here?" I ask, while looking back at my son. "Get dressed." I gesture to him then turn back to Jules for an answer.

"Shit."

"Yeah, shit. Nice job leaving him a cabinet full of liquor."

"Stabbing him for drinking isn't the best form of discipline."

Jack sets his luggage on the sofa and drops his towel. I'm about to cover Jules' eyes when she turns away and ignores the scene on her own.

I lean into her so he can't hear our conversation.

"Take him with you to clean up the garage."

"What?" She raises a brow. "I agree he needs to know more about you, but throwing him into a job like that seems a bit much on his first day. You think he's ready?"

I nod and look back at his bloody ears. He pulls on a black shirt and slips into a pair of baggy jeans before slumping onto the sofa, blowing a strand of hair from his temple.

"My ears hurt," he grumbles.

"Yep, my side too, but we'll live. Jules will bandage them for you, *after* you do a job for me."

"I'm not cleaning your pool in the dead of winter, at this time of the night, with bloody ears. Besides, you said I needed a work permit before I could start."

"Jack, stand up."

Nervous and keeping his guard, he stands slowly and

waits. "I'm not disrespecting you," he says softly.

He watches my every move as I'm whispering to Jules about being peeved because of the booze, but that we'll discuss it later.

"And don't cut the body into pieces," I say to her. "It's messy and you've never done it before."

"Yeah, but the bears are hibernating and the ground's too hard to dig a grave. Plus, your boats are in the garage for the winter. What's the plan if it's not a cut and burn? Cement? Barrel storage until the spring?"

"The septic system."

"Oh, please no," she says. "That's gross, Mark."

"The piss and shit will overpower the scent of rotting flesh."

"What rotting flesh? Are you talking about my ears?" he calls out.

It's good to see a worried look on his face as I walk toward him. Calm men are dead men. That's lesson two. Always be on guard.

I grasp the back of his neck and our foreheads meet. He swallows hard and inhales deeply as I tender a warm smile. I'd still do anything for him.

"I didn't hurt you because I hate you or because I no longer love you. It was to bring us closer together. One day you'll understand that and thank me for this night. Now, we'll discuss the rest of your evening with Jules over breakfast. Don't act out, follow her lead, respect her, and make me proud."

I kiss his head and swagger out, more positive about

our future together than ever before.

But... I'm still confused about all that shit with Jules.

Not her first kill?

SLY

Six hours.

It's five in the morning, my restaurant will soon be open for the breakfast buffet, and I've just finished a pleasant six-hour shift. Being away from my business is like leaving my rabbit hole then returning to find a snake suffocating my offspring. My hotel is my baby, and the piles of paperwork, orders, employee issues, and customer complaints are the smothering snake. It's a relief to have it skinned and simmering in a pot, giving me time to sleep the morning away and check on things again in the afternoon. My hotel managers are first-rate, but no one can run a business like me.

I check the corridors before heading to my suite, inhaling the smells of my hotel along the way. During the holiday season, my staff adds fresh cut pine branches, vanilla candles, and cinnamon sticks to the side-tables outside every room. And each morning, my guests will find a newspaper, a miniature simmering pot of coffee (serves two), and an invitation to breakfast resting next to the fresh scents and festive displays. Yeah, I'm a pussy when it comes to pleasing my guests, but I also make a fortune because of it.

I'm surprised when I enter my suite to see my son's asleep on the floor in front of the fireplace, wearing fleece pajamas and smelling of bath soap and cologne. He looks peaceful lying on his side with his hands between his legs, drool on the corner of his mouth, and his body curled into the fetal position. Small bandages cover his earlobes and a bottle of water is next to his head. I'm unsure why he's here, but delighted nonetheless. I guess his first *job* went well.

I take a blanket from my entryway closet and cover him from neck to toe, realizing I haven't physically cared for him since he was a toddler. He stirs, but doesn't wake, turning slightly to display a hint of whiskers on his face. Hell, he looks so grown-up, especially now that he shaves.

His face has thinned out and his jaw and cheekbones are more distinct, giving him the look of a high-class, New York model, yet his clothing tastes are still immature. He wears torn-up jeans, graphic tees, and black hooded sweatshirts. I suppose that's the look I should expect from a kid who now dreams of becoming a biker, or maybe it's just typical teenage boy clothing, who knows.

His blond hair is often tucked behind his ears or slicked back and is in need of a trim, although he wears it well. The longer look is decent when he covers it with one of his baseball caps and it hangs out the back. He's already tall and I can tell he'll end up around my height with a similar build—a definite heartbreaker in a few years, if he isn't already.

"He looks so much like you," Jules unwittingly concurs from the top of the stairs. She's draped in a white robe and motions for me to join her in our bedroom. I take one last look at my son, sound asleep, before following her into the room.

Her robe's on the foot of the bed and her nude body is hidden under our comforter. I'd fuck her straightaway if she weren't due to be spanked, and my need to discipline her this morning has nothing to do with sexual play. She drove home last night drunk, gave my son a suite with enough liquor in it to fill my pool, *and* she killed Mera Calloway.

That's the kicker.

Mera was her first kill, and she's kept it a secret for an entire year.

"Get the fuck up, stick out your ass, and present yourself to me."

I throw my sport coat on the chair by the bed and place my gun and shoulder harness on the dresser. My back's turned as I unbutton my shirt, but I can see her reflection in the mirror as she follows orders.

"Don't move a muscle. Keep your head down and your ass up." She obeys while I lock the bedroom door, maintaining a low voice so my son doesn't hear.

I stand next to the bed wearing only boxers, my hands on my hips and my head shaking in disbelief that such an outspoken woman could keep secrets from her man.

"I'm going to ask you a few questions." I rub my hands together. She knows I'm not looking for answers and she'll keep her mouth shut when I speak. This is merely my way of gaining control over the situation. It's how I work through a problem in our relationship without becoming too much of a prick. The alternative is having a fight—a shouting match that always puts me in a foul mood, but this form of domestic discipline will bring us closer together.

I steal the sash from her robe and tie her hands behind her back with the soft, silk fabric. Her hair is gently moved to the side while I remind her to relax and remain silent.

"I brought you into my life because you're the first person I've ever trusted." I massage her ass and she tenses. "Don't worry," I say tenderly. "Stay calm."

My hand gives her a light pat before a quick, second swing makes a smacking noise in the room. She holds steady and places her face into the pillow to muffle any emerging cries.

"Very good." I nibble along the side of her neck. "I've been trying to figure out all night why you kept Mera Calloway a secret. We're supposed to be one, remember? What happened? How will I ever trust you again?"

Smack.

"Oomph."

Smack.

"Uh!"

I caress her warm ass cheeks while watching the mark from my hand slowly disappear in the dim, morning light. She takes deep breaths, just like I taught her, and spreads her legs for better stability, signaling she can handle more. I step back and pace, trying to process what happened.

"That night... together we walked in the cold with that bitch over my shoulder... I thought I had killed her in my own way. Why did you take that away from me? When the hell did you do it? Did you go back that night after we fucked?" I let up for a second, getting a bag of weed out of my dresser drawer. I pack the glass bowl she bought me for Valentine's Day, and take a nice, long drag, then open my back door to disperse the smoke. A good buzz will help me through this.

"When I left you waiting with the flashlight and headed back to the tree on my own, my father's voice was in my head. He said he'd finally love me if I killed her. Then Sophia's voice was there, telling me to stop and let her go. I listened, walked, tried to block them out, then looked down at Mera and studied her face. I thought her eyes would give me the answer I needed." I speak slowly, making sure she can hear the disappointment in my voice. "I was looking for regret, remorse, anything, but her expression was only one of disgust. Then I remembered how much my sister had once loved her, although Daxton was also on my mind."

I set the bowl down after a second hit and shut the outside door, noticing Jules is shivering from the frigid air. Her arms are covered in goosebumps and her tied hands are in fists. I kneel and set both hands on her back, rubbing tenderly to warm her flesh. She stays quietly obedient, something I haven't experienced in the past. It tells me she knows she was in the wrong. Her silence is her apology.

"I trailed the length of Mera's legs with my eyes, ending on the knife I had left by her feet. I considered using it to slice her torso—straight down from her neck to her pussy. And when I picked it up, she turned away, expecting death to come at that moment."

My arm swings and my palm makes perfect contact with her ass. A loud *slap* fills the room, then a second, and a third. She turns with tightened lips, holding her cries inside. I offer nothing in return except a fourth *smack*.

Her head rests on the pillow as she waits patiently for me to finish. A reward might be in order after I'm through.

"I left her in the same position she was in when we first walked away. Mera Calloway would've died that night, either from the bears or the freezing temperature. I wanted her to suffer for hours, not minutes. And, I was happy. It was the right decision. My father's voice was pleased that I left her for dead, and Sophia's voice tapered off, content that I hadn't killed her with my own hands. I allowed nature to take its course. I got what I wanted, and so did they... so what the fuck were you thinking going back there to finish the job on your own? Tell me."

This time, the contact from my hand sends her head upward and she announces that she's sorry, another rarity from Jules. When those words leave her mouth, they're sincere, yet I still need answers.

I run my fingers through her straight blonde hair,

down her back, ass, and legs, before standing again to pace. "Speak," I request. "Why did you do that?"

"Daxton," she whispers. "It's a sin to harm a little boy. I don't give a shit if she was sorry, or if she thought it was okay because he was returned alive, or that she said it was payback for Dayne. That's all bullshit when it comes to a child. You left her for dead, I understood that, and I saw you take your knife so she couldn't escape, but I wanted to make sure... I needed to know she was gone for good. And more importantly, I wanted to punish her. I went back after you fell asleep and stabbed her multiple times on the side of the neck, stayed until she stopped breathing, untied her, and left the body slumped next to the tree."

Her voice started soft and slow, but it's rapidly growing faster as she relives the moment.

"It was wrong what she did! I have no regrets about killing that bitch after she harmed Daxton. No regrets whatsoever. Even if you're furious at me, I don't care!"

"Shh, shh, shh." I gently untie her hands and she rolls over, massaging her tired arms and wrists. She looks up with a red face and I nod that I understand. "And you were afraid I'd be upset?"

"Mark, what just happened? Yes, I knew you'd be upset, disappointed, hurt, and a dick. And besides all of that, I didn't want *him* to return. If I told you, then our lives would suck again."

I drop my head and exhale. She gets it. What she just said is the real reason I'm pissed about all of this.

"Your dad's voice disappeared that night and he hasn't been back since." She reaches for my hand and pulls me next to her on the bed. "That morning you said you were surprised he wasn't criticizing the mistakes you had made. You spent an hour staring at yourself in that mirror." She points toward the ceiling. "Then another hour gazing at yourself in the bathroom mirror, but you didn't talk to yourself or break the glass while you were in there. Then you walked out smiling, kissed me, and we made love. It was passionate and uninhibited."

The backs of my fingers touch her temple and cheek, caressing her pretty face. "That was the first time in years I didn't feel like someone was watching my every move." I drift my fingers across her skin, looking into her honey eyes. She killed Mera for Dax, and kept it to herself so my father would no longer haunt me. Hell, all I want right now is to be inside this beautiful woman—to possess her. My lips press tightly against her forehead and I hold that position, hoping the gesture is enough to express my love for what she did.

"I kept thinking Mera might be found," she continues, "so I went back two days later with a shovel, but you were right, an animal had devoured most of the corpse. I dug a small hole for what was left."

I clutch her cheeks, bringing her mouth to mine in a burst of affection. Our tongues play, strutting in and out, swinging together, and mine becomes its usual greedy bastard self. "Lie back." I roll on top, using my knees to spread her legs wide as she tugs my boxers down.

"Are we okay?" she asks, inhaling deeply when she feels my cock slide inside. "I'll take that as a yes."

I release a long, heated breath, rolling us back on our sides. "I didn't plan on fucking you this morning." She playfully restricts my dick with a repeated clench and release, causing my bottom lip to twitch. *Tease.* I set my head under her chin and enjoy her warm pussy without any further movement. I've never had such a fierce desire to be with another person, it's agonizingly painful. "I'm stronger with you in my life, though confused because you've turned me into a weakened douche."

She massages the back of my head and says she loves me too, making me smile.

"I'm sorry about driving home drunk, I just needed to get out of there. Next time I'll call."

"Forgiven," I affirm, kissing her wrist, traveling up the length of her arm, then coddling her tit while I suck and listen.

"And the liquor in Jack's suite was a big mistake. I'll be more careful around him."

"Forgiven." I lick and suck. Being on the pill has triggered her tits to grow into exquisite soft mounds. I've always loved her chest, but now it's better than most of the porn stars I've fucked... yeah, hers are so much nicer. Her natural figure is fucking sexy compared to those porn star whores.

"You're the first." I drive my hips and let out a carnal growl. "The only one." She's quickly following my momentum and ready to fuck. I glide back on top, my arms straight and body tense, looking down into her seductive eyes. "Uh, fuck." My lips part in pleasure. "Jules, you're the only person that's wanted to protect me from my dad." She grips my shoulders and guides me down until our bodies rejoin. "The only one," I mumble into her shoulder.

I'm subdued in her arms and smothered in kisses from my jawline to my ear. "I'd do anything for you and your family," she says.

"I know. I understand that now."

She holds my hips and her pussy powers into me, wanting more than my cock's offering. I inch out and drag my wet lips between her tits, down her stomach, and trace a heart shape around her clit with my tongue.

"You can have anything you want."

She laughs, kicking her feet. "You've been so sensitive and loving lately. It's the pot, right?"

"Not always." I smirk, feeling how wet she is. "Feet up." I tap my shoulders and she positions them without hesitation, resting upright on her elbows to watch the show.

"I fucking love pussy in the morning." I take a quick look back at my bedroom door then place my finger over my mouth, signaling to keep quiet. She's a screamer. One lick and she loses total control, shouting like she's birthing a fifty-pound baby. Let's see how far she can go before I have to bring out the duct tape or my gag.

"Yes!"

"Shh." I stop and scold.

"Just kidding." She winks. "Continue on, you rich, handsome, hotel owner. Hey, do your guests know you have a secret stash of sex toys under your bed?"

"Funny, Jules."

My thumb grazes the sensitive area above her clit and she quiets down, focused on the soft sweeping motion of my tongue. The sheets are clawed as I play in a longingly delicate way, nursing her engorged flesh. I spread her legs wider and she mouths the words, *God! yes! fuck!* every time our eyes connect.

I slide two fingers erotically inside my mouth then, slowly; one disappears inside her pussy while the other gradually enters her ass. *Oh, Jesus*, I think she just said. Her voice is soft, sounding like the wind whistling through the windows of an old house. *Hoooo, hoooo.*

I fucking love seeing and hearing her so aroused.

"Oh," pant, *"yes,"* pant, *"oh."*

She's caressed inside and out—short licks then a twist, long licks and a finger fuck.

"I'm, I'm, I'm gonna…" She leans back and covers her face with a pillow… two pillows. Her toes curl around my shoulders. She's ready.

I toss the pillows on the floor and fuck her madly. She enjoys my tongue until her orgasm starts, then my cock is in demand. This time, *her* mouth is the one being covered to stifle the cries. She screams into my palm, her head turns, and she cums.

"I love you," I whisper, feeling a spasm around my cock as we fuck. "I love everything about you, princess."

My body moves in turbulent waves with her jaw now locked in my hand. Her pussy's been deprived of my thick cum for ten hours. It's starved. I'm sure of it. I feel it pulsating from her orgasm, working to suck me off.

"Fuck, I'm gonna cum so hard." I thrust faster and watch her tits bounce until I feel my cock about to bust. "Fuck, yeah." I surge. A quick shot fires out. My arms shake and my dick raids with slow, long drives, feeding her flesh. One lengthy lunge, two, then I cease and enjoy the after-effects of a decent suck and fuck. That was a kickass spree... three cum shots in a day. Christ, I'm exhausted.

I give her a warm kiss and a smirk, then roll off and take her in my arms. We lie next to one another, staring at our reflections in the ceiling—my hand gently brushing her shoulder and our legs twisted as one while we relax and catch our breath.

"Your ass okay?"

She nods.

"Is your pussy full?"

Another nod.

"Did you know you have the nicest smelling twat in all of South Lake Tahoe?"

"Ha! I should have that printed on a shirt."

"Don't laugh, it's true... so are you happy?"

"Yes, you?"

"If my dick and nuts could speak, they'd end their sentence with multiple exclamation marks."

She kisses my cheek. "Cocky bastard."

I yawn while bringing the pillows back to the bed,

placing one under her head and the other under mine. Damn, I'm tired... and she's cold. She pulls on her robe while I slide into my boxers, our movements ending with our hands joined over my heart.

"Thanks for wanting to protect me from my dad. I always thought he disappeared because I killed a woman, something he had asked me to do in Vegas and I refused. Dayne and my dad's other brutes would always take care of them instead. Now, I believe it must've been because of you. My father despised love, absolutely detested it. I'm still unsure why he got hitched to my mother since he also hated marriage. But I think bringing you into my life is what shut him down."

"Mark, nothing made his voice disappear but you. It wasn't Mera's death or our love, it's all inside you."

"You wouldn't say that if you knew him." I sigh with heavy eyes. "How'd Jack do?"

"As expected. After all, he is *your* son."

"What does that mean?" I hold her arm as she tries to rise from the bed.

"You'll need to discuss it with him. I'm not being the mediator for you two."

I'm given a kiss before she escapes to get ready for work. It's my fault we're not on the same schedule; maybe tomorrow I'll get my shit together. I love working side-by-side, especially since I've moved her from the front desk to the main office to help with some of the paperwork. Now, I get to stalk her all fucking day and night.

She tugs the comforter over my body, saying she's

going to check on Jack and bring my breakfast upstairs. I listen to her movements in our suite… walking down the stairs, picking up the mail I'd tossed across the room last night, opening the door and bringing the roll cart inside, pouring my juice, then coming back into the bedroom. My breakfast and newspaper are placed on the nightstand, but I'm struggling to stay awake.

"Jack's still sound asleep." She sets her hand on my side. "Will you be down in the office this afternoon?"

"Mmm hmm…"

"Love you, Mark. Sleep well."

"Jules, wait." I muster enough energy to raise my hand, waiting for her to take hold. She brushes my fingers and asks what's up.

"You said you killed Mera because of Daxton, because you believe it's a sin to harm a child… so what about my son? Not that I give a shit, but was I wrong?"

"No," she says gently. "And 'not that you give a shit,' but Jack's no longer a little boy. I was unsure of that last year when I first saw him standing in your living room, waiting to drive one of the cars. He looked too young to get involved in any of our shit. Now, I believe he's at a point in his life where you can't refer to him as a child. If he's old enough to get a job, drive a car, and from what he says—able to drink and fuck whenever he wants, then he's more man than child."

Her hand slips away and she whispers, "Teach him well, but don't forget he's part of this family, and like the rest of us, he needs your love."

NEW RECRUIT

T he sound of someone racking the slide of a pistol will wake me from even my deepest sleep. I lie still with my eyes closed, listening to heavy breathing close by. Cold metal presses against my temple and a moment later the little bastard's cologne drifts into my nose. Oh yeah, he's fucking dead.

"Jack, put the gun down before I kick your ass."

"Do you always leave weapons in plain sight for your teenage son to find?" I open my eyes and he slumps into the cushioned chair next to the bed. His legs hang over one arm while he leans against the other, appearing self-assured that I'm under his command. The gun's still pointed at my head as I rise slowly and reach for my pants.

"Don't move." He holds the weapon in two shaky hands. "This isn't a joke."

"So you're going to kill me?"

"Will I get my inheritance money if I do?"

"No, you'll get arrested and spend many long years getting raped in prison. But Jules will be kind enough to mail you some lube, and your Aunt Sophia will send you cookies, that's always a plus. Go ahead, shoot. Kill me and become a pansy-ass, prison-bitch, jism-receptacle."

He grimaces, but doesn't back down. "Jules told me everything last night. Is it true?"

I smile, unsure what *everything* means. Obviously, he knows we killed the guy in the garage, but what else did she explain... how far did she go?

"Is it true?"

"Chill the fuck out before you make a mistake."

He closes one eye and raises the gun higher so it's aimed at my forehead.

"If that goes off, both our lives will be over, not just mine."

"You asshole. As usual, you're not listening," he complains. "Why can't you ever just talk to me?" He's flush with anger. "Are the things she said true, or not?"

He won't shoot me on purpose, he's only *playing* tough guy, but I am worried about that gun going off by accident. I don't believe he's ever held one... although he knew about the slide lock and release.

"Fine, let's do this. I haven't a clue what she told you, but just ask whatever you want and I'll answer."

He sits up, placing the gun in his lap, apparently happy with my response.

"Did you really kill that man in your garage and thousands of other men? I thought you were joking when you mentioned him, and now I find out there've been thousands."

Crap, leave it Jules to exaggerate. "A hundred, maybe, but no, not thousands. I hope she explained why. Did she

74

offer any specifics about the guy from last night?"

He looks down, giving me the perfect opportunity to snatch the gun, only the moment passes too quickly. Fuck, I hope he does that again.

"Yeah, she said he attacked her behind some bar in town. She also told me about David and Dayne Rosen, and that they were planning to hurt Uncle Cove and Aunt Sophia. Is all of that true? Did you protect them?"

"I did what needed to be done for the people that I love."

"What if someone hurt me or had tried to hurt mom before she died?"

"They'd be dead."

He runs a finger down the barrel of the pistol before using it to relieve an itch on his chin. I get shivers when I see him imitating my moves. This must be what Jules goes through whenever I do such dumbass things.

"Pay attention to how you're handling my gun."

He stares motionless for a good minute before leaning forward with the muzzle directed toward my chest.

"I don't understand why you didn't call the cops to deal with those men. Like the guy that hurt Jules, why not call it in and have the guy arrested?"

I swipe my hands down my face and exhale a deep breath. How am I going to explain this to a sixteen-year-old?

"Dad?"

"Give me a second, Jack."

"Dad..."

I look up and see a wild grin. He tosses the gun next to me and shakes his head, trying to contain his laughter.

"I'm just shitting you. I can't believe this! Holy crap! You're like some dark comic book hero!" He jumps up and walks energetically around the room, running his hand through his hair, just like Cove often does, only Jack's excited, not fucked in the head... well, yeah, he's fucked in the head, but in a different way than his uncle.

"So you kill people because they're evil? Like how often? Will you go out tonight and do it again? Can I come too? What about giving me my own gun?"

"Whoa, whoa, wait a second, buddy. That's not how this works. I think you've got the wrong idea—"

"No, I've seen guys like you in my favorite cable series. I can't believe I'm saying this, but you rock. This is incredible. My whole world changed last night when I saw that bloody body in your garage. Fuck, it was crazy! Fuck, fuck, fuck! I love it! And you knifed me. At first I wanted to punch your lights out, but then I thought it was kickass that a killer nicked me! Shit, I hope I get scars from your blade."

"You're using incorrect terms for all of—"

"Fucking hell. My dad's some sick, badass motherfucker. You're like the Prince of Darkness, no wait, that's Ozzy Osbourne or Marilyn Manson or somebody. What do you call yourself?"

"What? Slow down."

"Why didn't you tell me any of this before? Does... did... did mom know? And Jesus Christ, I got to touch the body. Jules let me put the pieces in the septic tank!"

"I'm sure she did. Wait, what pieces?"

"It was so nasty inside. The stench was sickening even with my scarf over my mouth, and it made my eyes water and burn. Still, it was cool climbing down the ladder into the tank with the body parts. I left them on the small concrete ledge above the sewage in case you wanna remove them in the spring. Jules said you'd likely bury the pieces when the weather's nicer, or sink 'em off your boat. Have you ever been in your septic tank?" He talks nonstop. "It's huge. I guess I shouldn't be surprised with five hundred people here a night. Guests, workers, diners, lots of shitting going on in the Jameson... you know, we could kill every day and even after a decade there'd be room for more bodies. And man-oh-man, fuck, your woman's awesome. She showed me where she knifed him and where you slit his throat. Then, then." He sounds like he's hyperventilating. "Then she used the tree pruner in your garage. Slice and dice." He does an overdramatic gesture with his hands. "That tool was hard to clean. Took a shitload of bleach. And I need a new jacket. It's a bloody, shitty mess. My sneakers too."

"You're wearing a hole in my floor, come over here and sit down so we can talk."

"When do I get a gun?"

Shit. I thought I created a monster with Jules, but he's far worse than her. "Jack, sit."

"Seriously, Dad. So when we lived in Vegas you did this too? Did you ever have bodies in our garage when I was a kid? Holy fucking Christ, I can't believe I even fell asleep last night with all the thoughts twisting in my head. And those cars last year? Did you kill those people too?"

He reclines in the chair with his legs over the arms once again, kicking his feet eagerly with a cheerful grin. "I can't wait to tell my friends."

"No!" I say with force. "You can't tell anyone, ever. This is between family members, no one else. The moment you tell one of your buddies, it's all over. You should never trust a soul with information about our lives. Only those already involved. It'll get us all arrested or dead."

"Not even—"

"Jack," I order. "No one. And I'm not going out each night to slay people, so get that image out of your head."

"Jules explained some things. I get most of it." He picks at a broken toenail, ripping it off and flicking it across the room, then continues swinging his legs like a four-year-old.

"Don't," I say. "That's disgusting. Sit up straight. You wanted to talk so we're gonna talk."

He asks about his mom again while setting his feet to the ground, his voice cracking when he mentions her name, as it will for some time.

"She knew a few things."

"Did she help?"

"No, you still don't understand. This is about—"

"But you enjoy it. Jules said you like to kill."

I rub the back of my neck, looking down at my bare

feet. I guess the old saying's true—*careful what you wish for.*

"Can I have some weed as payment for the job last night? I already know you smoke, so you must have some in here."

Careful what you wish for.

"Oh, and what you said yesterday, about us being closer because of this? I didn't understand what you meant, but after the cleanup and finally hearing some shit about your life, holy fuck! Don't you feel closer? I do. I get it. To think, my dad killed a guy to protect his woman and I got to help by putting the body in that tank, oh, and the access cover was frozen shut. Jules had to bring hot water out after we shoveled, then it took awhile, but we finally got it pried open... I did that, for you. It was amazing! Like, we all had death hands."

"Death hands? What the fuck does that mean? You need to slow down and breathe for a moment. I'm serious. And I believe you meant to say 'blood on our hands.'"

"Yeah, we all played a role. Was that my initiation? Am I good to go? Do I get a name? Weapons? And what about the pot? This is crazoids, I'm wide awake now."

"Stop." I raise my hand, in need of a break. *Careful what you wish for.*

"If I can dispose of a body I should be allowed to smoke. I haven't had any in months." He holds out his hands, palms up. "Dead guy." He raises one. "And weed." Then raises the other higher, teetering them up and down. "Dead guy, weed, dead guy, weed. Fuck, I'd say the dead guy could be more harmful to my future than smoking a little pot."

"Little fucking... you know, I'll do more than slice your ears if you get out of line again. And, no pot. I'm not providing a minor with drugs and alcohol. I'm opening up about my life so there *might* be a chance for us to be father and son. It's okay to protect and defend, and that's what you experienced in my garage, but drugs aren't a form of defense."

"For some people they are."

My voice rises. "If I get arrested, it's not going to be for pansy-ass shit like being my son's supplier... don't laugh! Don't open your mouth again until I'm finished speaking." I put my gun away and dress while he sits in silence, covering his bed head with his hoodie. Hopefully, he'll start to unwind.

I forgot what it's like being his age until just now. An endless amount of energy flows freely from every pore of your body and keeps you awake all night. You feel invincible and experience each conversation, drink, road trip, and fuck like it's the most exciting thing that's ever happened to you. You overreact and are obnoxiously boisterous, especially around your friends and family, not only for attention, but because your hormones are out of control, causing you to act like a dumbass... fuck, I think I just described myself in my late thirties.

And now, the kid has a mile-wide smile. I sit before him and he slowly presents a more balanced expression. "Better." I exhale, remembering Jules' words about loving him. I'll give it a shot, but so far, life was more relaxing when we hated one another.

"Let me try to explain this to you in a way you'll understand. If someone broke into your house back in Philly and was attacking your mom, would you call the cops?"

"Fuck no, I'd take one of my swords and cut his head off or use my zombie gutter to take him down. The cops wouldn't get there fast enough to help, and even after they arrived, the guy could escape in some way and never be caught."

Our eyes link and he copies my nod. I knew my son had issues, all teens do, but when did he become unsympathetic to the life of another human being? He should've awakened as a more timid, fearful kid after dealing with the body. Someone I could manipulate and train. Again, I get the award for being a shitty parent... here son, let me slice your ears, now dispose of the dead guy like a good little boy. Well, fuck me. *Closer together* meant he's supposed to be under my command. Double fuck me.

"Look, buddy, my father played a role in my ability to turn cold when taking a man's life, he was an evil man, but I also felt the need to kill before I was initiated into his world. I had craved it for years, yet I knew how to control it. That's important and something you need to learn. Take an asshole down when it will make the world a better place or when you're protecting a loved one, but random kills are bullshit. Don't search for them. We're better than that. A Jameson isn't a cowardly serial killer. Jameson's are vigilantes who protect people... I can tell by your endless nodding that you understand. Now, remember I don't ever seek men out—I let them come to me. If you're like me, you'll be able to sense the wickedness that hides inside of people. You'll hope their foul ways don't come into contact with your loved ones, because that's when things turn to shit."

He listens closely; his body reclined with his hands entwined in his lap, his eyes disappearing under his black hood while his tongue incessantly moistens his full, cracked lips. I pat his knee, leaning forward as I speak, trying to offer some fatherly advice, whatever the fuck that means.

"Real men kill to protect love, serial killers kill to destroy it, and the average man won't get involved in either of the two because he's a pussy."

He laughs and says that'll be his next tat.

"I'm serious."

"I think I get it. But when are you going to tell me about your dad? You never talk about him... you said he's evil. Did he kill a lot of people too? Thousands? More than you? Were you guys a dark duo?"

"Your grandfather told me what to do and I followed orders without opening my big mouth... most of the time." I point to his face, trying to get him to understand the pecking order. "Paul Jameson is six-feet under and he's not resurfacing, ever. Leave him there."

"Can I ask Aunt Sophia and Uncle Cove about him?"

"Never. I'll explain more about my life in time, but not him. It's bad luck to talk about the dead."

"Why?"

"Jack, enough about it." I check my watch and wince at the time. I can't believe I slept seven hours. Fuck, I've got a lot to do. "Change your clothes. I'm taking you to register for school. The local high school's okay, right?"

"Fine," he says with a groan. "Don't you need an appointment or something?"

"I guess we'll find out when we get there. And afterward, we'll pick up the driving handbook from the DMV. The world outside my septic tank still exists and I want you to stay focused on other things besides killing people. Keep your ears bandaged, and if anyone asks, say they're infected from having them pierced."

"Plugged. I wanted to get plugs, but that won't be possible now." He removes his hood and tightens his jaw with a serious expression that slowly changes to a warm grin. "I think I love you," he whispers. "You're finally starting to act like you care."

Wow, I can't remember the last time I heard him say those words. My heart races, then plummets into a dark hole. I hated my father because he was a malicious bastard, but I also loved him for it, and I coveted his power. My son might feel that he loves me now, and I bet it's for the same reason. He sees me as some dark hero he can admire. I'm sure he also desires my power, whether it's in this environment, in some biker club, or out on the open road.

"What do you want out of our relationship?" I

should've asked him that years ago, and maybe I did but never got an answer other than his request for material objects or cash. And asking now probably originates more from Jules than me. *Love him*, she says. *I'm done with him*, I say.

He bites the dried skin on his lips while staring over my shoulder.

"To be noticed and not tossed aside or forgotten about like I have been for years." He swallows hard and rubs his chin with his index finger before scanning the room. "For you to accept the fact that I may not want the same things or have the same goals in life as you." Our eyes meet and I can tell he's practiced this moment. The words are precise, like they've been written and reread over and over again. He's been waiting for center stage, but it feels unnatural, calculated, and fake.

"To be respected for who I am and not punished all the time for who I'm not."

"Oh."

He lets out a grunt, disappointed in my one-word response.

"Is that too much? What the fuck? Then why'd you ask?"

"Keep going." I motion for him to continue.

"All I have left to say is that I want to feel loved. Okay?"

He sounds perturbed. I bring him to my chest and cradle the back of his head, hoping he can sense that I'm listening. I said those same things to my dad, only I was called a wimp and had my face slammed into the wall.

"Jack, don't confuse your love for an illusory, dark superhero, over your true feelings for your father."

My embrace stops his disagreeing headshake. "Dad," he mumbles into my chest. "If you had to eat all the shit that came out of your mouth, you'd be the size of your hotel."

"Sounds like something Jules would say." I laugh and kiss the top of his head. "Welcome to the family, son."

ARTIFICIAL SON

J ack failed to tell me he hasn't attended school since last June. Well fuck, buddy, that would've been nice to know before we walked into the office to get you enrolled.

His mother allowed him to stay home this fall because she knew she was dying. She hired a college co-ed to tutor him who he claimed was a good fuck. Yes, my son seduced some twenty-year-old when he was supposed to be reading *The Great Gatsby*. I shook my head incessantly when he told me, explaining it's illegal in most states for him to be screwing women, to which he responded in the same way he did with the pot. *Pussy's less harmful to my future than the body in the septic tank.*

Snarky smartass. That's going to be his new line for everything.

So now, it looks like he'll be attending summer school to make up for lost time. Plus, the local high school doesn't want him to start until after the holidays. That's two weeks. Two fucking weeks until he's back on a schedule.

I've got to figure out how to keep him busy with something that isn't illegal; otherwise he'll get caught in a power trip thinking about what a badass he is, or worse, a downward spiral over the loss of his mom. I asked him if he wanted to get a model kit, like a plane or a car to work on to pass the time, and he responded in a typical Jack Jameson way... "Only if it comes with the *good* glue."

Screw that idea. No model kits for my son. He's too old for them anyway. Fortunately, he became enthusiastic when we got the driving manual at the DMV, and even more so when he saw all the kids his age at the ski resort. After purchasing a season pass, it took him two long hours to pick out a snowboard, jacket, and boots. Fuck, I haven't spent so much money since the gondola lift reservation for Jules. But it was worth it. That was three days ago and he's been living at the resort ever since.

Jack's a social butterfly and kids fall in love with his dirty mouth, graphic sex stories, big grin, and the confidence he exudes wherever he goes. He stands with his head held high, legs apart, and hands on his waist when he's around his buddies. And the past two days I've seen girls hanging on his every word as I wait for him to get his ass into my Tacoma. He nonchalantly brushes against them, puts his arm over their shoulders, and sweeps his hand across the back of their necks. He's a scabby eared, confident, cocky player.

I'm unsure if he's actually snowboarding or just hanging out at the snack bar and goofing off, but frankly, who gives a shit? As far as I know, he hasn't been drinking or getting into any fights, so the cost of the pass and equipment to keep him occupied is a win-win. He's busy,

I'm busy, and life's finally getting back to normal. We can now be an ordinary, habitual, bland, piece-of-shit family. Call me average Joe. Yep, that's all I can think about as I recline in my lobby chair, watching my guests check in for the evening. Hello, I'm average Joe, welcome to my goddamn hotel, you motherfuckers. Hope you brought the entire family for an extended stay. Don't forget to piss in my pool, vomit at the bar, and deposit cum all over my sheets.

"You in a foul mood?" Jules asks, placing a hand on my jerking leg.

"Ya think? I can't believe you trapped me into this."

"It's *talked* me into this."

"No, trapped."

The doors open and I look up, thinking it might be her parents, but it's only a group of twenty-something-year-old women. They 'ooh' and 'aah' at the thirty-foot pine covered in white lights and gold bulbs that towers next to the burning fireplace. My head shakes and I grimace as they track snow through the front door. With a stomp of their boots on the lush entryway carpet, they leave piles of white fluff that quickly melts into a slushy swamp.

"Wipe that irritated look off your face," Jules whispers. "You love your guests. Don't be such a fucking baby by taking your personal life out on them."

"Why here?"

"Would you have gone to dinner with us if it was downtown?"

"Nope." I rub my forehead to relieve the tension. "I deserve a big reward later tonight."

"This okay?" Jack walks toward us with his hands raised, showing off a grey button down shirt tucked into dark blue jeans and a black sport coat.

"Hell, you invited Jack?" I stand and tuck his shirt collar under his coat. "And when did you get a haircut?"

His thick hair is cut to a decent length and combed slightly to the side and forward with short wavy pieces framing his face. He takes mint ChapStick out of his front pocket and applies it leisurely across his thick lips while sitting across from Jules in one of the leather club chairs.

"He wanted me to take him somewhere to get it cut today, so I cut it."

"You did this? I'm impressed. It looks damn good."

"Thank you." She tilts her head with a confident smile. "And he's not coming with us, he's got a date."

"With who?" I turn to him.

"Her name's Emma. Just wait 'til you see her and her monster rack. She's got long black hair and wears violet contacts that are killer. Violet, Dad. Fuckin' hot! She's like the kickass characters in my favorite Manga comics. And she's not afraid to show off some skin either. I could stare at her cleavage all day," he responds.

I scan the room to make sure my guests aren't listening and realize the lobby music is off. No wonder Jack's voice is echoing through the space. After multiple finger snaps to get the attention of my front desk staff, I point to the overhead speakers and a moment later the sounds of vintage Christmas music fills the room.

"What else do you know about her besides her breast size?" I ask.

"Well, thankfully she's not a prude." He laughs. "And her mom works in the restaurant at the resort. I think she's a hostess. Emma said her mom lets her smoke and can stay in one of the cabins on the slopes for free. She can walk out her front door and ski all night if she wants."

"How old is she?"

"Sixteen. Smart and funny too."

Sounds like my dream girl at his age.

"If I'm lucky, her friends will be open to a threesome. I could use a little ménage in my life." He rolls his cuffs with a serious face, but a few minutes later, smirks and winks in reference to his comment. "I'm kidding."

"I'm not amused," I say. "Just keep your pants on tonight."

"Why?" he asks.

"Yeah, if she's okay with it, why?" Jules questions.

I don't have an answer. There'd be something wrong with a sixteen-year-old who didn't have pussy on his mind every second, so I decide to change my words... "Keep your pants on when you're on my property. Besides the illegal shit we've already discussed, I also don't want child services pounding at my door."

Tap, tap.

Tap, tap, tap.

A walking cane raps against my lobby floor, and all three of us turn toward the sound. An older man, much older, I'd say in his eighties, is sitting in one of the chairs next to the fireplace. His head's down like he's taking a nap, but his cane's tapping some overt message... or perhaps following the beat of the music. It's unusual to have someone his age at my hotel. I get baby-boomers every once in a while, but never anyone from the silent generation.

"That was weird," Jack whispers. "He did that right after you mentioned someone knocking at your door. Ya think he's listening? FBI? CIA? Do you have guys like that after you?"

"No. My life *is* black and white. There's no grey area or unknowns. Stop fantasizing." I look away from the old man and back at my son. "Where are you going and who's driving?"

"Well, I heard the food at the Jameson is outstanding—the perfect spot for a romantic dinner, especially if you can get us a table that overlooks the lake."

"Clever." I grin. "Everyone's using me for my restaurant this evening... just make sure you stay out of your suite."

"Cool, I heard pool sex is a lot of fun."

Fucking teenage boys. "Jack, I've got things to deal with other than making sure you behave inside my business. Try to act like a responsible adult."

He rises quickly and puts on a show as a young girl walks through my front door. Once her winter coat is in his arms, he sets his hand on the side of her neck and rubs her cheek, telling her she looks delectable.

Delectable? What is she, a piece of chocolate cake? Is my son talking about a dish in a food magazine, or her face?

They kiss... for way too fucking long I might add, and after she touches his hair, they walk past us without even saying hello. Down they go, toward the back of the hotel where my restaurant is tucked away.

"Did you see how short her dress is? And her heels are higher than mine."

"Oh yeah, trust me, I saw... I can see." I watch my son's hand sliding down her ass. "I don't understand where kids get so many tats from when they're underage, or how they can afford to pay for them."

"Right? She had a heart on her arm and wings on her chest, not to mention the birds on the back of her leg. The girl's cute, and I hate to say it, sexy too. Other than the fact that she's doused in patchouli, I'm jealous." She caresses my knee and studies the door, waiting for her parents to arrive.

"Jack cleans up well, thanks for taking care of him today. I'm assuming you bought the ChapStick too?"

She nods. "Have you had the sex chat with him?"

"What? Jesus Christ, sometimes talking to you is like having a conversation with Sophia. Such random shit pops into your head."

"It's not random. He was just talking about getting laid. I hope you've discussed it with him. Does he have condoms?"

"From ChapStick to buying condoms." My head falls

back and I stare at the flickering white lights that hang from my beamed ceiling, reminding me of dripping icicles. "No. He was too young for a discussion about sex when my ex and I were still together, and I haven't been around him in years. I was hoping she had gone over all that crap with him. And he's too old now."

"Don't be ignorant."

"Hey, I did alright without someone talking to me about things. Plus, I'm not going to embarrass him."

Tap-tap.

Tappity-tap.

"Embarrass him or yourself?" she asks.

Tap.

That old fucker's annoying.

I'm distracted from the rapping cane when Jules rushes to the door, putting her arms around a middle-aged woman while a man follows close behind. He brushes snow off his brown leather coat and nearly slips in the snowy entryway. After knocking the snow from his cowboy boots, he pulls Jules into a tight hug.

"Hi, peanut."

"I've missed you," she says. "You guys look great! Thanks for coming!"

"Are you kidding me? We finally get to meet this *mystery man* you've been keeping from us for a year."

The three of them turn and I'm put on the spot. Fuck, I hate this shit. I'd favor smoking pot or watching porn right about now. Or better yet, I'd rather my son stab me again than make small talk for the next two hours.

But for my beautiful woman, I stand, put on my best smile, and extend a hand. Her father gives me the firm, double-handed grasp.

"Mark, is it?"

"Yes, Mark Jameson."

He nods.

"Great to meet you, finally. Nice hotel you got here. It's a massive beast, isn't it?" He gazes at the two-story, log-beamed ceiling and opulent decorations, but his wife clearing her throat leads him back to the conversation.

"I'm Sam." He shakes my hand a second time then brings his wife closer. "And this is Karina."

"It's a pleasure, Mark. Thanks for inviting us," she says.

I didn't invite these people... "It's *my* pleasure. I'm glad you could come."

Sam and Karina Barringer. Their names sound like a couple of gangsters, but they remind me of real estate agents. She's a gorgeous, tall, athletic woman with golden blonde hair and tanning bed, tinted flesh, just like Jules. A beauty queen. I was told she'd won a few pageants back in her day, which I suppose would be about twenty-five years ago. She takes off her long winter coat to reveal a black sweater dress that, although ordinary, looks stunning because of her add-ons—a red silk scarf and large-stone, turquoise jewelry.

And Sam's also the type of guy who would've been prom king, standing like a marine, light brown hair neatly trimmed into a crew cut, broad shoulders, and wearing clothing that reminds me of something you'd find in Robert Redford's *Sundance* catalog. Affluent, mature, and the all-American western man, right down to the classic musk-scented cologne. The two are classy, something I never imagined, especially considering Jules' foul-mouth.

I motion for us to head to the restaurant, seeing Jules crack a smile. "Payback's a bitch, just wait," I whisper as we leave the lobby.

"It's worth it. I love seeing you squirm every once in a while."

"You're the one who'll be squirming later tonight."

"Hey, I told you we're not getting married until you meet my parents. Now buck up, buddy, and grow a pair. It's one night," she says under her breath.

"My nights are always long. Sometimes they can last weeks."

"What the fuck, Mark? Just shut up and open the door for us."

I walk ahead and hold the door of my restaurant open for her parents as they approach. The feeling in the pit of my stomach is exactly why I didn't want to do this shit. It's not nerves, more of a feeling of disgust for the common man. Yeah, sounds pathetic, but I've made it clear that I like to work, fuck, and get high, not have dinner with mommy and daddy.

"Wow, look at this place. It's like a holiday movie set from the '50s that makes you feel all warm and fuzzy inside. A winter wonderland." Karina's stunned reaction is exactly what I hope for from my guests. "Everything's silver and gold, and the red lilies on each table are such a festive touch. It's so beautiful!" She turns back to us and notices our outfits, Jules in a black dress with sparkling gold heels and me with a black suit and a silver-ish, light grey, dress shirt. "The two of you even match."

"Follow me." I grin, taking them to one of the tables overlooking the lake. "I have white Mariposa lilies on the tables year round, except during the holidays when red seems more appropriate."

"That's pretty, too." She points out the window to a row of pines covered in white lights, creating a glistening effect on the snow around my property.

"Mark has a brilliant designer who comes in every three months to update the hotel for the changing seasons and holidays. He's a fun guy. I got to work with him last time he was here."

"I'm impressed," Sam says, pulling a chair out for his wife. "Is it family money?"

"Dad, don't be rude," Jules scolds.

I notice Jack's to our left, a few tables away with Emma's hand in his. He's ordering for her, something he must've picked up from me at some point in his life. And there's that old fucker, across the room, staring at the four of us. There's no way it's a coincidence he's here. Who the hell is this guy? He doesn't look familiar... caterpillar eyebrows, deep forehead wrinkles, stern expression, and a fine black suit... whether on purpose or not; he's got the typical mob boss appearance.

Nonchalantly, I rub the left side of my chest to check

that my gun's in place, and I sense he knows the weapon's there. The guy's a giant red flag.

"Some of it *is* family money and some I earned, and I'm not ashamed of any of it," I finally answer.

"Earned how?" he asks.

"A couple of companies in Vegas."

"Mark, you don't have to get too detailed," Jules cautions.

"Well, I'd prefer if he did, especially if you plan on marrying the guy," he says. "What were the companies? Technology, insurance, pharmaceuticals, what?"

Our server pours four glasses of wine and I order a salad and the steak dinner for everyone. Thankfully, no one complains about it, and I'd say Sam's too busy with my personal life to care.

"Manufacturing companies? Construction, retail?"

"No, personal services and hospitality."

"Dad, drink some wine and stop harassing my man. I want to have a nice meal together, not an interview, okay? Please?"

"What do you mean by personal services? Like a massage parlor or an escort service?"

"In a sense, yeah."

He leans back and the two of us drink, keeping our eyes glued on one another. I pour us both a second glass and we drink again.

"And here we go." Karina smiles at Jules. "You know your dad needs to be in control."

"Yeah, but Mark does too."

"Should we make a bet over who'll rule the table at the end of the night?" she jokes.

"I think Dad will win. I've got more power over Mark than you do in your marriage, so if I tell him to back down, he—"

"Excuse me?" I show my best authoritative look.

"We're only teasing." She grins.

"Sam, honey, why don't you tell him what you do for a living."

He swirls his wine, looking curiously at Jules. "You've been together for a year and you haven't told him? How is it possible that my little peanut has kept her mouth shut for this long?"

"She told me you work in theater... that you do costume and makeup design. Which, I realize this will sound stereotypical, but I pictured you a little more feminine, less brawny, with more of the college professor look. Perhaps with longer hair and a beard. Maybe feminine is the wrong word. How 'bout, hippy-like?"

They laugh, but I was being serious.

"Yeah, that's quite the clichéd description," he says.

I shrug and glance at Jack, then to the older guy who's busy with a salad and a beer. He eats while keeping one hand on his cane, still tapping it every few minutes.

"What do you think an *embalmer* would look like?" Sam asks.

Embalmer? I study his face, wondering if he finds himself entertaining, only the guy's dead serious... an embalmer who's *dead* serious. Raising a brow at Jules, she bows her head and seals her lips. Her chair is pulled closer and her leg gripped tightly under the table. "And what, exactly, does your father mean by that?" I'm not even going to ask him... *she's* the one who needs to fess up. "You lied."

"What? No, I didn't."

"A makeup artist is a far cry from an embalmer."

"No, that's *exactly* how you would describe his job."

"What the fuck? Not even close. Why didn't you just tell me the truth?"

Her mouth drops open like I'm the one being an ass, especially for swearing in front of her parents, but she's the one in deep shit, not me. "A freakin' embalmer?"

"So what's the issue, Mark? I don't make enough money for you to marry my daughter, or are you worried that I'm morbid? Perhaps into necrophilia?"

"Dad!" Her face reddens.

"I've met a few people who are fond of dead bodies, so no big deal," I say.

"Mark!" She smacks my side.

"I've even seen a dead man first hand, and yep, felt a twinge in my pants for the guy. Now, if you'll excuse me, I just noticed my son's about to get me arrested."

As I walk away, I can hear Jules stressing that I wasn't being serious... "Don't listen to him. He's playing around like he always does, but just wait, eventually he'll crack a smile and tell you he's kidding."

The bottle of wine was on Jack's table, clear as day a moment ago. I'm sure of it, so he better not bitch when I call him out.

His date gets one of my warmest smiles as my hand rests firmly on his shoulder. "Son." I lean down for a private chat. "I'm not getting shut down for serving liquor to kids, and you sure as fuck don't want one of my guests to call CPS, so why don't you be a good boy and hand me the bottle before I reopen your scabby ears and make you cry in front of your date."

He laughs and reaches under the table, handing me the wine. "CPS would surely be on the way if you did that."

"You know how it goes, buddy. Your ears got caught on my cufflinks as I was reaching out to give you a hug. Shit happens."

"I wink at Emma and carry the bottle and their glasses back to my table. Someone's getting fired tonight. Fucking staff, serving my kid alcohol."

"Who gave him that?" Jules questions while her parents stalk my son. I wave the hostess over to find out what happened, watching her bright smile quickly change to a horrified expression.

"I'll check on it, Mr. Jameson. I'm so sorry." She hurries off, waving at the servers to follow her into the kitchen.

"So you were married?" Karina pries, curious as to Jack's presence in the room. "Sorry, that wasn't a polite thing to ask. And, I'm unsure why I did, Jules already mentioned it once or twice... or three times."

Ah, so this is indeed an issue with them. "Married

and divorced," I respond, feeling a line form between my bows while placing a dinner roll on my plate. She has no reaction, but surveys her daughter for any indication that my baggage bothers her, only Jules is focused more on the arrival of our food than my past.

I'm not going to allow the previous conversation to slide. And we're sure as fuck not going to discuss my ex... "How'd you get into the embalming business?"

"My father," he says. "What about you and yours?"

"Same."

We lift our knives, copycatting each slice into our tender, bloody steaks. My fork rises, his follows, and we chew simultaneously with forced smiles. I lick my lips, he licks his... and I imagine anyone watching would either think we're about to beat the pulp out of one another, or rip each other's clothes off and fuck. Yeah, it's that type of tension.

"Women tend to marry their fathers," I whisper, cutting another piece of meat.

"And men tend to marry women who look like their mothers," he strikes back. "And from your fair hair and the *Detail's*-wanna-be, cover model look you're sporting, I'd say that's true. Is your mother a cute and fit blonde, like my daughter?"

"Hold on, you two." Karina sets her wine down and takes her husband's hand. "This table is oozing with testosterone for no good reason. For crying out loud, you just met. Focus on the fact that you both love this beautiful, young woman sitting before us, and she loves *both* of you. Now, play nice." She takes a swig of wine and smiles at Jules.

"Well." Sam starts another attack. "He didn't get that mug from Paul."

"What the fuck?" I stand and reach for my gun while he follows suit. Goddammit, what the fuck is this shit?

"Whoa, whoa, wait." Jules grabs my hand and keeps my weapon concealed as Karina does the same at Sam's waist. "Sit down," she begs. "You have an audience."

"This is my fucking home, my hotel, my world."

"This is my daughter and I have the right to know who she's marrying."

Our jaws are clenched, muscles tense, and hands confined, hidden under our jackets. My son starts to walk over, but I motion for him to stay back. I can handle this prick without the kid getting in the way.

"Mark, seriously, you hate it when people cause a scene and now you're doing it. Breathe, love, just breathe. Let's talk this through."

My arm drops as I peer around the room, seeing my son looking at his date, then at me, the old man smiling, and the rest of my guests patiently waiting. With clenched fists pressed on the table, I lean forward and say, "Sit down."

He drops his hand and Karina relinquishes her firm hold. How the fuck does he know anything about my dad? I turn to Jules, immediately feeling conned. I should've known better.

Sam sits, and gestures for me to have a seat now that

he's followed orders.

"Maybe we should call it a night. I didn't picture things turning out this way," Jules says, visibly disappointed.

"Hell no." I pick up my steak knife, cutting furiously at my meat. She watches me shove a large piece into my mouth. I chew viciously then have a glance around the room. Jack's at his table, my guests are getting back to their conversations, my hostess is still speaking to the servers while pointing in our direction, and the old coot is giving me a silent hand clap. Fuckwad. Sam's first, but that guy's next in line.

"The evening's just getting started," I say to Jules, taking a huge gulp of wine before pointing my knife across the table. "Who the fuck are you?"

"Mark, what are you talking about? Don't act crazy," Jules pleads.

"It's alright, peanut. He has the right to know everything about me." He leans in. "Just like I have the right to know everything about you, Mark Jameson."

"So speak," I say.

"No, you'll start. Tell me how you made your fortune. I want to hear you say it."

"Oh, God." Jules rests her face in the palms of her hands. "Can we please go back to discussing the pretty decorations and red lilies?"

"Porn," I say proudly. "And casinos. My father started the Fox Palace in Vegas, built a couple more, one in Reno that didn't do as well as the others. He was also the front man for Jameson Industries. After he was *murdered*." Karina winces when she hears the word, but I continue on. "I inherited the casinos and some money, my sister got about the same, although a lot of our father's assets were seized, including the house and all of his belongings. The casinos and porn industry were two separate accounts so we didn't get entirely screwed. Then one of my dad's partners, the main man behind the scenes of Jameson Industries, began rebuilding the company. He put me in charge."

"David Rosen," he says. "The guy who committed suicide?"

"Yes," I say harshly. "So you've already heard this fucking story? Talk, asshole."

"Shh." Jules reaches to stop my hand from cutting frantically into every piece of food on my plate. The steak, green beans, potatoes... hell, even the roll is in tiny half-inch bits.

I toss my knife and say it again. "Talk."

He signals to his daughter to leave, but she won't budge.

"No, I want to know what's going on. I haven't told you any of this. What gives?"

"Good show," I whisper.

"I'm serious, Mark," she insists.

"Mr. Jameson?" My hostess interrupts our argument. "None of the staff served your son the wine. I was able to track down all the bottles from the evening, and the only one unaccounted for was ordered by the older gentleman who was sitting right over there." She points to an empty seat. "He left about five minutes ago."

"Find out his name and what room he's in." I lean back and trace a finger across my lips, waiting for her to leave so Sam can answer my question. Now, I've got three fuckers to worry about tonight, Sam, my son, and the old man. Four... yep, four, since my shit list with Jules keeps growing.

"Jules, honey, your dad and I hired a private detective to find out a little more about Mark."

"What?" I snap.

"What the hell?!" Jules exclaims, sounding devastated.

"We know nothing about him," she says. "You've never brought him around to meet us, and it was only recently that you mentioned his last name. Once we found out, we were worried. He just appeared in our town a few years ago and built a castle in the pines, no one ever sees him downtown or anywhere besides his own property, and our friends who come here to eat said they've heard him mumbling about trolls. What were we supposed to do?"

"You could've asked or trusted her judgment." I spit fire. "What else did you dig up? Did you find out my mother's been in and out of psych wards? Or that my father molested and beat the shit out of my brother-in-law when he was a kid? Oh, and did you know I used to be a porn star? Go ahead; tell me you watched some of my scenes. Did you like 'em? Can you picture me doing that shit to your daughter?"

"Fuck this." Jules tosses her napkin on the table and

struts off, either embarrassed or pissed to hell at all of us. Karina follows her, leaving Sam and I to glower.

I snap for our server and request a third bottle of wine, having finished off our original and what was left of my son's.

"Might as well get shitfaced," I say under my breath.

"Might as well," he repeats. "What are you packing?" He looks at my chest.

"Today, my Sig P226. You?"

"An SR9."

I nod. "Both are cheap, easy to conceal, and get the job done."

"What job is that?"

"Protection, nothing more. What about you?"

"Same. Ever use it?" he questions. "Or was the talk about feeling aroused from the dead all bullshit?"

"Have you?"

"I work with the dead every day."

"And being a porn star was like working with the dead every day, so yeah, maybe I've been aroused by them."

"You're a real piece of work. How'd you end up brainwashing my daughter? She's never been so fooled by anyone before."

"Really? You don't know jack shit. Why don't you tell me how a man could leave his daughter high and dry to sleep in her car? She could've been raped, beaten, killed, not to mention the cold temperatures. You're lucky she didn't freeze to death."

Finally, he turns away and shuts his mouth. I watch him squirm, trying to seem occupied by adjusting the buttons on his jacket... clearly he realizes I'm right.

"I admit that was poor parenting on my part, but to some extent it was her choice. She said it was time to break free. Plus, it was between Karina and Jules at first. And I thought she was staying each night with friends or at the church, not in her car, only her mom was aware of that, and—"

"What other shit did your *detective* dig up about me?" I interrupt, not wanting to listen to a litany of excuses.

"About you? Nothing. Everything he found was about Paul. You, on the other hand, are a complete mystery. You didn't exist before your divorce. The records he found were about the sales of your businesses in Vegas during and after your divorce, and building the Jameson, other than that, you're a ghost. Why?"

"Maybe because there isn't anything. I made porn and that's about it."

He lets out a heavy sigh as Karina and Jules return to the table.

"So you've seen photos of my dad? His murder? The trials? Things about my brother-in-law and his family?"

He nods.

"Enough," Jules says. "I've had it with both of you. I expect this shit from Mark, but Dad... what the hell? You've never acted this way before."

"You've never kept a secret from us before."

"Oh, trust me, I have." Her face is a deeper red than

the lilies in the room, her knuckles whiter than the snow falling outside our window, and her voice harsher than the winter wind. I'm fucked. We're all fucked.

"For Christ's sake, what's wrong with the two of you?"

"Peanut, we just—"

"No." She points to her father. "Don't call me that. I'm so furious right now that I think you all deserve a stab in the ass with my blade."

"What?" her parents say in unison as I start to laugh. That's my woman.

"Don't laugh, Mark. Shut your mouth before I knock your teeth out and make you swallow them so they cut into your colon as you shit them out."

"Julia!" Karina shouts. "Act like a lady!"

"Why, because I have a vagina between my legs? Screw that shit. Mom, listen to me. I love this man, and he doesn't control me. We have a wonderful, supportive, caring relationship."

Sam laughs and tosses his napkin on the table. "Jesus, you sound coached, sweetheart."

She points again. "And he treats me better than any man I've ever known. We share a love that no one will ever understand, so don't judge us or judge me. Next time you want to know something about him, fucking ask, and if I don't want to tell you, then respect our privacy... damn it! Damn you! All of you!" She tosses back a glass of wine, refills it, and starts to chug another. I reach to take it away, but she gives me her best, *fuck off, asshole*, look.

I can't keep from laughing. She's flat-out adorable when she's being such a badass. A strong woman is a smoking hot woman and after those words and her expression, I sure as fuck won't be able to stand with this erection anytime soon. But shit, Jack's getting up to leave... I excuse myself, making sure my stiff cock is concealed under my suit jacket.

"Hey," I call out to him. "Wait a sec."

He stops and approaches me, leaving Emma behind.

"I'm taking her to the lobby. Her mother's on the way," he says as I motion him off to the side.

"Did that old guy say anything to you when he gave you the wine?"

He shrugs.

"I'm serious. Every detail's important."

"The only thing he said was 'have fun, sonny boy.'"

"That's it? Nothing else?"

He shakes his head.

"Okay." I pause and scan the room, then grip his shoulders and whisper, "I need you to pay attention to everything and everyone around you. Be careful until I figure out who he is. Don't talk to him, go anywhere with him, and if you see him, walk in the opposite direction."

"I knew it."

"Jack," I say in my lowest voice, taking out my pocketknife. "I can't watch you twenty-four hours a day." I slip it into his hand. "It's only for an emergency and don't even think about using it on me or I'll beat your ass."

"Thanks," he says with a giant grin, sauntering over to his date like he's the toughest guy in the room.

"And Jack," I call out. "You better be telling me the truth."

The hostess catches me on the way back to the table as Jack and Emma leave the room. I feel like a net's about to fall over my head, snaring me in my own home.

"Mr. Jameson, the older gentleman paid with cash and the front desk has no record of him. We don't believe he's a guest at the hotel."

"Of course," I say. "Fuck... if you see him again, call me right away."

"Will do."

She walks off and I take a moment to shake hands with a few of my guests, asking them if they're enjoying the food and their stay. The longer I spend bullshitting with people around the room, the less time I have to spend bitching with the Barringers.

After a few minutes, Jules gestures that I should return. I can feel the wine kicking in as I make my way back to the table. I'm drunk, not sloshed, just drunk. And I can tell the rest of the group is too. With red cheeks and upturned lips, the liquor is choking out the hatred we all feel for one another, at least for the moment.

"Now," Jules says in a calmer voice and a deep exhale. "We're going to have an enjoyable dessert then Mark can show you around his place before you turn in for the night." Her nails dig into my thigh, silencing any comments I might have about them staying here. "No more arguing, no remarks or questions, no leader of the pack, alpha-male wars, or wrestling matches to see who's king of the hill."

"It's king of the mountain. And since my hotel is at the top—"

"Shut up, you fucker!" Her face twists. I laugh hysterically and Sam cracks a smile. "Damn it, one more word Mark... one more."

"Hey, I'm trying to lighten the mood."

"Well ain't that a switch. Lighten the mood? After telling my parents you were a porn star?"

"It's okay," Karina says. "Your dad and I have gone through this information a hundred times—up, down, left, right, inside and out."

"And?" she questions.

"Well, everyone knows you can't choose your family."

"No fucking shit." I drink.

Sam leans forward to continue. "Although, he does seem a bit crazy."

"He? Don't treat me like I'm not here."

"Yes, however he's unbelievably handsome and has money," Karina teases, nearly spilling her wine as a drunken laugh escapes her mouth.

"But, he also has a short fuse," Sam says.

Her parents are deliberating about my character right in front of me? Fuck that.

"And, the porn was and is a concern." Sam lifts his wine glass and pretends he's giving me a toast.

"More *was* than *is*." Karina pats his hand before

111

grinning at her daughter. "We want to make sure he's clean. I suppose it's too late now since the two of you already live together, but..."

Oh, what the hell, I feel like being a total shit again. "I can whip out my dick if you want to inspect it." I reach for my zipper and Jules quickly slaps my hand.

"And besides that area." Karina points to my cock. "His mouth is atrocious, just filthy, but so is yours, so perhaps you have found the man of your dreams."

"Well, *we're* no saints," Sam says as Karina nods in agreement. "And you have to understand our actions were out of love."

"That's laughable," I mutter.

"Mark, hush," Jules demands. "So you know his background, but wanted to hear it from us?"

"Yep," Sam says. "If he denied these things or made up some other cockamamie story, then we'd be worried. I can't fucking stand liars."

My fingers tap anxiously at the table. *Tappity-tap, tap, tap*, sounding like the old asshole's pattering cane. Fuck, what is it about her dad? Besides the fact that he's a dick like me, maybe the unease is because we're close in age.

"I can feel the tension around us," he says. "The veins in your neck are throbbing."

Our shoulders rise and fall together in steady breaths. He glares at my neck then down to where my concealed gun rests. He's pushing me again, seeing if I'll snap, testing to see what'll take for me to boil over. I thought this game was over, but if he's not backing down, neither am I. "You know, Sam, younger guys are like minnows, undeveloped and useless, swimming aimlessly in circles, but they do come in handy because you can use them as bait. And older men remind me of seahorses, the slowest fish on the planet. They're easy to walk away from and ignore. But you... you're more like a hagfish. You kill your prey by covering it in slime. You live off decaying corpses and when you come across a large carcass, you dig inside and eat your way out. And if someone tries to eat you, he'll gag on the slime you've shot inside his mouth. But trust me, I'm good at eating people. Think of me as a troll... *and I'll eat you, for supper,*" I sing.

"Don't go there," Jules says. "Mark stop. Dad, stop."

"Nope, you're wrong about one thing," he responds. "The slowest fish are dead fish."

"I used to be a call girl," Karina blurts out, trying to distract the two of us. "It's how I paid my way through college. We'd be hypocrites to be too upset over Mark and his past, or how he acts today because of it. Right, honey?" she says to Sam.

"Wha-what?" Jules' mouth drops open... "Oh, wow." She pauses, then a few seconds later she tries to respond, pauses again... opens her mouth... speechless... utterly speechless.

The table is quieter than the dead guy in my septic tank. Karina tightens her lips and looks to her husband for assistance. He shrugs, I shrug, and poor Jules says, "Gah!"

No one speaks.

Minutes pass, and still, nothing. Not a word.

After four slices of pumpkin pie and a carafe of decaf coffee, we're still waiting for something, but none of us are exactly sure what that something is—perhaps an apology, a confession, more details, or wanting to turn back time to know less. Less is better. Jesus fucking Christ, I can't stand it.

I inhale deeply as everyone waits for the *only* voice of reason to save the evening. Sam leans in, Karina looks up, Jules grimaces and shakes her head, and I say brashly,

"So... how 'bout them Cowboys?"

GOOD NIGHT

T he door of our suite slams shut and Jules attacks. It's a full on, palm smacking, cheek reddening, groin bashing, maximum impact, one-sided brawl. I set my hands on my hips and take it, which pisses her off even more.

"How dare you!"

Smack.

My head turns and I smile. This shit gets me erect quicker than a lick and suck from her mouth. I fucking love it.

"I can't believe you find this amusing!"

I wipe the grin off my face, spread my legs, and clasp my hands behind my back, presenting my body for whatever punishment I deserve.

"Five minutes! It wasn't even five fucking minutes before you and my dad were at war!"

Smack.

My hair falls forward with that one. Fuck, I hope she hits me again.

"Rude, Mark. So fucking rude."

"Well, your dad—"

115

"Don't talk." Her finger is an inch from my face.

I bite my top lip and bow my head, listening to her throw a fit.

"I can't believe they hired someone to dig up shit on you. Do you think the guy was snooping around here? They, or he, better not be looking for more. Argh! I need to talk to my parents. Gah!"

I shake my head. "I'm sure the detective found whatever he needed online and that was enough to please them. They could've found the same crap on their own if they searched hard enough. It's not like my father's murder and the other shit with Cove is under lock and key from the world."

"But the porn, Mark! Seriously! Did you *have* to go there? I had my fingers crossed that just once you'd put on your big boy panties and act like a man instead of a foolish dick fairy."

"I don't own any panties," I say. "What the hell is a foolish dick fai—"

"Shut up! What the fuck were you thinking when you said, *can you picture me doing that shit to your daughter?*" she says in a deep voice, mocking my inability to stay in control. "You couldn't act like an adult for one fucking night. You couldn't do that for me? For *me*!" She stomps upstairs and I run after her, grabbing her arm at the top of the stairs.

Smack.

Okay, that one hurt... I think my lip's bleeding. My tongue glides across it, tasting blood. Fucking hell, that got the pre-cum flowing.

"You done?" I ask. "Wait, where are you going? Put the fucking suitcase down." I reach for it, but get pushed away.

"I'm not staying here tonight."

"Where ya gonna go? You're not taking one of my trucks."

"You fuckhole! For the past year they were *our* trucks. Now they're yours? Screw you."

"That's not what I meant."

"Yeah, I know. And you didn't mean anything you said during dinner either, right?" She dashes to the bathroom and grabs a handful of items, tossing them into the bag. She zips it and rushes down the stairs.

"Freakin' A, Jules. I let your little 'makeup artist' fib slide so cut me some slack. You're no sweet angel. And your fucking parents could've been a hell of a lot nicer to me."

"No, they were our guests. They didn't have to be nice."

"What? So everyone gets to beat on Mark Jameson? That's the game we're playing now?"

"Stop referring to yourself in the third person!" she screams.

"Mark Jameson disagrees."

"My God, is there anyone you like? Anyone you get along with other than yourself? Fuck, and what are we, some white trash couple who can't have a nice meal and a decent conversation with another couple without getting into a brawl? Reaching for a gun? Were you going to shoot my father?" She takes a deep breath before continuing. "I know I had my moments and was a total bitch, but I sure as fuck didn't start the evening out that way until you and my dad went after each other like a couple of wolves. And believe me, I'm peeved at him, but you? I was hoping for more. You know? Seems like all you need is my pussy to be happy. That's what your life is about. You fuck and fall asleep, then tomorrow you'll get up and work all day, then fuck, then you'll smoke, then fuck, then sleep, then fuck, then work, then smoke, then fuck again, and sleep."

"Holy hell," I mutter.

"Yeah, Mark, holy fuckin' hell! It was one fucking dinner!"

"You're really pissed at me."

"Uh!" She throws her arms in the air. "No, I'm not angry. The evening was satisfying and pleasant. It was fan-titty-tastic. Can't wait to do it again. How 'bout tomorrow? Now fuck off!"

"Hey, wait!"

The door slams and I quickly rush over and follow her out, catching her down the corridor.

"Where the fuck are you going?" I ask, smiling at guests as I walk by.

"Gee, there're two hundred twenty-two rooms in this place, see if you can find me."

"Two hundred twenty-one minus ours." I let her go, watching her drag the suitcase toward the elevator. "Two hundred twenty, minus Jack's suite," I say.

A woman in the hall voices her support with a, "you go girl," after Jules holds her head high and her middle finger higher.

"Oh, and minus your parents' room, that would be two hundred and nineteen, darlin'. And I've got cameras. I'll find you," I shout, no longer giving a shit if I'm heard. If I want to profess my love for her, so be it. "You'll fucking miss me!"

The elevator dings and she vanishes inside, not responding to my loving words.

"Fuck," I say under my breath. "Shit." I turn and head back to the suite. "What a nightmare."

Tap, tap.

No, damn it. That fucker, *he's* my nightmare. I spin around, only the corridor's empty. I swear I heard that fucking cane again, but the interior corridors of my hotel have carpeting, so that's impossible, unless it echoed from the lobby... no, it was too close.

I take a slow stroll around the second floor, stopping every twenty feet, listening to the gentle holiday music, smelling the pine branches outside each room, listening for the cane, walking, listening, walking... reaching the opposite end of the hotel and smelling... yep, goddamn patchouli.

Jack and Emma were sitting in the lobby when I left the restaurant with Jules and her parents. He smiled at the four of us, then I'm sure he brought Emma upstairs the moment we were out of sight. I was a complete fucking idiot not to realize this was going to happen.

"Well played, son. Well played. Get ready for a new approach from your old man."

I swipe my key card and quietly enter the suite. It's pitch black, darker than a moonless night, and as motionless as a frozen lake. Slowly, my eyes adjust and I'm able to make my way through the living room, up the stairs, and to the master bedroom suite where I'm overcome by the smell of pot. It floats out the open door, overpowering the patchouli I've been following to this point.

A popping noise comes from the bed. It sounds like he's either cooking bacon or has a fire burning under the sheets. Which I suppose isn't far from the truth when you're about to get laid.

I lean against the dresser with my arms crossed, watching a bowl burn red before someone lets out a hoarse cough. That's Jack. I follow the trail of the lit bowl to the side table, unable to see his arms or face, but hearing the popping noise continue.

"Incredible." He laughs hysterically and coughs again. "That's wicked good. I can't believe I haven't tried this before."

"Jack," I say calmly.

"Oh, fuck. Dad. Get real! You can't bust in on me like this. Not now."

There's a rustling movement in the bed and a crunching, popping, crackling noise. I turn on the light and see Emma's head emerge from under the sheets. Her hair's messy, lipstick's smeared, shoulders bare, and she's holding a package of Pop Rocks.

"What the fuck are you doing?" I ask, trying to stay calm. She opens her mouth and the candy pops wildly.

"You just ruined what was going to be the best night of head, ever!"

I raise my hand, breathing in, closing my eyes, and trying my best not to lose my shit in front of this sixteen-year-old girl. But who am I kidding? If I lost it in front of Jules' parents...

"Emma, I'm going to say this one time, and one time only. Get dressed and wait downstairs. Do it quickly. Do it now."

"I thought you said your dad was cool," she whispers, giving him a kiss on the cheek as he hands her a wrinkled dress.

"The man's jealous." He tugs her back for another kiss. "Make sure you save some of that candy for next time."

I turn away, allowing them to dress in private, using the time to bring up security on my cell. When her footsteps reach the stairs, I turn back to Jack while speaking to my staff.

"Joe, that you?" I ask.

"Yes, everything good, Mr. Jameson?"

"I need you to come upstairs to escort a young girl to the lobby then wait with her until her mother arrives. Can you meet me in the corridor in a few minutes?"

"Be right there."

I end the call and approach Jack with hesitation. My

intent's unclear, and after an already fucked up night, I'm debating if this shit is worth my time. It should be. Right? I'm supposed to be a *Dad*.

"Wipe the foolish grin off your face."

"That's gonna be tough since I'm kinda stoned."

I look down at him, knowing I need to remain in control, verbally and physically in control. You can do this, Mark.

"For some reason, you think it's alright to abuse the few rules I've set for you. I asked you not to fuck, drink, or smoke on my property, and tonight you've done all three. You're underage and jeopardizing my business and my life."

"You'd make a good politician. Always promising, never delivering, saying one thing, yet doing something else. Flip-flop, flip-flop."

"Stand up," I request.

"Hey buddy, do this illegal thing for me, oh, but don't do anything illegal on your own. So, Dad, what are you gonna do, cut me again? For fuck's sake, did you see the chick you forced out of my bed? What would you have done with her? Shake her hand goodnight or fuck her? Come off your high horse. You were so cool earlier, now you're acting like a fucking reserved businessman again. You're full of empty threats and empty promises. And look at your face, I bet your girl even smacks you around. Ya pussy. And fuck, you're ruining my high! I'm furious you came in here and fucked up my night!"

Oh, it's time. This little shit needs more than a small

nick from my blade, he's getting his ass kicked. I'm not taking a step back, but a step forward—his life's about to crumble. After clenching my fists and feeling the anger and frustration exploding inside... fuck, I hit my son. And it's not a pussy slap either. He gets a hard smack across the top of his head then a fisted strike to his jaw before his neck's held tight. I want to choke the life out of him.

His mouth drops open and he cradles his face with an expression of total disgust. After my release, an attempted retaliation swing ends in failure when his wrist is caught, body turned, and his face shoved into the bed.

"Stop kicking your feet like a madman."

"You bastard!" he shouts into the sheets.

"Jack." I grin in victory. "Do you still think I'm full of empty threats? Well here's another. You're grounded for the weekend. I'll give you three minutes to gather what you need then you're coming to my suite."

"Grounded? No one's ever grounded me before."

"I'm fine with hitting you again if you want to disobey. Keep mouthing off. Just try me." I release his head.

"I've never been grounded," he repeats, with a hard kick to the mattress.

"Good, I'll throw a party and we can celebrate, and Jules will bake you a *Happy Grounded for the Weekend* cake. Now get up, get your things, and come downstairs."

I head to the living room and see Emma waiting patiently by the door. "Empty threats," I mumble. "I'll show you what an empty threat is."

"I'm sorry, Mr. Jameson," she whispers.

I open the door and she scurries out with her tail between her legs.

"Was that your pot?"

She nods as we walk down the corridor.

"Do you have it, or did you leave it with him?"

"I took it," she says in a mousy voice.

"Don't bring drugs into my hotel again."

"But Jack said you smoked."

After I present her with my best side-eye, she hustles into her coat with sealed lips, smart enough not to argue back.

"Joe."

I shake hands with my security guard then introduce him to Emma, repeating my instructions and emphasizing not to let her out of his sight until her mother arrives. As soon as they disappear, Jack emerges, making his way down the corridor with a bag in hand and animalistic grunts spewing from his mouth. He reaches my suite, types the code, then stomps inside, slamming the door in my face. His actions, like Jules, make me smile madly. I mean, how could someone not love *me*? The people in my life have some serious personality issues.

He's already in the upstairs bedroom when I enter. "Jack! Come down and let's talk. I wasn't serious about the cake. How 'bout brownies instead?" I smirk. "I heard that! Don't break my stuff!"

Sounded like a table lamp was smashed against the wall. "Clean it up!" I yell. "And don't cut yourself!"

I'm tired of yelling. I'm tired of being disrespected. And I'm just plain tired.

"My kid's a fucking asshole." I sigh, running a finger slowly along the liquor bottles in my cabinet. "Let's see." I scan the labels. "What's it gonna be tonight... eenie, meenie, miney... Jameson. Jameson Irish Whiskey."

I pour a shot, wishing I were the one who had thought of such a great company. I suppose then I'd be copying Cove. I have to admit, his Dark Scarlett wine is some of the best I've tasted.

My cell rings as I'm pouring a second shot... incoming call from the front desk.

"Mr. Jameson?"

"Yeah, go ahead, Chloe."

"Vanessa from the restaurant mentioned we should keep an eye out for an older gentleman... like, in his eighties, with a cane?"

"That's him. Is he there?"

"He was. He tried to check in, only he wanted to pay cash and he didn't have a driver's license or a credit card. He showed me a birth certificate instead."

The whiskey shot is downed, the glass slammed on the counter, and I want answers. "Who is it? What's the guy's name."

"Well... it was a bit odd."

"Yeah, my whole fucking life is odd. Just say it."

"You. The birth certificate said Mark Jameson. Were you born February second to Elizabeth and Paul?"

I rub my forehead, trying to reduce the ever-growing

stress in my life. Dear fucking lord, what the fucking hell is this old fuck doing?

"He still down there?"

"No. I told him he needed a credit card, but it was obvious by the cab waiting outside that he already knew that. He hobbled off, got in, and was driven away."

"When?" I ask, heading for the safe in my office.

"Like, a minute ago."

"Don't hesitate next time, call if he returns." I hang up and open the small steel door under my desk. My birth certificate is in my possession, plain as the light of day, along with all my other important papers. It must've been a copy.

For fuck's sake, what gives? My family's all dead except for my mom and Sophia. I wonder if this is a company man. One of David Rosen's or my father's heavies from back in the day, coming around to collect an old debt, or revenge for some shit I know nothing about. Whoever the fuck he is, he's taunting me, but he'll find out soon enough I don't play well with others. As a matter a fact, in high school I was voted most likely *never* to play well with others. So back off, shitfuck. I have no reservations about killing a guy who can barely walk. Just like the joke about the kid in the neighborhood who loses his legs. You don't feel sorry for him; you ask his parents if you can have his bike—it's not shameful, it's life. Okay... maybe that analogy doesn't work well in this instance, nevertheless it's funny as fuck. Yeah, go ahead, be a dick to me, see what you get, whether you're sixteen like Jack, or eighty, I don't care.

I look upstairs, thinking he's been quiet for some time. "Hey buddy, why don't you come downstairs so we can talk."

No answer.

"Jack!" I listen by the stairwell, but besides the sound of a ticking clock and the furnace kicking in, it's uncomfortably quiet. I walk upstairs and slowly open the door. He's on the bed curled into a tiny ball, wearing a pair of black sleep pants with a hoodie pulled over his head. There's sniffling and a soft cry, and when he hears me enter, he covers his face with a pillow.

"Hey." I sit next to him with a hand on his side. He rolls over and pushes me away, repositioning the pillow so I can't see his tears. "You pissed at me or did I really hurt you?" I exhale, noticing the pocketknife I gave him earlier on the side table. Since he's not leaving my suite for a few days, I take it back. There's no point in him carrying it around.

"I suppose I'd be angry too, but that doesn't mean you're right and I'm wrong. Although if you're hurt, then I fucked up and maybe we should talk it out. So which is it?"

"Mom," he says in a soft, tearful voice. "I miss mom. I want to see her. I need to talk to her."

"Oh." I breathe out, looking around the room for some magical instructions to appear. "I don't, I don't know what I can—"

"Leave me alone." He sniffs.

I pause and fiddle with my watch then check that my gun's in place while trying to think of something to say. An apology won't do shit, but I don't have any other words at the moment. "I'm sorry. And I'm sorry I hit you."

"Just go away. I seriously don't care anymore."

I nod and look at the floor with clasped hands. It's amazing how quickly you can feel in command of a relationship, having total power and control, only to realize those things can just as easily turn to regret. Feeling remorse is something I never admit to, and maybe it's all the alcohol that's fucking with my emotions, but right now I just hit a ten on the guilt meter.

I untie and slide off my shoes then lie next to him with an arm raised, hovering, debating, then slowly lowering it across his body. "It's okay to cry."

"I'm not crying." He sniffs. "I'm not a wuss."

I move closer and surprisingly, he submits, taking my hand and bringing it closer to his chest. "I hate that she's not here, especially at night when I'm all alone and have nothing to do except think. I can't turn off my brain. Sometimes, her scent is on my clothing, or I find one of her hairs in my things."

"Is that why you slept in front of my fireplace the other night?"

He says 'yes' with a heaving chest while he fights to hold in his sobs. "I wanted Emma here tonight. It wasn't about fucking; I just didn't want to be alone. The pot I asked you for could've blocked my thoughts about her suicide, and the alcohol from that guy in the restaurant would've done the same, and Emma... I just don't want to think about what happened. She left me. Mom left me." He starts to cry.

"She didn't have a choice, Jack," I say softly. "She wanted you to remember her before..." I can't believe I'm choking up. God, I wish I hadn't done those shots. Whiskey unlocks the *loving* creature in me.

"I'll take anything right now, any drug, any girl, I don't care as long as I don't have to think about her. Why don't you go ahead and hit me again. It took away a lot of the other pain I was feeling. Just fucking hit me!"

"You're describing how addictions start. You want a fix to stifle something in your life instead of facing it head on. I'm not sorry I took those things away from you tonight. I did it because of your attitude and because you're underage. I'm the one responsible if the shit hits the fan and the cops show up at my door. But also, I did it because I care about you, whether you realize it or not. This bullshit at your age is normal, but I didn't... there are other ways... you can't... you need to..." What the hell am I doing? Jack's a mini me and for fuck's sake, why is there anything wrong with that?

"What?" he asks.

"I don't know anymore." I rise and sit on the edge of the bed, head in my hands, and feet tapping the floor. I'm useless when it comes to dealing with grief, and I'm screwing his life up worse than my dad did mine.

It's ironic that most teens his age will end up in a

hotel room for a night to fuck, yet Jack stays in a hotel every night and I'm saying 'no,' not here. I'm trying to have all of the control, including when and where he fucks, or smokes, or does whatever, knowing it's gonna happen anyway... and if not here, then where? At the resort in some restroom? Out on the slopes in the bitter cold with skiers passing by? Or maybe he'll go off and drink on his own and end up face down, frozen in a snowdrift—all because I didn't want to deal with any unknowns or surprises in my life, or him... *my son.* Well, have some fucking goddamn balls, Mark, and stop being such a dick.

"Fuck, I can't figure out what I'm doing."

I ease into the club chair in the corner of the room, unbuttoning my jacket and rubbing my lips with two fingers, watching him, eyeing every breath, up and down. I've never felt so lost and confused about a situation in my life. Everything with him seems like a mistake. And I know, I've been saying that to myself for years. All I can do is try another approach, take another shot, and keep guessing my way through fatherhood.

"Jack, we'll work something out, only don't lie to me and sneak around behind my back. There's too much shit that could go wrong. If you need something, we'll discuss it, but my business isn't going to turn into a brothel for a bunch of your friends or a house of weed."

He moves the pillow away from his face and listens.

"You're still grounded, but in a few days you can have Emma or someone else over, and you can smoke here, upstairs, where the smell isn't going to drift into the corridors for my guests to track. And I don't want anyone to see you take some young girl into a room. The suite you're staying in on the other side of the hotel is for you alone, no one else. If you have friends over, you can use the pool, the weight room, the restaurant, or stay in *my* suite, but don't take anyone into any of the other rooms. Got it?"

"Yes," he mumbles. "Thanks... and you didn't need to apologize for hitting me. I wanted you to. The throbbing in my jaw is a perfect distraction from everything in my life. I knew if I provoked you enough you'd lose your cool."

Sounds like a good cover. He's clearly embarrassed I took him down. But if pain distracts him, then he's got the temperament to become a cutter, and fuck, I'd rather see the kid smoke weed than slice his flesh.

I leave for a second and get the metal container from my dresser. "New road, new method, take another shot at this," I declare, packing a bowl before returning to the room.

"You still high?" I ask.

"Only a little bit. Emma smoked before me while I was eating her out, so I only had one drag before you walked in," he says.

"Here." I set it on the nightstand, ignoring his sex comment. "Hell, I can't believe I'm doing this, but... if you need it to ease the pain about your mom or to help you sleep... it's... it's here."

131

"Really?" He turns and sees the bowl on the nightstand. "So, use drugs? That's the solution? Another one-eighty?" He smiles and wipes the tears off his face.

"Watch yourself. Don't switch back into a smartass so quickly or I'll change my mind."

"This is awesome." He gives me a thumbs-up with an instant change in demeanor. "You're the best."

"Yeah, I know, I'm such a wonderful dad when I cut people's throats and give drugs to my son; the perfect father and the perfect guy for any woman. That's why Jules is MIA at the moment."

"I thought so." He sits up and takes a hit then passes it along, but I decline. I may be a dumbfuck for giving him pot, but I'm not going to smoke it with him too. "Dad, try the Pop Rocks on her. Place some inside with your finger then start licking. I swear she'll forgive you for whatever you did, you gotta try it. And when she uses them on you, oh man." He laughs. "Dang, this is good stuff." He looks at the bowl and takes another hit.

"Are you okay for a while?"

"Yeah." He wipes the remaining tears off his cheeks and grins. "Am I allowed to talk to my friends online? They're waiting for the details about Emma. That okay so I don't have to be alone?"

"Are you telling them the part where I walked in on you?"

"Hell no," he says.

"And it didn't happen in my hotel, right?"

"Nope. Won't mention it."

"You're learning." I pick up my shoes and head to my bedroom to change.

"Except I'll tell them I albino clammed her!" he shouts with a burst of laughter.

"Fucking teenage boys," I grumble. At least he stopped crying. I know he's gonna break down at his age, especially over his mom, but I'm not the best at dealing with that shit. That's why I love Jules—the badass that she is; she rarely sheds a tear.

Now, where is my princess?

EXCUSES, EXCUSES

T he room's dark except for the flickering lights from the hotel grounds that pervade the window. I can smell her perfume and see her silhouette stretched out on the bed, but she's not asleep. I know because she says *cocksucker* and *fuckhead* as I undress. I slide alongside her warm, nearly nude body and kiss her shoulder down to her forearm, gazing at her illuminated tits. I lovingly profess that she's beautiful, feeling my cock rise and nudge against her flesh.

She drops her underwear partway down and spreads her ass. "Is this what you came here for?" she asks in a defeated voice. "Go ahead, Mark. Do your thing."

I tug them back up and pull her close so I can view her face. "No. I came to apologize to an alluring, strong, caring woman who deserves better than a prick like me." I brush her cheek with the back of my hand. "And after I apologize, I want to make love to her."

She rejects my touch and turns away. "I hope you came with a wheelbarrow full of flowers and chocolates," she says. "Did you track me on your security cam?"

"Yes."

"Why? Because you can't stand to lose and you need to be in control of everyone and everything at all times?"

My fingers run gracefully along her back, tracing the word *dick* as a second apology.

"That's exactly what you are, and you reek of booze. How much did you drink tonight?"

She's angry, yet she knew I'd be here since she's not hiding under a robe or flannel pajamas. That means she's craving my touch, but I'll have to beg if I want anything in return.

"I'm sorry. This is my fault, right?" Her voice is lifeless. "You said you didn't want to meet my parents and I should've listened. I should know by now how much you hate people."

"Don't turn things around and blame yourself. That's an evil trick to make me feel like shit, and it's working... and I don't hate people... just... I'm not... eh." I exhale. "Your mom was nice, but men are assholes, including your dad."

"So you should be the lone man on this planet?"

"That would be great, but I'm also an ass so I guess I fit right in with the rest of them. But yes, if it was just me, life would be grand."

"You need help... and what about Cove?"

"He's like a woman so he can stay."

That produced a fraction of a laugh; good, I'm making a comeback.

"I'm aggravated, Mark, and what really sucks is my mother asked if I knew the guy who went missing the

135

other night from the bar. Her question took me by surprise. I hope they don't have someone snooping around us still. I can't imagine them finding out I'm a murderer."

I can tell by her cracking voice that she's worried, more about her parents than killing the guy. I didn't realize before tonight how much she cares about them, and her concern over what they think about her. She was trying to put on a good show, wanted to impress them, and I destroyed the entire night.

"You're a victim, not a murderer. And everything's been taken care of. The cops are focused on the guy's friend who was with him that night at the bar. Plus, I read in the paper that a snowplow went through the back lot and alley that morning, sweeping the scene. I had already checked and cleared the area, but that plow did double duty for us. Everything's fine and it will remain a missing persons case forever." She faces me and our eyes finally meet. "Jules." I place my hand on the side of her neck and cradle her jaw. "I'm sorry for treating your parents like shit. I was a disrespectful fuckwit who embarrassed you in front of your family. I should've walked into the situation like it was a business deal. That's the only time I'm ever charming and civil around people, especially men. And don't..." I cover her lips with a finger before she has a chance to protest my pathetic rationalization. "Don't be offended that I just said that. You're the most important business deal of my life, and coming from a guy like me, you should take it as..."

Her head turns to detach from my finger and she

says, "A compliment. It's flattering, but only coming from you because you're such a bastard."

"I'll make everything up to you."

"Yeah, you will." She digs her fingernails into my ass and draws my body closer. "Believe me, I'm annoyed and plan on giving you a hard time for days, but I'm not going to let your bad behavior take away from my needs. Keeping my legs shut because you screwed up would punish both of us, and why should I suffer? Now, I want a visit from your cock—an extremely *slow* visit. Enter and admit your guilt, then make your request for forgiveness on your way out." She removes and tosses her underwear across the room. "I'll decide after a few remorseful departures whether you deserve to continue on."

"Mmm, I love your games."

She spreads her legs wide, yielding me the right of entry. I pause, my tip snug between her inner lips while my mouth hangs open like a drooling junkie waiting for a fix.

"You're powerless," she says with an erotic hiss. "Defenseless, and my prisoner until you cum."

I seize her chin and move slowly like she asked, deep inside with my mouth pressed delicately to hers.

"Repent," she demands.

I slide back gradually and kiss her again, hoping my look of adoration, sensual movements, and compassionate touch will convey the regret that I feel. With my forehead resting on hers, I travel calmly in, exhale, and retreat with a second intense rush of air. Repeat... gently, feeling every tiny spasm inside her pussy, every slick fluid secreted over my dick, and hanging on every inciting, amorous remark between her warm breaths.

Inch by inch, I gift her my hard cock with confidence, knowing I've been forgiven. We've become lost in a steady motion. Her lips are nibbled, mouth occupied, and hypnotic tits caressed.

"Oh," she says in a quiet, loving voice. "Mark."

I remain graceful, moving on top and pulling her legs around my waist. Her pussy is seduced, aching, rubbing across my groin, being enticed to cum.

We kiss, pant, and fuck. Kiss, pant, and...

"Mark." Her hands move in a whirl down my chest and up my back. "It's perfect. I love you." She fondles her tits then lowers her fingers to her clit. "Jesus, Mark," she whispers. "Fuck me. Keep fucking me."

Her words are whispered as I coax her clit and kiss her precious skin. She knows saying my name when we fuck makes my heart skip and cock swell. I only wish she could feel how incredible this is from my end. The nerve endings in my dick are on fire and my head's spinning like a dancing devil.

"Can't wait to hear you cum. I'll hold out for as long as it takes." Licking my lips in anticipation, "I can see your muscles tightening, your tits swelling. It's so fucking good, isn't it?"

"Mark..."

"That's right." I straighten my arms and watch her body rock under mine. "Feel it. Focus on my cock. Let it control you."

She lifts her chest off the bed. Her arms and legs tense while she holds her breath. There's a soft *ohh, ohh,* wavering from a low to high pitch while she powers toward my dick. Her head tilts back, she clutches my flesh, and an eruptive outpouring of, "I'm cumming. Oh God, I'm cumming," is a rewarding song to my ears.

We pant and convulse as one until I lower over her heaving chest to taste her plump, salty lips. Her neck and chest blaze like welding sparks, lit from the outdoor lights. Gorgeous. She's beautiful.

"Forgive and forget." Her fingers run provocatively down my back, across my ass then back up my sides. I shudder from the arousing touch, my dick still gliding in her pussy. "I can never stay angry with you for long. I'd miss the sex too much." A warm, glowing, smile appears. "Do you want me?" she asks.

"Yes."

"You need to get off?"

"Yes," I repeat, drunk, and acting like an innocent, submissive boy.

"I suppose you've been good and deserve to cum. Stand next to the bed," she says. I pull out and stand with my stiff cock bouncing eagerly. She kneels on the bed and gives it a long, wet lick. "I know how much you love a titty fuck, so slide in."

I hold her chest with a grin, squeezing her tits together onto my cock. She's so fucking right; I'll take a good tit fuck any day of the week, especially from her...

only from her... and that wild tongue of hers. Damn.

I moan and watch my dick slither through her sweaty tits. Her tongue gives it a good lick on the way up... yep, there it is again. Fuck, I love it. Fuck.

"Oh, getting off fast tonight?" she teases. "Bet you can't wait to shoot that cum onto my face."

"Yes." I pant.

"All... over... my face," she says in her sluttiest voice. "I just love it when your warm cum covers me, dripping from my lips, down my chin, then falling onto my tits. Is it coming? Are you gonna shoot it out all over me?"

"Fuckin' hell. St-stop. I mean, don't. Don't stop. Don't." I push her down and hurdle on top, my legs straddling her chest, riding her like the crazed sex fiend that I am. "Uh, I'm gonna cum, open your mouth, open it. Open it now!"

She raises her head and the first shot hits her forehead, but the second and third land deep inside. She grins with a lick of her lips, giving me a suggestive look as she lets it run down her chin.

"Oh, hell yeah." I collapse. "That face, that look... I can't wait to think about it next time I jerk off. Hell fucking yeah... man... I just want to stay in this state forever. Shit. Oh fucking, fucking, fucking, fuck, shit."

She laughs and wipes her face on the sheet as I lie with my arms and legs spread wide on the bed. "I'll never move from this spot again. Just come see me twice a day, get me off, bring me some food, and... and... oh... oh, crap." That old guy just came to mind.

"Oh crap, what?"

"Nothing. My head's a mess. I don't know what I'm saying." I'll wait until the cum's off her face to tell her about the incident with my birth certificate. "Jules." I touch her arm softly. "You know I love you, but it's also in my nature to feel superior to men. I'm an arrogant ass who needs to be in charge. That's what happened at dinner."

She rolls her eyes. "Excuses, excuses."

"Hey, you've known since day one that I'm like this."

"It *is* part of the reason why I love you."

"So, we good? Because I don't want to wake up tomorrow and find out you're still fuming about what happened at dinner. If that's the case, I won't go back to being a fuckhead until you give me the okay... maybe."

"I'm not *as* angry, but I still need to talk to my dad, and just so you know, I'm not marrying you anytime soon. After last night, it'll be awhile before that subject gets discussed again."

She ignores my look of disappointment while gliding her fingertips down my chest and abdomen, floating in a circular motion until she reaches my stitches. "How is it?" she asks about the wound.

"It hurt like hell for days, though it's fine now."

Her hand continues to drift, poking at my slack dick, exploring my abs and nipples before coming to rest on my shoulder.

"I think it's great you came crawling back. How does it feel to be a pussy?" she teases like a bitch.

"Well, let me tell you something, beautiful princess,"

I say in my finest sarcastic voice. "That's been my life's dream ever since I saw my first porno mag. All I ever wanted was to become a soft, moist, pussy. And now that I've become one, I can fuck myself all day and all night. So I'll take it as a compliment. Thanks."

"Mark?"

"Hmm?"

"Don't ever use the term moist in the same sentence as pussy. Brownies are moist, not snatches."

"Mark Jameson disagrees."

"You're starting again." She laughs. "And while we're on the subject, princess is such an overused pet name."

"What?" I sit up, slightly offended that she's now, on top of everything else, going to tell me what I can call her.

"Well, I guess it's not as bad as baby, babe, or kitten."

"There're only so many fucking names out there. And most of them I wouldn't use on an animal, let alone the woman I love."

"Maybe you can call me princess *and* something else, switch it up occasionally. It'll be fun and romantic."

"Sure." I get dressed, tossing her clothing on the bed. "I'll call you shithead from now on."

"Mark, seriously."

"Oh, I'm serious, shithead."

"Sometimes, I can't tell if you're joking or just unwell."

"The latter. Picture this—a giant *moist* pussy walking around the hotel, carrying a knife, rubbing against its victims to get off while shouting, 'princess, oh princess.'

That'll be me."

"What are you talking about?"

"It doesn't matter because I'm insane."

"Oh, I forgot..." She dresses and zips her suitcase then stands by the door... "You've been drinking."

"Yep, though not enough. I'm getting tanked when we get back to the suite. I'm still trying to process the fact that your dad's an embalmer. Liquor might help me laugh it off." I smirk. "Talk about complete opposites. I kill and your father preserves."

"If I were you, I'd consider getting on his good side. He *is* my dad."

I open the door. "You ready? I don't want to leave Jack alone for long. He's having a rough night."

"He's at our place?"

"He's grounded for a few days. Don't ask."

"Grounded?" She laughs. "He let you do that? What the hell happened?"

I walk silently, giving her a headshake to let it go. Plus, I just fucking told her not to ask.

"Mark?" She presses for an answer, only my focus is on the scene ahead.

Our place.

Our door.

Is open.

I check the corridor for guests then pull out my gun as Jules quickly notices the issue. A split-second later, her blade is out.

"You think Jack left and forgot to close it?" she

whispers. I shake my head, holding up a hand to keep quiet and stay back.

My heart trots then starts to gallop when I set my hand on the door. Blood gushes through my veins like a river after a heavy rainstorm. I'm all fight and no flight. I listen to the sound of the crackling fireplace in the suite. It wasn't lit when I left. I swear, if anyone hurt my son...

Jules hides her knife when a woman steps off the elevator, but I'm not letting my guard down. The gun stays out and I *will* fucking use it on whoever the fuck's in my suite. When you don't know what you're walking into, or whether or not an intruder's armed, a gun always takes precedence over a blade. I'll kill a bastard for breaking and entering, and in a case like this, I don't give two-shits how messy it is. This is my fucking property, my home, and if I want to shoot a rat fuck in the face for trespassing, I will.

I step stealthily inside the entryway, listen, and take in a whiff of air, searching for any odor or clue to who's inside.

"Smells like pizza," she says, using her softest voice. I smell it too, except there's something else.

My nose twitches from the strong scent of women's perfume. It's different from Emma's patchouli and Jules' delicate scents, much heavier, like vanilla and roses. And my gut feeling tells me this has nothing to do with Jack.

With my gun raised, I take a short step into the living room...

"What the fuck is this?"

PART FIVE

BASTARD

I lower my gun. Confused.

The fireplace illuminates two young boys sleeping soundly on the floor, bare feet poking out from under fleece blankets, mouths open wide, arms and legs overlapping—one holding a half-eaten slice of pizza and the other clinging to a cell phone. The place is a mess— open suitcases, clothing flung everywhere, fast food and used napkins on my coffee table and floor. Christ, I've only been gone an hour. Fucking kids. Jack too. He's also asleep on the floor, getting his hair massaged by a beautiful woman... my sister, Sophia.

"Reminds me of marble cake." Jules nods toward the crew. "Two dark tufts of hair next to your son's golden locks."

The Everton boys are back, Dax and Xav, but Cove's nowhere to be seen.

"What are you doing here?" I whisper, putting my gun away before my nephews wake up.

Sophia places a finger to her lips for me to hush, then points to my son's ears and the red mark on his jaw, signaling with a troubling headshake that I'm an ass.

Either she believes I'm not taking care of him, or she knows I caused the damage to his flesh. I shrug in response, not giving a shit. If she knew the preceding events, his bitching and disrespect, she wouldn't pity him.

I motion her to the kitchen and she rises slowly, trying not to wake the boys. Jack looks up and smiles, watching the three of us leave the room.

"What the fuck are you doing here? I just talked to you on the phone and you didn't mention anything about a visit. And where's Cove?" I pour another shot of Jameson whiskey only to have it stolen away and guzzled by my sister.

"Give me another," she demands.

"No, answer me. You traveled two thousand miles to my hotel. What the hell? And where's your husband?"

"I left him," she says in a sullen voice. "I'm not putting up with his drinking and depression anymore. I can't handle it, and it's affecting the boys. I caught Daxton with a bottle of beer in our backyard the other evening. My kids are only eleven. They're too young to be experimenting... and I know it's because of Cove."

Jules reaches out and places a hand on my sister's shoulder before bringing her close for a hug.

"I've been telling you for years the guy self-medicates with booze. It's bullshit," I say, pouring myself more liquor as I rage about her drunkard husband. His alcoholism may drive *me* to drink. "Why the fuck won't he get any help?"

"He's tried a few times, but always backs off whenever

the difficult discussions about his past come up. He wants to get help without having to talk about his time with Dad."

"That's not gonna happen." I hold my glass in front of her with a finger pointing toward her face. "You've known this shit forever. Why now? Why not years ago? You're either not telling me something or you've got the seven-year itch, in which case you need to go back to the guy. If you're bored, deal with it. Your whiny ass runs away from anything and everything when it hits a rough patch. And there's no way you came two thousand fucking miles just to get away from him. Why didn't you get a hotel in St. Louis and try to work things out? You ran, like always. Why?"

"Our entire lives have been a rough patch! And it's not a seven-year itch—it's twelve! And who's running away from life? You could be a bit more considerate for once."

"I'm saying these things out of love. I'm sympathetic, but I also know the two of you like the back of my hand. You're both a couple of kids in adult bodies. It's freaky. Your boys could take better care of you than you do." I cut her off as she tries to attack back. "And you'd think I'd say 'thank fuck, you finally left the pussy,' but the reality is, you need him. Think about it Soph, no one else would be able to deal with your immaturity other than him. If the two of you split, then you'll both be on your own forever. And you suck at being single. You'll never find another guy at your age. You'll sleep, eat, shower, shit, masturbate, and die alone."

"You asshole!" she shouts. "How dare you!"

"Shit, don't hit me." I rub my cheek. "Everyone's fucking smacking me today. Must be National Abuse Mark Jameson Day... stop."

"He's been drinking," Jules says. She turns back to the boys and notices Jack's listening to our conversation.

"Oh, great. This is just wonderful." Sophia stomps off to the living room.

"See, she's a kid. A baby."

"I leave one drunk and end up in the home of another. You're right. I should go back to St. Louis and get a hotel room. Never mind that you, my big brother who's supposed to take care of me, my brother the *hotel* owner, might have a room I could stay in. My brother, the skunk head!"

Her kids stir, moaning and stretching their scrawny arms.

"Dax, Xav, and I will spend this holiday by ourselves in some crappy St. Louis hotel, *if* we can get one this time of the year. And we'll eat spam and potato chips on paper plates for our Christmas dinner."

"Mark, don't make me apologize for you," Jules says. "Do it now or you're toast."

"Fine, but my apologies are worse than watching cows being put through a meat grinder. I only know how to say I'm sorry with my dick, and it's never coming out for family. I'm not a fan of incest, and—"

"Just go do it!"

I put the shot glass down and follow Jules to the living room. "Soph, I told you I was saying all that shit out of love. Besides, it's all true."

"Can we stay here or not?" she asks, holding two suitcases. "Just until I figure out what I'm gonna do."

"You mean, until you see if Cove comes running after you? Isn't that what you want?"

"And?"

"It proves my point that you're childish. Did he hit you? Did he smack you around and beat your ass?"

"No, of course not."

"Then there's no issue. I don't get it. Why did you leave again? Because he gets sloshed?"

She gestures to Xav and Dax. "They deserve better." Then she motions to Jack. "And for fuck's sake, Mark. So does your son. What the hell happened to him? He was stoned when we got here and he looks like he got in a fight."

"You want to take him? Go ahead if you think you can do a better job."

"Such coldness coming from my bastard father." Jack smirks while Dax and Xav rise, picking up on his scornful remark.

"Yeah, Uncle Mark, you're a bastard." Dax yawns.

"Yeah, a dirty bastard." Xav drops his slice of pizza on my floor and takes a suitcase from his mom. "We going back to that dark prison suite we stayed in last year?"

"Fuck no, the other suite in this hellhole is *my* place," Jack says. "And I don't want your grimy, sticky, baby fingers all over my stuff!"

"Of course you can stay in that suite." I smother my son's assertive statement. "Jack's grounded so feel free to use it for a couple of days. That's the perfect place for you and the boys. I'm sure Cove will be here tomorrow to sweep you off your feet for the hundredth time anyway."

"Dad!" Jack complains.

"Give 'em your key card," I order. "Or if you prefer, they can stay with you upstairs in my guest bedroom." I signal toward his temporary room.

He babbles a volume of obscenities on his way upstairs to fetch the card, protesting by tossing it over the stairwell on his way down. It lands at Jules' feet and she hands it to Sophia, offering to walk her and the boys to the other side of the hotel.

"Perfect, we can catch up and you can tell me what a jerk Mark's been lately."

Tap.

Tappity-tap.

Tap.

I turn rapidly, staring at the door. He's back. This time I'm gonna find out what that motherfucker wants.

"Huh." Sophia inhales, alert to the sound. Her reaction catches me off guard and I stop partway through the room. She's heard it before, Dax and Xav too. They stare motionless, their faces fearful of the noise echoing in my corridor.

"The cane man," the boys eerily speak in unison. They step back and turn to Sophia for comfort. "Mom?"

"Shush," she says. "It's not him."

"Yeah, it *is* a cane man. An old fucker who knocks his cane around like he's on a throne with a staff in his hand and we're his peasants cowering in the corner like terrified animals. How do you know this guy?" I ask, stepping quickly to the door.

"Don't open it!" Xavier screams. "Uncle Mark! Don't! Dad said to run from him!" He races past everyone, pushing Jack out of the way on his way up the stairs, locking himself in the bathroom. "He's gonna get us!" His words are muffled through the closed door. "Run!"

"Sophia, what the hell's going on?" I open the door to look down the corridor, smile at a few guests, but as always, the shitwad's not around. I close and lock the door then demand an answer.

"He's gone?" she asks.

"What do you think? Do you see him in here, face to the ground, begging for his life?"

"See Mom, I told you to call Uncle Mark. He'll get him." Dax puts his hands in his pockets and rocks on his heels with a big grin. "That woman who took me last year said Uncle Mark's a killer. We don't have to be afraid when he's around."

"Should've listened to your kid, Soph. Why the fuck didn't you tell me the asshole was bothering you? What happened anyway?"

She sets the suitcase down and walks over to Dax, sweeping his hair from his face. After a pinch to his cheek she turns to me with arms crossed. It's usually a protective stance, but I'd say she's frustrated more than anything—annoyed at Cove, me, and now this.

"That old man spent three days at the Scarlett." She hesitates, looking at Dax who's eager to hear the story. "He sat at the same table each night, ordered wine, watched Cove and me, and always paid with cash. We were tired of him coming in and gawking at us, irritated at how unsettling it was with him around."

"He's truly creepy," Jules says.

Sophia nods in agreement. "One night, we decided to talk to him, only he got up and left when we approached his table."

"And you didn't follow after him?"

"We're not about to cause a scene in our business, besides he didn't do anything wrong. There was no reason to stop him."

"You're a couple of cowards."

Daxton laughs as Sophia takes a step in my direction, tired of my cockiness. "Watching people in a wine bar isn't illegal. If he was there the next night we would've spoken to him then, only he never returned. We decided we had overreacted, especially considering the man's age. Then the boys came into our bedroom one night and said a man was in our backyard running a stick along our fence."

"Let me guess, no one was there when you looked."

"Exactly. We told the boys it was probably a teenager fooling around, but the next day they ran inside the house yelling that the same man with the stick was at the bus stop a few doors down. He was knocking it against the plastic window in the bus shelter, trying to get their attention. I went outside and saw *him*, the same guy who was at the Scarlett, getting on a bus. That's when I realized the boys had thought his cane was a stick."

"Morons." Jack laughs. "Haven't you ever seen a fucking cane before?"

"Shut it or you'll find out what a cane feels like on your ass," I scold.

"Right on, keep beating me, Dad."

I have to ignore his comment or our bickering will continue long into the night. "Soph, why the hell didn't you tell me?"

"You know Cove's not going to call you to come out to St. Louis."

"*You*, Sophia. *You* should've called, not your husband. What's Cove gonna do to protect you anyway? Vomit on the guy? That seems to be his only form of defense."

Dax looks offended by my comment about his dad and immediately crosses his arms like Sophia.

"Go check on your brother," I say, knowing we can't discuss certain things with him around. "And Jack, it's time for you to disappear too. Don't bitch about it either," I command, wanting to clear the room. I wait until they're out of earshot then tell Soph to continue.

"Cove thinks it's one of the originals who raped him when he was just a young teen. One of Dad's *clients*. He said the face looks familiar, but he can't be certain."

"Fuck. That was over twenty years ago. Why would the guy come looking for any of us now?"

"Personally, I didn't believe Cove at the time. He feels that way about most of the people at the Scarlett who cause problems. He distrusts everyone. Says every asshole has something to do with Dad. But seeing that the guy's now *here*, I've changed my mind. He must be from the Industry. It's the only thing you and Cove have in common."

"You smell that?" Jules whispers.

"I sure as fuck do. Jack!" I shout toward the guest bedroom.

"Weed?" Sophia sniffs. "Is he giving my children drugs? What the fuck, Mark?" She races upstairs and I'm one step behind, only we never make it to the guest bedroom. Instead, Sophia stops like a jammed brake in front of my open bedroom door. "Oh my God! Put that down!" she shouts.

"Fuck." I push past her and seize my gun from Daxton's hand. "Don't touch anything in my suite. Nothing! This room's off limits!"

He sprints out and his brother yells for him to hide in the bathroom. I hear the door lock and the two are self-jailed in the small space.

"I'm done." I strap on my ankle holster and position my extra gun in place. "I'm tired of this shit." I slip into a clean sport coat and mutter continuously about the fucking kids.

"You." I direct a finger at my sister. "Don't leave this

suite. Stay here tonight. The little piss ants can sleep in the bathroom for all I care. They'll fit in the tub." Her kids shriek when my fist hits the wall next to the bathroom before kicking the guest bedroom door open. "And you," I snap at Jack. "My dope smoking, a-hole, kid from hell, stand up and get your ass on the sofa downstairs. This is your aunt's room tonight."

"Screw you." He's sprawled on the bed, gazing at the ceiling. "I'm baked. Nothing's gonna move me." His laughter lasts less than a second, changing to 'no' and 'eeeyouch' as he gets dragged down the stairs with my fingers shoved up his nose.

"Lie down," I demand. "I'm in no mood for anything else to happen tonight. Not another word, grunt, or fucking obscenity leaves your mouth." His head emerges over the back of the sofa, Sophia's looking down from the second floor, and Jules is sitting on the top step shaking her head at my performance. "And you." I stare back at her. "Go clean our sex toys like a good woman."

"What toys?" Daxton opens the bathroom door. "Can I play?"

"Yeah, clean the sex toys, Jules," Jack calls out to her. "He needs to get laid. Maybe then he won't be such a douche."

"Mark, chill out," Sophia says, ticked off.

"Fuck that, you all need to chill the fuck out. No more surprises, secrets, drama, and not one ounce of protest, nada! Roll over and play dead like good little dogs."

"Thanks for the warm welcome!"

Jules, still shaking her head, turns to my sister and says, "It's a combination of the alcohol and feeling suffocated by the number of people invading his space. He's also livid that he doesn't have total control of our lives. Not *his* life, ours. Typical Mark shit. He'll feel better once he kills..." She looks at Daxton and changes her words. "Once he has the opportunity to put a man in his place. And you better watch out Jack, it might be you."

"Oh yeah, twat queen. Well maybe it will be him. He's the one who better keep his guard up."

I can't stand it. They're still yapping. I slam the door on my way out, mumbling, *"It's one thing after another. If it's not my son, it's the old fuck, if it's not him, it's Sophia and the terror twins, if it's not them..."* I head down the corridor, muttering, holding my gun under my coat, not having a clue where I'm going or what pushed me over the edge. Has to be the old man. Has to be him. All I wanted was to get wasted tonight. Should've opted to smoke a bowl instead. And I can sense Jules is following. I know she's behind me.

"I left my husband..." I say under my breath, thinking of my family's bullshit. *"I hate you, Dad... Go ahead and fuck me, Mark. It's all you want from me..."*

"I told you there's something wrong with him," Sam says to Karina as I pass them standing outside their room.

Hell, I forgot about them. That's more shit to add to the pile.

"You fucked up the best night of head ever, Dad... Mark,

you better apologize... you better get along with him, he is my dad." I wish Jules would stop following me. I know she's behind me. "Go back to the suite, I need to be alone."

"Is he talking to us?" Karina asks.

I turn and watch her parents enter their room, then scan the corridor, expecting to see her following me, but landing on a pair of shiny black oxfords instead. It's him. Standing outside my suite, his cane placed directly in front of his body with both hands resting on top. His shoulders back, feet spread, chin up, and cane being raised. He knocks it against one of the tables in the hall then sets it back on the carpet, flashing timeworn, yellow-teeth.

I step forward and he gestures with one finger to stop. To hell with him. I approach, only with each step forward, he moves toward the room closest to my suite. I walk faster, noticing the key card in his hand.

He swipes and enters the room, the door shuts, locks, and I'm a second too late. I use my card in haste, but he's set the inside latch, forcing me to smack the door with my palm in frustration.

"Open the door. Tell me what you want," I say firmly. "Don't be a fucking wuss. You're here to start something, now open the door and let's get it started."

Croaky, ill-sounding words pierce my ears. "Give me thirty minutes, sonny boy." He expels a rattling cough and his grisly breath seeps through the door. "Let me prep."

A tremor of dread fills my body and my fingers turn cold. Never has a man cloaked me in fear. Lucky me, the grim-fucking-reaper has entered my hotel.

"Thirty minutes, Mark." He wheezes. "Make time for death."

CONFIRMATION

Ny fingernails drum the lobby desk as I hover over
Chloe, bearing a brightly lit face of scorn.

"Mr. Jameson, I would've called you. He must've
checked in while I was on break." She looks up at the
security cam, knowing straightaway she's caught in a lie.

"How much did he pay you?"

"He didn't—"

"How much?" I lean in, projecting my strongest
voice.

"Five hundred dollars for me not to mention he was
here." She lowers her head. "But he had I.D. this time."

"So that makes it okay? Pack your stuff and get the
hell out of here."

"I was doing my job. You can't fire me for checking a
man into a hotel room. What's the issue?"

"How about bribery and deceit? Is that a big enough
issue for you? It is to me. What else do you do around
here for a little extra cash? My hotel manager said we have
food missing from the kitchen. You selling turkeys and
cranberry sauce to people? Or are you accepting money on
the side for guests to have a room with a view of the lake?

No second chances, not with something like this. Time to check out of the Jameson."

Her head hangs low as she takes her things from the back office, dragging her feet past the towering Christmas tree, burning fireplace, leather chairs, and out the front door.

I call Jules to come downstairs, then search the lobby computer for the guy's information.

"Here we go." I type in the room number. "Checked in for one night, one king bed, one guest. His Pennsylvania license was scanned, name is... uh."

"Hi," a woman says. She waves a sheet of paper in front of my face, trying to get my attention. "Here's our itinerary, can you check us in? Hello?"

"Yes." I nod with a deep exhale, puzzled by the name on the screen. It has to be a fake license.

"How about *now* instead of tomorrow?"

Bitch. I take her papers with an artificial smile and retrieve the reservation, getting the key cards together, and I'm pleased when Jules arrives.

"Let me finish this for you." She takes on the simple task while beaming cheerfully at the guest. Warm and welcoming, that's what I always say. It's the only way to run a successful business, yet I've fucked up twice recently by running my mouth throughout the second floor corridor.

Kindliness isn't in my blood at this moment. My head's clouded. I saunter into the back office, take a seat and lean back.

Could it really be him, and more importantly, why? Why would he be here? I access his check-in information on my desktop, certain my drunken mind's playing tricks on me. I need to see it again.

"The pool's down the hall and to your right, weight room and tanning beds directly across from the pool area, the restaurant and bar toward the back, and you have a lovely room on the second floor. Enjoy your stay and please don't hesitate to call us if you need anything."

I don't believe it. Either the guy made this bogus license to fuck with me, like he did with my birth certificate, or someone has a shitload of explaining to do.

"Where's Chloe?" Jules walks in and parks her ass on the desk in front of the screen.

"Fired." I look up and she cocks her head, noticing the strain in my face.

"Why? What's going on?"

"She took a bribe from the old guy. He's in the room next to our suite."

"No shit?"

"Yeah. Are Soph and the kids locked in?"

"They're settled for the night, and she won't open the door if he comes knocking, that's for damn sure. What do you think he wants?"

With fixed eyes on my computer, I stroke her bare legs tenderly. She crosses them and lowers her head, drawing me out of my zone.

"Mark?"

Her hand rests on mine and I move it leisurely to the

side of my face, smelling her flesh. "You high?" I whisper.

"No. I was putting away the stuff from Jack's room. Handling the bowl must've left a scent on my fingers."

She slides onto my lap, her arms and back caressed as I study her pretty face.

"I love you, Jules. I wish I could put into words why I'm unsettled. Just remember that I love you."

"Remember? Are you okay?"

I pull her closer and rest my head against her chest, taking deep breaths. "No, princess. Not this time."

She lifts my chin, yielding a look of concern. "You've never said that before."

"I know. This unease has only happened one other time in my life—when my dad was shot. I knew something was wrong, just didn't know what until I got the call that he'd been killed. It's the same feeling."

"No one in your family's going to die." She makes an effort to calm my nerves. "This is so unlike you... extra wasted tonight or what?"

"Maybe." I stare at the screen, debating if I should call *her* and ask... find out for sure if it's him, or just talk to the fucker first. "It's more than the booze. There's been abundant chaos every single goddamn day since my son arrived... he stabbed me and I hit the little prick, turns out your dad's an embalmer and we came close to beating the shit out of one another, Cove and Sophia split, you refuse to marry me, and a demon con artist is breathing down my neck."

"Who? The old guy? He's no match for any of us.

AVEN JAYCE

Even your sister could take him. And she and Cove will be fine. Sometimes people have marital problems, *we* do, and we haven't even said our vows yet. And Jack, he's a typical teen with an atypical father. If you think about it, our lives are no different than they were last week, last month, or last year."

I shouldn't expect her to understand. Normally, I'd say kill the bastard upstairs and be done with him, only he's an oddity and I'm a inquisitive fucker, so I can't. Not this time.

"Can you cover Chloe's shift? The system shows there're still two guests who haven't arrived. I need to do something then I'll be back down. Security's around if you need anything. He's probably checking the corridors or the pool, should be back in the lobby soon."

"I won't clean the bloody mess this time unless I can participate."

"Is that right?" I grin. "Share the kill? I'm supposed to share everything with you except my last name?"

"Yep."

"You're like Jack with the lousy attitude." She gets an ass smack, the back of her neck gripped, and a frisky bite on her chin. "Tell me that you'll be my wife. Say it. I need to hear those words tonight."

Her lips trace mine in a slow, suggestive manner.

"Jules, we have thirty days before our marriage license expires. There's no reason to wait. Besides, I'm the best thing that's ever happened to you."

She pats my cheek, making fun of my words. "You're

164

the 'cream of the crop,' the finest, loveliest, most delightful murderer I've ever met, and all of those things go double for what's in your pants… but don't rush it. In fact, I believe impatience killed the cat, not curiosity, and you're impatient about everything. As soon as you stop asking, step back and relax, it will be time."

"Ah, so it's all about *you* having control again, you, you, you," I tease.

"No, it's about *patience*."

"Say it," I request. "Just in case."

"In case what? Stop this juvenile act like you're turning into a little chicken shit. You want me to go upstairs and stick a knife in his head, twist, and kill? Are you holding back because of his age?" She kisses me, taps my nose and walks back to the lobby, swaying her ass in my face.

An evil, smart, badass troll is what she is.

"Who's holding back? I'll eat the old bastard for breakfast and shit him out for dinner!" I shout.

"Hello. Welcome to Jameson Hotel. Mr. and Mrs. Clark, we have a beautiful room waiting for you. Was the weather nice on your drive in?"

Fuck. Guests are here. Fuck, fuck, I'm an idiot.

Her head surfaces, leaning around the doorframe with a shameless smirk. "Just kidding. The lobby's empty."

"Great, I'm stressed out and you're pranking me? Just wait. My belt will be off before dawn."

She leaves in laughter and a minute later a wiggling ass appears. Her skirt rises, revealing the best black Sharpie message I've ever read... *Owned by Mark Jameson*, with an arrow pointing to her asshole.

And the woman wonders why I want to marry her. "Very clever, princess. Thank you."

"No problem, future husband," she says, lifting her sweater to flaunt a second message on her abdomen. *Mrs. Julia Jameson.*

"See, now that's better." I point to the name. "If you're trying to get me out of this funk, that will help."

The sound of luggage rolling through the front door interrupts our remaining time together before I head upstairs. She leaves to greet the arrivals and I check my watch.

He said *make time for death*. I'm ready. My guns are in place, blade in my pocket, and whatever the fuck he came here for... I'm ready.

I scrawl a final note to Jules, slipping it in her skirt pocket on my way past the desk...

I ruled our relationship because I loved you last.

A(I)NCESTRY

The corridor walls that surround his room dissolve into a blur while I focus on the peephole, knowing he's inside, watching, possibly stroking the door, trying to feel me as his endless, raspy breaths are ingested and spit out. My palms rest against the doorframe, high above my head, leaving me vulnerable for a shot to the chest. Presenting myself this way should convince him of my power—back off.

A television blares a few doors down, but the other rooms surrounding us are unoccupied. I imagine when he checked in, he requested to be by my suite. For my own privacy, the rooms around my place are always the last to be booked. He got what he wanted from Chloe. It's amazing what people will do for a small amount of cash... and now the two of us are alone.

I power my words through the closed door. "You're a fraud. Don't mock my family."

The inside latch opens and the deadbolt is turned. There're no words, only the sound of sluggish feet trailing along the carpeted floor. The loud breathing fades and the glowing light coming from the gap under the door turns to darkness.

Don't overthink. Enough of the *what-ifs*.

With my gun drawn, I pause in the entryway to survey the space. One dimly lit corner lamp casts a warm yellow glow throughout the room. A brown suitcase is spread open on the floor next to the bed, and beside it are bony, bare feet. I follow his stark-white, hairless legs to a shriveled dick, flabby stomach, saggy-breasted chest covered in moles, up to a wrinkled neck and weathered face. He sits on the edge of the bed with the small kitchenette table pulled before him, cane in one hand and patting the mattress with the other, wanting me to have a seat.

"Who the fuck are you?" I continue to stand by the door, making sure the room is secure. The bathroom's dark and no one else seems to be here. "You alone?"

"Sit down, Mark. Close to me."

"Fuck that." I point my gun at his head. "Take out your weapon and place it on the table. Cut the shit."

He laughs then nearly coughs up a lung, his face turning red and dick bouncing with each gasp for air. "Your inquisitive Jameson mind won't allow you to kill me, not yet. Trust me, take a seat and listen. Be good, hear me out, then you can shoot."

He touches himself like he's trying to jerk off. Thank fuck *it* remains slack. The sight is more disturbing than viewing his name on the license.

"I have no weapon, but I have a story to share that will make you whole."

"Make me whole? What, like I'm not a man? Jesus Christ, are you broke? You need money? People come begging and expect a handout from me all the time. Is that why you're here?"

"Your money?" He coughs. "No, kiddo, money isn't a necessity any longer."

My pulse just did a long stride over the starting line and isn't going to slow until it reaches the finish. "What did you say?"

He looks up and for the first time I'm close enough to see he's suffering from glaucoma. The man lacks any distinguishing characteristics, including eye color, though they look brown under the clouded areas. He has a few strands of greasy white hair tucked behind his big ears, but no tats, scars, or any other identifying information.

"Kiddo," he repeats.

That's a coincidence. A term my father always used. The guy must've been a client of Jameson Industries. I bet he heard my dad say it back in Vegas. And I bet this old bastard's dying. He's here because he's longing for one last fuck from Marcus Wild. What a way to go. Hell, I don't blame him. I'd fuck myself before my death if I could.

"The way you're fondling your dick, I'd say you want something I'm not offering."

"There'd be no choice on your part if I were thirty years younger," he says with a raspy voice. "Now, listen up, accept the truth, then you can put me to sleep." He reaches into his suitcase and takes out a black wallet. It's flipped open to display a badge and set in front of him on the table.

Shit, I take a look and should've known—the guy's a detective, that's how he obtained the birth certificate and license. And he must be lying about being unarmed.

"Tilted head and full of fright?" He questions my expression. I guess his vision isn't all that bad. "I doubt you're the type to shy away. Can't be if you're like Paul."

"No fear," I answer with authority, pulling a chair to the table to sit across from him. "Did you work on my dad's murder case or the child porn ring with Cove? You from Vegas?" I reach for the wallet, reading the name on his I.D. card that's opposite the badge. Fuck, same as the license he used to check in. Fuck, fuck, fuck.

"Shall we begin?" he asks, swaying his cane in a hypnotizing motion. "Take out your cell and make the call."

Waiting, he places a hand on the table, his finger passing over his name while he instructs me. "Call her. I can tell you haven't, now's the time. The truth can only come from her."

My gun's pointed at his chest as I take out my cell. Peeved, I tap the number. I was going to do this before I came up here, but decided to wait to see how things played out.

"You won't kill me just yet. Put the gun down. Story time comes first." He slides the wallet across the table and I lower the gun. The fucker's right. It's only raised out of habit. Even if he's armed, he's too slow to shoot first.

"Mark? It's... it's after midnight here."

I knew she'd be asleep.

"Are you okay? Is Jack alright? What's... what's happening?" Her mouth sounds full of saliva.

"Mom."

"Is it Sophia? Is she okay? She hasn't called in years, and what's your excuse? We used to talk all the time; these days it's only once a month. What have you been up to?"

"Get to it," he says.

I inhale until my lungs can no longer expand, holding the breath while waiting to form the correct sentence. "Tell me again about Granddad." I pick up the wallet and stare at the name... Jameson.

"What? At this time of the night? You haven't asked me about your grandparents since you were a kid."

"I know, but I'm curious to learn more."

Her bed creaks and I hear a lamp turn on. A hard swallow precedes a loud moan with clear intent to express aggravation. "I'm your mother, make time for me at a decent hour, mister."

I fucking hate it when she calls me *mister*.

"Why haven't you called? Are you angry about her death? Saddened by the news? Any reaction at all? You and your sister are so inconsiderate. It's like I raised a couple of selfish monsters."

Boy, she woke up fast.

"You kids, I'm out here trying to repair this house so I can sell it and live the rest of my days in a senior community, and the two of you are enjoying the high life, gallivanting around like I don't even exist. I could use a little help out here."

"I'll hire a handyman for you."

"A stranger? No."

"I don't have time to discuss this, the house, or my feelings about my ex-wife's death right now. I haven't called recently because Jack and I are both exhausted from the funeral and I'm trying to get him settled."

"I don't give a damn! You need to make time for me!"

That nasty, high-pitched, witch voice of hers just kicked in. I can picture her sitting in bed, wearing a baggy pair of jogging pants and a loose top with a pile of used tissues on the nightstand. She's been letting her body and the house deteriorate for years. Depression is the main reason, but I'd suspect there're others as well, like age. Fuck, I wish she'd just stay on the subject.

"Are you going to answer my question, or not?"

"Why don't you care? How can you not care?" She begins to sob.

"If you want to know the truth, yeah, it fucking sucks that she got cancer and died. I hate seeing Jack so upset, this is killing him and he's going to be fucked up for a long-ass time. Today was the first day in weeks he actually laughed."

"Marky." My name's spoken like I'm an ignorant toddler. "I was referring to me. Why don't you love *me*?"

"Of course." I sigh. "Of course you were."

This is a perfect example of the source of my sister's personality. My mom's selfish and she produces a rapid-fire flip of emotions. She either explodes into a rage or ignores you *and* the subject being discussed like it never existed. It's so fucking passive-aggressive. "Hello?" I say harshly. "Fucking answer me!"

"They're dead." She exhales. "Both of your grandfathers died from heart attacks. I've told you that. Why are you asking?"

This is ridiculous. I don't know who the fuck this guy is, but...

"Tell her I said hello," he interrupts. "Ask her if she misses my dick."

"Excuse me?" My gun raises back to his head. "What the fuck just came out of your mouth?"

"Mark?" my mother whispers. "Where are... who is that?"

"Tell me about Abram, Abram Jameson," I say in a steady and firm tone. "When did he die?"

"Your father's father?" she questions. "It was a long time ago. I don't remember the exact date. Why? Why are you calling here this late to ask about him?"

"Was he in the hospital after he had a heart attack? Did you see the body? Was there a funeral?"

He shows his elderly teeth and laughs, enjoying the fact that I'm starting to squirm.

"I don't remember," she says softly.

He's touching his tired dick again, trying to get erect. And my mom... she's fucking lying. I can hear it in her voice. I'm stuck between an intrusion and an evasion.

I concentrate on the badge, still seeing his arm jerking out of the corner of my eye.

"What did he do for a living?" I exhale, wishing I could turn away, but needing to keep him in sight.

"He worked for the county."

"Doing what?" Jesus, I'm tired of having to ask twenty questions to get a direct answer.

"I don't remember."

"Great, are you finished lying to your son? I swear, Mom, you've been the only one who hasn't fucked with me. You've never been deceitful. What the hell? Was he a detective or not?"

"Where did you hear that?" She gasps. "How did you get that information?"

"Did he work for the fucking goddamn police department or not?" I yell.

He reaches into his suitcase and takes out an envelope, shoving it across the table with a snorting chuckle. My mother asks me again who's there, but I ignore her to open the envelope.

Photographs... a handful of photographs. One is of my father when he was a kid, standing next to a much younger version of the man in front of me. There's another one of... "Oh, dear Lord." I look away and start to panic, searching for air. What the fuck's going on? The dread of seeing... I look again. "Jesus Christ." I toss the photo of this creep molesting my dad and stand like I've been set on fire, pacing, rubbing my chin with my gun, listening to my mother ask me what's wrong... "Fuck!" I keep pacing, my body temperature an easy thousand degrees as my blood races through my ignited veins.

"Tell me about Abram Jameson!" I shout. "Tell me!"

She's silent, and I know. It's him, Paul's father. My grandfather. He's here.

"Mark." She pauses, and starts to cry. "If he's there with you... you need to get out of the room."

"So he's alive?" I laugh. "Fuck you, Mom. Fuck you. I can't believe you lied about this. Why? What the hell are you hiding?"

"Listen to me." She sobs. "Walk away. Get away as quickly as you can. Don't talk to him. Don't listen to—"

I pitch my cell into the wall, watching it break apart and fall to the floor. The fury I feel that this guy sought me out, came to my fucking home to taunt me, and carries photos around of him molesting his son... fuck, I'm killing this bastard. I don't care if he's family. He's dead.

My knife comes out and he holds up a finger, nodding for me to sit.

"No, I'll stand," I say. "You touched your own son? Is that why my dad was so fucked in the head? I thought he was cruel all on his own, but no, it was you. *You* fucked him up."

"Sons are created to submit, serve, and obey their fathers. Isn't that how you feel about Jack? Sit, sonny." He pats the bed. "Be an obedient boy, like Paul was. Try it for me." He touches himself. "I'm only asking for one last erection before I die."

"Screw you, you vile shit." I almost spit in his face, but administer a solid drop kick to his chest instead. He falls back and holds his ribs, winded and emitting a low moan. In anger, I swipe the pile of photos, spreading them wide across the table. I can't believe this fucker photographed himself fucking his own son, and he kept them all these years. A fucking detective, no less.

"You..." My jaw drops at the sight of one of the photographs. I pick it up with a trembling hand. "You fucked my mother?" I speak like thunder, staring at the image. "You fu... f-fucked my mother." The photo's from the '80s, I can tell by my mom's hair. It's night, shot outdoors with a flash. "You fucked..." Two cops are in the scene. Abram's one. He must've been an officer before he became a detective. He's in uniform, smiling and holding a baton around her neck as she cries. He's got his dick in her while another guy is raping her mouth.

"No, you didn't fuck her, you raped her."

My world just shattered.

The photo floats out of my hand and I follow its descending path, wide-eyed and breathless. "Fuck."

He laughs... the wheezing piece of shit laughs.

I jump on him, blade out, slamming it hard into his chest, excited when a gush of air whizzes from his mouth. I pull out and raise my arm to strike again, only my wrist is gripped as he begs for me to wait.

"We're not finished."

"You're a sick fuck, worse than my dad. I can't believe I'm saying that, but yeah, you asshole, you're worse than my dad."

"Mark." His trembling hand rests over his wound while his forehead furrows from the pain. "She should've aborted you."

"What?" The word expels in a spectral midst, hovering between us with a massive question mark fixed on the end. What is he saying?

"That faithful Catholic bitch, she wouldn't get an abortion. I should've cut you out of her myself... son."

"No." I lean back with a shudder. The room spins and a blast of heat passes through my body. Horror and angst surge as I clutch my knife.

"Paul was your brother." He coughs for a good minute while I move away.

I can't look at him. I can't.

"He was my possession before you came along and tore our relationship apart—a boy who always obeyed, even when he was in college. If I wanted him, he was mine." He stops to catch his breath, bringing his bloody hand to his face in a gaze. "His last year," he continues. "He said he met a woman who was different than his usual frat house whores. She was innocent and wholesome, and not uptight or threatening to his manhood." He tilts his hand, examining the sticky red coating on his flesh as it glows in the dim light. "That's hard to find in a college girl. She wasn't one of those females who needed to have a career in order to prove she was just as good, if not better than, a man. That's no woman for a Jameson."

I shake my head at his wretched words.

"And she was sympathetic to his past... I'll assume she was the first and only person he ever opened up to about our perfect father son bond." His breathing becomes more labored. My first stab won't kill him unless he bleeds to death, and that could take hours. The fucker's just old and tired, taking breaks between long sentences. "She was a recluse, a woman who would keep his secrets safe. It was such a switch for Paul, and I suppose that was the attraction." One long agonizing breath. "And it was good, my son could finally tell someone about his life." Two long breaths. "But, I wanted a taste of her... so I fucked her behind his frat house at his graduation party. Hard and long." Three long breaths. "Then he wanted me dead."

"You raped her!" I rage and pace. "Were you jealous? Didn't want him to start a life without you? What?" I twirl my blade and pace. "You're weak." I spit and pace. "You're nothing but a cowardly sack of shit!"

"And you're just like me."

The corners of his mouth turn upward as I come to a grinding halt and contemplate my two weapons. Gun or blade? I set them both on the table and remove my sport coat, rolling my sleeves.

"Show me more," he says, massaging his junk. "Take off your shirt."

I stand cross-armed, stricken with an unsound mind, transforming into a savage, cold-hearted animal.

"I think he felt sorry for that bitch when he saw my dick in her. He had only seen me fuck his mother in the past... apparently sharing another woman made him jealous."

"What do mean, sharing another woman?"

"My boy did what I said. He slept in the same room as my wife and me. She was his first."

"Keep your trap shut. I don't want to hear anything else!"

"I bet he liked your mother because they shared a special bond." He laughs. "Me."

I pick up my gun and introduce the fucker to a decent pistol-whipping. One, twice, until I see a wide laceration and blood gushing from his cheek. He doesn't make a sound. No yelps or moans, only a dying voice thudding about the room.

"Paul tried to be someone he wasn't when he met that woman. She was pretty back then, maybe not so much today."

I'm finished listening to his shit. He's wasting his breath describing *his* account of my family's past. Time to tune out and focus on his rust-scented blood instead. Seeing the deep red is a pleasurable thrill for my brain and as pacifying as a sedative, which I need right now. It flows down his face and leaves spots on my heavily bleached hotel sheets. *Drip. Drip.*

"He tried for a few years to escape his past. Everyone craves normalcy on occasion, but having you in his life, having to raise his brother..." He laughs. "You killed any chance he ever had of breaking free."

I inhale deeply and turn his body to the side of the bed, dragging him to the edge so his head hangs over and his neck's exposed.

"You, my boy, were a constant reminder to him of his

own father. He couldn't escape me if he tried."

I know the feeling. Paul's hatred for me has been a noose around my neck since I was a child, and now this fucker will be too.

"My Paul turned you into a splendid killer. I saw you in action from a distance once in Vegas." He stops to take a wheezing breath. "It was late one night... after I had left a boy on the front steps of Paul's house. A *loving* anonymous gift."

"When you what?"

With his head hanging over the edge of the bed, he views me upside-down. "If I had to guess, I'd say..." He takes a deep breath. "If I ever surfaced in Vegas..." Perishing breath. "His plan was to have you kill me. He was as skilled at manipulating people to do his dirty work for him as you are at taking a man's life... my two magnificent sons." His hand reaches for my dick. "Please... let me touch you before I die."

"Ergh!" My gun beats his face causing a spurt of blood to shoot out his nose. A second full swing and a gash splits open on his forehead. His lip bleeds from my third hit, but he still doesn't let on that he's in pain.

Gravity pulls the blood to his head where it trickles onto my damask carpet. I don't care if the entire room is coated in his putrid, sticky blood. My heart is as hard as metal and every bit as cold. I switch my gun out for my blade, holding it steadily against his neck.

"It's time," he says with a busted face. "I got to see my grandkids, Sophia and Jack, and passed my existence onto you. But I'm done living. I no longer need this life or want to be in this old frail body. Nothing on me works. Everything aches. So kill me," he demands. "I'll be with you forever, Mark. That was my plan—to meet you and pass along the truth. Now, please, do it… I want to die by way of my boy."

I foam at the mouth, having been infected by a rabid animal—another Jameson virus. Abram's disease will embark on a long voyage within my body by damaging my heart and slaying my mind, just as Paul did for so many years.

"Fuck!" I rage, sinking the blade into his neck and handling him like a slab of meat. I work through his flesh, euphoric from the butchery and even more delighted that he finally expresses pain, pointing his feet upward, and digging his nails into the bed. Cutting into a man's neck is the most painful of all deaths. His skin is tough and thyroid membrane firm as I cut my way to his trachea. I hold my breath while he succumbs… ordinarily an exquisite sight, though not tonight. Tonight I see the blood of my own life flowing from this man—a man who I'll *never* call my father.

His dying expression is as warm as the blood surging onto my leg. The fluid seeps through my clothing, trying to attach to my body, forcing its way under my skin.

My life-long desire to kill my father has been fulfilled because of the foul invasion of a stranger. A man who resided in my body from the moment I was conceived, a phantom follower who so kindly blessed me with his presence on the day he wanted to die...

Sick. Sinister. Rapist.

Is it possible to hate someone you've just met more than a person you've known your entire life? Well, I do. I fucking hate the bastard. And I wish I had held out and made his painful death last throughout the night.

Once his fixed pupils dilate and his face is slack, I plead for him to return. "Breathe so I can kill you all over again." My fist slams into his chest, causing his head to bob and more blood to color the room. "Breathe!"

His vacant stare is too goddamn peaceful. I want more. He needs to rise so we can have a badass fight. Then he has to pray for forgiveness while I'm killing him. "Get up!" I pace next to the bed, shouting at the carcass. "Get the fuck up!"

The photos spread across the table pry their way into my heart. They mock my very existence. Blocking them out isn't an option, especially my mom... she... Paul.

All women should be worshipped and protected. Paul... he was a pussy like every man I've ever met. If a sack of shit did that to my wife, ex-wife, even if we loathed each other, I still would've stepped in, rolled up my sleeves, and put the scum in his place. And what did *he* do about it? Nothing. He let Abram get away with that shit. I would've killed him on the spot. I swear I'm the only man in this world with balls. Fuckers. All of them! A bunch of dumbass fuckers.

"Freakin' A." I rub my temples then glance at my blood-coated hands. I try brushing the evil away, swiping them together, wiping them on my pants, but it won't come off. He's hanging on. The man's under my skin, soaking in... damn it... "I can't..." I pant. "I can't..." Calm the fuck down, Mark. Calm the fuck down.

"No."

I climb over him, my gun raised; beating his face over and over until his teeth break and nose is bashed in. I want his jaw to crack, his eyes to disappear, his cheeks to sink, and, and, and...

"I'm a troll!" I roar.

Whack.

Punch.

"I'm a fierce fucking troll!"

Strike.

"You wicked... son of a... motherfuck! You're malicious! You didn't have to come here! I didn't need to know any of this!"

Whack.

"I'll fucking eat you for supper!"

Smack.

How the hell could you do this to me! I was fine not hearing *any* of this!

Slap.

To hell with you!

A whistling sound halts my psychosis. My arm's raised high, prepared for a final swing, only someone else is in the room.

Of course it's him... my kid.

He's shirtless, leaning against the low dresser with his

tat reflected in the mirror, trimming his nails, and yes, whistling. Nonchalantly whistling while I'm breaking the face of a dead man with a sliced open neck.

"What the fuck are you doing in here?" I lower my arm.

He looks up, then resumes cutting his nails. "I went into your home office to use the computer. Did you know you have security cams in some of these rooms?" He smirks.

"Yeah, Jack, I know." I stand and rub my split knuckles.

"This is my granddad?" He motions with the nail clippers toward the heap on the bed, and I nod. "Your dad?" I nod again. "Well... that sucks."

"Get out." I haul him to the door, leaving a bloody handprint on his arm. "How the fuck did you get in here anyway?"

"Jules' master key card was on the kitchen counter."

Good one, princess.

"Go back to the suite and wash up for bed. It's late, and I shouldn't have to remind you that you're grounded."

"You want my help?" he asks.

"This is personal."

He stands in the corridor, giving me the once-over, and positions his foot between the door and the wall to halt its closure.

"Dad." He cocks his head, crossing his arms with an authoritative expression. "Life sucks. That's what you told me. Now, you can either put one foot forward and make the best of it or be a miserable fucker and see where it gets you. Words to live by, right?"

I love and hate that little shit.

DECONTAMINATE

T he water in my hotel never runs cold. My plan is to lay spread eagle on my tiled shower floor until I resemble a shivering kitten... I mean a pussy... a pussy that's been abandoned in the rain. Only I'm more of the type to smoke a bowl, wash the blood off, and go back to work.

Still, the incident in that room screwed with my head. Just a bit. A wee-tiny-bit. A little-teeny-minuscule... shit, I need a fuckload of *temporarily inactive Mark time* to piece my brain back together before I can do anything, and that includes remembering how to walk.

I couldn't stay in there. Didn't want to look at him. I needed to get away for a while. So here I am, chillin' on my shower floor. For now, I'll just stay right here with water spattering my abdomen and my dick a shriveled prune. Jules will be okay with that. She likes fruit.

The good thing is, my life-long question of whether or not my father loved me is settled—I've decided he never existed... and that's the end of it. It's too fucking painful to head down the road of always guessing, always questioning, so I've deserted the idea that I even had a dad. Yep. I pulled out the Windex and wiped the mirror clean. No Paul. No Abram. From here on out, I'm the creation of a virginal conception. My mother never had sex... ever, at least not with those beasts. And Sophia? Hell, she'll always be my baby sis. There's no way I'd ever consider her my niece. She's my sister forever. And I'm *not* the product of a rape.

Okay, who the fuck am I kidding?

"Hey," Jules says softly, trying not to startle me as she opens the glass door and steps inside. "I read the Jameson name on our check-in then Jack came downstairs to fill me in on the rest. He saw everything on your private cams."

"I know. He's also been sneaking around with your master key card."

She kneels next to me, her clothing soaked as she places a hand over my heart. "I'm sorry. You okay?"

My head shakes in disappointment.

"I noticed his license was expired when I cleared his information from the hotel records. I looked him up online and found an obituary from last month. He's been planning this, Mark. Faked his own death so he wouldn't leave a trail."

"*Postponed* his death, not faked, and I doubt he did that for me. Who's watching the front desk?"

She reaches for the washcloth and soap, wetting both under the stream before lathering the cloth and wiping my chest and neck. Being pampered isn't what I need, but I'm in no mood to protest. "I called a replacement to cover for

Chloe, but she'll be returning to work tomorrow. You can't fire her."

"No, fuck that shit."

"Mark, the last thing you need is for her to tell people she got fired for giving *him* a room. She saw his name. You don't want that information to get around. Fire her in the future if she fucks up again, not over this. Don't screw yourself just because you're upset. And everything's fine in the lobby, try not to think about it."

"You're right." I lift my hand to see the blood still stained on my flesh.

"Are you hurt or is that from him?"

I flip it back and forth to view the dried traces of my father. "Funny, isn't it?"

"What?" She places my hand under the water, scrubbing my fingers until they're no longer contaminated with swine.

"Funny that I always wished for a different Dad, and now given a choice between the two, I'd keep the original. Paul never looked so good before today."

"Hmm." She scrubs, taking my other hand then gently using the washcloth to clean my face. "Cut knuckles, bloody face, and a dead man in one of our rooms. I've only been gone for two hours. Did you at least talk to him? You were quick, I mean, you always dive right in. There's no fucking around when it comes to your butcheries."

"True." I grin. "The longer these situations linger, the messier they become. Week-long, month-long, or year-long games aren't my thing. My dad..." I pause, fighting to use that word. "Paul took me places to kill. Walk in, do the deed, and leave. Life's too short to shoot the shit with a man you're going to murder. I've got better things to do with my time."

She smiles, humoring my daft rationalization. "I understand being tied down to a job that lingers makes you anxious, but this was a family member. Your dad."

"*Dad* is a relative term. It means nothing to me. Besides, all Jameson men are like this."

"Wrong. Don't feed me that bull and contradict yourself. Paul controlled your entire life, even from the grave. And look at you lying there. Since when do you mope around feeling sorry for yourself?"

"That's *not* how I feel. I'm perfectly fine."

"Lies... lies... lies..." She opens the shower door, removing her soaked clothing before walking away buck-naked.

"Hey, a guy can have a nervous breakdown every once in a while. Now get my bowl!" I pull myself up and wash the leftover soap and blood from my face. With my palm at chest level, I watch the filth rinse away, changing from brown to clear in a matter of seconds. "Where are you?" I ask, reclining back to my original position. "I'm not fine! I'm a tortured soul and I need more drugs... and a good woman would be sharing my pain! My misery is your misery! Hustle back!"

She returns with our laundry basket, shaking her head at my exaggerated suffering. "You're such a numbskull,

Mark."

"What is that... oh, nice."

She dumps our sex toys playfully over top of me. They bounce off my chest and onto the floor, some rolling around, a few bobbing, and a couple doing a hilarious hula-hoop dance.

"Shit, you trying to tell me something? I don't think I can get through all of these in one night." I turn and see one of my cock rings fall by my side. "Although this might help during the third or fourth round. No, not my leather dog hood!" I fling it away from the water. "That and my leather mitts cost over two hundred bucks. Don't get those wet. They can get sweaty, but not soaked."

She drops next to me, sitting cross-legged with a bottle of our toy cleaner in hand. My *Vickie Quickie* sucker is picked up, misted, rubbed, and rinsed.

"Killing two birds with one stone?" I question.

"If it makes you smile, yes. And you asked me to clean the toys."

"I was only being a dick."

Her tongue pearl is scrubbed from top to bottom, and one of the dildos, then another dildo, and another. She strokes each shaft under the jetting water, humming as she washes the flesh colored silicone pieces. The volume's soothing at first, but slowly grows in intensity until it changes to a high and boisterous pitch.

"Watching you a moment ago was one of the most erotic things I've ever seen, then you had to go and ruin it with your 'Alfalfa' voice. Why are you singing that anyway?"

"Jack has it on repeat downstairs."

"He's listening to *Cats in the Cradle*?" I let out a short laugh. "I'm surprised a kid his age even knows that song."

"It's a cover, not the original."

"I can't hear it over the water and the fan... though I know the lyrics well... *he's just like me*, isn't he?"

"And you believe you're just like your dad, only you're not."

"How do you know? Where you come from shapes who you are. They're me, I'm them. Both Paul and Abram."

"Listen up, would you? Listen, listen." I'm whacked with our purple Doc Johnson anal slider. "You grew up with a reclusive, bipolar mother who kept you locked away from the world, and the more I learn about your past, the more I believe she was trying to protect you. And that's exactly who you are today—a hermit-loner, who's fucked in the head, but will do anything to keep his family safe. Where you came from *did* shape who you are today."

"Thanks, love you too," I say cynically. "You're not helping by saying I'm like my mother, besides that's not what I meant."

"Yes, it *is*. You're just not looking at the whole picture. And don't take this the wrong way, but your son's disturbed beyond what I had imagined. I thought he'd settle into this lifestyle over the years, gradually, not overnight. Nothing fazes him. When he came to the lobby earlier, he was cracking his knuckles and beaming while explaining in great detail what you did to Abram... said he tried to act cool in front of you like it was no big deal, hoping you'd find him mature enough to join the next kill. He can't wait. He's excited, then eerily composed, then angry and rebellious... his behavior flips because he's trying out different things with us until he gets his way."

"He's also depressed."

"Well, he wants in. And he's singing those lyrics like it's his theme song, seeking attention, but still feeling ignored. I mean, it's great that he looks up to you. However, the kid needs to level out."

"He's perfectly fine in public. My son attended the best private schools back in Philly. I don't have to keep him locked in a cage."

She laughs. "Not a cage, just our spare bedroom. And now that I think about it, I just realized you're right, he has better manners than you... what I'm trying to say is he can be brutal like us, only not twenty-four hours a day. You have moments when you're loving and kind, that must've come from somewhere, and it certainly didn't come from Paul."

"Well, it's not from my mother either."

"Fine, but you didn't turn out this way because of one specific thing. Neither will Jack. We have multiple influences in our lives. Stop focusing on those two asinine men and think about the other people who have been around you. I'm sure Jack has a sweet side from being raised by his mom. He's not entirely a mini-Mark. Plus, I'm going to rub off on him while he's living here."

"God help the poor kid." I move away from the splashing water and sit with my back against the mosaic wall, picking up my black dog hood that's in the corner, and giving Jules a wink. I place it over my head and zip the neck so it's secure before taking the anal slider from her hand, waving it high like it's a magic wand. "I spent my entire life trying to get attention from a man who wasn't even my dad." I lower my arm and drop my head in disappointment. The weight on my shoulders should've lifted after all this shit; tonight they're even heavier. I'm balancing larger concrete blocks than ever before. "Unbelievable. Un-fucking-believable."

"My hands were full when I carried in our toys so I didn't bring your bowl. You want me to get it for you now?"

I shake my head and drop my head even further until my chin nearly touches my chest. Her soft feet brush against mine, and our toes mingle under the streaming shower.

"I never imagined I'd see you like this... didn't even know it was possible. I'm sorry, Mark."

"Sitting naked wearing a leather hood isn't all that unusual for me."

"The anal slider in your hand would already be in my ass if you were acting normal."

I look down at the sex toy and shrug.

"That and the fact that you're not being cocky."

"Rest assured, it hasn't disappeared for long. Why don't you go ahead and stand in front of me and spread 'em."

"Oh, fucking hell. Why me?" Sophia says, with her cell in hand and an arm covering her eyes. "I can't believe what I just saw and heard. For crying out loud, a dog hood? And why are you surrounded by that stuff! I understand owning a few playthings. But you could open a store!"

"Why the fuck are you walking into my bathroom?" I cover my dick with two washcloths.

"The door was open so I thought it'd be okay."

"And you didn't hear the shower? What the hell, sis?"

"Mom won't stop calling my number. Something's wrong. She hasn't called in years. See, that's her again."

"Don't be such a baby, just answer it. What are you so afraid of?"

"Why isn't your cell ringing? What does she want?" Her voice cracks in panic.

"You need to get over being scared of that woman. Give me the goddamn cell, but don't look."

"Are you crazy? I won't look!" She smacks into the glass while trying to find her way in the dark. I reach out and take her cell, waiting 'til she leaves to answer.

"Mom?"

"Mark! Why aren't you picking up? What's going on? Is he there? Are you still with him?"

I lean against the wall and look toward the ceiling. "He's gone... he's not coming back."

She exhales and says, "Did he hurt you?"

"He's in his eighties, I think I can take him."

"Oh Jesus... I was so worried. Are you sure he's gone?"

"Yeah, I'm sure. Trust me, he's not coming back, ever."

She's quiet for a moment before whispering, "I'm sorry."

"Don't. I'm upset that you kept it from me, but don't apologize for that piece of shit, or for what happened. That bastard destroyed our entire family. You, Paul, me. At least he never got to Sophia, not directly anyway. He fucked Paul up though, and Soph and I got to experience the after-effects of that. And it's no wonder you're so angry and depressed all the time. Was it an ongoing thing? Did he hurt you more than once?"

"Be careful," Jules says gently. "Don't push for details."

"I don't know if... I don't know."

"Yes or no?"

"Stop," Jules warns.

"Fine." I sigh. "Everything's my fault anyway. Paul would've been a different person if I hadn't been born. I knew he left because of me."

"Not because of you, for you," my mother says. "Paul couldn't change no matter how hard he tried. He knew he was like his dad and that form of temptation tortured his soul and eventually took control."

"You're saying he left us when I was a kid so he wouldn't rape me?"

"Mark, he caught you touching yourself... you were

around nine. He knew it was time to leave before he did something he'd later regret. After seeing you... he just knew he was like Abram, just like him."

"Ah, for Christ's sake, see it *is* my fault."

"No, honey."

I rub one of the leather dog ears between my thumb and forefinger, wishing I could actually feel the kneading massage.

"He gave up and gave in. I heard from him on and off over the years, and each time we spoke he sounded worse—insensitive and numb. After a while, I hated answering his calls... then I just stopped altogether. He left so he wouldn't harm his *son*."

"*Pretend* son. My childhood was a sham. And you know he eventually found a boy who could've passed as his real son, more than I ever could. Same features as him. Did that make it okay? Raping someone was okay because he wasn't family—he just looked the part? I bet that's how he rationalized he wasn't completely like Abram, because the kid wasn't related to him."

"What do you mean, *found* a boy?"

"That's unnecessary," Jules warns again.

"I mean he molested kids, that's what. And one in particular he wished was his son." I cover the cell and whisper to Jules, "I'm not holding back on this shit."

"But not *you*." She starts to cry. "Not *my* son."

"No," I mumble through the hood. "Not me..."

Her tears put a halt to my words. I've always kept certain things about Paul to myself. Like how he enjoyed watching me fuck other porn stars, sometimes staying in the room with his robe open and his hand on his dick, other times requesting that I get off in front of him, which I never did. Right now, those moments don't seem much different than if he had touched me as a kid.

"A bunch of sick fucks in my life." I exhale.

And he loved it when I was with Cove. Our first fuck was in my father's bed. Paul was lounging in a chair, smoking a cigar, and when I finished and the cameras were off, he crawled into that bed with him. Cove didn't come out of his room for hours.

"Mark?"

"I'm still here."

"I'm glad you're my son."

"I have to go."

"Can you call me soon, please? I need to hear that you're okay."

"I will. Promise." I hang up and slide forward, turning the water off with my foot. My head hangs low, hands rest between my legs, and my back arches forward. "Their marriage failed because of money. Fuck. That's the lie they told us. My mother spent their savings and my father left for that reason and because he couldn't deal with her depression. I think he said it so many times that he came to believe it himself."

She moves closer and puts her hand on my thigh.

"But he really left because of my dick."

"Don't do this."

"We didn't have any money when I was a kid, so

perhaps it's partly true, maybe she did spend their savings. I don't blame her. She must've been so unhappy having me around. Both of them. Later she was jealous of my dad's wealth, possibly mine too. I never sent her much money because of what I had heard. I thought she'd gamble it away or spend it in a day. I'm a fool… or I was treated like a fool."

"Okay. You're done." She stands and grabs two towels. "Get up. This isn't the Mark I know and I'm not going to allow you to punish yourself for something you had no control over."

I drop the anal slider and stagger to my feet, feeling unstable from exhaustion and all the emotions from a long night. "I told you sometimes my nights can last for weeks."

She wraps the towel around my body and rubs my arms, torso, and legs, then motions for me to bend down so she can dry my hair. I take off the dog hood and she blots the top of my head like it's an open wound, trying to stop the blood from flowing out. When finished, she tenders an adoring gaze toward my tousled mop.

"Don't get used to it." I try fixing it in the mirror, but get pulled over to the bed—delayed from bringing myself back to the handsome fuck that I am.

"Lie down."

"I need to take care of things."

"No one's going in that room tonight so take it easy. I'll help you clean it in the morning. Before anything else, you need to relax. Do as your told or I'm bringing out the cuffs."

She pulls down our comforter and I submit, setting Sophia's cell on the nightstand, and crawling right in.

"See, not even a comment about the cuffs. I'm trying to make you laugh. Tell me what I can do to help."

"I don't know. I've never felt this way before. I just... the bastard was a cop at one time then a detective. I wonder how much evidence he tampered with, especially for other men like him. I can't even process that. Of all things, a rapist cop."

"That's twisted." She covers me then stands with her hands on her hips and one side of her mouth curled upward as if she's coming up with a plan.

"The man's supposed to see the light and be lifted out of the darkness."

"What?" I question.

"The big change. You're a damaged man and some great event occurs in your life, then a shift takes place, and you're supposed to become a different person. I mean, it's supposed to be because of me, your princess, but I'm not that egotistical to believe it will happen that way."

"Oh dear fuck, what are you talking about?"

"You're going through the change..."

"What? Like menopause? I'm not a woman."

"A significant transformation after killing the man who started it all. Only you're fighting it." She looks at me with a straight face and deep lines set into her forehead.

"Cow shit," I say, noticing her quivering lips holding back a smile. I start to chuckle, a little at first before I lose it, breaking into a full-blown robust laugh, one I can't stop. The kind of laughter that makes your eyes water and your cheeks hurt. "The change." I crack up. "What a crock of shit. You're good, but I'm not going to follow the rules. This crap happened so, I'm what, supposed to stop killing? Buy a fucking house and get married? Then we have kids? Get rid of all my weapons and become a family man? Bring home the bacon to my wifey? Buy a giant Christmas tree for our place? Maybe purchase a boat?" My laughter slows and I turn to her, realizing we already have most of those things. "Fuck," I say, and she laughs. "No kids though, and no house. I have a giant house right here."

"That's my man." She heads for the bathroom to dry off. "But you know, I can't stand the fact that we live and work in the same place. We need to get away sometimes."

"No. I own a hotel. There's no need for a house when we live in a mansion with a pool. Fucking homemaker," I mutter.

Sophia's cell buzzes with an incoming text while Jules is in the bathroom. I don't even ponder whether or not I'm going to snoop. It has to be Cove and I want to read what the ass has to say. And it better be a groveling, take me back, I'm a pussy, I promise to stop drinking, apology. And if Soph is crashing here with the kids, yeah, her privacy is gone. I'm checking her messages.

Leaving in the morning. Got my suit. The dress fit? Is Jules ready?

What the...

Then a second text appears...

How about the rings? Bet your brother's clueless.

I sit up in a burst of emotion. My heart on fire. Pulse quickening. The words glowing on the screen.

Suit.

Dress.

Jules.

Rings.

I'm clueless.

No. Fucking. Shit.

DELIGHT

The mouth of my dog hood is unzipped. I push my tongue playfully through the hole as I pant over her, all while packing a bowl. She giggles, stoned, and rubs her leather mitted hands over my dick. After two drags, I set the weed on the nightstand and reach for our lube, place a little on the mitts, and sit back, enjoying slick leather gliding over my cock. "Fuck, that's nice." I grin wildly.

The morning sun emits reviving energy after a night of erratic sleep. I couldn't relax knowing I left Abram's body in that room. I should've moved him to the garage. And I was disturbed about Paul and the photographs, especially the one of my mom. Why the fuck did I leave those in there? Then being keyed up over the texts... a mix of anger and excitement raced through my veins all night.

But I'm feeling better with Jules' pretty little mitts on my dick. What a clever woman I've found. Ingenious, I should say. Leave it to her to plan a surprise wedding. I'll play along, wouldn't want to ruin her fun. Damn, this is going to be magnificent, especially with Cove. Can't wait to mess with him when he arrives. Try to fool me? Never.

"You happy under that hood?"

"Woof," I joke.

"Good doggy." She laughs, scratching my abs to get my back leg to kick.

I've worn the hood for her in the past, usually when she requests I be her submissive for the night, but this time it's to help me ease back into my frisky self. It's a new day, time to play. Oh shit, I forgot. What an ideal opportunity to use that children's book line on her.

I begin slowly, in a low, growling voice...

I'm the Gingerbread Doggy who comes prancing along. And with my Pussy I want to play.

We both laugh and I change to a higher tone for her part...

Pussy says, "No, please go away," and slides further up on the bed.

She lowers the mitts and plays along, sliding away on our bed.

I bark and I bite then lick my sweet Puss, saying, "Spread your twat for my big head to slay."

And she does. Her legs are wide, pussy exposed, and I glide inside. Beautiful.

This interaction is what's been missing from my life since I was a teen. Sex as a kid was spent trying to figure everything out. There's too much pressure to ever enjoy getting laid at that age. Then, when I got married, it felt like a job. And of course the porn company *was* a job. And all those one-nighters that came after leaving Vegas were nothing more than a quick dampening of my dick—dull and monotonous. No comfort, no love. Get in, get out, wipe off, zip up.

Jules gives me what I've always desired and our fucks are fun, not a task. We're not uptight around one another and she doesn't always need that romantic bullshit, just every so often, and I'm fine giving her that type of love on the rare occasions when she asks.

It's a sure sign you've found the right person when you're comfortable enough to put on a dog hood and bark over top of her while she paws at your cock.

Oh fuck, the *change*. I start to laugh, thinking that she might be right. Am I becoming a sensitive douche?

"You just high or are you laughing at me?" she asks.

"Laughing at you? No. You're spectacular. I'm laughing at myself."

I pull her forward until she's upright, take off the hood, and plant a sensual kiss on her lips. She removes the mitts and grips my unkempt hair, her warm tongue slipping over mine, causing my dick to rise even higher.

"I'm pussy-whipped this morning," I whisper. "Don't you wish we could stay in bed and fuck all day?"

"More than anything."

She turns and marvels at the snowflakes twirling past our bedroom window, set into motion by a light wind. With a smile, her fingers mirror their descent, weaving down my chest and stopping at the base of my dick.

Desire radiates from her bronzed skin while her body awakens mine. I follow her hairline down to her jaw and lift her chin for another passionate kiss, savoring this moment before we start to fuck. Her willing mouth opens—excited for a loving frolic with mine. Our eager lips touch. Blood flows. My mind's clouded.

"I'm overwhelmed," I say softly, holding back any explanation. She nods like she understands, though she hasn't a clue my emotions are for her—not the events from last night, or my dad, just her.

"Follow me." I pick up the hood and offer my arm, leading her to the window. She faces the glittering snowflakes, her hands on the frame with a tilted head. I take the bait, tasting the sweet flesh of her shoulder as she enjoys the winter landscape.

"Mmm. Heated kisses. Your dick pressed between my ass cheeks. A steady finger massaging my clit and the sensation of leather touching my breast... this is heaven." She spreads her legs and arches her back. "The snow's captivating when I'm stoned... it's like..." She laughs. "Like..." My lips brush over her ear, triggering a long sigh. "God, that feels good. Every time you tease my ears, I lose my train of thought."

I nip and tug at her lobe, slide my tongue around, tenderly up and down, then bite her neck.

"Eeee, you're giving me goosebumps."

Slowly, while holding her side, my cock parts her awakened lips.

"Nice... again."

I thrust and she says, "Uh, again."

Repeat.

The leather hood is on, an excited growl emerges from my mouth, and I'm fired up to fuck my perfect woman with quick, ball smacking drives from behind. She steadies herself with a hand to each side of the window while soft moans fill the room...

Her clit's massaged.

The sun rises.

Wind blows.

Snow gusts.

Sweat forms.

Birds fly past... and we fuck.

I move lustfully, devoting my hands to every inch of her figure, becoming more and more aroused by her warm flesh. The sun's rays blaze across her back and her blonde hair shimmers like sparkling waves.

"I'm thinking like a pussy again," I admit. "I look like a badass mutt on the outside, but my inner thoughts are as affectionate as a purring cat."

"Meow." She laughs. "Have I ruined you in some way?"

"In some way? You've ruined me in every way." I pull out and order her to the bed. "I'm a crazed junkie and it's all your fault... you, you with your fucking gorgeous tits and never-ending requests for my dick."

"Me?"

"Yeah, you. Don't act so innocent. Every few hours you crave my lips and once we kiss all I can think to do is eat you up." She blushes as we play, my engorged cock becoming a nonstop machine. "And tell me your secret. How is your pussy always so wet?" I toss the hood and grin at my sliding cock, lubed with her stimulation.

"God."

Our hips move in elated harmony.

"I'm so close, beautiful."

We start to fuck harder, crueler, faster—her legs over my shoulders and hands on my hips. Quickening breaths escape our mouths as our flesh slaps, creating the sound of a thrilling spank on the ass.

"Fuck me, Mark!"

And with those words, it's time. My mouth keeps her occupied, kissing her madly until I get my nightstand open and the thing unwrapped... my vibrating thimble. It fits on the tip of my finger and shakes over her clit.

"Fucking hell!" She gasps, turning her head from side to side. She loves it, and I can tell from the claws in my back that she's about to explode.

"Jules, I'm so close. Cum with me this time."

Her fingertips shake, trying to dig deeper into my flesh. Our arms stretch and tighten. Her legs quiver. I erupt.

"Fuck!"

Her tits are constricted in my hands like I'm suffocating my prey while she clutches frantically at my abs. With an open mouth and shut eyes, she has a silent orgasm... her favorite kind... nothing's better than when the rush is so intense you can't speak.

"Cum princess, cum for me. Yes, yes, yes."

A minute passes before she finally hunts for air, panting with a surging chest. I give her another minute to relax, before saying, "Nice one. And good morning."

"Good morning." She smiles, stretching her arms high above her head. "That was incredible. Did you cum?"

"Me?" I laugh. "Did *I* cum? Seriously? What the fuck kind of question is that?" I ask, putting a finger in her pussy and offering up a taste. "Convinced?"

"Yummy," she says. "I was kidding. I felt it during my orgasm. Awesome timing. Rare and awesome."

I put on my boxers and head for the bathroom. "We can do it that way more often if you'd like, but I'd prefer your pussy pulsating on its own without my shooting dick getting in the way."

I close the door and take a piss, seeing my sore red cock reflected in the mirror. "Need a vacation, buddy? You're looking a bit overused."

"Mark!" she calls out. "Don't start talking to yourself in there again!"

"I was talking to my dick. Stop listening!"

Damn it, I've lost all my privacy. I can't kill a man without my son showing up. I can't take a shower without my sister walking in. And I can't take a piss and have a conversation with my dick without my woman checking in on me. On the other hand, why is my suite so quiet this morning? No high-pitched pre-teen voices squealing in my living room, Sophia's not knocking on the bedroom door to get her cell phone, and Jack's not begging for pot.

"And you, Mark Jameson, you look like shit. Since when do you wake up with dark circles under your eyes? Your hair's a fucking mess too. Fix it. Fix it now."

It's slicked into place with a wet comb.

"Hello, handsome. You look smashing."

"Mark! Final warning!" she shouts.

"It's impolite to eavesdrop!" I open the door and strut out, scratching my nuts. "Have you heard anyone this morning?"

"No, you?"

I shake my head and open our closet, dressing in a pair of tattered jeans and a hoodie. "I'll go check on them while you get ready. Let's get an early start on that room before work. The sooner it's taken care of, the sooner our lives will be back to normal."

"I thought this was normal." She rises and slips into her robe. "Just so you know, I'm having a girls' day out after we finish cleaning."

"A day off?"

"Yes, a day off! It's been two weeks. I worked every single fucking day while you were in Philly. I deserve this."

"Of course you do."

"So what's with the look of disappointment on your face? Oh, I get it. You're upset because I'm leaving the hotel? Is that the cause of your wrinkled forehead? Because you have to work and won't be able to follow me?"

"I don't *have* to work today either."

"You also don't *have* to spy on us."

"Who? Tell me where you're going and who's tagging along?"

"No." She disappears in the bathroom and locks the door.

"If you don't tell me, then I'm keeping my dick in my

pants for an entire day... no, ten hours... or maybe eight. Okay, four! You hear me? Four hours without a glimpse of my giant cock!"

"Not a problem! We have plenty of toys to keep me satisfied!" she teases.

"Go ahead and keep secrets from me. I'll hang out with my sister and nephews today."

"Sophia and the kids are coming with me!"

I knew it. Her day out has something to do with the wedding. Still, I need to act like a prick so she doesn't suspect that I know. There can't be any change from my usual bastard self.

And where the hell is everyone?

"Jack? You better be here or I'm extending your punishment... Jack!" There's no response. "Soph?" That's odd. They must be at breakfast, although I can't imagine a sixteen-year-old being awake this early. The place is spotless too. Remarkably clean.

Dax and Xav were asleep in front of the fireplace and surrounded by pizza and napkins when I staggered in last night, and luckily they didn't wake to see me covered in blood. Now, I can't even tell they were here. The fresh scent of a recent shower hovers in the air, but the suite's empty. Clean as a whistle. The fast food's been picked up and the clothing and blankets folded and placed in a tidy pile on the sofa.

"Looks like they borrowed a laundry cart from housekeeping to clean up the mess." She points toward the main door on her way down the stairs. "Jesus, is that blood?"

For a brief moment, my pessimism overpowers my sanity and I can only imagine the worst-case scenario when I see the red stains on the cart—Abram isn't dead. He broke in and killed my family and the four of them are stuffed inside that cart. Or maybe my mind wants me to believe that tale over reality, because my reality is just as twisted—my son stuffed my dad inside the cart and brought him to me like a cat brings a dead mouse to his owner.

The scene gets bloodier as I approach. A hand is exposed and a black oxford shoe is on top of the pile of bloody sheets. There's a note under the shoe along with Jules' key card.

"What does it say?" she asks.

"Clean up in aisle seven." I exhale. "There's nothing worse than a sixteen-year-old trying to be amusing in a somber situation. He's not catching on that this isn't a form of entertainment."

I move the sheets to see Abram's lifeless body and shake my head at the sight of his open neck. Gruesome. They always look different in the sunlight.

"I really lost my shit."

"That man ruined many lives. Don't second-guess yourself this morning." She pushes the cart into the laundry room, hides it behind the door, and asks what we're going to do with him.

"Living next to a lake that never freezes has its benefits. I didn't plan on going boating this month, but I think I'll take Jack for a scenic ride before dinner, seeing how eager he is to be involved. One body on my property was fine, but not two, and not him." I point toward the laundry room. "Besides, it's time for a discussion about life and death with my son, and I'll have Abram and the body parts from the septic tank in tow as examples."

"Yeah, I forgot about the other guy. Just be careful, especially with Jack."

"I'll make him wear a life preserver." We walk into the corridor; curious to see what's left to clean.

"I meant be careful he doesn't push you into the freezing water," she warns, following me to the door.

I ignore the comment and swipe my card, wiping a small spot of blood from the doorframe before entering the room.

It's light. The blinds are open and fresh linens cover the bed. Pieces of carpet have been cut and removed. The nightstand and other furniture are impeccable. I'm impressed.

We pull the sheets back to reveal a white mattress.

"Holy crap," she says. "Either he flipped it or your son's a magician."

"I'll still need to have it replaced."

She tugs the sheets further down, exposing more and more of the mattress, stopping at the area that contained his blood.

"He cut it. I was right that he flipped it over, but there's a chunk missing where the blood must've been. Clever kid."

"There was a lot. I can't imagine he got it all."

"Looks like it to me." She nods toward the table. "And what's all that?"

His open suitcase is there, along with the detective badge, a gun set atop a pile of papers, and prescription bottles on display in a line.

"I'm surprised Jack didn't walk off with the gun."

"No shit," I say. "But it does make me wonder what he did take."

"Didn't you look through this last night?" she asks, reading the labels on the meds. "A diuretic... sedatives... hmm, antidepressants and more sedatives."

"I needed to get the fuck out of here. What the hell is this?" I move the badge and pick up the top paper, letting her read along over my shoulder. She makes a questioning noise and once I catch on to what I'm holding, I put it quickly out of sight. "Get dressed and figure out where everyone's at," I request faintly. "And take Sophia's cell with you. I'm sure she's looking for it."

"Is that—"

"Jules, give me some time here."

She steps away slowly, then leaves the room without sound or protest, understanding how serious this is... far worse than I ever could've imagined. Even for a guy like me, this is beyond disturbing.

I slump into the chair next to the table, getting lost in the sound of the heater. "Room, you have permission to distract me from this evil," I say to the empty space, looking for a diversion—something to lead me in another direction, to another place, somewhere other than Abram's life.

The curtains sway, drawing me to the outside view of my cold and desolate property. Grey wintry clouds have moved in, bringing large snowflakes that smother out the sun. It's a drastic shift from thirty minutes ago. Even the pine needles have become a ghostly white. And I imagine the temperature has dropped with the loss of the sun. Everything has changed. A split second, and a heated morning has turned to ice.

The paper is back in my hand. I read through it, stopping to take deep breaths, my hand alternating between covering my mouth and rubbing my forehead as I fall deeper into a troubled state. Page after page, learning more about this man's life, trying to comprehend all of this... I just don't get it. People can call me an evil shit if they want—say that I'm fucked in the head and unstable, but Jules is right, I'm nothing like Paul or Abram... thank fucking God I'm nothing like either one of them.

Compare the slimy assholes that deserved to leave this earth by my hands to innocent young lives that my dad made a profit from, both my dads for that matter, and the difference between right and wrong is clear. An eye for an eye in my book is not the same type of criminal wickedness as senseless trade, based on sex or age.

The pages before me are independent adoption papers and I can tell they're not legit. Abram's name is signed as a witness at the bottom of every one of them. It's a total scam. As a detective, I'm sure families found him trustworthy and the process authentic. A detective helped these parents find the right family for their child.

There's also documentation of his profits from the exchanges, but what bothers me the most is the adoptions are for a specific gender and age... my mind wants to block that part out... not only did Abram make a profit from this, that's shitty in itself, but on top of that, it was a form of sex trafficking. I'm sure the families weren't even aware that this was happening. Either that, or the parents didn't give a rat's ass and sold their kids to make a buck... the addresses are all from dirt-poor neighborhoods... it's possible some of these kids were never even missed.

"Mark?"

Jules stands in the entryway, looking for permission to enter. I wave her in and toss the papers on the table.

"I know you wanted to be alone, but I had to come back. Were those adoption papers?"

I nod.

"For you and Paul? I saw Abram's name on the bottom."

"No. Random boys from where I grew up, not us, we actually sprouted from the monster. We weren't sold by him."

She sighs and sits next to me, taking a look, flipping through page after page. "There're so many."

"At least a hundred. He made twenty grand off each one... is Jack downstairs?"

"Downstairs, wide awake, and wearing a suit."

"A suit?"

"Yeah, he's eating with my parents and asking my father how he can become an embalmer."

I rub my forehead and sigh. "I suppose that's the perfect profession for him. Legal at least."

"The rest of your family's also at breakfast."

"It's *your* family too."

After setting the papers down, she looks at me adoringly, holding my hand in a firm grip. "I'm sorry all over again. I don't know how many times I can say that before it loses all meaning."

"And I don't know if I can do anything about this, or why it was even brought to my attention. I guess it's all a power trip."

"I'd say so."

Wind gusts into the window, causing a low vibrating noise to sound throughout the room. The shuddering glass imitates my shaky pulse as I detach from her hand.

"I fucking hate this shit." I tap the papers. "It's exactly why I wanted out of the porn industry."

A heavier snow begins to fall, darkening the room. In the mountains, a foot of snow can fall in a short amount of time. It worries me that she's going out, even if it's for good reason.

"Stay here today," I request, feeling anxious. "The weather's unpredictable and the roads will be icy."

"I can't scratch these plans, besides it's only a ten-minute drive downtown. And if the weather's too extreme for a girl's day out, you're not going out on a boat."

"You can go tomorrow."

"Can you dump the bodies tomorrow?" She pauses, peering out the window and scrunching her nose at the scene. "Shit, that does look bad... I can't cancel though. It has to be done today. How about we make it a quick trip and I invite my friends here for the evening? We were going to end the day with a dinner, but we'll cut the trip short and eat here instead."

"Just tell me where the hell you're going," I demand, beginning to place the items in the suitcase. With the scene still fresh in my mind, I feel restless and need to get the fuck out of here.

"It's the holiday season, Mark. Duh. We're going Christmas shopping. And I won't ruin the surprise by telling you what your gifts are, now drop it."

"I'm sure you can order everything online without leaving our front door."

"Why are you such a curmudgeon about these things? And not just you, men in general are assholes when it comes to shopping. There's much more to it than just purchasing gifts. Decorative lights, holiday music, the smell of burning wood and cookies, plus being out in the snow, that's all part of the experience. It's festive and makes you feel warm and cuddly inside."

"I'm never warm and cuddly." I close the suitcase and take a final look around the room.

"Ha, baloney. I'll try to record you on my cell next time you act that way."

"Not gonna happen. And if that's the experience you want, you have it all right here."

"Ugh."

"I'm serious. Why don't you and your friends sit in the lobby and shop on your laptops while admiring my decorations and the lights on my tree? You can experience the snow from the hotel windows, listen to the holiday music on the lobby speakers, inhale the scent of burning wood from the massive fireplace, and order a plate of cookies from the restaurant."

"Seriously?"

"Yep."

"Men are so fucking stupid," she teases as we leave the room. "Why don't you launch the boat in the pool and get rid of the bodies there? That's similar to going out on the lake. You have everything you need right here."

"You can't compare what I said about shopping to the disposal of bodies."

"Perhaps not... so what are you going to do with that?" she asks, looking at the suitcase.

"Go over a few more things before storing it in my safe. Then, in time, I'll burn it."

"What about your sister?"

"I'll tell her the cane man is gone and that she no longer has to worry."

"And what about you?"

"I'm *not* worried."

"No." She rolls her eyes. "I mean, what about *all* of this?"

"Well, I'll be tainted by it for a while, that's for damn sure, but remarkably, I also believe all of this verifies how significant my life is. I'm a man who keeps shitheads like this one." I swing thc suitcase. "Out of society and away from innocent people. This kill is the ultimate confirmation of that. I was young and immature when I set foot in Paul's domain and clearly should've killed him back then, but now that I'm older and have better wits about me, it's clear I've got the biggest brass balls in this family. I'm in a class all by myself."

She grins playfully at my emotional toughness. "I love it when *arrogant Mark* appears. Missed you."

It doesn't matter whether I'm serious or I'm putting on a show, as long as it makes her smile.

"When are your parents taking off? I guess I should say goodbye."

"Ya think?" Her head shakes. "They're staying another day."

"What for?" I ask with a curious look as I open our suite.

"For one, you need to apologize. I'm not allowing my parents to walk out of here when you and my dad are on such bad terms."

"We're fine.

"You're *not* fine."

"Okay, if I go downstairs right now and say I'm sorry, will they check out?"

"Mark!"

"I'm kidding. Fuck. I'm not going down there anyway, I need to get to work and clear my head. But if you want, we can try dinner with them again after Jack and I return from our boat trip."

She looks at me like I'm insane.

"What? It wasn't that bad last night."

Still glaring.

"Okay, maybe dinner didn't go so well. What if I promise to behave and we give it another shot?"

"You shouldn't have to promise, you should just do it. Didn't you just mention something about being older and having better wits about yourself?"

"Touché, my love."

She returns to our entryway. "I'm going back down to eat breakfast. Food is calling my name. Oh, did you hear the kitchen is missing a turkey and some other stuff? You think one of our staff is stealing? I mean, how can someone walk off with a whole bird without being seen?"

"I'll check the security cams when I have time, but it's not that important considering everything else that's going on. I'm sure we'll figure it out eventually. And if it's a turkey, that's usually a sign someone needs to feed their family."

"Let's add a larger holiday bonus to the checks this week to make sure people have enough to enjoy a decent holiday meal."

"That's fine. I'll take care of it today. Remind me when you're coming home again? Noon?"

"Three!"

"I'll expect you at two."

"Three!" She closes the door in laughter. "Three!" I hear her shout as she walks down the corridor.

"Two o'clock it is, beautiful! Don't mess with the power of twos!"

Lucky number two... two of us will take two dead men out on a lake that's twenty-two miles long on this twentieth day of the twelfth month. It can't be done tomorrow. We have to do it today.

KNAVE

"According to dictionary.com, *knave* means an unprincipled, untrustworthy, or dishonest person, although in earlier times it was used as a term for a male servant." Jack scrolls through his new iPhone, a gift I picked up for him when I replaced mine during my lunch break earlier today. It's keeping him occupied as I continue to steer the boat the two miles back to shore.

He did well for a first-timer—following directions precisely, securing the concrete blocks like a champ, and when the time came, he happily rolled the two men into the water—Abram as one big lump, and the other guy in pieces, wrapped in a large tarp. He mentioned his disappointment in how quickly they sank and that they weren't still alive when they dropped in. He said they both deserved to die horrible, painful deaths, especially his grandfather.

"Are you saying you feel like my servant?" I ask, pulling my winter hat over my ears.

"Nope. Just shooting the shit. You want to hear some of the synonyms?"

"Sure."

The moisture in his breath hits the cold air and a small cloud forms with each word. "Fraud. Bastard. Lowlife. Rascal. Scamp. Scoundrel. Swindler. And this one, Dad, this one is my second favorite... villain. Villain is such a fascinating word, isn't it?"

"It certainly is, son."

The snow stopped at noon and Jules made it back to the hotel safe and sound, bringing her friends along for dinner as we discussed. They're at the bar for now, waiting for me to return so we can all eat together, and that means her parents too.

"Aren't you going to ask me what my favorite synonym of the word is? I said villain was my second favorite. You listening, or not?"

"Oh, sorry. What's your favorite synonym for knave?"

"Jack." He grins. "Isn't that cool? I never thought of it before this moment, but I'm like the Jack on a deck of playing cards. Your little soldier." He bows with one hand raised in the air. "At your service, my master."

"You said you were just shooting the shit? So now it has meaning?"

"Tell me you're not amused by all of this. At least give me some praise that I thought to look it up."

"Why did you anyway?" I slow the boat as we approach the dock. "What goes through that pea-sized brain of yours, stuff like this?"

"I'll pretend your pea comment didn't just hurt my feelings. Don't you get curious about things? Or are you too old? I hear words I don't recognize all the time, like on

223

cable and online. I want to find out what they mean. Do you think you already know everything?"

"I get it. I get it."

"From now on, you can refer to me as your dishonest, swindling, bastard knave. Or your servant boy is fine too."

"That's not funny."

"*Nothing's* funny, is it?"

"I find humor in everything and nothing at the same time."

He sighs and sets his hand in the water. "Fuck, that's ice cold. How long do you think a man could survive in this lake if he fell in?"

"At this time of the year? I'd say a minute, tops."

"If I push you in and tell the cops you accidently fell over the side, you think they'd believe me?"

I offer a side-eye with a taut mouth and a look of disgust over his comment. "You have an odd sense of humor, buddy. Why don't you work on being witty instead of sounding like a dumbass? You'll pick up a lot more women that way."

"A girlfriend, plus some side chicks and honey dips." He laughs.

"There you go again. And trust me, one's enough. You don't need extras on the side. Don't be a cheating dipshit." I cut the motor and tie the boat to the dock.

"Lighten up, would ya? I'm sixteen and grounded... trying to make the best of things right now."

I help him step onto the platform and we start to walk toward the truck. "Watch your footing. The dock may be icy under this fresh snowfall."

"Are you sad?" he asks, grabbing my wrist as he slips.

I put my arm over his shoulder and pull him close; making sure he doesn't fall off the edge.

"You know my friends back home in Philly used to call me Jester. It was a decent nickname, better than when you refer to me as a *little prick*."

I open the passenger door and he slides in, continuously talking. His behavior's playful, like it was years ago when we were still living in Vegas.

"I have fun clowning around, but you think I'm obnoxious. Most people would've figured out by now it's how I hide my depression... I don't think you get that."

"I know you're depressed." I shut his door, get in the driver's side, start the truck, shift it into four-wheel drive, and back down the ramp to the edge of the lake. "Stay here while I get the boat on the trailer."

"No, I want to help." He jumps out and walks toward the water.

"Wait at the edge and I'll walk it over."

He nods, standing with his hands in his pockets, kicking the fluffy snow with his dress shoes. That's why he can't get his footing—the kid's dressed like a gangster today. I told him to change into old clothes for the trip and he refused. He said you're supposed to dress your best for a funeral. A funeral. This is a disposal, not an observance. Dump and go. He even wore his suit into the septic tank to grab the body parts.

I won't complain too much though, he did mention

he had a greater understanding of why I kill certain men and not others. That's a step in the right direction.

What lives are worth taking and why? He said the two men would have met the same demise if they had crossed his path under similar circumstances. That's my boy. That's who I want him to be—not a pussy or a wimp, and not a bully or a psychopath, just a man somewhere in-between. I want him to enjoy a good life, stay away from the cops, and take care of business when necessary.

"I do like your suit," I say, cranking the boat onto the trailer. "I don't think you should refer to this as a funeral, but you look good when you dress in something besides baggy jeans and a black hoodie."

"It's the emergence of my alter-ego. I've decided to dress like the owner of a fancy hotel, except when I go snowboarding, then I need to wear something that will get me laid."

I smirk. "I get laid plenty when I wear my suits."

"God, you never catch on to anything I'm trying to say. I could hold up a sign in front of your face that says, *thank you*, and you'd think it said *fuck you*." He hops back into the truck and I attempt to drive up the ramp. The tires slip, forcing me to put it in reverse and repeat the climb for better traction. After three attempts we're able to make it up the incline and out of the private launch area.

"I'm trying to say thank you."

"For what?" I ask.

He inhales a deep breath and looks at his cell, replying to a text before answering my question. "For one, you didn't get upset that I cleaned the room."

"You did a fine job, almost as good as Jules and I would've done. I only need to replace the mattress, but the rest is flawless."

He looks out the window at the snowcapped mountains then turns his entire body to face me. "Thanks for being better than him. I didn't know shit like that happened to people. I mean... I saw those papers and didn't know... I'm dressed like this because I admire you today."

"Today?" I raise a brow and glance over to see him grinning.

"Yep. Today. Maybe tomorrow too, we'll see."

"Now *that* one I get. That's funny."

"What are you gonna do with that stuff?"

"The papers? Nothing. It's from decades ago and I have no way of explaining how I came across it if I take it to the authorities. It's just another family secret to add to the pile."

His cell buzzes and he sends out another text, mentioning it's Emma and she wants to see him. "I'm not happy that I'm grounded like an eight-year-old, and I want my suite back before my cousins' sticky fingers ruin my things, but it was cool that you let me do this. It was like *take your son to work day*, only not at the boring hotel—I got to tag along with you to your exciting job."

"Glad you enjoyed it." I follow the snowy road into the mountains, heading back to my *unexciting* hotel. "Why don't you like the Jameson?"

He shrugs. "I guess because it's like a prison. Everyone's placed in a cell and they gather in the mess hall for a meal then go back to their cells. Sometimes they come out for an hour and walk around the yard to get some exercise, but they stay in their cliques. And like prison, they could get stabbed if they get out of line."

"That's an interesting way of looking at it." I notice the boat swerving in the rear-view mirror and slow the truck so we don't slide into the ditch. Large, wet flakes start to cover my windshield and I'm glad we made it off the lake before this next wave of snow rolled in.

"Jack, the note you left in the laundry cart this morning was immature, but besides that, I'm proud of you."

"Really? Cool. Does that mean I'm not grounded anymore?"

"No."

"Fuck. Well, can I at least finish unpacking the rest of my stuff tonight? I promise to come back to your suite as soon as I'm done."

"Midnight," I say.

"Yes!" He holds a fist in the air and tightens his lips in excitement.

"Don't even think about inviting anyone over or you'll be grounded for a year. And do me a favor. Change out of that suit. It smells like sewage."

"No problem."

I hit the button for my garage door and back the boat into one of the stalls, unlatch it, and park the truck. We head up the stairs and enter an empty suite. I nod that it's okay for him to go ahead and unpack and he's out the door in the blink of an eye.

After a quick shower and a change into nicer clothing for our dinner, I set my blade and gun in place, fix my tie, place a dab of cologne on my wrists, and make my way downstairs to join the party. This is going to be another one of those awkward nights. Not only do I need to make a good impression with Jules' friends, but I also have to apologize to Sam and keep my mouth shut, no matter how many times I'm poked with a stick.

No confrontations. I'll keep repeating that in my head.

"Mark!"

Oh, perfect. My woman's showing cleavage and I can tell by her crooked walk and red face that she's drunk. Wasted. Thank fuck. I might be able to get away with more than I originally thought.

"You're shit-faced," I whisper, giving her a kiss on the cheek and taking her wine glass away before she spills it down the front of my suit jacket. I take a sip as I'm dragged over to the bar, nodding to her friend.

"Angie, this is my fiancé, Mark."

She puts out her hand and we shake. "Wow. Gorgeous, like a model, just like Jules mentioned millions and zillions of times. You're almost as handsome as my husband."

"You're married? That's a surprise. Jules never mentioned any of her friends had husbands."

"For three years. His name's Marc, but he spells it

229

with a 'c' not a 'k'." She points to my name on the bottom of the bar menu. "And he's only twenty-five. What are you, like fifty?" Her cheeks match the color of her red hair; flush from the alcohol, and round like a chipmunk's.

"Sixty," I respond.

"Eeew."

"He's only in his late thirties, don't let his grey hair fool you."

"I don't have any grey hair." I take a quick look in the bar mirror and frown at their ribbing.

"It's so nice to finally meet you." She regains composure and we clink wine glasses.

"Where is everyone?"

"This is it. My other friends only stopped in for a drink, they have family in town for the holidays and couldn't stay for dinner. And Sophia and her kids are busy... don't ask, it's a secret."

"Another holiday surprise?"

"Something like that. You ready? My parents are waiting for us in the restaurant."

"As ready as I'll ever be."

Angie stands and straightens her velvet brown dress, bringing a small gold clutch purse and her wine glass along. "What's that about? Don't you like the Barringers?"

"My dad and Mark clash." Jules speaks for me.

"What? Your dad's great. Remember years ago when he took us to see Lady Gaga and he wore a gas mask to the concert? It was amazing. He fit right in with our friends and the rest of the crowd. We all thought your dad was the bomb." Jules catches her as she tumbles in her heels.

"Careful, girl." She helps her friend get steady and they laugh.

This is gonna work out beautifully. Thank fuck for alcohol. The two of them can act like fools and take the pressure off me to carry the conversation. Drunken women are always good for a laugh, unless they're vomiting. It's all fun and games when you're wasted until someone starts puking up their guts.

I hold the door open for the tall, attractive women to enter the restaurant, winking at mine as she heads inside.

"My dad only wore that gas mask because he heard there'd be a lot of pot at the show. He wasn't trying to be hip."

"Another reason not to like the guy," I say under my breath. "You look pretty, by the way. New dress?"

"Yes, black, your favorite. And heels." She kicks up a foot. "New panties too."

"Don't show me those just yet." I raise a hand. "Surprise me later."

We walk to one of the private rooms overlooking the lake where a long table is glowing with silver and gold candles. The room has a fireplace and is complete with warm decor, hopefully soothing enough to keep us all tame.

Unexpectedly, Sam rises when we reach the table, offering his hand before I have the chance.

"Sorry about last night, Mark. No hard feelings, I hope." He pats my arm and gives his daughter a kiss on the cheek, confiscating my role of champion. Damn him, I wanted to say that.

"I'm the one who needs to apologize. I'm sure I came across as vulgar and egotistical. You'll experience the real Mark this evening," I declare, pulling a chair out for Jules before sitting across from her at the table. Angie's by her side and her mother's next to me, while I let Sam claim the head of the table next to his wife, leaving the end next to Jules and me empty.

"I hope you're enjoying your stay." My fingers snap for the waiter at the door to enter. "Wine for everyone, bread, and bring me a dirty martini, wet, stirred, and on the rocks."

"I'll have the same," Sam says.

"Oh, I want one," Jules says.

"Me too," Angie agrees.

"Wine is fine for me," Karina remarks.

"Four then," I say. "Plus two bottles of wine, bread, and the special for everyone." I think for a moment then call our waiter back. "Hold up. On second thought, I'll have the special, but go ahead and tell everyone what's on the menu tonight." The waiter sounds off a long list of choices from the kitchen and after everyone orders, I feel a soft foot rubbing my pant leg in appreciation. Jules removed her heel. I lift my brow playfully and she nods that I did the right thing.

"So, Mark." Sam leans forward—he and his wife dressed attractively, like socialites wearing all black with a trace of turquoise jewelry.

The table falls silent as everyone waits for a quarrel to begin. My head turns and I remain calm. No matter what he says, whatever it is, remember to keep your mouth shut.

"You a gambling man?" he asks.

"Betting isn't my thing."

"You're not a big risk taker?"

Jules foot slides up my pants as I keep a relaxed state.

"No." I direct my words toward him while gazing directly into her eyes. She tilts her head friskily in awe that her touch is helping me chill out.

"I think there'd be a significant risk to selling off all of your possessions in Vegas and starting over in this area, especially since you didn't know anyone out in our neck of the woods. I'm not saying this didn't work out for you, just looking around your place I can tell you're a smart and successful businessman. It's a splendid hotel."

"Is there a question coming?" I ask.

"I'm sure there is," Jules mumbles. She draws as close as she can to the table and reaches for my hand. "Everything is about me, just keep that in mind. It's all about his daughter."

I nod.

"That's true," he says. "I'm curious if you plan on doing it again." He scans the room and property as the drinks and bread are set on the table. The table comes alive while everyone reaches for their glasses to stay occupied during our exchange. "You gonna sell and take off in the near future? And if so, is my daughter going with you or are you leaving her here?"

"Oh, Dad." She sighs.

"It's okay." I put my hand out to let her know I can handle this, even though it's a trick question. He wants to know if I'll be moving his daughter away from him or if I plan on breaking her heart. Either way, I'm an ass, although with a guy like him, he'd prefer the latter—me taking off, Jules being crushed, and him getting his daughter back.

"You're taking an awfully long time to answer a simple question," he says.

"Honey, let them be tonight," Karina insists.

"This is a civil conversation and a simple question," he replies.

"He's right," I say. "And I have no plans on leaving the area. I'm extremely fond of my property and hotel."

"What if it starts to fail?" he asks.

"Then I'll build a casino. South Lake Tahoe could use another one."

"I don't believe that's wise."

"It's only an example. What I'm saying is, I'll make it work. There's always a way if you're levelheaded, intelligent, and have the correct resources. Plus, a little charm never hurt anyone."

"And you have all those things, correct?"

"That's exactly right. And a good woman by my side to tell me when I'm out of line." Her foot's back, this time rising higher. I catch it in my hand and smirk.

"So you're not going to sell and move?"

"I haven't even considered it."

He picks up his drink and gestures for the rest of us to follow. "Well then, cheers."

"Cheers." We shadow him and drink.

This could get interesting... and I'm not referring to Sam. I can tell he's opting out of another head-on collision. Undoubtedly, he got a lecture from Karina *and* Jules about his behavior last night. There's no way I'm the only one who was reprimanded.

But what's going on under the table... this sneaky foot of hers that keeps tiptoeing up my leg. That's what I mean by interesting. It stops over my cock and wants inside my pants. I shake my head, but she refuses to abandon the idea of a little sexual play during dinner.

"I wouldn't want to leave either." Karina distracts me with a warm smile. "Your hotel is reminiscent of the castles I used to read about as a child. I feel safe and perky inside these rooms."

"Mom, perky is a good word for breasts, not—"

"Okay, then vibrant." She stops Jules from finishing. "I feel sprightly and vibrant."

"Aren't sprites like goblins or leprechauns?" Angie asks, making us all laugh. "Are you saying you've found a pot of gold at the end of the rainbow?"

"Can I speak without my two favorite, but intoxicated women, correcting my choice of descriptors? And yes, in a way, that's true. That *is* what I'm saying. The massive stone fireplaces, crackling and full of glowing embers, the pretty lights and soft holiday music in the background, the magnificent food and breathtaking views..." She turns to the landscape. "I'm waiting for a white horse to prance through the snow outside this window."

"And a fair-haired prince to sweep you off your feet?" Sam laughs, but stops when the three women turn and gawk at me.

I raise my glass and smile warmly. "Cheers, Sam."

"Shit, I set myself up for that one," he mutters. His wife takes his hand as two of my waiters arrive with our food. They set the steaming plates of winter beef stew, pork loin with sweet potato, and tortellini stuffed eggplant before us, leaving a cranberry and goat cheese dinner salad beside each of our plates. I was only partly wrong—three of us did want the special.

"And the most significant thing I've noticed," Karina continues, "is my daughter's radiant face. She's in love. Julia's never looked so joyful, and that makes the two of us incredibly happy. Isn't that right, honey?" She turns to her husband.

"I suppose." He gives in, blowing on a spoon full of stew to cool his first taste. He nods in delight after taking a bite and wipes his mouth with a napkin before pulling his wife nearer for a private discussion. I take the opportunity to lean in and tell Jules to knock it off. The last thing I need is to walk out of here with an erection. I'm not wearing the same jacket I had on last night and this shorter length isn't going to cover a bulge.

"You're behaving," she says quietly. "You deserve a

treat." She pulls back and whispers something to Angie, who nods like she's agreeing to a mischievous plan. The two speak to Jules' parents—the classic; *remember when* conversation that people can never get enough of—a walk down memory lane that keeps everyone occupied and in good spirits, and a ploy to distract them from what's *up-and-coming* under the opposite end of the table.

The sensation of her toes wandering around my shaft makes me blush. She's frisky, rubbing her instep over my dick until it swells.

"That's good," I declare, and she joins me in a celebratory drink.

I pull the tablecloth over my lap, lean forward, and pray to God no one hears the sound of my zipper. I can't believe I'm doing this... but that's just it... I've never done this. I've never experienced any type of foot play over an evening meal.

I'm fucking game. Bring it.

The toes walk up my leg and ecstatically discover my bare skin, wiggling in delight.

Freakin' A, it feels better than... no... oh fuck, she wouldn't. She can't. She is!

My eyes are the size of her tits as she discreetly, with a guiltless snicker, smears butter over her fingers. Her hand disappears under the table and I inhale a deep breath when the feeling of slick toes slide over my cock. Oh, dear fuck. She wins. Damn, she really wins this time. The outcome of this is going to drive everyone screaming from the table. Hell, I can just imagine my cum shooting out and landing on her friend's leg.

"Not all the way," I whisper.

She conceals a big grin behind her drink and swipes the sole of her foot around my crown.

"Uh." I accidently release a grunt and swiftly emit a fake cough to cover the sound. "Must've swallowed wrong." I suggest to her parents and finish my drink.

Jules continues to hold a nonchalant conversation with everyone while secretly fluttering her toes over every inch of my dick. At one point I become so worked up I sound like a babbling idiot.

... Mmm, this is exciting, I mean touching. Stroking and touching. No, I mean... it's nice. It's a nice dinner, everyone. Glad you're all here. Toes and all...

What a douche.

And that look—damn she's proud of herself, presenting me with an endless flash of her pearly whites.

My voice upsurges and breaks whenever I speak, providing Sam the belief that my nervousness is on account of him. The man's in heaven with how uncomfortable I am, and I'm in heaven with his daughter's foot gliding over my dick. His thoughts and mine are like night and day.

I'm aroused by soft, lubed, skin that passionately performs all the way through dessert. She rolls a cherry over her tongue and I dab my forehead, playing along with her games. This is the longest I've ever been teased, the quietest I've had to remain, and the closest I've come to climax without a release, not just once, or twice, but multiple times throughout the night.

She's fucked. She *will* be fucked. I'm so ready.

"That was great." Angie sets her napkin on the table and puts her hand on Jules' arm in an adoring manner. "I'm so happy for you, and it's wonderful you found someone who isn't threatened by the fact that you used to be a man."

"Oh, the secret's out." Jules places her elbows on the table and rests her face in her hands. "I wasn't going to tell him until our wedding night. I wanted our first time to be extra-special."

I laugh. "Hey, as long as you're equipped with something down there and it works without batteries, we're good. Heck, I'm okay even if it requires batteries. We'll make it work somehow."

Sam struggles with our playfulness, standing with his wife to leave. "I can only hear so much about my daughter's 'future bedroom activities,'" he gestures quote marks, "before I need to eradicate it from my mind by watching some cable melodrama so I can sleep."

Jules and Angie share a moment of whispering before her friend stands, purse in hand, with a thank you and a finger wave.

"You okay to drive?" I ask.

"Jules drove me here so I'm taking a cab home... mind if I join you on the way out?" she asks the Barringers.

"No, not at all," Karina says, surprising me with a kiss on the cheek. I smile and rise slightly to shake Sam's hand, making sure not to stand upright so the tablecloth doesn't drop from my waist. Again, he feels superior that I'm lingering beneath him, inferior to him like a servant boy... a knave, as Jack would say. And to be honest, it doesn't bother me one bit since I know his daughter, my soon-to-be wife, her ass, is about to be fucked in five... they give her hug and start to leave... four... I smile as they walk out... three... Jules stands and slides the door to the private room shut... two... she walks over and sits on my lap... one.

"Hi."

"Fuck me," I demand. "Now."

She lifts her skirt and moves her new panties to the side, sliding in.

"No." I take my blade from my pocket and cut them off, then pull out. "Anal."

"Man of few words," she whispers, taking a clump of butter in her hands and rubbing it over my cock.

"Uh." My mouth opens and eyes blur.

"Whoa, I didn't realize you were so close."

"Now."

She rubs my tip over her hole and slowly lowers, bringing me partway in.

The dessert plates are slid away, her back hits the table, and legs wrap around my waist. "You cruel tease. Damn, your ass is so fucking tight." I pound into her. "Fuck, fuck. I can't believe you kept me on the brink for so long." I give her a hard thrust and hold steady, then repeat to power and possess. "Fuck." And with another push into her crushing-tight space, I finally eclipse the exhaustive peak I've been trapped in all night.

"Oh, Mark. You're cumming. Yes." She touches my cheeks as my forearms hit the table.

Her dress is gnawed to confine my moans. It's quick and intense—the spasms deep, my passion obvious, and her love prized.

"Dear woman." I gasp.

I've been at climax for a fucking hour, waiting for the tension to be released and my head to level out.

"*My* woman."

We kiss affectionately and I say, "Mine."

RID

"The sight of butter will forever give me an erection."

My suit jacket's folded over my forearm, covering the stains on my pants as we leave the restaurant.

"You think the busboy overheard? He was standing next to the door when we came out."

"Probably, but who cares? As long as no one walked in while I was cumming in your ass... I'd rather have people hear me fuck, than watch. What do you call that type of sex anyway? Getting the butt end of the butter stick?"

We laugh and hold hands, walking down the corridor toward the lobby. It's a busy night. People are arriving for the holidays, needing a place to stay when visiting relatives. Shit, speaking of which...

"Oh crap," Jules says with dropped shoulders. "Leave him alone. You're not supposed to know he's here."

"Hmm." I smirk. "I was just about to mention how perfect this day was, perfect, perfect. Everything went down without a hitch. And there, before my eyes, as the night's coming to a beautiful end, is my favorite brother-in-law sneaking into my bar. The day just keeps getting better and better. Hell, I've missed him."

I take a step forward and she pulls me back.

"No. I'm serious. Sophia doesn't want you to know he's here, not yet. Pretend you never saw him."

"What? Pretend I never saw him? Why? I knew he'd come here and apologize, that's no secret. I'm just gonna say hello..."

"Please, let them work things out first. Keep your nose out of their business."

I sigh and shake my head. "I'll meet you upstairs. One drink, just one, and I'll be up."

"No." She clutches my hand even tighter, practically cutting off my circulation.

"What are you so worried about?" She's nervous. Afraid I'll find out about the wedding, and if Cove's wasted, who knows what he'll say.

"Don't ask him any questions about today."

"Like what?"

"Oh fuck, forget it. I'm coming with you."

"No, you're not." I laugh.

"Mark, don't be upset with him about his marriage. Sophia doesn't want the two of you to get into a fight, that's why we didn't mention he was here. You don't have all the details."

I place my hands on my hips and give her my best *bullshit* look.

"Listen to me." She points at my face.

"No, you listen. It's drink time with my bro."

"With your what? Your *bro*? Dear Lord, this is going in that direction? You're going to sound like a dumbass again to make me laugh so I'll lighten up and you can get your way?"

"Umm, yes?"

"Would you please lower your hands and cover that butter stain."

I look down, forgetting it was there.

"You can't go in there all buttered up."

I laugh. "Surprisingly, I've heard that line before."

"Gah!"

"Cove doesn't care. He'll get a kick out of the soft creamy spread story."

"No!"

"See ya in a bit." I turn and walk toward the bar.

"Hey, wait." She sounds troubled. "I have to tell you something."

"Later. I'll be upstairs soon enough. Thirty minutes?"

"No, wait... Cove doesn't know... we went... I didn't tell everyone today that... don't get angry, okay?"

"You don't have to tell me anything... hold on, don't get angry at what?" My voice deepens. Now I'm confused.

"Promise me you won't yell."

"Spill it," I demand.

"Fuck. If I tell you, don't ask why."

"I don't have a clue what you're referring to. What?"

She bites her bottom lip and looks around like her hand's caught in the cookie jar.

"Did you kill someone?"

She giggles nervously. "I wish. At least I could go into detail about something like that. No, I had to go to Reno today, but no questions."

"That far? In this weather? Wait, you said you were going downtown, a ten-minute drive. *Downtown is only a ten-minute drive.*" I say, impersonating her high-pitched voice.

"It was for something special. No questions!"

"Well what the fuck's the issue with Cove then?"

"We picked him up from the airport in Reno. I know he won't mention the shopping, but he may say we were out there to get him. I wanted to tell you I was there before he did."

"Wait a second. How the fuck did you do that trip in the amount of time we discussed?"

She bites her lip even harder.

"Jules?"

"We left this morning," she says quickly. "The moment you started working. Not at noon, a few hours earlier."

"During the heavy snow?" My hands are back on my hips.

"Mark, the stains."

"Jules, the fucking weather. I don't want to lose you, or anyone else for that matter. You took Soph and the kids too? How'd all of you fit in the truck?"

"I... we... I took the Sequoia. The one used to take guests places."

"You did what?" My brow lifts. "Wow, okay. Let me get this straight. You lied about the time you left, where you were going, stole the hotel's SUV, and risked your life and the lives of my family for a goddamn shopping trip? Am I hearing you correctly?"

A guest walks past and looks at my groin.

"Answer me!"

"You're making it sound worse than it is."

"So you believe it's not that bad? But for some reason you didn't want to tell me? Jesus, your ass is grass. How can I be so madly in love with you one minute, and want to bury you neck-deep in the snow the next?"

"I'm sorry."

"Go home."

"You're kidding, right? Don't walk away from me!"

I reach the bar, alone. To hell if I'm going to say, *oh that's okay, princess, go ahead and lie to me any time you'd like.* Then again, it *is* for the wedding. I'm torn on this one, like she is. I guess I'm so upset because I love her to death. Genuinely upset, not just playing along this time...

"Hello, handsome. Come here often?"

Cove lets out a long exhale with his hand covering his face, indicating he wants to be left alone.

"I was hoping you didn't see me."

"You can't hide behind that tiny girlie hand." I gesture for my bartender.

"That's not what I meant."

"I know exactly what you meant... give me the same." I motion to Cove's drink and watch a glass of Coke being poured and set in front of me, no liquor, just Coke. "What are you doing in here if you're not drinking?"

"Like I said..." He takes a sip and sighs. "It was a duck and escape."

I sit next to him and set my jacket over my crotch, covering any evidence of dessert. "How are you?"

"I'm fixing everything with Sophia, so don't piss on me."

"Who's pissing? You see my dick out? I'm asking you a friendly question. How the fuck are you, man?"

He swirls his glass and sips it like it's liquor. "Life's bland, for the most part, so that makes me happy."

"See. That's good. Happy, like ha-ha I'm a drunk, or happy like, I love my life?"

His head finally raises and I smile when I see his dark features.

"Or happy because *you're so good looking?*"

He relaxes, and I'm surprised he caught on to my Seinfeld reference, tossing one back in good fun...

"These pretzels are making me thirsty." He takes a drink of soda with a grin.

"You're so much better at that than me, being emotionless and deadpan when you're sober. It works for you."

"How's Jack doing?" he asks.

"Ah, he's alright."

The lights dim, replaced by a string of glowing holiday decorations along the liquor shelf. Must be eight. The evening bar specials and room transformation has begun.

"He's up and down all the time like the rest of us, a true Jameson, only slightly crazier. Sometimes I think he's gonna kill me in my sleep."

Guests' eyes are drawn to the glowing bottles of golden liquids, red flickering bulbs skip to the music, and the smell of stale beer and cinnamon are heavy in the air. Cove crosses his legs, dressed in black jeans and a pair of Chelsea style boots. His finger traces the etched pine trees on the tumbler drinking glass before taking another sip, stopping to roll his flannel sleeves to expose his watch. He checks the time then decides to continue the conversation.

"What about you? Holding up okay?" he asks.

"With Jack? I feel terrible when he gets depressed. Other than that, we're doing okay."

"I was referring more about this refuge in the pines and your sanity. I heard you went on a boat trip today. This time of the year, that can only mean one thing." He holds up a finger for a refill.

"Easy buddy," I tease. "Too much caffeine and you won't be able to sleep."

One of my servers lights the candles on the tables throughout the room then places a couple of logs in the corner fireplace. It's peaceful in here, but still early. At ten, the place will transform into another world.

"Things are taken care of and I'm stable. We don't need to discuss the boat."

"Was it for the guy who was in St. Louis? Soph said he's here."

"Not any longer. No need to be troubled over the asshole."

"Gone?"

"Living at the bottom of the twenty-two mile lake."

He sneers and releases a wounding remark. "That relentless, flippant attitude you have about death is what makes you Paul's son. At ease with taking a man's life like it has no meaning."

"I'm not him."

"That's right, you're a man who kills people, or protects people... protects, that's the magic word, isn't it Mark? So here's the thing—that asshole, as you call him, was in *my* bar, screwing with *my* family. I deserve to know what the hell's going on. You killed him. Why? Who is he?"

"Give me a shot of anything," I shout to my bartender. "Make it a double."

"Fuck, that bad?"

"Cove, trust me when I say you don't want to know. Let's talk about something else."

"I should just go back to our suite," he mumbles. "I needed to walk around after a long day of travel, but I didn't realize I'd run into you. Soph will be fuming if she finds out I'm here anyway."

"You ever think about divorcing her?" I ask.

"What? Oh, don't start this shit. No, I'm not leaving my wife."

"So she's here because *she* wants out, not you?"

"No. Neither one of those things are true."

"Are you sure? That's not what she said yesterday. She's leaving your ass, wants out of the marriage, and can't wait to get away from your boozing... look at you, sitting here, chugging all those sodas... pathetic." I down the shots and hold back a grin. "You're a disgrace, Mr. Everton... how long you been sober? It can't be for only *one* day. No way, not with such calm hands. They should be a shaky mess right now. I'd say you haven't had a drink for some time, but according to my sister, she left for that reason." I turn rapidly and place a hand on his back. "Did I ever tell you how much I hate surprises?"

"Where the hell is this going?" He pulls away.

"A surprise is a secret that was born from a lie."

"A what is a what?"

"I'd choose getting my teeth pulled without any Novocain, over being lied to by someone wanting to keep a secret that ends in a god-awful surprise. And that's what my life's been all about. The cane man opened my eyes to that, and I'm tired of it. All of it. No more." I wave my hand like I'm casting it all away.

"Ahh, I get it." He inhales with a continual nod. "Another one of your cryptic stories? Is this one a comedy or a tragedy?"

"Both... I think. Listen."

"I *am* listening."

I take a deep breath, and say, "You can learn a lot about your past once people around you are finished denying it."

He sets his drink on the bar and stares blankly.

"Let it sink in for a few years."

"I'm thinking," he says.

"It's not a question, there's no answer."

"But it's a reference to one of us. That guy must be from Paul's company. Why else would he want to haunt both you *and* me? We have no other connection."

"It was a family issue, nothing more. Everyone from Paul's company has either moved on, forgotten about us, or is dead. I can't think of anyone else we have to lose sleep over."

"We're family. Tell me—"

"We are?" I laugh. "That's the first time I've heard you say that."

He stares ahead with a tight mouth, swirling his drink in the air. "We are," he whispers. "That's why I'm here."

"Yeah?" I smirk. "Okay then... nearest and dearest brother-in-law... since you put it that way, Paul and I do have something in common. We both married over a pregnancy. Only I did it because I was young and I thought it was the manly thing to do. His motivation, I can only guess, was based on a shared experience, something he was trying to conquer, or perhaps a last-ditch chance to escape... fuck, I'll never know the whole truth. Each fucker would give me a different story if they were still alive. All secrets, all lies, one big surprise."

He leans back and swivels the bar stool, twisting the ring on his finger. "You know, don't you? That's what all this is about. The steady stream of nonsense about surprises and why you and Paul married. You know."

Damn, he's so fucking dense. I'm talking about my dad and he's talking about a wedding. "What?" I ask innocently.

He turns toward the entryway, definitely checking for Soph. "Honestly, do you hate surprises that much?"

My hands rise and my jaw drops. "Have you *not* been listening to me?" I ask sarcastically. "Hello?"

"Mark." He sighs. "Sophia and I are renewing our vows."

"What? Horseshit."

"Why do you think we're here?"

"Hold on, what?" Damn it.

"Soph asked if we could have a small wedding since she never had one, remember, we got married in the courthouse? Now she wants some old-fashioned, sleigh-ride type, enchanted wedding in the mountains... with *her* family. You're it. This is it." He raises his hands as mine slowly lower. "I agreed, as long as we're back in St. Louis to celebrate the holiday with my parents. She gets four days here to have a small, but magical wedding, I get to marry my Dove for a second time, and we still get to be in our own home on Christmas morning with the kids."

"No way."

"I don't want you to ruin this for her just because you hate surprises." His hand slithers nervously through his hair... the little sly snake... all three of them... snakes.

"Why the fuck didn't anyone tell me?"

"So you can take control of the entire event? No way. The women wanted to be in charge. Jules is helping put things together. And if you had known, I bet our faces would be plastered on banners all around the hotel, not to mention you'd hire a two hundred-piece orchestra, have choirs in every corridor, and lilies carpeting all the floors."

"What the hell's wrong with lilies?"

"*And...* you would've pulled some stunt, like kidnapping your sister and holding her in a room so we couldn't fuck until our wedding night."

"True. I still might." I rub my chin, considering all the ways I could accomplish that.

"Just once, could you let someone else be in charge? Jesus. You've teased her since she was a kid and played some evil games with both of us, let her believe she's finally tricked you, and won."

"You said Jules is helping with all of this?"

He nods as I send her a text... *Sorry, princess. Luv U.*

"We couldn't have done it without her. And what about a date for your wedding? Sophia's convinced you'll be married by Easter, but after talking to Jules, my guess is another year."

Is my ass grass, or not? She responds.

Your ass is a golden ray of sunshine. I kid.

A smiley face appears on my screen. Great, she liked that one. Let's try something else...

When are we getting married?

"Mark?" Cove nudges my arm. "Mark... fuck, I think I know that guy."

"Who?" I look up and see Sam sitting on the other side of the bar. A second later, a frowning emoji lights up my cell. Fucking balls, I'll never get that woman to marry me.

"He's much older now, but I'm almost positive that's the embalmer," he says.

"How'd you know what he does for a living?"

"So you recognize him? I'm right? That's really him?" He stands and backs away, his face pale while Sam's eyes are locked on us. "Shit, why's he here? Does it have something to do with the other guy? Or is he working for you?"

"What?" I ask. "Ho-hold up. What other guy? The one in the lake? Cove, stop. How'd you know her dad's an embalmer?"

"Whose dad?"

"Jules'."

"Son of a bitch." He rubs the tension in his neck and stands wearily next to me. "I thought you no longer worked with guys from the company? Now you're engaged to the daughter of one of them? That's not leaving Vegas behind."

I ignore my ringing cell, tilt my head and wince as my heart plummets. I replay the words, trying to rearrange what he just said so it emerges differently. No luck.

He sees the twitch on my bottom lip, detecting my anger and confusion as I check my gun, making sure it's in my jacket pocket.

"Didn't Paul ever take you to Reno?"

My head shakes... my cell rings... my heart shatters.

"You're being set up if you don't know."

I hear a text.

"Dump her," he says. "Trust me. I don't get what the fuck's going on, but something's rotten if you didn't know that sick bastard worked for Paul."

I open the text... another emoji... a blonde-haired, bride.

"Mark, you can't trust that guy, especially if he hasn't mentioned he knew your dad. And what about Jules? What the fuck is she hiding?"

Another emoji appears, this time it's a pair of rings. Fuck, I can't think straight. What the hell's going on?

"Get rid of her quickly, before you find yourself on his embalming table."

I'm fighting my blade... it wants to see the light of day then the darkness of a gut.

My cell's ringing incessantly, Cove's worrying, Sam won't stop grinning, and Frank Sinatra refuses to shut his goddamn mouth. Fucking feel-good holiday music. Who the hell wants to hear *Have Yourself a Merry Little Christmas* at this moment?

"Say something." His hand's on my shoulder. "I can tell you're about to fly into a rage. Can you get past this one without a winter boat ride?"

"Doubt it."

"Call it off with her and move on."

"Fuck, who keeps calling me?" It rings for the third time and I finally take a look, seeing Sophia's name.

"What?" I answer.

"Get your ass up to our suite ASAP, like now, pronto,

you have to take care of something. I'm totally freaking out!"

"What's wrong?"

"I can't say in front of the boys, just get up here! Quick!"

The call ends... what the hell was that all about? "What's Soph up to?"

"She's making cookies tonight with the boys. They got the ingredients from your kitchen staff, why?"

I stare at my cell, studying the texts, wondering if Jules will stab me with the blade I bought her, then I look at Sam's devilish face, glowing red from the holiday lights, and Cove standing by my side with his arms crossed and legs wide, holding steady, nervous, and waiting.

"I wish I were drunk," he whispers.

And I think again about Sophia's frenzied voice, summoning me to the suite... shit, Jack's up there, unpacking tonight.

"Sometimes I wonder if I'm protecting the right people, or if my family will end up killing me in the end."

PART SIX

BETSY

"What's the problem?" I ask Sophia, seeing Dax and Xav standing in the kitchen. The boys are wearing matching red turtlenecks, sleeves rolled, and their chests spotted with flour. "You burning down my hotel or what?"

"Uncle Mark!" Xav dashes over with an unbaked cookie twisting in his hand. "Look! What color do you want yours to be?"

"What is that? A penis?"

"Mark!" Sophia scolds. "Xav, go back to the kitchen and finish what you're doing. Don't get flour all over the room."

"I told you they looked like penises!" Daxton yells.

"They're rockets," Sophia says, pulling me to the stairwell and pointing toward the main bedroom. "You've got a penis to deal with upstairs."

"What? Damn it. I told him he couldn't have anyone over. Is it Emma?" I start up the staircase.

"Oh, is that what he calls *it*? Emma? Just go! I'm shocked by what I saw in that room. I pray that's not what I have to look forward to with my boys. It's damn disturbing, Mark. Talk to him!"

"I'm going, I'm going."

I can only imagine... I bet it's another Pop Rocks incident. That would freak her out.

I tap on the door first, not wanting to walk in on some young girl. "Jack. Cover yourself and whoever you're with."

"He's wearing headphones," Sophia says. "If he didn't hear me shriek when I walked in, he sure isn't going to hear you knock on the door."

"Go back to your cock cookies and let me deal with him alone," I say, irritated with having to hold my jacket over the butter stains. Why can't I have one night of peace around here?

"Don't worry." She throws her hands in the air and walks off mumbling. "I'm not going in there again... never sleeping in that room again either... crazy teenage boys."

I open the door, but only for a split second, needing to rapidly close it, shocked by the scene.

"Oh, fucking Christ."

"Told you!" she calls up.

My head rests alongside the wall as I try to talk myself through this. How am I going to stop it? Or maybe I shouldn't. No, I *have* to. Fuck, I can't let him do weird shit.

"You've seen worse, Mark. It's not that bad. He's just a horny teen," I whisper. Uhh, why couldn't it be a sex doll? Why? Why? Anything else, heck, even a pillow hump would be easier to get through than...

I bite the bullet and step inside. My son, Jack Jameson, the little prick, knave, jester, whatever he wants to be called, or should be called, is... it... it's like one of those scenes from a raunchy teen comedy where a kid fucks a pie, only my son is having *sexual relations* with a raw turkey that he obviously stole from the kitchen—a goddamn turkey for crying out loud.

"Jack!" I say sharply. The music's blasting from his headphones, it's so damn loud he can't hear me. "Jack!" I yell at the top of my lungs, this time causing him to jump back, covering his waist with a shirt as cranberry sauce drips out of the turkey's hole.

"No! Dad!"

"Sweet Jesus." I lean against the dresser, looking at the floor with a hand on my forehead, providing him a minute to wipe off, pull up, and zip. Where do I even begin? How do you start a conversation with your teenage son about... about the suitable way to stuff and baste a turkey?

"I thought you went to dinner!" His voice is flustered, fighting between aggravation and embarrassment. "You're not supposed to be here!"

"Your Aunt Sophia called me to come over."

"She saw me? No! I thought all of you were gone tonight? Fuck, fuck! I feel like such a dickweasel."

"Let's not think about dicks and weasels. This is bad enough."

"Don't turn my life into a joke!" he screams, feeling humiliated. He crosses his arms, turning his back to stare at the wall.

A glob of cranberry sauce slides out of the turkey and onto the desk. At least he thought to lay a towel under the scene of the crime.

"This sucks ass. If I can't have a woman in my bed, I should at least be able to jack off with a piece of thawed meat. For fuck's sake, I'm only human. What harm could it do?"

"It may be a form of animal abuse."

"It's a carcass! The thing's dead! It has no head!"

"Calm down and sit," I direct.

He collapses on the bed like he's been shot and is surrendering to death, staring at the ceiling with his knees up, feet tapping, and hands over his pants. "So eating it and shitting it out isn't abusive, but sticking your dick inside it is?"

"Shut your mouth for a moment so I can think." I peer under my jacket at the grease stains on my clothing, shaking my head at this family's shameful antics. I've got a lot of crap to take care of tonight with Sam and Jules, and getting into a shouting match over a turkey fuck isn't my main concern, especially taking my own butter play into consideration. The incident's absurd, and to some extent, laughable. My rage would be better spent elsewhere, not on this.

"Do you want me to buy you a few, or some, um..." I fidget with my shirt collar, feeling choked by my words. "I can, I've got, do you need toys, or lube or something?"

"God, no! I don't want my dad buying me sex toys!

Can you just forget you ever saw this and go away?"

"No." I sigh. "You're inquisitive and creative, Jack."

"Stop it! Please!" He sticks his fingers in his ears. "Mom never would've done this... she would've left me alone," he mutters. "She always let me do what ever the fuck I wanted. Always."

"That's part of the problem."

He's upright in a flash, sharing his middle finger and a pissy scowl.

"Okay, I'm not heading down that road tonight, and you're not fucking any more meat, do you understand?" I wonder how many times I'm going to repeat that line over the next couple of years.

He hangs his head, displaying a feigned performance of regret. With entwined fingers in his lap, he follows my every move as I pick up the towel and use it to wrap the *leftovers* and sauce. Then, after cleaning the desk I say, "Sorry, buddy," with a pat on his shoulder.

"Ah, man. It was fun while it lasted." He pouts, wiping a fake tear from the corner of his eye. "Whatever you decide to do with her, make it quick. I can't bear the thought of Betsy being in pain."

"Betsy? That's one of your jokes, right? Cut the act and stand up, it's time to place you back in your cage for the rest of the night. And don't mention any of this on our way out, not in front of your cousins. Hang your head low and exit."

"No apologies?"

"Jesus Christ, no. What would you say? *Sorry you*

walked in and saw me fucking a turkey, Aunt Sophia. Trust me, she'll be ecstatic never to hear about it again."

We leave the bedroom, Jack running ahead of me, *Betsy* under my arm, and my jacket in front of my dick. I'm one hundred percent certain that boy came from my seed. Tonight, he fucked a Butterball while I was lucky enough to get buttered balls. No one else... no one else but the two of us...

Soph holds the door open, shaking her head at the cargo, and shooing us hurriedly away.

"Has your douchebag husband come groveling back yet? When's he gonna show up and drive you back to St. Louis in his liquor wagon?"

The door's shut in my face and I'm ignored, left to dispose of the twenty-pound turkey. I wonder how disgusting it would be to take it back to the kitchen and serve it to my guests?

I smirk while walking toward my suite, knowing I'd never do such a thing. Though, I wouldn't mind force-feeding it to Sam... that motherfucker knew Paul all along and he made up all that bullshit about hiring a detective to find out my background? And what the hell happened between him and Cove?

There's no doubt in my mind Sam will be the next man to walk down the aisle with my blade.

"I wish you'd stop smiling about this. It will give me a complex. I'm damaged already, ya know? Think about everything you've put me through since I arrived. You're killing me with your shit."

I nudge him on to continue. "I'm taking notes. Go ahead."

"That's a first. Good, listen up, Dad... so I was forced to stitch you up, got my ears cut, cleaned up after your kill, twice, let you hit me, not to mention you drove my woman out of my bed, forced me to smoke weed, and practically tossed me onto that boat."

"Yes, it's true. I know you detested all of those things. Especially the dope."

"Shh, listen," he scolds. "Now, you take the *only* thing I have left and you're going to pitch her in the trash? Your interference is cowshit. One night with a thawed piece of meat would've been rejuvenating. And you strut down this corridor, smiling your butt off like you've beaten me again. Ha-ha-ha." His voice is deep, imitating mine. "Son, go to your room."

My smile widens. "You're a little ham, aren't you?"

"Nope. Just being a turkey." He flashes a grin.

I'm beginning to question many of the arguments we've had over the years. Was he genuinely being a shithead, or did I just never catch onto his sense of humor? The kid's brilliant—a witty beast.

"You get those one-liners from me you know."

"Good looks and a way with women too." He laughs, stepping inside the suite and gesturing toward the towel. "How about you let me take her out to the trash?"

"How about you stop trying to con me and you spend the rest of the night doing something rewarding, like reading a book."

He takes the iPad from the kitchen counter and makes his way up the stairwell, mumbling that he reads a hell of a lot more than I do.

"And Jack... how the fuck did you come up with this idea?" I point to Betsy.

"One of my friends posted a shot of himself doing it to his family's Thanksgiving turkey the night before it was cooked. He said everyone should try it. He was right, it's big fun."

"No iPad tonight!" I call out as he closes the bedroom door. "Stay offline and away from kids posting photos like that! And don't you dare post any explicit photos of yourself either. It's a felony! I've told you before, I don't want the cops showing up at my door... and don't steal any more food from my restaurant!"

I hear him laughing while my bedroom door swings open. Jules walks out, wearing only a robe while brushing her hair. She's gorgeous, the way Eve conceivably looked as she handed the apple to Adam... deceitful wench.

"What was that all about?" she asks.

I dump the turkey in the kitchen trash and walk upstairs, yanking her by the forearm into the bedroom. The door's shut and locked. My tie's off, gun placed in my holster, jacket tossed, shirt unbuttoned, sleeves rolled, and greasy pants left on the floor. I'm left wearing boxers, an open shirt, and a gun.

"What did Cove say to you?" She frowns. "I can tell by how quiet you're being and your rapid actions that you're upset."

"Sit." I move the desk chair to the middle of the room. She looks at it with a hand clasping the neck of her robe, closing it like she's hiding her body from a stranger.

"I said, sit down."

"Is this a sexual thing? We just did it an hour ago. You can't possibly—"

"Sit the fuck down!"

"No." She takes a step back. "Tell me what's wrong?"

The rage I felt while speaking with Cove in the bar has returned. I walk past her; fuming that she won't listen to my command. The nightstand's opened in haste and two pairs of cuffs brought out and cracked in the air.

"What are you doing?"

I position her arms behind her back, cuffing her wrists and ankles to the chair. She tries to knee my nuts, calling me a fuckwad this and a bastard that.

"Where's your blade?" I ask.

"What the hell? I'm not answering until you tell me whether or not this is for fun."

"Ohhh, yeah. It's a very special game. Where's JAB?"

"It's always under my pillow at night." She tilts her head toward the bed. "Mark, you just came. The butter's still on your boxers and I can see you're not erect. Give it a rest."

"I don't need to be erect for this, besides you'll be the one at rest when this is over, not me." The blade flips open and I place it over her lips. After two long, exaggerated breaths, she gives in, believing it's time for foreplay. Her tongue emerges, gliding along the metal, leaving a slick trail of saliva. With a nod of her head to her waist, she opens her legs, wanting me to lick her pussy.

"Where are you going now?" she asks. "Oh, I hear that dresser drawer... should've known you'd smoke before you put your mouth on me. Weed first, pussy second. At least give me a hit." She tries to turn the chair in my direction, leaning until it tips—then saying, 'fuck,' when she's near a sideward fall. Her weight shifts in an instant so she doesn't drop to the floor. "I'm not feeling this tonight... hey, Mark?"

My leather backless slippers disappear under the drifted snow as I walk onto the deck off my bedroom... my dick cowers from the blast of cold air and my nipples go hard.

I light the bowl and inhale. Eyes closed. Smoke blown. Another drag... another puff into the winter night. *Shit, I don't want to kill her. I hope she doesn't know.*

"Mark, it's freezing in here. Can you close the door?"

Soft moonlight breaks through the clouds, causing the distant pines to become black silhouettes. Their shadows dance on the snow covered ground each time the wind cuts across my property. There's a splash in the pool to my left, steam rising over the water, and the sound of an owl *whoo-hoooing* to my right, hiding in the trees. The snowflakes tumbling to the ground have become sporadic, no longer blanketing my hotel in a blinding descent.

"My girl, my girl, don't lie to me," I sing in my faintest voice. *"I'm going where the cold wind blows... In the pines, in the pines, where the sun no longer shines..."*

Goddamn pussy ruins my life every time.

I take a final drag from the bowl, exhaling toward the clouded sky, watching a lone star flicker and disappear. Precision. Clear your thoughts. Be sure.

Who-hooo. Who-hooo.

"Shut the fuck up."

Who-hooo.

I pull out my gun and point it at a distant pine.

"Mark! It's cold in here."

"Bang. One shot and you're dead, pop-eyed, thick-clawed, piece of shit prey." I pretend to shoot then blow on the muzzle like I just finished a duel in a classic '50s western, putting the gun back in my holster before heading inside.

"Why aren't you talking?" she asks.

I tip the chair and drag her next to the bed.

"Hello? Mark Jameson? Open your fucking mouth and say something! Are you going to play a man in the dark shadows all night? I don't like it one bit. You know how much I enjoy hearing your voice, even when you're being a dick, it's better than the silent treatment... hey, talk to me!"

I sit before her, grasp the back of her legs, and slide the chair closer to the bed.

"Go ahead. Go down on me if this is what we're doing. I promise I won't close my legs on your head to get you back for being such a prick." Her knees separate and the white robe falls open, exposing a tit. Perfect. The blade runs along her neck, to her chest, and circles an erect nipple. "Damn it, please say something."

I take out my cell and make a call.

"Yeah?" Cove answers.

"Did you tell Soph we had a nice conversation in the bar?"

"No."

"You still down there?"

"Yeah."

"He still there?"

"No."

"You have time to come to my suite?"

"Yep."

"Remember my code?"

"Yeah."

"You doing okay, or what?"

"No. I'm a bit on edge... and I'm trying to text Xavier while talking to you. Having two conversations at once... but I'll be right there."

I toss the cell on the nightstand and lean back, resting on my elbows. "We need to talk, princess."

"Finally. Why's Cove coming over? You better not have some sick idea of a threesome, that's not my thing. I already told you—"

"Shut the fuck up!"

"Stop," she whispers. "You're scaring me."

"Well then, let's go ahead and start with all the alarming bullshit I heard tonight, 'cause you're scaring me. We'll start with something easy... are Cove and Sophia renewing their vows?"

"Damn it. Why did he tell you? It's supposed to be a secret! I knew you shouldn't have gone to the bar. So this is why you're angry?"

"Secrets. I fucking hate them." The blade travels back to her neck, resting over her jugular. "And you know I hate liars even more."

"Not telling you isn't a lie! Uncuff me!" She wiggles for freedom, her face on fire. If she's released, I'm sure I'll be slapped. "I don't understand why you'd be so upset over such a special event. It's your sister after all."

I clutch her thighs, stopping her movement. "Look at me." I lower my head. "Look at my face when I say this... you never told me you were living in your car, you lied about Mera, you didn't call after the incident behind the bar, I'm unsure I'd even know you knifed that guy if I wasn't there." She tries to turn her head, but I capture her chin, holding it steady. "Fucking look at me."

"Don't," she cautions. "Why are you doing this?"

"Listen, I can't even count the number of lies you told me about the fucking shopping trip, and I'm sure there were many more over the past year."

"Mark." Her lip quivers, and a puzzled expression appears. "What's wrong?"

"All of those moments are nothing, meaningless next to the news I heard about your father. First, is there a reason you didn't tell me he was an embalmer? And for fuck's sake, you better have a good answer." I release her chin, hearing the entry door click open.

"Mark?"

"Upstairs!" I shout to Cove.

"Why is he here?" she asks in a faint voice. "I don't understand what's happening."

He walks in, holding his cell, shaking his head at the scene.

"What did she say?" he asks.

"Nothing, yet." I motion to the club chair next to the nightstand. "Join us. I need you here for this."

"Only if you close her robe, put on a pair of pants, and put away the knife, otherwise I'm outta here, especially if you plan on cutting her open."

"What? Oh, fuck that. Stop goofing around and let me go. This is ridiculous. Why get so upset about a stupid fib over a wedding? And my Dad? Yes, he's an embalmer. So fucking what? Why is that an issue? I didn't lie!" She twists her body fiercely for an escape, becoming a tornadic wind. Her hair swings. The chair tilts. And down she goes—flat on her back.

"Ow!" Her feet wiggle and she screams. "My arms! Let me go, it hurts! The chair's on my arms!"

I can't stand it when she gets frenzied like this. Makes me want to stuff her mouth with a sock. And it'd be worse if I hadn't cuffed her. This out-of-control burst in behavior would be directed toward me, but at this moment it's aimed at her release.

"Stop jerking, or next time I'll leave you on the floor," I say, pulling her back to our level and securing her robe shut. "We're going to have a conversation, the three of us, and I want *you,*" I point at her, "to keep your head up, body still, and pay attention. Not another word except to answer our questions."

"Fuck you, Mark. If this is a prank, it stinks to high heaven! It's not funny! Stop smoking so much dope and be nice to me!"

"No pranks."

Cove slouches in the chair and kicks my leg. "I bet she doesn't even know. Think about Sophia. She was clueless about Paul until she went to Vegas."

"That's why you're here. You're going to talk to her."

"Me? Just ask her... and cover your dick."

"Ask me what?"

I walk to the closet and slide into a pair of jeans, take the roll of tape from under my bed, and tear a piece to seal her mouth.

"You're the only person I've ever met who keeps duct tape under his bed," he mutters. "What's the point of that anyway? I thought you wanted her to answer our questions."

"She's going to listen first, then we'll have a heart-to-heart."

I stand in front of the chair and see her mouth downturned, cheeks red, and those killer honey eyes looking sadder than a caged puppy in a pet store. Damn. Damn her! Why the fuck did I fall in love? Why can't she be an ugly, hairy bitch with no teeth and a dead-mouse-scented twat? Why is she so alluring in looks and heart? Why does she have to be so assertive, clever, and strong?

Why is she so fixed in my head?

"Please." She shies away. "Why are you so angry with me?"

I let the tape fall to the floor before reclining on the bed, uttering a pained growl. My mirrored ceiling reflects the top of Cove and Jules' heads, his hair tidy and stylish, hers disheveled like she's been out in a storm. They watch me run the blade across my chest, stopping over my gut.

"I'm not a badass like Paul wanted... not when it comes to her. She's the only reason... the only... I refuse to be cruel to the woman who's worked her way deep into my heart, even if she has the balls to lie to my face. I love her too fucking much... damn it, what am I doing? Go fuck yourself, Paul. Fuck you and fuck your friends." My stoner grin battles my true mood. "You didn't hear me say that, Cove. Delete it from your memory."

"Erased. So what are we doing and what do you want from me?"

"I want to know how you met him. What he was doing with Paul. What happened. Everything. And she needs to hear it, not a recap from me, but directly from you."

"Met who?" Jules asks.

"Does she know? I mean, about Paul and me. I'm not saying shit if she doesn't have the background of what I've been through, it won't make any sense to her."

"She knows," I say in a lowly voice. "Princess, pin your ears back, listen to his story..."

RENO

"*The kid's still alive. What the fuck, Paul? You said you had a body, not a living, breathing, shitting, human being. I'm not doing this. Get him outta here,*" Sam says.

"*The fuck you aren't. You said you had a closed casket funeral in the morning. He's going in the coffin with the other guy. There's room. Now, get your tools ready. Whatever you need to embalm him.*"

"*Alive? Hell no. What if the owner of the funeral home comes back tonight?*" He turns away, crossing his arms and lowering his head. "*Please get him out of here. I'm not killing a man. I'll handle the disposal of your bodies up this way, but I'm not killing anyone. No way.*"

"*There's ten grand in that bag for you.*"

"*I don't want your filthy porn money!*"

"*Okay, you wanna fuck him as payment? I can fulfill those terms, on condition that I get to go first then can watch you fuck him, and as long as you don't mind your dick being coated in my cum. You may like it though—sloppy seconds can be a big turn on, especially when it's in the ass. It's some great lube. This one's tight so you'll need it. No matter how many times I work him over, he never loosens up.*"

"Enough!" He turns, holding a surgical blade with a step forward and his hand trembling in the air. "You've persuaded me to take care of a couple of bodies a year... bodies, Paul! Fucking dead men! Look at him. The tears on his face, his mouth and hands bound, the frantic search for air whenever you cover his nose, and fuck, his entire body's trembling. Oh, to hell! That's puke. That's puke coming out his nose. Uncover his mouth!"

"He'll be dead soon so what does it matter?"

"I'm not killing him!"

Paul yanks the gag off, allowing the vomit to flow out, thrilled from the torturous episode. He smiles at Sam, grabbing the erection through his pants.

"Fuck yeah, Star. Maybe we should fuck one last time." He holds Cove's hips, pressing his groin tightly against him. "I know you'll miss my dick. Bet you wish I'd take you back home for a long night of fun in my bed. Remember that. Always remember this was your choice. You said you wanted out and here you are... Sam will treat you well. You won't even feel the blood being drained and the formaldehyde flowing inside after a few minutes have passed, but fuck, I wish I could stay to see how painful it's gonna be in the beginning."

"Who is this kid?" He lowers the blade, stepping back as Cove slides to the floor.

"Kid? Ahh, he's eighteen, could be nineteen by now." He kicks him. "I wish he was a kid. He's getting too old for me. Hah."

"Sick, you're disgusting. He's already in so much pain.

And his tears, it's, oh fuck me, just put him out of his misery."

Paul smiles and lifts Cove onto the metal table. "Ya hear that, Star? Sam wants you dead too."

"No. What I want is for you to get the hell out of this room and never come back."

"I've heard that one before, and the guy who said it disappeared. Poof! Gone. His wife and baby too. Never heard from again. Sucks when people leave this world without a trace. Doesn't it, you fucking pussy? I was hoping you'd stick around for some time. What are you, like twenty-five?"

"Eight. T-twenty-eight," he stutters.

"You dumb shit. You're too young to make such a life changing decision... I mean, end of life decision. You hear me? I need this setup. There're no decent dumping grounds in Reno, not like the lake and my construction sites in Vegas, and I'm not hauling a body back home in the trunk of my car, or having my guys do it when it can be dealt with right here. So take the fucking cash and shut your pretty little mouth before I rip it open with my dick. This is a simple disposal. Easier than digging a hole or burning a body in this city."

Sam swallows and lowers the knife. "Bring 'em to me already dead and I'll help you out, that was the deal. There was no discussion about murder."

"We have no deal. You do whatever the fuck I want, nod your fucking head, and say, yes sir. Now, go ahead and start. He'll die when you drain his fluids."

"I'm holding the knife, and I say, no."

"I'm holding the massive cock with the big bucks and the

men behind me to cut off your head and shove it up your ass."
Paul steps forward, covering Cove's face as tears pool over his
jawline. "I say, yes. You toss my throwaways into these coffins
and you get paid. It's that easy." He moves closer to Cove,
brushing the hair away from his face and whispering in his
ear, "I love you, son. Be a man for once and hold in your tears
while you die."

"Fuck, is this your kid?"

"I'll be around at sunrise... Samuel."

"Sam."

He leaves and Sam nearly collapses, using the stainless
steel sink for support while his shaky hands cover his face.
Anxious. Rattled. Fearful... his fingers separate, gazing at the
traumatized man on the metal table.

"We stared at one another for a good hour. I can
remember his worried expression, every pore, whisker, and
bead of sweat on his face. He kept asking if I was Paul's
son, but I couldn't speak. I couldn't. I was given some
drug before we arrived that made it difficult to
communicate other than a few groans and cries. It took
him a while to catch on that I was out of it." Cove's head
lowers. Tight fists have formed, causing his knuckles to
turn white. His voice often breaks, diminishing to a
murmur before cutting back in. I've never heard him be so
detailed about his past.

It's the lack of self-meds... he's able to speak freely
without hiding behind the alcohol.

I watch Jules' reaction closely, feeling her out as he

exposes the truth. Her tear-stained cheeks offer a sign that she's truly heartbroken by the information. So far, I don't believe she knew about her dad. It seems my biggest concern might be her few white lies.

"He wrapped me in a material like cellophane. I didn't understand if it was part of the preserving process, if I was going to be buried alive, or what the fuck was happening. It went from my feet to under my nose. My head was the only part exposed against the cold table. The smell of chemicals and cleaner pervaded my nose. I prayed I wouldn't vomit again, knowing I'd choke... though my stomach and brain always fought each other in those moments. The panic... the terror... and it got worse. He blindfolded me and left the room. I waited. My eyes remained open under the cloth. I had to piss, but I couldn't relax enough to let it flow. Every muscle and bone ached... fuck, for the millionth time, I couldn't wait to die."

I can't sit still as I listen to his suffering. Paul's easy to picture in that scene, saying all that crap, and to hear more information of how he destroyed a man that I love is revolting. I disconnect from my victims, showing no remorse because of their actions, but my heart breaks for Cove because of his innocence. He was a decent kid who became my father's permanent prey, like a cat that catches and paws a mouse for hours, never killing it, just having fun until it surrenders and no longer strives to escape.

"The average teen would've started college that year, but I was cut off from the world and confined inside

Paul's mansion. Everything happening was punishment for turning traitor and attempting to go to the cops... it was Paul's control, his retaliation, and it lasted for months. On the drive to Reno, he said it was the end. He assured me I'd be on a plane back to St. Louis from there, which I knew was bullshit. How many times had I heard that? When we got there, he checked on business first, met with a few men, dragging me along for show... his handsome product. By evening, I was in the basement with Sam... and Sam returned after I had spent hours on the icy table, my vision stolen and movements confined."

He rubs the back of his ear, reluctant to carry on.

"That's more than enough. We get the gist if the rest is too difficult to talk about."

Jules remains silent. It's an unfamiliar behavior I'm unable to read.

"It wasn't until Sam returned that I learned he was heartless like the rest of Paul's crew. He wasn't the type to be incited by Paul's sexual razzing, and he struggled with the request to kill me, but he sure as fuck didn't mind formulating a sick plan to save his own ass. I'd been tormented before, but never experienced anything more chilling than my night with him. And although I couldn't see, I sure as fuck could feel what he was doing. He placed hard pieces of either metal or wood along the length of my body and wrapped more of the cellophane material around me so I couldn't bend or twist any of my limbs. He wrapped my head too, right over the blindfold and my mouth and nose. I thought I was going to suffocate, but after a minute of not having any air, a sharp pain grew under my nose. He sliced a tiny hole through the wrap, nicking my skin. It was enough air to keep me alive."

"My dad wouldn't treat a man so horribly. He has respect for his profession and would never abuse his license. He's not like that."

Her words are faint and behavior vacant.

"He might say the same about you if he knew the things you've done." I'm a jerk for saying that, but its something she should be thinking about while we're immersed in this situation. "Cove, keep going if you can."

"Yeah, I can... the fucker stuck me in a coffin with the dead, like Paul wanted. I was wheeled upstairs and a second later found myself being rolled inside a tight space. Even without my sight, I knew I was with a body by the shape next to mine. Sam told me not to move, not to make a sound, no crying, pissing, or puking. He said the man next to me had his face blown off so no one would be opening the coffin, said he'd do his best to get me out after Paul checked in the morning to see if I was inside. He apologized, yet added, *no promises kid. If Paul shows up and the funeral's already on it's way, you're shit out of luck.* Then he lifted my head and put a cord, or rope, or something around my neck."

He clears his throat, replying to a text before recounting the rest. "It's Soph," he whispers. "I told her I'm admiring the holiday lights."

"Uncuff me," Jules interrupts, her voice dim and weak. I release her and attempt to wipe her tears, but my hand's shoved away. Rubbing her wrists she utters, "tell me the end so I can leave."

"Alright... so... he closed the lid and I was confined for the rest of the night... and the cord pressed into my neck whenever I tried to move. It must've been attached to the coffin. I was certain I'd be strangled if I stirred. The drug Paul gave me was slowly wearing off, and the more alert I became, the more I panicked." He stops, swallows, leans back, and takes a full breath. "With the cellophane covering my face, the cord now pressing into my neck, and being scared shitless, it was impossible to even grunt. Trying to make the smallest noise was enough of a movement to tighten the cord. I spent hours in agony. All I could think about was what would kill me first. Would I suffocate? Was the cord going to cut off my airway? Was I going to vomit again and choke to death? Or would I be buried alive next to a man with a missing face? I'd been confined inside boxes, trunks, and closets before, but being placed in a coffin with a dead person was gruesome beyond what I can describe. Paul was fucked up, and Sam was just like all the others who worked for him. He only thought of himself... although, I suppose everyone in this world's that way."

"No," I say, prohibiting him to fall into a state of depression. "Not you. You don't always think of yourself, and Jules doesn't either."

She walks to the window, turning her back on me. All of her expressions, words, actions... she didn't know. She honestly didn't know. What the fuck was I thinking, cuffing her to the chair?

"He came back for me. Paul did. The coffin opened and I heard his wicked laugh. After I was unwrapped and the blindfold was removed, I saw his smirk... fuck, he was an expert at turning me into a passive bitch. I worshipped him for weeks after that night. If he wanted me on my knees, I dropped. I didn't give a shit... and Sam? Paul knew the type... he was certain he wouldn't have the balls to kill me, said he waited in the lot all night, kept watch, made sure I wasn't released... he always tested his new guys. I just happened to be the bait. Lucky me."

"Did you see my dad again after that day?" Jules asks.

"No. I never went back to Reno, not until Mark moved here and I had no choice except to fly into that city. It's the closest airport to this hotel. And although your dad didn't physically harm me, he did fuck me up emotionally. He must not have known Paul all that well either, thinking he'd be able to trick him into believing I was dead, then set me free. I wouldn't doubt if he got a fist in the face for that stunt. Paul was brilliant, nothing got past him, not until the end... and Sam... that bastard knew I could've died from all the shit he did to me. He's far from innocent."

Jules disappears inside our closet, coming out wearing a pair of jeans and a grey sweater. She pulls her hair into a ponytail, takes her purse, and grabs the blade from my hand.

"Don't you dare think about killing my dad, I'll take care of this. And don't follow me."

There's no eye contact and she doesn't say another word, leaving with a determined stride. She's out the door before I can make it to the stairs, incapable of catching her when I'm stoned.

"Fffffuck."

"I could've told you this wasn't going to end well."

"Damn it." I head to the bathroom and splash cold water on my face, more because of Cove's troubling story than her plans, whatever they are. "Damn it. Damn it." The towel slides down my face, dragging my skin along. I can't bear to view my reflection. "Fuck you all over again."

He leans against the doorframe, crossing his arms and feet. "Fuck me? Fuck you asswipe. You're the one who wanted to hear it."

"No, that's not..." I lean forward; placing my hands flat on the counter and watching my fingers ripple from my high. I can feel him staring at me, waiting for an apology. "I was talking to Paul, not you. And Jules is right... she said not to think about killing her dad. She knows me too well. But I am. I want to beat his ass into the ground. Motherfucker did that to you and now he has the nerve to come to my home and put on a show? Acting all innocent like he never knew about my family? That's fucked up... and I could tell Jules didn't know about any of this."

"Yeah, me too."

"She's wounded by it. When she cries and stays silent, I know she's troubled. And fuckin' A, I'm sorry. I'm fucking sorry for everything I've done to you." My head shakes in disappointment. I want to hug him, but I know he detests being touched.

"I've heard that before and it's not what I need."

"Well, it sucks I can't figure out what *anyone* needs. And you should beat the shit out of me for all the times I've been an ass to you."

"It's in your nature. You're his son."

"Stop saying that!" I rage, seeing him take a step back. And there it is, my goddamn lack of control bursting out again. "Oh fuck." I exhale, gazing at the ceiling. "Fuck, fuck, fuck."

"Chill the hell out for once and figure out what you're going to do, if anything."

"What do you mean, *if anything*?"

"Maybe you should let it slide."

"Wait a sec, you were the one who said I was being set up and I needed to call it off with Jules. You got me all worked up and now you're saying I should let it go?"

"That was before I saw her reaction. This has nothing to do with her. I'm just paranoid about these things."

"What things?"

"Arranged relationships."

"Jesus. Just because Paul played matchmaker with you and Sophia, doesn't mean the same thing's happening here. I'm not that dumb."

"Excuse me? I'm not an idiot either."

"I mean, she didn't come knocking on my door and fall into my arms. I had to work for months just to get her to spread her legs. This wasn't planned. Plus, there's no rhyme or reason to why it would be."

"Money. Revenge."

"And he waited an entire year for that? I doubt it. And if you hadn't recognized him, I still wouldn't know. He's terrified his daughter's with me and he doesn't want her to find out about his past. That's why he was such a douche yesterday. He wants me out of her life because he's afraid."

"See. That's the reason I said you should let it slide. Too fucking bad you didn't work this through before you cuffed her. It's a simple case of a father wanting to protect his baby girl. He doesn't know how different you are from Paul—" He halts. "I didn't say that."

I grin and match his crossed arms. "Yes you did. And I loved it. Say it again."

He glances at his cell and mumbles that he has to go.

"Wait!"

He heads out and I follow two steps behind, down the stairs and to my entryway, stopping when he reaches the door. The new sober man before me is fascinating. He's being forthright, with little paranoid hesitation like I usually get from him.

"You're *almost* as irresistible as me." My smile goes unseen, unlike his extended middle finger, scratching the back of his head.

"Yeah, almost." We stand in silence for a short time, and I know he's debating whether he should reveal what's on his mind.

Say it, Cove. Throw in the towel and say it.

285

After shuffling his feet and a few passes of his fingers through his thick dark hair, he continues... "I've always mentioned you're like your dad because I know how livid it makes you. You're not the only one who's good at tormenting his brother-in-law."

"Yep, but my badgering is all in good fun because I adore you. We differ in that regard."

He sighs and peers over his shoulder, making sure I'm paying close attention to his words. "I meant what I said about him... there's no resemblance between you two, no connection other than your last name. And don't take offense, but you became someone he would've hated. I know you struggle with that, and you shouldn't. Screw him. Pretend you're the milkman's son." He throws in a timeless joke to lighten the mood, one with more meaning than he realizes. "Was there a blue-eyed blond delivery man in your neighborhood?" He faces the door, scratching a spot in front of him that looks like dried pizza sauce; likely from one of his sons' grimy hands... or, it's Abram's blood. "I can think clearer now that I'm sober. It's much easier to talk to you when I'm not always angry." He licks his finger and rubs the spot, causing it to smear into a wider blotch on my light grey door. "Is this blood?"

"Cove... I'm not Paul's son."

FORGIVE ME

MVT. It doesn't stand for the "Mean Value Theorem" I learned way back in calculus class, and it's not "Modern Vintage Today" or "Mesa Valley Transit."

It's "Mark's Vigilante Transformation."

Jules put that shit about *the change* in my head and now I'm jinxed. It's all a plot to turn me into a pussy. That's my bet. Subconsciously, she wants me to kick the devil off my shoulder. And damn her because it's working. I know it is because I told Cove about Abram.

His words touched me and I wanted to give him something in return—a reward for being forthcoming. I showed him the paperwork from Abram's suitcase and passed along the story. His eyes were wet with sadness to learn about the twisted bastard and shocked that I'm not Paul's son. He couldn't wait to tell Soph. Fuck, I didn't think that far ahead. With persistence and a few warnings that I could make his life miserable over the next two days, he was convinced to keep it to himself, at least for now. Besides, I'm not supposed to know he's at the hotel until they renew their vows. We are still playing up the surprise wedding, and the lie that his drunkenness compelled her to flee their home...

... and the secrets continue to grow.

The next time I decide to spill my guts to him about something that could disturb my sister, I need to make sure I have a fake foot on hand to cram down my throat.

The upside is, a few hours ago my nephews came knocking at my door and gifted me a plate of penis cookies—decorated with pink and white icing and a small cinnamon candy on the tip. They insisted it was fire, but I assured them I'm keen on how eleven-year-old boys' minds work—there was no debating it was a plate of dicks, not rocket ships. They called me a bastard, handed me their *Santa Mark X-mas Wish Lists,* full of overly expensive things they want for the holiday, like go-karts and video games, then took off in a race down my corridor. I called out after them, asking where they were going to ride a go-kart in the middle of St. Louis, only to get a simultaneous, "we love you Uncle Mark... buy us lots of presents!" shouted back.

Christ, they always do this to me at the last minute. Little asshats. It sucks they're old enough to know Santa isn't real. I'd love to be the one to tell them I killed him.

That was six hours ago, and yeah, the cookie bribe *was* the upside.

The downside? Jules hasn't returned. She hasn't answered my texts or calls and I'm worried sick. The only thing racing through my mind is she no longer considers this her home.

It's clear by Cove's story her dad wouldn't hurt her, I

mean, the guy sounds like a tool. Still, that doesn't mean I'm not concerned about her emotional state and our relationship.

And I know I'm in the doghouse. I might as well place the leather hood back over my head and get down on all fours, waiting for her to come in and chain me outside for the night. However she chooses to punish me, I deserve it, although her not coming home or responding to my messages is punishment enough.

Why'd she take her knife? Was that out of habit, or is she using it?

I've been checking the security cams every fifteen minutes and I know she entered her parents' room, but I haven't seen anyone come out. I doubt they'd take off in the middle of the night on these icy roads. They have to be in that room, only there's no sound whatsoever when I stroll past. No voices, movement, or even a whisper. Damn, why didn't I install a camera in *every* room?

Reclining on the sofa with crumbs on my robe, feet on the coffee table in front of the glowing fireplace, and cell phone in hand, I text her for the twentieth time.

Forgive me.

I wait, but there's no answer. Nothing.

"Come on, Jules. What the fuck?" I toss the cell on the coffee table. "At least call me a shithead or tell me to go to hell."

"Dad?" Jack questions my whereabouts, standing outside my bedroom door.

"Yeah, I'm downstairs, buddy."

He leans over the landing with the iPad and asks, "Why are you awake?"

"I have a lot on my mind, you?"

"Did you kill someone?"

"Not tonight. You doing okay? Why are you up at four in the morning?"

"Can I help next time you do? I know I'd be good at it, you just have to let me try." He ignores my question.

Come down here so we can talk.

His slippered feet shuffle down the stairs and he takes a seat in front of the fireplace, raising his hands before the flames. The iPad glows in his lap, open to some online site.

"What are you looking at?"

"Nothing." His voice cracks, always a sign he's been crying. "Mindless searches. Looking at stuff I want. Thinking about mom... you know... stuff like that." He pauses and looks at the screen while stroking his scabby ears. "She would've asked me a month ago what I wanted for Christmas... it's a few days away and you still haven't asked."

"Don't worry. You won't be left empty-handed on Christmas morning."

"You didn't talk to me about it, Dad." He leans forward with his palms covering his face. "Jules did, but you didn't."

He hasn't a clue I've been viewing his search history. I know exactly what he wants... and unfortunately, I also know he's researched Paul and Abram, and he watches a shitload of porn.

"Mom knows what I want. I told her." He hands me the iPad and returns to the fire. The screen displays his mother's Facebook account. It's her final message before she died.

I love you forever and always, Jacky Bear... think of me. Know I can always hear you. Talk to me and I'll be listening. I'll follow you through life until we're together again. You're my baby. When you view my words years from now, you'll still be my little boy, always in my heart, no matter your age. I love you so very much. Please, be strong for me. Be brave. Love hard. Live joyfully. Have no regrets... ~ Mom

I've seen it before. He views her digital afterlife multiple times a day.

"She loved me," he says softly with his back turned. "I'm fucking stressed out by her death. Why can't we have control over these things? You seem to have a say when people live and when they die, why not with mom? I c-can't... can't push the memories of her aside. I have no choice but to think about her and deal with it the best I can... it-it's hard... when the lights are off and the room's silent, I can't get her out of my head." He sighs, rubbing his eyes. "What do you think about when you can't sleep? Is it me, or am I not important enough?"

"Oh, buddy." I lament. Maybe it's the age or the way he's trying to make sense of death, but man, this needy, self-reflective behavior is challenging. I put myself in his shoes, trying to figure out what he wants, how he feels—I know it's all about isolation and abandonment. Soph and I have discussed the desertion and loneliness we felt growing up. I know how much that empty feeling eats away at you.

"Jack, I'm sorry. Sit on the sofa next to me." I raise my arm and he looks back, hesitates, and finally slithers to my side. He's held, setting his head on my chest and feeling comforted, I hope. I caress his hair and kiss the top of his head.

"Don't think I'm a sissy for crying every night."

"I don't. There's nothing wrong with shedding a few tears, especially for your mother."

He picks at his fingernails as we talk, smelling of cologne and cranberries. "I'm just trying to fit in. I mean, in your life, except it's tough because I miss mom's love and our routine. She used to check in on me every night, asking how my day was and if I needed anything. You don't."

"It's two different worlds, though I can certainly start if you want."

"I shouldn't have to ask, it should happen on its own." He slides a cookie off the plate and turns it front to back, tilting his head inquisitively. "Are these—"

"Rockets." I stop him.

After two bites, he nods that they're good, taking another off the plate and putting his feet on the coffee table.

"I love these black Jameson robes. We match," he

says, attempting to change the subject to suppress his pain.

"That we do."

"Where's the old lady?" His mouth is full as he drops crumbs everywhere. I shrug and he kicks my foot. "You gotta put that chick on a leash so she doesn't leave the yard."

"Not if she's the one who *owns* the yard."

He disapproves with a headshake. "I knew she was the one in control and not the other way around. She's gonna walk off with all of my inheritance money, isn't she?"

"There's plenty for everyone," I mutter.

He shoves the rest of the cookie in his mouth, chomping away while jerking his feet, clearly in a better mood now that he's occupied with conversation and no longer alone. "How long has she been gone?"

"All night."

"Yeah? That's a long time to go without snatch." He nudges his elbow into my side and I can tell something's brewing in his brain. Quick with a quip, that kid. Crumbs tumble from his mouth as he continues chewing the sugary treat, letting out a short laugh—a signal to his looming tease. "Umm... Dad... I've got... you want me to buy you some sex toys? I got lube. I could pull Betsy out of the trash for ya." He snorts.

"Son." I exhale. "Here's some fatherly advice... don't speak when your mouth's full of dick."

He laughs harder, choking on the cookie. His face turns red and eyes water, but he keeps taking bites and nodding that he's fine. Dumbass.

"I have a serious question for you, Jack. No joking this time. Swallow that thing and pay attention."

He puts the cookie down and wipes his mouth on the back of his hand. Ready to listen.

"Do you think you could kill a man? If a guy was beating the hell out of you, and you knew it was your life or his, would you stab him? Or if the two of us were in a situation where a man had a gun on me, would you shoot him to save my life?"

"No," he says with confidence.

"Really? I didn't expect that answer. How come?"

"Because you haven't given me any fucking weapons yet, that's how come."

"Oh, Jesus Christ. For once, stop being such a literal shit and answer my question."

"Okay, then yes, without a doubt I would. In fact, the guy would be dead before he even drew his weapon. Mine would be out first, not his."

"That's a good answer. So, what if you're dating a girl and you find out her father hurt one of your cousins decades ago? And be serious, don't say they wouldn't be born yet or any of that crap. This is hypothetically speaking."

"Only dating the chick or do I love her?"

"Love."

"Hmm. I thought killing was like a defense, something that's happening right this sec and you have to deal with it quickly. I don't know." He ponders, tapping a finger against his lips. "I suppose the woman has nothing to do with it."

Huh. He gets a gold star for that response. "True, smarty pants."

"If you really think about it, your answer is at the bottom of Lake Tahoe." He brushes the crumbs off his robe and walks to the kitchen for a glass of juice. "That fucker," he hollers back to me. "You took Abram out just for that reason. You killed him because of what happened in the past, not the present."

"I killed him for many reasons." A text sounds on my cell and Jack comes back, looking over my shoulder as I read the single word response from Jules.

No.

"No what?"

"I asked her to forgive me," I whisper.

"Sssshit, she burned your ass."

Another text sounds...

U weren't supposed to cuff me.

"Whoa. Is this a sex thing with you two?"

And another...

Now, I'm reconsidering.

I move my cell from his sight and text her back.

Reconsidering what? Our relationship? Get your ass home.

I call, but it goes to voicemail. Call again, same. And again.

"Damn her! Fuck, I don't want to have to club her over the head and drag her back to my cave like some brute."

"Gee, that's the way to win her love."

"I *have* her love!"

"Nope. Don't think so," he says, with his feet on the coffee table and his hands behind his head.

"You comfortable?"

"Yep. Could use some popcorn for the show... and you just got another text."

"I know I did!"

Come home? Why, Mark? More punishment?

"Ehh." *I overreacted. I love you. Sorry.*

No response.

Jack swings his feet and starts to hum, amused by my irritated strut in front of the fireplace. His head turns back and forth, following my march.

I message her, *Let's fuck. You'll feel better.*

No response.

Please?

No response.

"Why don't you just go talk to her?" he asks.

"Because I'll end up killing the person she's with."

"Who? Sam?" He leans forward. "Why? Is this that shit you were talking about? Your hypomanic question?"

"*Hypothetical...* yes."

"Ahh. Then I take back what I said. The girl *is* part of the problem. You can't kill her dad. She loves him."

"The best case scenario is she's so furious tonight that she kills him."

"Or, I do."

I shake my head at his ridiculous response while another text lights up my cell.

U wanted to take JAB! My engagement blade! A frown appears on my screen. *U R a piece of shit! I should flush U! Only U'd get stuck and come back, flooding my world!*

I am your world. I respond, wishing I had hit *delete* instead of *send*. Big mistake. Yep... my cell's ringing. Here we go.

"I gave it back," I say, answering the call. "I gave the blade back."

"*I* took it back! And how dare you treat me like I'm one of your targets. I was going to be your wife, Mark. Your wife!"

"Going to be? Stop it. I made a mistake, alright? I'm not proud of what I did, but think about how I felt after hearing our dads knew one another."

"No! For once, get it through your smelly asshole that everything *I've* done has been for you and your family. *You* need to think about how I feel and stop calling me a liar!"

"Jules—"

"You're so fucking lucky my dad's in bigger trouble than you, considering what he put Cove through. But when I'm finished with him, you're going to get a fat lip for thinking my love for you was fake. What the fuck?"

"What are you doing right now? Where are you?"

"I'm doing nothing and I'm nowhere."

"Come home so we can talk."

"We are talking."

"Face-to-face."

"I don't want to see your irksome face."

"Irksome? Cut the shit, Jules."

"Irksome! Irksome! Irksome!"

"Mark Jameson finds you exasperating."

Jack laughs, and I'm sure he can hear both sides of the conversation.

"I'll be home in the morning," she says. "Get some sleep."

"It *is* morning!"

"I'm not coming home to argue with you. We're both a couple of hotheads who need to mellow out, besides, I'm not finished!"

"With what? Hello? Fuck, she hung up."

"I'd dump her," he says.

"Well, you're sixteen and not engaged or in love."

"That did *not* sound like love."

"This is exactly what love sounds like! You wait and see."

I sigh and pace, then decide to message her my defense. What the hell can it hurt?

Cut me some slack... under a lot of stress... Jack, Sam, Abram, you, work, the holidays, Cove and Soph... need to keep watch on everything and everyone...

And I add an excuse...

You're engaged to a former porn star turned hotel owner who's a bit f'd in the head. Expect nothing less than irksome.

There's no reply, not that I want one... yes, yes I do. Goddammit, I do. Pay attention to me, princess.

I wait a few more minutes before sending a final apology in my usual, self-entertaining tone...

Sorry I thought about killing you, used our handcuffs for non-sexual play, and ate all the cock cookies before you got home. Please, forgive me.

WRETCHED MORNING

"We're too much alike for me to stay angry. I can picture myself doing the same bullshit... in fact, put your hands behind your back for me." She gives orders while we're in bed. "Give me your hands and you have my word I won't kill you or beat your ass."

I'm barely awake, listening to her steady voice as I lie on my side and face the wall. When did she come home? How long have I been asleep?

She smells of strawberry shampoo and soap, and I feel the cold wet strands of her hair on my shoulder, a distinct contrast to the firm fingers running down my side. No, not fingers. That's a blade.

"Do you trust me, Mark?"

"What did you do last night?"

"Hushhh. Your hands... place yourself in a vulnerable position... prove our relationship can move forward and that you trust me. I refuse to be engaged to a man who doesn't have faith in my love."

"It's not all about what I've done wrong. You shouldn't have kept so much from me."

"Oh." She uses a soft, seductive voice, persuading me

to follow her commands. "My handsome man's being difficult. Why? I did something for you last night that no other woman would ever do, and you can't place your strong hands behind your back in return?"

What the fuck did she do this time? And that blade's moving down my back, making its way to my ass. "I could have that knife in your neck in less than a second."

"It would've been in my neck two minutes ago if you were truly worried, but you haven't moved an inch." She flaunts the weapon in front of my face; the shiny metal edge flickers, displaying her initials.

"Julia Alison Barringer," I say her full name so she's aware I'm paying close attention, not worried or nervous, just listening and contemplating her words as I examine her hand. "Your knuckle's busted up. What the fuck did you do?"

She snubs my question, continuing on like it was never asked. "I'm aware this doesn't frighten you, not like it does when other people see a blade, but I do know you're terrified that I'll leave you."

"It's called being *marginally on edge,* not terrified."

"It's called *you better fucking listen to your fiancé.*"

Speaking in this calm, gentle tone must be killing her. Although, she's not fully tranquil... I can hear gnashing teeth, other than that, she's managed to keep her emotions in check. No shouting or slaps to the face... she just wants my hands. Why not give in to her request in order to fix this? Besides, being cuffed is a simple punishment.

"This is about me proving my love, you proving

yours, and our commitment to one another. Put your hands behind your back, please."

"You don't need to do this. I was wrong and I apologized."

"You apologize time after time for the same thing, and I'm tired of always going through this with you. I don't want you to question my love any longer."

My hands drift slowly behind my back and she whispers, "good husband." I love it when she calls me that. And I adore the way she manages to bring a thrill to even our most difficult times together.

The cold metal closes around my wrists and I'm detained. I hear the desk chair moved and her melodic voice telling me to sit. I do as she says, turning to see her gorgeous face and nude body for the first time today.

"I want you," I beg.

"Sit. We're talking, not fucking."

"I meant forever."

My morning wood creates a massive bulge in my briefs, and when I ease into the chair, the cold leather against my back triggers my bladder—a pressuring command that I need to take a piss.

She sits before me, on top of the desk with her feet to either side of my thighs. Her legs spread wide with the blade held steadily between us.

"In your heart, you know everything I've withheld was to protect you or to help your family in some way. Don't turn me into a malicious beast."

The blade parts the front exit pocket of my briefs,

allowing my cock to spring free. Fuck. Oh, shit... the dull metal edge travels along my shaft, stopping at the base of my dick.

"It's time to deal with the consequences of treating me poorly."

Her head tilts and I inhale, swallowing hard before declaring my trust. "I'd never willingly put myself in this position with anyone else. I'm lost when you're not by my side; you know that. If you don't stay, then go ahead and cut it off. I won't need it without you."

She grins. "Good answer."

The knife slides across my stomach, making its way to my heart—the spot where she first cut me on the night I gifted her the blade.

"It's a small fucking world," she mutters. "I'm sorry about Cove. And believe me, my father is too. More than you could ever imagine." She sets JAB on the table and leans forward, brushing my hair to the side and caressing the back of my ear. "When I was a kid, he'd always be waiting for me when I got home from school. We'd sit at the dining room table and talk about my day, each of us with two cookies and a cup of tea. He smiled a lot, listening to what I had learned and the crazy activities that took place with my friends—normal kid stuff... but he *listened*. He wanted to hear about everything. And each day, around dinnertime, he left for Reno. Traveling an hour to and from work. During those years and because of his line of work, not once did I ask him about his job or what he was doing. Not how he felt or what he was thinking. The conversation was always one-sided, everything about me, never about him. To my dad, I was more important than what he was going through. I *always* came first. That's why he hired someone to dig into your past. That wasn't some concocted story. I'm his daughter and he knows nothing about the man I'm going to marry. He wasn't even aware you were related to Paul until he received the information from the detective. According to my mom, he went nuts when he found out."

"She knows about all of this?"

"They discuss *everything*. It was her idea for him to quit his job to get away from Paul."

"I doubt that happened, no one could hide from him."

"He wasn't hiding. If he wasn't working at the funeral home, he couldn't do what Paul wanted. He worked as a UPS driver for a year until he thought it was safe to go back to being an embalmer, except he found a job in our hometown, not Reno."

"He's lying."

"No, Mark." She peers at me like I'm acting paranoid. "My dad isn't lying to me. He's not out to get us."

"You can be close to someone and never truly know anything about him."

Her hand brushes along my cheek and sadness clouds her features. "Not us," she assures. "And heads up, I've asked him to speak to Cove. He owes him an apology."

"Cove and Sam? What?"

"They're having breakfast together this morning so my dad can clarify a few things, and more importantly, express regret and offer an apology."

"That's not a good—"

"Hey, it *is* a good idea." She lifts my chin and nods that it's fine.

I had high hopes she killed him last night. There goes that wonderful thought. "An apology's not enough."

"It's a start. And I understand how you must feel, but let me make something clear—no violence against my dad unless it's my decision and I do it myself. He's *my* father. You're not killing him over something he had no control over. Period."

"I have to find out more about him, then I'll decide whether or not he deserves to live."

"No. Look at me. Look. At. Me!"

She holds my chin tightly and I start to feel anxious, wanting out of the cuffs... and her blade... my throat... the blade's now against my throat. Damn her.

"I've had enough, Jules. Get the key."

"I'm not giving you control over this situation. Not this time. And I'm talking about control over your freedom *and* my dad."

"This is a load of shit."

"No, it's what you did to me last night."

"Wrong. I cuffed you because I didn't t-trust..." I stop, not wanting to say it.

"Yes, I understand."

I try slipping my hand out of the cuff, but no-go.

"You're better than this."

"Not really. I thought I just mentioned how alike the two of us are."

"For fuck's sake." I huff. "Come on. We can talk without my hands being confined."

"We can? Only last night we couldn't? Not with little, harmless me?"

"I get it... ha-ha, now uncuff me." I stand, turning around for my release.

"Mark, sit."

"No. I need to piss. I'm serious. My bladder's gonna explode."

"Make it quick."

I feel sweat beading on my forehead from the restraint. "You've ruined me. A fucking badass woman has destroyed my life!" I walk to the bathroom with my hands behind my back. "I love and hate the danger of being with you! It's the dead of winter and you're making me sweat!" I grunt, lifting the toilet seat with my foot and quickly realizing I'm in a jam.

"Hey, beautiful?"

"I'm not helping."

"I'm not amused. I can't position my erect cock toward the bowl. It's bad enough when I try to do this in the morning without any limitations."

"I hope it hits you in the face." she calls out.

"You're such a bitch!"

"No, I'm not. I bet many men have urinated with an erection while their hands were tied. Join the club."

Fine... I'll just... no, I'll... I'll try this... fuck. I move around the bowl, having no choice except to sit like a fucking girl. This is one of the lowest forms of humiliation... and fuck, my dick won't go under the damn... oh, come on... please.

I slide back and forth, stand and lower... stand and lower, until I finally get my dick under the front of the seat and below the rim. Uh, this sucks balls.

"Payback, Mark. Suck it up."

"By now, it should be obvious how much I love your ass!"

"You'll be rewarded tomorrow."

"Tomorrow? On top of all of this, we're not going to fuck and make up? I have to wait?"

She cackles like a witch, spreading her legs apart when I return to the room.

"I've figured it out, Jules. Being confined so I get an impression of how you felt last night isn't my real punishment—being treated like your submissive is. My woman controls my whole world, but it's supposed to be the other way around."

"Women rule the entire world, not just yours. Took you long enough to realize that... though it's good you finally figured it out and can admit it, considering some men never begin to see the light. Those are the guys who'll be alone forever."

"No more cutting remarks this morning, are we gonna fuck, or what?"

She points to her clit and says, "kiss," and I want to

point to my dick and say, "suck," only I can't.

"Kiss," she repeats.

"Fuck," I say.

"No." She smirks. "We're not fucking until tomorrow night."

I look at my erection. "Then suck me off."

She jerks her head, no. "You proved your commitment and trust the moment I snapped the cuffs shut, now the rest of this is about punishment... "Kiss."

"Wait... did you say we're not fucking until tomorrow night? Says who?"

"Cove and Sophia."

"What the hell? They don't control my dick."

"I talked to them this morning. They're sleeping in separate rooms until the wedding. Isn't that romantic? I think we should do something like that to show our support."

"Are you fucking crazy? Release me so I can throw my hands in the air. I need to gesture my frustration. Cove would never go for that crap... come to think of it, Soph wouldn't refrain from sex either. Is this a joke? Another part of my wretched morning?"

"Of course not. Think of it as practice for when we get married. We should refrain too." She guides me to the chair by my cock. "You said you didn't beat off when you went to Philly. One day isn't going to kill you."

"You weren't in eye-sight when I was there... and you fucking believed me?"

"I'll forget you said that. Now think about this. It will

be fun to wait..."

"No it won't."

"Can I finish my sentence? It'll be fun. We can get wasted tomorrow at the reception and fuck like it's our wedding night. That's how Sophia's looking at it, something a little different from the rest of her life, you know? She said she wants this to be old-fashioned, and what she means by that is *normal*."

"Old-fashioned means behind the times, and I don't need to practice celibacy. I did that for the first fourteen years of my life. How about we fuck now, get wasted tonight and fuck, then get wasted tomorrow and fuck again. Just do it, go ahead and yank it. Whack me off."

"Mark," she whines.

"Jules," I complain back. "We live together. We've been fucking for over a year. I shouldn't have to wait."

"No."

"Okay, okay... then we get to fuck three times tomorrow night... don't... don't laugh. I can do it! Four times. We'll shoot for four. Four big loads in your face and on your tits!"

She sits on the desk with her arms crossed and legs open, looking at her twat and back at me. Twat. Mark. Twat. Mark. Up. Down.

"Kiss it," she demands. "But no sex, just a little play, then we'll stop until tomorrow."

"Stop? That sounds dreadful."

She touches her pink pussy lips, snubbing my words to get right down to the seductive performance, replete with fluttering eyelashes and a puckered mouth. The sight and sounds of her moans make me salivate, inciting a lick of my lips and a drip of pre-cum on my cock. She's so fucking skillful at making me desire her all hours of the day.

With fingers holding her folds open, and a hand on the back of my head, I'm drawn closer for the tongue action she craves.

"The only thing missing from my life at this moment is a bottle of whiskey," she says.

I open my mouth slightly, enough to bring the core of her arousal spot between my lips.

"Oh."

Hold steady.

"Fuck, that first touch is sensational."

Possess her. Don't move.

"Please... more."

Cradle the flesh between my lips.

"You're teasing."

Endure. Hang on. Warm breaths.

"Lick."

My tongue meets the sensitive area, swirling once, twice, while hearing another passionate sound. I stop, holding the tip of my tender tongue over her clit. Not moving... not breathing... waiting... a small twitch arises... waiting...

"Oh, Jesus. Move!"

I'm the master at making sweet love to her pussy. My tongue fucks start with a casual taunt, leading to lively lunges to find the most responsive places, then exploring each one until she says her head's going to explode. Nibble and flick. Kiss and lick. Glide in and out. Whatever she wants, I obey. And the 'add-ons' make me a god. I bring her close to arousal, stopping short, and leaning back to watch her hands clutch at the desk and her legs shake. When she catches her breath, my hair is pulled and my face forced back between her legs. I fake her out a few times by scarcely touching her clit before it gets twirled and caressed.

"You're so good at that."

"I know."

She lowers onto my lap taking my head in both hands. My eyes close when her nose brushes alongside mine, leading to the words, "I love you," coming from her soft lips before we kiss.

"Wait," I complain. She's leaving me.

"We should get ready for work. It's after nine. I'm late, and you're always late."

"This is my hotel, I'm never late. I could show up next week and still be on time... and I need to cum. Look at me. Look at *it*. He's a throbbing, jerking fiend."

She gives it a once-over before reaching under the bed, finding the key to unlock the handcuffs. Once I'm free, my Jesse Jane Fleshlight and a bottle of warming lube are set on my lap.

"What gives?"

"Do the deed while I get ready."

I survey her tits, peer at my cock, and look at the toy.

"Ugh."

She pulls a bra from the dresser and hustles to the closet.

"Aren't you going to do it for me?"

"Ha!"

"I'm serious."

"No way. This is the last part of your punishment. No sex together until tomorrow... have fun masturbating."

I pick up the toy and get the lube set... "Fuck, okay then, big buddy. Looks like it's you, Jesse, and me this morning. We haven't had a date with her in months. Bet you missed... oh, hello. Look at how happy my massive dick is to see you, precious Jesse Jane. He's smiling... you're smiling..."

"Mark?" Her head pokes out of the closet. "You're lucky I get your sense of humor, any other woman would be running out the door the moment her man started talking to a sex toy."

"Hey, I'm busy. Don't disturb us... Jesse Fleshie doesn't like hearing another woman's voice during playtime."

She flees my whack off session, taking her clothing to the bathroom and shutting the door. Her blow dryer turns on, giving me five minutes of privacy to grunt and cum.

Five minutes.

Five, lackluster, lonely minutes of suction sounds, ending with a jizz shot into a porn star's fake pussy.

What a dreadful way to kick off the day.

"Mr. Jameson?"

The voice comes from my cell phone watch that's sitting on the dresser. The device is something I'm using now to communicate with my head staff members, and only if there's an emergency. I realize immediately there's a problem.

I drop Jesse, sprint to the dresser, and hit the talk button.

"What's going on?"

"Mr. Jameson, the police are in the lobby. They'd like to speak with you."

My heart tightens and blood surges through my veins. "Be right down," I say in a shooting breath, sure they can hear my response on the intercom app.

I toss the watch and dress quickly, demanding Jules stay put. She's too involved to come with me, especially if they start probing about Mera or the guy missing from the bar. The last thing I need is for them to put her on the spot if this has something to do with the dead.

Fuck. What *is* it about?

I'm out the door without her protesting or tagging along, and there's no doubt in my mind she'll be spying on the security cams anyway. In a near sprint, I have just enough time to button my dress shirt and finger comb my hair on my way to the lobby.

"Shit." I feel my chest and hips, searching for my gun—relieved it was left in the suite. I don't need to show up armed. The decent, law-abiding citizen façade is crucial for getting through this.

The hairs on the back of my neck rise when I round

the corner, seeing two officers admiring the thirty-foot pine. I'm noticed straightaway and they head in my direction. One extends his hand and we shake.

"Mr. Jameson?"

"Yes sir. Is there a problem?"

"How'd you get this tree in your lobby?" one asks.

I point to the double doors and he studies their width and the size of the tree before taking out a pen and flipping a notepad open.

"Again, is there something I can help you with or are you here because my tree's in violation of a city code?" I say with a playful smile, acting friendly, yet eager to get them the hell off my property.

"Is there a place we can speak in private?"

Holy Mother of God... it's the private conversation request. This can't be good, but there're only two of them, and they haven't pulled their weapons or presented a warrant, so as far as I can tell, this isn't an arrest.

I lead them to the main office and ask my hotel manager to give us some privacy. He closes the door on the way out and I gesture for the men to have a seat; both in uniform, wearing black snow boots and heavy winter coats. The cops from *Fargo* come to mind as they sit before me doing nothing more than scanning the room. I swivel nervously in my chair, waiting, but not pushing them with any questions until they're ready.

"Nice hotel." The shorter one with the buzz cut says—the same dumbass who asked about the tree. "My wife keeps asking me to bring her here for dinner, only we never seem to have the time... you know, kids and stuff... you have any kids, Mr. Jameson?"

"You can call me Mark."

The older one's eyes bore into him, causing him to seal his mouth and lean back. Okay, it's obvious who's in charge.

"Mr. Jameson, do you own a gun?"

"Yes. Two. And they're both registered. I keep them in my suite. Never been fired." Fuckin' A, I haven't cleaned the one I used to beat Abram's face in. I'm sure his flesh, blood, and DNA are all over that weapon.

"Are you carrying now?"

"No sir."

"What's their main use?"

"Protection." I open the security cams for the grounds and turn the desktop screen in their direction. "This is a vast property. I have hundreds of guests who come and go each night, over two hundred rooms, a restaurant, pool, weight room, and a bar, plus a few private areas, like the tanning bed rooms, and acres of forest... nothing but pines for miles. It's a five-minute drive down the driveway to the main road and another ten minutes to any form of civilization... my hotel is similar to a chateau that sits on a mountaintop. Total seclusion. Yes. I own guns. Legally. They provide me with a sense of security in case something goes wrong out in the woods. I'm in need of a form of defense since it would take the police at least twenty minutes to arrive in an emergency." I turn the screen back in my direction, wishing they'd get to the fucking point.

"Alrighty then."

Jesus, they are *Fargo* cops, and they should've introduced themselves when we shook hands. "Can I see your badges and ID's?" I want their names, just in case this turns ugly. Though right now, they seem as useless and non-threatening as a couple of sidekick characters, like Robin and Aqualad.

"George Patterson and Handy Luke?" I look at the badge numbers and ID's, flipping their cards over, dumbfounded by the names parents give their children. I need to take a second look to be sure it's not a joke. His name is Handy? The guy from the bar was Lucky? I wouldn't be surprised if the two weren't brothers.

I slide the items across the desk while noticing Jack on one of the security cams, walking toward the lobby.

"Mr. Jameson."

"Like I said, call me Mark."

Cops who are on the level and state their purpose and intentions the moment they arrive are tolerable, but when you wait minutes for these slow, chatty ones to get to the point because they're trying to feel you out, you end up wanting to stab and bury them with the rest of the asswipes who've crossed your path.

"Mr. Jameson."

The fucker won't say my first name.

"Do you own a revolver?"

"A revolver? No."

He looks at the younger cop and they both nod. "You

see; we're here because we received a call from one of your guests that a juvenile was observed entering your suite in possession of one."

"A juvenile?"

"I'm sure you're aware it's illegal for anyone under eighteen to carry unless it's for marksmanship training purposes or hunting, not to mention having it openly in his hand in such a populated setting. The situation is grounds for arrest."

"I don't know anything about this." Fuck, that kid of mine is screwed this time. I check the screen and see he's sitting in one of the club chairs by the door, wearing his snowboarding jacket. Where the fuck does he think he's going?

"This is the photo we received of the incident. A guest took it with his cell."

I don't need to see it, but I pretend that I'm curious and feign surprise at the image.

"It's my son." I sigh, drawing my lower lip between my teeth, trying to think of an explanation for the kid—a clarification so they'll leave at once, only I'm not a fool when dealing with law enforcement. I have no idea where the gun came from and if I lie, it'll come back and bite me in the ass. Think, Mark, think.

"Were you aware he had a revolver in his possession?"

"No sir, I wasn't." Motherfucking fuck. I can tell what's coming next.

"Mr. Jameson, as a parent, my children are my whole world, from morning 'til night they're on my mind and in my heart. I worry about their every encounter and the decisions they make from day to day. So believe me when I say I hate this part of my job. Dealing with crimes committed by teens is never pleasant for the family, but unfortunately, you'll need to call him down here. We need to interview him."

"In *my* presence," I insist. "Not downtown at the station when he's isolated and coerced into saying anything and everything because he's scared shitless."

"Yes, a parent must be present for the interview."

"Here. You question him in my presence, here."

"That's fine. This isn't... it's not that extreme of a situation. He'll be arrested for illegally possessing a weapon, but as a minor, and if it's his first offense..."

I swivel in my chair, glaring at the older man while he speaks, my finger tapping my lips as I mull over the thought of paying them off, or better yet, a torture session. Except making them disappear will cause more cops to show up looking for these dimwits, then I'll have to take them out too... all so Jack doesn't have a record at the young age of sixteen... so he doesn't suffer through community service, a rehab program, or the worse case scenario, six months to a year in jail.

"Mr. Jameson?"

And the gun... where the fuck did he get the revolver from? I bet he bought it from a kid at the ski resort or it's Emma's. She looks like the type to carry a weapon. "Would you excuse me for a moment?" My chair flies back and hits the wall. The younger cop stands, but he's given a gesture to hold back, allowing me the opportunity to willingly comply to their request.

My pace is aggressive, heading in a direct line for my son. He slouches in the chair, trying to hide out, sensing my anger. This is an insult to our family and how we... how *I* do business... he's put my life in jeopardy.

"Jack!" I shout when he races to the door. "Where the f... where the heck are you going?"

"Christmas shopping."

"You're grounded! Get in the office. Now!"

"Mark, wait." Sophia rushes toward us, wearing a winter coat and carrying her purse. "I'm taking him to buy gifts. I can't believe no one's driven him to any of the downtown shops yet. That's so unfair."

"Stay out of this," I demand, pulling him away from the doors.

"Dad, I want to get you something special. Please!"

Perfect. Just perfect. The shirt he's wearing under his jacket reads *You think I give a shit?* and his raggedy jeans are full of holes, not to mention there's a skull pendant necklace hanging around his neck. What an outfit to be arrested in. He looks like a criminal. Why couldn't he have on a dress shirt or that suit? Damn it to hell.

"I want to go out. Aunt Sophia will make sure I don't have any fun while I'm grounded. We'll be back by noon. Dad... listen to me!"

I drag his ass to the office with Sophia defending him left and right.

"It's the holidays, Mark. Let him have a couple of

hours to celebrate. It's a generous act, wanting to buy everyone gifts. Give him a break."

"Stop following, Soph. Go upstairs." Time to be a prick so she'll get riled and take off. "It's not like you to let your kids out of your sight. You're a horrible mother."

"They're watching cartoons."

"So you were going to take off with Jack and not bring them along?"

"They're coming too." She lies, not mentioning that Cove's upstairs with them.

The older officer appears in the doorway, watching the scene. He tilts his head, talking into his chest-walkie while motioning to bring him in.

"What's going on?" She steps closer.

"It's private."

"No. Don't you dare do this to me. I'm your sister. What? What is it?" she questions while I usher him past the cop and motion for him to take the seat at my desk. I close the door, cutting Sophia out of the conversation, but she pushes her way through in protest.

"He's my nephew. I need to be here."

I lean against the wall with crossed arms, ignoring her for now. The little villain, on the other hand, gets my undivided attention.

"Jack, this is Officer Patterson and Officer Luke from the South Lake Tahoe Police Department. They'd like to ask you a few questions."

"No," he says.

The cops are taken aback, although Soph and I are

used to his shit.

"I'll rephrase that. These men are going to ask you some questions and you better answer them truthfully. Got it, hotshot?"

His eyes narrow, my nostrils flare, his mouth twists, my jaw tightens, and finally he surrenders with a smirk and the wave of his hand to go ahead... like the hellion had a choice.

"It's Jack, correct?" Officer Patterson begins. I monitor his defensive body language, arms crossed tightly and his hands hidden in his armpits as he's advised of his Miranda rights, informed of the offense, shown the photo, and asked about the weapon. "Where's the gun? Is it still on the premises?"

He swivels in the chair, copying my actions from earlier, surely with the same thoughts of how to get out of this and whether or not *I'm* going to kill them.

"Speak." I command. "Sit up straight and take this seriously. Think about their questions and answer wisely and honestly."

His hand disappears behind his back, causing the officers to draw their weapons. I react with clenched fists, ready to swing if they harm him. Bastard cops.

"Slowly," I say. "Bring it out slowly with your other hand raised. No sudden movements, buddy. This isn't a game. Place it on the desk and let them pick it up before you move another muscle."

Officer Luke checks the cylinder, confirming it's empty as he passes it along to the other guy. Relief. That has to be good. The gun's not loaded. Okay, I have hope we can make it through this without jail time. He didn't threaten anyone and there're no bullets. Good, good, good.

"Where'd you get it?"

"My grandfather."

Bad! Bad, bad, bad. Oh fuck. Fuck me. Fuck me! He must've found it when he cleaned Abram's room.

I shift and Sophia steps forward.

"He gave it to me before he died."

"Jesus, Jack."

"You said be honest."

"What do you mean before he died?" She steps closer. "Your mother's father is still alive. He lives outside of Philly."

"My *other* grandfather," he says, turning to the officers. "He gave me the revolver a year ago. It was the only time I ever met him."

Holy fuck. What he is doing?

"This is a lie," Sophia interrupts. "Don't do this, you'll only fall deeper into trouble. Tell these officers the truth."

"He approached me in the park where I used to play hoops after school."

"Stop it," she says. "My father, your grandfather, died over a decade ago."

"He did say he was dying, but wanted to meet me before his time was up. We talked for a few hours until it was getting dark and I needed to head home for dinner...

and to do my homework."

That's a bit extreme. Homework?

"Before I left, he gave me the gun as a gift. It's the only thing I have of his."

"Sophia, step out," I whisper, keeping watch over him as he creates this absurd, yet picture-perfect story. He's going to save everyone's ass. Jules, his, and mine.

"No. What the hell is this? Our dad's dead. Why is he lying?"

He's so quick. My son's a genius. He knows the cops are gonna trace the gun back to Abram, and he's leading them away from the hotel, back to Philly. He got the gun in Philly. Abram was never here. Good boy.

"I just moved here and... my mom... sh-she died two weeks ago." He fights back tears. "My stuff arrived the other day and my dad has two living quarters in the hotel... suites on opposite ends... I-I was moving things from one to the other. I'm sorry, I didn't think to hide the gun when I was unpacking and moving my things because to me it's not a weapon..." He starts crying. Good show, Jack. "It's my g-grandfather's only gift to me. I'm sorry. I didn't mean any harm!"

Fucking brilliant.

"We'll need to run a check on the revolver and bring you to the station to answer more questions, plus get some paperwork filled out. As long as you don't have a prior record, I firmly believe hours of community service and a rehabilitation program are in your future. I can't see any court sending you to jail for something like this."

His palms cover his face as he sobs, showing remorse and putting on a glorious performance. Thank fuck he researched that bastard online. He knew he faked his death months ago. We're in the clear.

"What's your grandfather's name?" Officer Patterson asks.

No.

"Soph, get out." I take her arm, tugging her to the door.

"A-a-ab," he stutters. Damn, he wouldn't. Not with her in the room.

"Abram Jameson."

SILENT NIGHT

G reasy, fatty, meat.

The scent has permeated my clothing and hair, filling the Tacoma as Jack and I eat mystery shit. That's what I call this cheap, unrecognizable meat—*mystery shit*. No need for a definition, the term speaks for itself.

I haven't had food so vile since high school, and after today, I doubt I'll step into another *two burgers for a buck,* drive-thru dive ever again. I'm only eating it to please my son. He said we needed to have dinner together, that it would make him feel loved after being treated so poorly by the cops. Poorly? Not even close, buddy. They were decent guys.

But when we left the police station, he insisted food was a top priority, saying, "The cops tortured me. I didn't get a bite to eat. They held me for six hours! I think I'm gonna pass out from starvation. Eat with me, Dad. Join me in an after arrest meal."

Poor lying baby.

I stopped at the first place we came across on the way back to the hotel... now my truck smells like we just finished our shifts at the *Meat Palace*—a mix of salty fries, fatty burgers, and sugary apple pies.

I hold the wheel and lick salt from my lips, concentrating on the snowy, dark road, craving nothing more than a relaxing night. Shit, I feel like I've said that a few times this week. One night. Just one, is all I desire.

I peer at Jack, observing a continual gummy smile plastered across his face as he eats. Hamburger bun is stuck between his teeth and onion pieces are on his jacket. His happy-go-lucky expression is nonstop this evening.

Taking big bites of food, he chews noisily and swallows hard, always ending with a smile. Bite, chew, swallow, smile, and repeat. He tilts his head back and dumps the remaining fries into his mouth, crumbles the fast food bag into a ball, and pitches it over his shoulder into the back seat.

"That was too close, Jack. Way too fucking close. Jesus Christ, I hate dealing with cops."

He whistles softly, swiping his hands free of crumbs before texting on his cell, remaining unresponsive to my comment.

"Phweep, phweee... phweeeep, fweee, fuuuuit."

In my eyes, my son became a man today. I pull his hand away from his cell and give it a squeeze. Our relationship is more important than some goddamn text.

I love him. I love his sense of humor, his playful approach to life, his curiosity and cleverness, and the loyalty he showed to our family today.

"Carrying that revolver in plain sight was a childish mistake, but—"

"I always carried my swords around the house back in Philly." His cell's put away as he defends his slip-up.

"The corridors of my hotel aren't a home. It's a business." I calmly finish my sentence. "It was a childish mistake, but you handled it like a man."

He sighs. "How long is my punishment extended for this time?"

Car lights blind me before I can answer. My arm straightens in front of his chest, protecting him as the approaching car crosses into our lane.

"Hold tight!" I caution, swerving my truck onto the narrow shoulder then quickly steering back once the car passes.

"What the fuck?" I see the lights in the rear view mirror disappear down the mountain road. "See, that's why you're taking driver's ed... and I'm *not* buying you a motorcycle until you're forty. The roads up here are dangerous, especially in the winter. It's a different world than Vegas and Philly."

"No fucking shit. Why'd you pick this area anyway? Out of all the cities to choose from, you came here. Why not Portland, or Seattle, or hell, why not Boulder? You know, weed's legal in all of those cities. They have a better music scene too. I keep looking online and in the paper for something to do around here and I can't believe there aren't any bands that play out at night. I'm gonna be bored shitless once snowboarding season's over."

"Try focusing on homework and a job."

"How lame. Oh, I forgot I'm gonna be one of your

pool boys. Do I get a weapon before then? Cuz if it's just gonna be me and a bunch of drunken guests out there each day, I'll need something. What if I get attacked?"

"Okay."

"Okay?" He turns. "Just like that you're gonna give me a gun."

"No."

"Fuck, wishful thinking on my part."

"A blade. My number two."

"Your what? What does that mean?"

I turn onto the hotel drive, following the flickering white lights leading us forward like an airport runway. The scent of burning wood from the hotel fireplaces replaces the smell of fast food. Ahh. Home sweet home. The weather's calm and the sky's cloudless. A full moon's expected...

"Hello? You know you zone out all the time." He stirs me back to the conversation.

"My number two," I continue. "The second blade I ever bought and one that I've always treasured. One day I'll pass it on to you. That day's getting nearer, especially considering the commitment you showed to Jules and me today. You're now my favorite kid."

"Only kid." He laughs. "I'm your only kid so that doesn't count."

"Of course it does. Remember who it's coming from. It's the nicest thing I've ever said to you." I mess around, relieved that this situation's over for now. "I think as long as you behave in court, you'll end up in counseling and doing community service—and both will do you some good. I'd be happy with that outcome. It's a far better punishment than sitting in a juvenile detention center. And Jack..." He watches the garage door open while I place my hand on his shoulder. "That performance with the cops was fucking extraordinary."

"What performance?"

"The one... in the... wait, what do you... I get it; you're being a comical brat. Tell me you're kidding."

"I don't know what you're talking about."

"The fucking gun!" I jerk my hand away. "You found it when you cleaned the bloody mess. You got it in that room."

"Hmmm. I suppose."

"Jack!"

"What?"

"It's Abram's gun—from the room—yes or no."

"Yes or no to which part?"

I study his face, searching for a slight twitch, the beginnings of a smirk, a scratch of his nose, anything to get a sense that he's fooling around, except he holds steady.

"Be straight with me."

"I told you, I got it from Abram."

"Where? Did he seek you out in Philly? Did that actually happen?"

He shrugs and begins a string of questions. "Can I have the knife tonight? How big is it? Is it like a pocketknife, a switchblade, or a machete? How many men have you killed with it? Is there blood on it? Is it a kickass handmade one from a specialty shop like you bought for Jules?"

I park in the garage and get out of my truck, my son trailing behind, still mumbling about the weapon as I ponder his words.

We walk up the two flights of stairs and enter a dark living room. Jules is nowhere to be seen in the quiet suite. Good, more time to talk.

"Tell me about Abram's gun."

"Okay." After a deep breath, he wipes the smile off his face. "The truth is, since you're asking and all, I lie about most everything in my life." He removes his jacket, raising his shirt to expose his back. "Like this tat. It's sweet. Too high of a quality to be done by some kid in his parents' garage, don't ya think? I got it from a shop in Philly. Cut a deal with a wicked female. She hired me to torment her ex-boyfriend in exchange for this badass tat. Her loser ex was messing with her, so I keyed his car and slashed his tires. Oh, and I got her dog back. That was the big request. I broke into his garage where he was starving the poor thing in a cage. Total bullshit. Why steal an animal from your ex and not take care of it?" He lowers his shirt with a headshake. "What was your question again?" There's a pause. "Oh, the gun. Yeah, I took it from his hotel room." He sprints up the stairs and I'm left to question yet another strange conversation with my son.

"Was that another lie? Hey, did that really happen with the tat? And where'd you get the gun? Is that the truth? Stop being such a Jameson and give me a straight answer!"

He glares at me from the landing, looking smug with his shoulders back, a tight mouth, and his hands in his pockets. "Thanks for staying by my side today. The truth is, I love you," he says before vanishing into the bedroom.

"You damn well better!" I shout.

It sucks that he's making me wonder if he met Abram a year ago in Philly. I guess even if he did, what does it matter now?

"You're an ass."

"Fuck!" I do a quick U-turn, hearing Sophia's voice jetting from the dark living room.

"I'm glad Jack's home," she says, turning on the lamp next to the sofa. "That means things went well at the station."

"One of the easiest interactions I've had with the cops." I walk to my liquor, down a shot, and set my hands on the counter. "I was hoping for a breather tonight... looks like I'm shit outta luck. So you want to tell me why I'm an ass this time?"

"Don't act dumb. What the fuck, Mark? Cove told me everything about Abram."

"Of course he did."

"You could've let me talk to him. I didn't even have a chance to meet him. He was my grandfather! What the hell's wrong with you?"

"Goddammit!" I collapse in a chair next to her, setting my fingers on my forehead. "If Cove told you everything, then there's no need to even discuss this."

"Wrong!"

"Don't be so upset with me, the man was worse than Paul."

"I'm not denying that." Her arms cross and she leans back, squinting her eyes until I catch on to the real issue. She's upset about our relationship. "It's not fair that these things keep happening to us. I thought we were growing closer. You and I, we're... aren't you upset we're not brother and sister?"

"I'm still Elizabeth Jameson's son, which makes us brother and sister."

"No, you're Abram's son, which makes you my uncle."

"I'll always be your big brother, Soph," I say tenderly, leaning forward in the chair with my fingers entwined between my legs. "I'm *mom's* son, so don't start calling me Uncle Mark because of Abram. That's not who I want to be. I'll never consider Paul to be my brother. I just can't. He's my dad. And I spent my entire life having a baby sister, that's not going to change."

She smiles and wipes a tear from her cheek with a sniffle and a nod. "Cove said you have a photo of Mom and Abram."

I start to get up, but she raises a hand to stop. "No, I don't want to see it. It just made me wonder about a lot of things from our childhood. You think that's why she was so mean to me? Because of what she experienced."

I sit next to her and set my feet on the coffee table,

gazing at the beamed ceiling. "Yes and no. I'd say as teenagers, she didn't want anything to happen to us. The way we couldn't leave the house or have friends over could've stemmed from fear. She was tough on you because of your slutty ways. Think about all the men you slept with back then. You opened your legs for anyone. That must've been hard on her considering she's a rape survivor. I'm sure she despised the way you acted. I also wouldn't be surprised if Abram raped her more than once. He was pure evil. And I know this is a shitty thing to say, but I got away with being a manwhore because I'm a guy. It sucks, it's sexist, but unfortunately we all know things haven't changed much in that regard over the years. Men are treated differently when it comes to getting laid, no matter what their age. Besides all of that, you have to remember Mom is mentally ill. There's no denying it. Some of her problems are from Abram and Paul, but not all."

"I wish I had known," she says.

"Well, no shit. How do you think I felt finding out? I won't tell you how disturbing our short time together was. Be glad you never talked to him."

"So he went to St. Louis just to *look* at me? Just to see my sons?"

"I bet he's done it before, we just never noticed. The older people get, the more invisible they become. Would you have remembered some old guy passing you on the street or him sitting at the bus stop by your house if he didn't cause a scene? Trust me; there were other times. He just never made a sound until the end. At least, that's my take on it."

"Spooky. And I can't believe he was a detective."

"Yep. A spooky son of a bitch detective."

"So he wasn't going to hurt us?"

"Not physically, he just wanted to seep inside me before he died."

"I'm sorry." She places her head on my shoulder. "I hope you're okay."

"Thanks, Soph." I pat her hand, hearing the entryway door open. My head tilts backward and Jules, Cove, and my nephews enter the suite. "The privacy's over."

"Mom!" The boys jump on the sofa, one of them kneeing my nuts as they fight to give her a hug.

"We tried this new thing called Eddie Money for dinner. Eddie tastes awesome!" Xavier's full of excitement.

"Eddie Money?" Sophia peers at Cove. "Sounds like your Dad's playing games with you again."

"What the fuck, Dad? You said it was called Eddie Money?"

"Watch the language," Sophia scolds.

"Tell us what it's called," he demands.

Cove takes a seat next to the fireplace and smirks.

"What the hell are you doing here?" I ask. "Am I supposed to know you've arrived? Just like that. A tiny magical fairy has flown in and sprinkled *interpretation dust* on my head and it's no big deal that you're here."

"Dad, come on!"

"It's called edamame."

"See, he said Eddie Money. Told you."

"Dax." Cove laughs. "Listen, it's pronounced, ed-a-*mommy*."

Jules flops on the sofa and exhales a deep breath, blowing a strand of hair off her face. She takes my hand and gives it a light kiss before snuggling by my side.

"In case you didn't hear me," I say. "Why are you showing your face?"

"Because it wasn't worth the trouble, not after the shit with Jack today. I had to tell Soph the story of your dad when she came whining about what happened with the cops."

"I don't whine!"

"Like that." He laughs, taking a quick gaze around the suite. "Everything work out okay?"

"He's home and in his room."

"Kids, go upstairs and hang out with your cousin," he requests.

"Knock before you enter," Sophia calls out as they fight to see who can reach the landing first. "Don't fall! Boys, knock!"

Cove resumes the explanation when the kids are out of sight. "I told her that you know about the wedding. I decided it wasn't worth the trouble to continue the surprise, since it wasn't going to be one anyway."

"That's the dumbest thing I've ever heard. Why did you even come up with such a bogus plan in the first place?" I point to Sophia and say, "You show up and mess with me, saying you're at my hotel because Cove's a drunken asshole so you left him, then I find him drinking Coke in the bar. He tells me you wanted to surprise me with your wedding, since for some odd reason you think I'm a control freak and you didn't want me to manage things, which is what I do best by the way, and now he comes in and it wasn't worth the trouble? Fuck! What a way to mistreat your big brother." I sarcastically jerk my head, my mouth setting in a hard line. "You guys make me feel like I live in a fucking circus."

"Well, you win as usual, Mark," she admonishes.

"Yeah, I win seeing you happy and marrying this nutball... why is that bad? You win, not me. You've always been the champion, Soph. You landed this... this... this..."

"Loving and sensitive man?" She raises a brow.

"No, that's not it."

"Hey! That *is* it." He remains laid-back about the tease.

"Cove never would've married a guy like me, so you win, sis. You got him. Choose your prize. Would you like the stuffed gorilla or the portable television set?"

We laugh, then Jules' random question, "Why do you smell like meat?" cracks us up even more.

"See, I got stuck with this thing." My thumb motions her way as we continue laughing. "How was your day, princess?"

"Same-old, same-old. I took over the hotel while you were out trying to take over the world."

"I love it." Sophia smiles. "The two of you are so cute together. I hope you have lots of babies."

"No!" Another burst of laughter starts, this time directed toward me. "That's not funny."

"Aww, admit it, you love a good sibling tease."

"That I do..." I lean closer to Jules and whisper, "go get the weed. The new bag."

"That sounds like the perfect evening." She stands and straightens her skirt. "I'm exhausted and could use a mellow night after working all afternoon on the wedding." She smiles at my sister and leaves to get the pot.

"Check on the kids, too," I request.

Sophia turns with her legs tucked under her body, facing me and placing a hand on my forearm. "She did so much work today. The decorations are tasteful and look fantastic. Oh, and we had so much fun working together, getting everything ready. I love her to death."

"Me too. What time tomorrow?"

"Two. Did you see her poor hand? Last night we were working late and she got it caught in the ladder. Her knuckles are swollen and red."

"I saw." Fuck, I was hoping she had beaten the crap out of Sam. At least one hard punch to his nose or jaw. I guess thinking every wound comes from a fight is pretty cliché. "How many people?" I ask.

"With the kids and us, Jules' parents and a few of her friends, maybe twelve?"

"Small's good."

"I want it to be quaint. This is about love and new beginnings—a ceremony marking the next stage of our lives together. These are going to be our best years yet."

She tilts her head adoringly at Cove. "And just wait 'til you see how pretty the room looks."

"Which one?"

"We're using one of the private dining spaces. Is that okay?"

"Of course."

Cove cuts in, "Have things always been this way? Was I too drunk to realize it, or is this weird to you, too? Why aren't we arguing and calling each other fuckheads?"

I smile and raise my hand for the weed delivery as Jules returns from upstairs. She says the boys are fine, watching the cartoon network while Jack's talking on his cell.

"Thanks." I hold a flame over the bowl and inhale, pause and enjoy the fact that none of them are making a sound, then lean back and exhale. "Fuck, that was such a long ass day... and to answer your question," I pass him the bowl, "we've *always* been extremely loving and kind to one another. See what you've missed being liquored up?"

"Not funny." Sophia elbows me where I was stabbed. I cringe for a second before changing quickly to a grin by the thought of Jack's face after he dropped the bloody knife in the snow. I can't wait to see how he reacts the next time he tries to stab someone, and hopefully it's not me.

"You're right." I continue holding the bowl in his direction, coming back to the conversation. "I *am* proud of you. I know it's not easy. I mean, weed's not even addictive and I can't give it up. It calms my nerves. And these days, I seem to need it every fucking day. You're a better man than me for quitting."

He looks at the closed bedroom door and back at Soph. They're debating because of the kids.

"We can have fun sometimes. It's not like we do this more than once a year," she says to him. "I'm okay with it, and it's not booze, so you won't be breaking your sobriety."

"Shit, this could be a fucking after school special," he jokes, carrying the bowl to the kitchen to take a hit with Sophia following close behind. They're hidden from the bedroom, just in case the boys walk out. Smart.

"Good, isn't it?" Jules asks, taking the next drag when they return.

"Excellent." Cove's dimples show, his beaming expression lighting the room. "What's gonna happen to Jack?"

"Ffffuck. I don't want to talk about this when I'm high." I gaze at the ceiling with a hand behind my head, feeling Jules' thumb circling my palm. My heart pounds faster and harder than usual. I think that fucking greasy shit I ate for dinner is doing a number on my arteries. An instant blockage from two burgers, I just know it. "He'll be fine," I finally respond, deciding to discourage them from asking more questions by giving a real answer. "Nothing's gonna happen to my kid. The court won't do shit to a first-time offender. But I'll talk to him." I look at Cove who's nodding slowly, not from my comment—because he's stoned. I keep talking, unsure if he has a clue he's in this discussion. That's what happens to people who don't smoke often, even with one hit, he's toast, or maybe craving toast. "I can't change Jack at his age, and I don't want to either. So I need to make sure he makes wise decisions, like not carrying a gun in plain sight. Though part of that's my fault. I haven't taught him the where, when, why, and how of handling weapons. That's coming... is anyone listening to me?"

"Yes, darling." Jules laughs. "You're always heard. Now go get some ice. I could use a cold glass of water."

"Ice? Just grab some snow from the windowsill."

"Mark." She frowns.

"I'll get it," Sophia says. "You want a lot in a bucket or just a glass?"

"*I'll* get it." I lean forward and exhale. "Can we use some of it later in bed? I think that whole 'holding out' crap for Cove and Sophia's wedding is void once the ice enters our suite."

"Ha! You're making him wait because of us? That's brilliant." He relishes in a hard laugh over her power. "Oh man, if you could see your face... hell, where's my cell, I'll take a pic. I have to capture this moment."

"I believe you. There's no need for a photo when I'm fully aware my fiancé owns my dick. Trust me, the payback between us is always worth the torture we put one another through. She wants to wait? Well fuck, I wouldn't want to be her tomorrow night when the time's up and a full night of wild screwing begins. She won't be walking for days."

"Exactly," Jules says as the bedroom door opens. Jack walks out with is nose in the air, sniffing like a hound. He puts two fingers to his mouth, gesturing that he wants a hit.

"Nope." I shake my head and point for him to go back into the doghouse where he belongs. He drags his feet with a bowed head, cracking all of us up with his exaggerated performance.

"Later, buddy. When your cousins leave."

I take another hit after he's gone, find the ice container in the kitchen, and head for the door.

"I'll be back in a flash."

"Wait, kiss me," she says.

"I thought you wanted ice?"

"I want both." Her arms lift playfully and she puckers her lips. "We haven't kissed all day."

"Uhh." I give her a soft kiss. "You smell like strawberries again. Fucking sexy."

"I love you, Mark."

"Aww, me too, Mark. I love you, man." Cove laughs.

"I love my big brother, too!" Sophia grins.

"I love me the most." I smirk.

On the way out, Cove starts telling Sophia about the breakfast he had with Sam, explaining that to some extent it was friendly... yeah, I have questions for him when I return. Like, how the fuck did Sam break ties with Paul without ending up dead? I can't imagine him walking away without broken ribs or missing toes. Something must have happened. No one walks away from Paul Jameson.

The corridor's dark and the carpet pattern distorts in blurry waves. I always feel this way when I walk around my hotel stoned. The space tends to close in on me and colors fade. I clear my throat and take rapid steps to the ice machine. At least I think my pace is rapid. Maybe I'm walking slowly... or is it a normal stride? Will I seem graceless if a guest sees me? No, that's not me. I'm classy and refined... don't overthink it. I'm okay. Fuck, no I'm not. I think this new batch of weed is different from what I normally buy. It's hitting me hard.

Stop for a moment... smell the cinnamon sticks and pine branches on the corridor tables. Get your shit together. Breathe in, relax. Breathe out, relax.

Silent night, holy night,
all is calm, all is bright
round yon virgin mother and child.

Holiday music plays softly and the lights dim. The pot's tricking my senses... hell, I wish my world always looked and sounded so beautiful. And this song can bring tears to my eyes when sung by the right person, like in this Nat King Cole version that's playing. Slow down. Take a breath. Listen.

Holy infant, so tender and mild,
sleep in heavenly peace,
sleep in heavenly peace.

I sang this back in grammar school as part of our Christmas pageant. Poor Sophia was a sheep. I got to be one of the "wise men"—the one bringing the gift of myrrh. I complained at first, wanting one of the star roles, but was told I was too small to play Joseph, and too large to be Jesus. Then it was cool to learn myrrh was used for burial embalming, including Jesus' burial. So I started calling myself the *Myrrh Man*.

Silent night, holy night,
shepherds quake at the sight;
glories stream from heaven afar,
heavenly hosts sing Hallelujah.

I'll have to ask Soph if she remembers any of that, and Cove will get a kick out of the fact that she was a sheep.

Silent night, holy night,
Son of God, love's pure light;

The motion sensor activates the light in the small alcove where the ice machine's installed. I open the front and place a large scoop in the container, humming along with the music.

This will be the first Christmas in years that Jack and I will spend together. I can't wait to see his face when I give him the dirt bike he's been admiring online. No motorcycle. Not yet. But he can ride off-road on my property. We'll have to work on clearing a trail so he doesn't run into a tree and break his neck... I bet he's gonna love it. I know it...

"Fuck! Uh!"

I grab at the machine, trying to hold steady while a sharp object pierces my back. It twists and I feel it moving further inside my body.

"No!" Jules shouts from behind. "Stop!"

Warm blood drips down my flesh... the ice container slips out of my hand... cubes bounce and roll onto the floor...

Hallelujah to our King;
Christ the Savior is born.

SCREWED

"What the fuck happened?" Cove rushes to the door, seeing Jules helping me inside the suite with a weapon sticking out of my back. She's frantic, and her hands shake in fright.

"Mark!" Sophia shouts.

Jack races out of the bedroom and yells, "Dad!"

Dax and Xav look over the landing and shriek in terror, running in circles, looking for a place to hide.

Sophia runs upstairs, shutting her kids inside the bedroom, as Cove takes over for Jules, assisting me up the stairs.

"What the fuck?!" he exclaims. "There's something in your back!"

"Don't touch it."

"Mark stay down here," Jules pleads. "We need to take you to the hospital!"

"No, my bedroom."

"Dad, what do I do?"

"Stay calm... Cove, bedroom... Jules, kill that fucker or I will."

"Absolutely not!" She races to my side, helping Cove

take me to my room. "Jack, get out of here, now!"

"No, it's my dad! Who did this?"

"Get out!" she demands, pushing him toward the door.

He falls to the floor, grabbing her legs and taking her down. "No! I'm not leaving!"

"Enough! Stop being beasts! All of you! Jack, let go of her, now! Jules, leave him alone!"

"Don't tell him who it is!" she shouts. "I'll deal with him!"

"Uh, Jesus H. Christ." I clutch the dresser in pain, turning to see an odd-shaped handle sticking out of my back.

"You're going to the hospital," Cove says.

"No." I try to reach the weapon, seeing how painful a small tug is... "Oww! Fuck!" I drop my hand, taking short breaths. "I'm gonna kill that fucker!"

"No!" Jules says. "You won't! Don't even think about it! I'll take care of him!"

"Julia," Sam's deep voice calls from the bedroom doorway.

"I can't believe you followed us in here!" she screams. "Get out!" She sprints toward him and smacks her palms into his chest. "How dare you!"

"You're not marrying into this family. You have no idea what you're getting yourself into."

"Oh, I know!" She points her finger at his face. "I fucking know! You tried to kill him! You bastard!" She tries to clock him, but her hand's caught mid-swing.

"This is a warning for him to disappear. That's all."

"A warning?" I yell. "I don't do warnings, Sam. This was an attack and once I get this fucking thing out of my back, you're dead. You don't just stab me and walk away. You're going in the ground!"

"Stop it! This isn't happening! Don't make me choose between you!" She displays a look of desperation.

I'm between a rock and a hard place. This is the first time the act of killing someone would destroy the person I love. "Princess," I mutter.

Jack runs past her, striking Sam in the jaw. That's my boy. He swings a second time, but Sam snatches his arm, pulling it behind his back. His face is pushed into the wall making a loud *thud*.

"You fuck!" I open my dresser drawer and take out one of my switchblades. "Don't you ever touch my son!"

"What's happening?" Daxton screams from the bedroom as Sophia darts to my side. "Mom! What's going on?"

"Mark, put it away," she orders. "Focus on yourself, not him. You're not moving another inch until we get this knife out of you." She examines the wound as I watch the scene unfold. Cove pulls Jack away and Sam's pushed out of the room by Jules.

"This family destroyed my life," he says to her. "I spent years living in fear when you were a kid... I quit my job in Reno because of a fucking Jameson. We're just lucky I was so insignificant to Paul. He never bothered with me other than sending a guy to give me a souvenir of a fist in my stomach, a knee to my jaw, and a kick out of a moving car into a ditch. You walk *away* from men like this. You hear me. You walk away. You don't fight them, trick them, or fucking marry one of them! I won't allow it!"

They argue as Sophia feels the area around the puncture wound, trying to figure out if she can help.

"That's all about you and Paul! You know nothing about me, about us, about Mark!"

"Why didn't you tell me his name a year ago? I could've gotten you out of this then."

"I don't want out of this!"

"And when you finally said his last name my heart dropped into my stomach. I prayed he wasn't related to Paul. And why the fuck isn't there any information about his life online? That should be a massive warning to you!"

"Paul didn't use Mark's name in the company. He didn't want anyone to know he had a son! Stop this, now!"

"Hurry up, Soph. Pull it out," I say anxiously.

"I had to hire that detective to find out they were related. His name wasn't even listed in Paul's obituary. No one was. That's fucked up!" Sam rages. "The detective found out because Mark was the executor to Paul's estate!"

"You shoulda asked!"

"And you kept referring to him as 'just a guy' at first, then 'just a guy' turned into 'Mark,' but you waited until a month ago to tell me his last name! Why? I kept thinking he forced you to keep quiet, that he knew who I was, and he was planning to kill me or harm you!"

"You're fucking crazy! I'm not being used to get to you! That's insane!" she shouts at the top of her lungs.

"Yeah, well if that's not it, then ask him if he truly loves you or if he's going to use your body and toss you away like all the whorish porn stars he's fucked."

"That's bullshit!" I call out. "Soph, yank this thing out of me so I can move freely and break his face."

"I can't. What if I hurt you?"

"I'm already hurt!"

"It's too dangerous. What if I make it worse? And I'm freaking out from this weed, and it's two hundred degrees in here, and my head's spinning, and my legs are gonna give out!" she whines.

"Jack, get your ass over here and yank this thing out of me."

"Mom! What's happening?" Xavier screams.

"Stay in the room, boys! Don't come out!" she yells. "Cove, come help us."

He walks over and examines the blade, moving my bunched shirt. "Shit, what is that? It looks like... it's a corkscrew."

"What? Jack, get this motherfucking thing out of me. Don't waste anymore time! Just do it!"

He grasps the handle and places a firm hold on my shoulder.

"Ready?"

"Turn it... don't forget to twist on the way out. Oww! Fuck!" My head goes down and I take deep breaths, setting my palms on the top of the dresser. He didn't count to three; he just turned and pulled. "Thank you." I gasp.

He sets it between my hands and Cove laughs at the size of the bloody thing. I realize Sophia's spot on—we're all fucking stoned out of our minds. That should *not* have hurt like it did.

"Wuss," Cove says. "That's shorter than a fork."

"It could've damaged something. It's two inches and it hurt like fuck."

"It didn't go all the way in, maybe an inch."

"Damn, it's not like me to feel so much pain from such an insignificant wound. I can't believe how this batch of pot's fucking with my head. It's gotta be a different kind than I normally buy. My eyes are burning and my body feels like I'm trying to run in four feet of water. How's my back? That thing felt like it went right through my torso. Is it all fucked up? A deep wound? Or is the weed seriously fucking with my senses?"

"It left about a quarter inch hole that's oozing blood," Jack says. "It's kinda cool. Can I keep the weapon?"

"No!" the three of us say in unison.

"Gah!" Jules grunts outside the door. I can hear the anger and frustration in her voice. I'm ready to gouge Sam's heart out for this, but Sophia grabs my arm and draws me back before I can do any harm.

"Dad, you need to leave, and I'm not referring to the hotel, I mean my life. I can't say for how long... maybe forever."

"I d-didn't know what to do." Sam sounds defeated

and remorseful. "You can't stay here. I thought I'd feel differently after meeting him, only I feel worse. This isn't your life. You shouldn't be involved with people like this... they're... they're scum."

"Excuse me?" Sophia steps forward. "Who the fuck do you think you are?"

"We're not scum!" Daxton shouts. "Mom, can we come out? I wanna kick this guy in the nuts."

The four of us move to the doorway, seeing Jules with her hands on her hips, dishing out her usual badass attitude.

"How could you say such a thing? Leave. Leave, before something horrible happens. I won't be able to stop Mark or anyone else in this suite if they come after you, including me. And trust me, I'm close to doing it."

"Listen to yourself." His head shakes pleadingly.

"You acted like a madman tonight for no reason except you're resentful of someone who's been dead for years. The choice you just made may have cost you our relationship, forever. I know you're jealous of Mark for taking me away from you, but I'm not a fucking little girl!" She rubs her forehead, looking worn out and in a state of confusion over the mess. "And no, you didn't want to kill him, but you didn't think twice about hurting him. You stabbed him in the back like a coward, for Christ's sake!"

"Peanut—"

"Please Dad, don't. You need to leave. Now."

"No." Jack steps forward, pushing past everyone and

stepping right up to Sam. He crosses his arms with his jaw muscles twitching. "I'm gonna kill him."

"Get your ass back in the bedroom," I say.

Sam's head jerks as Jules' blade juts open, ready to plunge it into my son if he makes a wrong move.

"Jesus Christ, is this happening, or is it the pot?" Sophia starts to freak out. "Are all of you playing games with me? Is this a big joke to fuck with me when I'm—"

"Shh," Cove hushes her. "Take a breath."

"Except," Jack says. "If I did, if I killed you, Sam, then I'd be hurting Jules. I wouldn't do that to her. I'm still dealing with the loss of my mom, and no one should experience something like that. Which is why I can't believe you'd want to take the man she loves away from her. You fucking jackass. And let me tell you something..." He looks back at me, bites his bottom lip, then turns to Sam and continues. "Scum are people who are worthless. They're the lowest of the low, men who beat the shit out of women, pimps and pedophiles, rapists and animal abusers—they act like big brave men, but they're nothing more than pitiful cowards. They're the men my dad defends us from. He's not the scum. If anything, you should be thanking him for keeping your daughter safe. He'd do anything for her..." He pauses and places his hands in his pockets, having good reason to act superior since he's the only real man in the room. "As a Jameson, I can tell you we enjoy our liquor, a little weed, and have a good appetite for fucking, but we're not scum. We live for each other. We'd die for each other. And if you can't handle that, then you can go straight to hell." He walks past him, knocking shoulders, and stating he'll be in his room if we need him.

Sam gives us the once-over before dropping his gaze and heading quietly down the stairs, not saying a word after being schooled by a sixteen-year-old.

The entryway door closes and Sophia rushes to see her boys.

"I'm so sorry." Jules wraps her arms around me, causing a shudder of pain when her hand touches the puncture wound. "Oh, Jesus, Mark. What did he do to you?" She raises the back of my shirt and I lower my head, starting to feel dizzy and slightly paranoid. Okay... a lot paranoid.

"You alright?" Cove asks.

"I don't know, are you?"

"I think I am, but you're the one who got stabbed. Fuck, someone should've stayed straight tonight. My hearing's all fucked up. Everyone sounds like they're screaming, then voices are muffled like I'm wearing earplugs."

"I think we were screaming. At least I was," Jules says. "What the fuck? I can't believe this happened, and Mark, you look pale."

I walk into the bathroom, unsteady on my feet and nauseous, the taste of salt and greasy meat still lingering in my mouth. Cove joins me and we splash cold water on our faces; the two of us looking at our mirrored reflections, patting our flesh dry while emitting short-lived, agitated laughs, and brief headshakes.

"That could've been the end," I whisper.

"Not even close, man. We've still got a long time together as a family."

"Yeah, I suppose it's good to get stabbed in the back every once in a while, especially by your fiancé's father. Makes you realize you're marrying the right woman."

"Makes me feel like white-trash," Jules says from the doorway as Jack sneaks past her.

"Dad, this website says you're going to die if you're stabbed with a corkscrew." He holds up the iPad.

"That right?"

"Yeah. It says toenail fungus can kill you too. Do you have that?"

"Come here."

"Another stitch job?" He walks over, standing next to me without a fuss.

"No, not this time." I look at him admiringly and offer my warmest smile, my hands firmly gripping his shoulders so we're connected as one. "You should know I spent years trying to impress my dad... Paul. I'd do anything to hear the words 'I love you,' come from that man. Even once would've been enough. But he never gave me that. Many times, I tried to be just like him so he'd notice me... now... all I want is to be like my son." I lift his chin as tears begin to shimmer in his eyes. "I love you, Jack."

~~I THEE WED~~

LET'S FUCK

S he's beautiful.

I stand next to the bed, admiring her nude body with a lily in my hand. The stem twirls between my thumb and forefinger, causing the flower to spread open and a petal to float gently down to her nipple. Her hands are above her head as she stretches and yawns in the early-afternoon light, and a loving smile appears when I set the lily on her stomach.

My shoes and sport coat are removed before I slide by her side, taking her cheek in the palm of my hand and gifting her an affectionate kiss. Our tongues dance and teeth tug at one another's lips, producing arousing moans befitting the blustering wind outside the window.

"Who knew I'd end up with a soft spot in my heart for another person," I whisper.

"I did." She grins, smelling the flower. "What a nice surprise this morning. I thought we only had red ones in the hotel right now."

"A mix of white and red just arrived in the lobby."

"Sweet. I bet the bouquets look like candy canes."

"I ordered them special, just for you. I know you miss having the white ones in the corridors."

"I like the red too." She sniffs the petals and runs the flower down to her pussy. "Are you being nice because you want something?"

I nod and start to unbutton my shirt. "Hell yeah, yesterday was bleak. I could use a good fuck."

"Not yet." The flower taps my hands. "You were so good last night, but not 'til after the ceremony... how's your back?"

"Fine." I press my stiff cock against her side, not giving up. "My dick wants inside. Let me massage your clit and make love to you." My fingers tiptoe up her thigh, separating her lips and touching her wet pussy. "Mmm."

"Shame on you." My hand's pushed away and her legs snap shut. She's not giving in.

"You can't blame me for wanting to fuck when you're spread out nude in our bed." I rest my head on her pillow and place my arm across my chest, holding her close. Her hair's messy and mascara smeared, having crashed at three in the morning.

"Tell me the truth. Is your back really okay?"

"It is. Did you see him run off after he stabbed me? He knew he was in the wrong. Most men don't act like pussies, they stand their ground and defend themselves. They won't admit they've done anything wrong, but he knew. He was fully aware that mistake could cost his life. He fucking ran."

"Well, I can't believe he came back... he followed us

into the suite. And my mother told me on the phone last night that he's heartbroken over this."

"Good."

"I know." She gazes at the ceiling with her forearm over her head. "Is that the first time?"

"What?"

"That you let someone go."

"Who said I let him go? He's still dead."

"Mark, be serious."

"Alright, it's like Jack said, I thought it, only he was man enough to step forward and say it... hurting Sam would be hurting you." I kiss the back of her hand once, twice, then rest it next to my face to smell her skin. "And I won't hurt you... except when I'm an ass and cuff you to a chair, but you should be getting used to that by now."

"How could I not expect that from such a hot-headed, controlling, man-imal." She laughs.

"True. But just remember, your dad's fucked if he hurts you or anyone else. I can handle a corkscrew in the back, nothing else. He's not touching any of you."

"He won't."

"After seeing him run off like a baby, I know you're right. Fuck, I can't believe I didn't pull it out of my back right then and there and stick it in his neck."

"You didn't know what it was. I didn't either. I only saw his arm swing forward and the ice bucket drop. I'm just glad I was tagging behind you."

"Hey, did you want something when you did that?"

"Just another kiss without Cove and Sophia watching.

The one you gave me was way tame."

"Like this?" I kiss her lightly, making a *smooch-smooch* noise.

"Yeah. That sucks."

"How's this?" I roll on top of her, hold her jaw, and press my lips to hers, giving her a long, wholehearted kiss.

"Better... and thank you. You've killed for me, but this time you stepped away because of me. That's pretty fucking cool. It truly is love."

I unzip my pants, uncomfortable from being confined and needing to reposition the brute. "You're driving me mad. How about oral? No fucking, just give me head and I'll finish what we started yesterday when my hands were cuffed... I love eating you out." My tongue swipes my lips, taking another crack at having some pussy fun.

"Nope." She zips me up. "What time is it anyway? Eleven?"

"I'm on my lunch break so it's twelve-thirty."

"What?" She pushes me off and jumps out of bed. "You've been at work all morning? And you didn't call and wake me? And the wedding! Oh my God! I was supposed to meet Sophia at noon so we could fix one another's hair."

"I just saw her. Told her you were probably still asleep."

"I can't believe I slept this late!"

"You needed to after such a long night." I sit up and straighten the bed, watching her move frantically about the room, grabbing a dress from the closet and clean underwear. "How about the black lace pair? I like those."

"Please tell me you're taking the afternoon off." She tosses the underwear back in the drawer, looking for the black ones.

"Of course I am."

"Good, make sure you dress well."

"Excuse me? I know what to wear to these things. Jules, slow down, you're going nuts."

"It's late!"

"Just shower and dry your hair and slip into the dress. That should take thirty minutes, tops."

"I'm not a man! I've got to prep. I need to shave and—"

"Shave what?"

"My legs!"

I look down and shake my head. "They look fine to me."

"I have stubble! And I need to do my makeup! And my hair! I'm late with my hair!"

"Chill. Is this what I have to look forward to for our wedding?"

"Yes!" She runs into the bathroom, turning on the shower. "Find something to wear!" she calls out. "I want to approve it!"

"Approve it? No. You are *not* dressing me."

"Wear black."

"I always do!" God, sometimes she can be such a woman. Fuck, not sometimes, all the time. "I was going to wear one of my black Jameson Hotel robes—the one with the gold stitching. Elegant, swanky, and easy access after the 'I do's' for the two of us to fuck. Just untie and go."

I look to the bathroom doorway, hearing a tapping foot on the tile floor. Yep, arms crossed, mouth twisted, brows furrowed... "What?" I ask.

"You're such a romantic. Get dressed. Wear the Armani."

"Ah, how predictable. Why don't I wear a sign around my neck that says 'I've fallen into the groove of human boredom.'"

"What is with you this morning? Lack of sex? Is all that sperm building up, making it's way to your head, drowning what few brain cells you have left?"

"Yep."

"Mark!"

I chuckle and open the closet door, thumbing through my suits, coming across one that has a Christmas gift for her in the front packet. I place the small box in my pants and walk out. "Just trying to make you laugh. It's going to be a great day, I can tell already. It's forty-five degrees, the sun's out, birds are singing..."

"Okay, enough. You sound like a girl."

"... your tits are in need of a good fuck, your ass, pussy, and mouth too. Perhaps an ear."

"Now that sounds more like you. Don't forget my armpit, you wouldn't want to pass up a good armpit fuck."

"Never."

The shower door closes as a text sounds on my cell.

Cove. I wonder if he's this frenzied too.

Hey. You there?

No. I reply.

Funny. What's your song?

Huh?

Soph and I have a song. U wanna dance with Jules after ours? YOUR song?

I think for a moment, sending something clever back to him. *I'm a troll. Fol-de-rol.*

Fucktard. He responds.

OK... Centerfold, J. Geils Band.

Holy old school. U weren't even born yet. So NOT classy. Think about Jules.

Easy... Super Freak, Rick James.

Cut the shit.

Hold on then.

"Jules! Cove's getting some tunes together for the wedding. What song do you want to dance to?" I step into the shower room and place my hand on the misted glass, watching her blurred body as she shaves her legs. Only small glimpses of her flesh can be seen through the rising steam and clouded door... a hip, a moment later a breast, then the back of her neck, all beautifully arousing. I request a better view once the blade is back on the caddy. "Give me a window so I can see you."

She uses her middle finger to wipe the fog, playfully sticking out her tongue when I peer inside.

"Thanks. Anyway, did you hear me? A song for the wedding. It sounds like we have the second dance."

"Oh! *My Humps.* The Black Eyed Peas."

"Fuck that. I'll think of something on my own if you're tossing out chick music. Sounds like he doesn't want anything old school anyway."

"If it's *our* dance, it shouldn't matter what Cove wants. I say screw him and tell him what *you* like."

"Good point. How come you don't have a song for us? That's a woman thing."

"I beg your pardon?" The water stops and she grabs a towel from outside the door, drying off before wrapping her hair, turban style. "Since you were acting sweet earlier, I bet you can come up with one."

"If you'd stop acting all mannish, you'd already have one. Get in the mood. Put on something pink and paint your nails all sparkly and shit, I bet the song will come to you."

"Fuck off... why haven't you changed?" she asks.

"Fuck off yourself. Because I still have an hour and forty-five minutes. In man years, that's like two days."

"Man years? Like dog years? See, there's something really weird about you today. If it's not from lack of sex, maybe it has something to do with walking away from murdering my dad... wow, that sounds so crazy, doesn't it? Gee, thanks for not killing my dad," she says satirically. "You *are* a changed man, now think of something that reminds you of our year together and that can be our song."

"Perfect. *Stupid Hoe* by Nicki Minaj it is."

"If you text him that, then tell him I want Lady

Gaga's *Bad Romance*."

"How about *She Bangs*?"

"*Blah Blah Blah* by Ke$ha is my response to that!"

"Okay." I think for a moment. "I suppose we can agree on Jimmy Buffett's *Why Don't We Get Drunk and Screw* since that's how we spend all of our days."

"That can't be the title of a song." She applies deodorant and puts on her bra.

"It's before your time... and mine, shit, I just thought of one that will work." I text him my request, refusing to tell her what it is, she'll catch on when she hears it. "By the way, Jimmy gets bonus points for that drunk, screwing song. The lyrics mention that he buys a waterbed. The ultimate lovemaking machine, just a few rocks and the waves do all the work."

"Yuck. Sounds like it's right out of a bad porno... bow-chicka-wow-wow! I'd be gone, out the door if you owned one of those."

"Mental note made—another way to end our relationship if you get outta line. Bring home a waterbed and watch you flee. That's a hell of a lot easier than burying you under my garage."

She pinches my cheek, letting me know she's enjoying my lively mood. "Let's check your wound before you change into your outfit for the wedding."

My shirt's lifted and the bandage removed. She wets a washcloth and proceeds to clean the small hole.

"I got screwed."

"That you did," she says in a focused tone, her head

lowered, poking around the area. "I think it needs a few stitches."

"Still bleeding?"

"A little. The flesh looks mangled, like it was twisted through a meat grinder."

"In a way, that's what happened."

"Give me the medical kit and I'll make you brand spanking new again."

She takes the needle to the dresser, sterilizing the tip with my lighter, ready to thread.

"I like this... you and me, together. It's good," I say when she walks back to the bathroom.

"It's always good when no one else is around."

"That's what turns our lives to shit, interacting with other people."

"We can't live in a cave."

"Hmm. Maybe a house in the woods?"

"That's what the Jameson is, a castle in the pines." After three needle piercings, she pulls the suture, snips, and ties it, placing a small bandage over the area and patting me on the side when she's finished. "You want a sucker?"

"What I want is for you to open this." I take out the small red box, the gift I picked up from the closet when I was thumbing through my suits. "An early Christmas present."

Her hands shake and lips are tight in excitement. "Last time you gave me a gift this size it was my engagement blade... is it another weapon? Or a necklace?

Can't be a ring. That's unlike you. Must be a sex toy. Another thimble vibrator?"

"Not saying. Just open it."

The black bow is tugged and comes undone. She lifts the red velvet lid and takes out a slip of paper. "What is this?" She unfolds it curiously. "An address?"

"Ours."

"What? Land?"

My head shakes, no.

"You bought us a house!"

"No." I raise my hand. "Wait. Before you get too excited, I bought a getaway cabin. One day a week, you can have the distance you need away from my luxury hotel. Go off on an escape. That's what it is, an *escape*. Thirty minutes from here, higher up in the mountains, still a nice view of the lake... four acres. Small but charming, and you can be away from the hundreds of people who stay here each night."

"No fucking way!" she screams, jumping into my arms. "This is amazing! I can't believe you broke down and did this for me! Holy shitballs. Oh my God!"

I knew she'd love it.

"You're coming with me though. It's *ours*, not mine. *Our* retreat?"

"You and me, endless nights of hot sex in *our* new place. I can't wait."

"Sounds perfect. Oh, I can't wait to see it! Does it have electricity?"

"What?" I laugh. "Maybe I shouldn't have called it a

cabin. It's a home, a log cabin home. It has everything you'd find in a house downtown, minus the noise. Like I said, we'll take off one night a week and return here in the morning, spend the holidays there too."

"Two nights a week?"

"Maybe."

"And what about Jack?"

"Short term, I'm gonna let him spend Christmas Eve at the ski resort. I saw on his Facebook feed that Emma's having a party at her cabin. He's bitching that he can't go. I thought it would be a fun gift for him, and it will give us some time alone. If he doesn't do anything foolish that night, like get so piss ass drunk he can't stand, then maybe he can stay with his friends on the nights we spend at the cabin."

"Incredible. Thank you." She gives me a kiss and grins wildly. "This is beyond anything I'd ever imagined." Her hands run down my chest. "Especially you."

"Alright, that's enough. We're both starting to sound like a couple of starry-eyed twats." I smack her ass, heading back to the closet when someone knocks. "Bet that's Sophia."

"Can you get it and tell her to come upstairs? Then explain to me what a starry-eyed twat is?"

I whistle on my way down, stopping for a quick shot of bourbon. Hell, two shots of bourbon. It's a wedding. I'm getting drunk.

"Mark, let her in!"

Too late, Sophia uses the keypad and lets herself in,

hurrying past me with Angie and a blonde in tow. Must be Jules' friend, Michelle. They're wearing identical mid-length black dresses, likely what they picked up in Reno, and they already have their hair done. I didn't realize this was gonna be such a production.

The door to the bathroom's closed when I get back upstairs. High-pitched voices and loud bursts of laughter explode over a whirring hairdryer. This is what it must be like to have teenage girls, only these are grown women. I wonder if they've already hit the bottle, like me.

I dress in my finest black suit, finger comb my hair; put on cufflinks and a dab of cologne. I'm set. Check, check, and check.

I hear the words *cake, rings, sex,* and *cabin* on my way to the entryway door. Chatty, gossipy women.

Girl talk. Time to get the fuck out of here.

"Well, look at you," I say to Jack, watching him slip out the suite door right behind me. "Nice suit."

He straightens his tie, swipes his sleeves, and tugs on the bottom of the jacket. "Stylish?"

"And mature."

"Where to?"

"A stroll. Making the rounds."

He follows a few feet behind as I walk the second floor corridor. I stop at the tables, fixing the pine branches, noticing he's watching my every move. When I straighten, he straightens another table. If I pick up a piece of fuzz from the carpet, he looks for one too. I adjust a wall sconce and walk by another that has a burned out bulb, pointing with a whisper to get it replaced. He points and whispers to have it replaced.

"You bored?" I ask.

"Curious."

"This isn't what I do. It's just a spot check. My job's down in the office eight hours a day, sometimes ten."

I continue walking, inspecting everything in all the spaces, checking the pool, dressing areas, weight room, and ending in the lobby. I sit in one of the club chairs and cross my legs while Jack joins me in a chair to my left. Cove strolls in with his sons, the three well-dressed in suits like us. He sits in a chair to my right while the boys keep busy, trying to guess the number of ornaments on the tree.

"Three men, next to a blazing fire in the middle of the Sierra Nevada Mountains, got our guns ready, waitin' to kill us a bear," I say in my best western cowboy drawl.

"I feel like a mobster," Jack says, leaning back with one arm over the back of the chair. "Cowboys are lame, Dad. We're all in black suits, and you're the boss of the family, sitting between us. Uncle Cove and I will protect you from any gangsters that come through the door."

I pull him closer and tousle his hair out of love. "Whattaya think, Cove?"

He snaps at Dax to come out from under the tree before saying, "I think cowboys are crude, mob bosses are brutal, and business men in well-tailored suits who care about their futures, their wives, and what their vibrant sons are going to become as they grow older, are refined."

I pat his knee and mutter, "I can always depend on

my little brother-in-law to shine a light on what's important. Are you doing okay? You ready?"

"Everything's happening so fast. I don't remember feeling this way when we got married in the courthouse. The boys are all sugared up from Christmas cookies, Sophia's in a rush, and there're women here I've never even met."

"That's what weddings are like. Everyone's racing around and the whole day becomes a blur. You'll remember half of it."

We sit back and admire the afternoon lunch rush, watching the guests come and go, either on their way downtown or to my restaurant. I realized years ago that I'll never know the majority of these people. They pay to use one of my beds for a night then disappear in the morning. I guess in some ways that makes me a pimp. I make a buck selling beds. Kind of ironic considering my dad paid people to fuck in them.

"Wow, did you—"

"I see 'em," I reply to Cove, noticing the women heading to the restaurant. "They cleaned up well, at least mine did."

"I wouldn't repeat that in front of them unless you want a heel up your ass."

"More than one heel, I'm sure."

The twins run ahead as Jack lags behind on our way to the private room in the restaurant. I'm reminded of what a difference a few years makes with these kids. "The never-ending balls of energy will soon become girl-crazed, social media obsessed, drooling, zombies. Then they'll move out of the house and you'll wish you had your zombies back, because having a zombie around is better than nothing." I nod toward our crew of kids. Jack's nose is planted in his cell and his middle finger flies high. "Lower it for now. You can flip me off once we're in the private room."

"You worried about Sam?" Cove asks.

"Not one bit. What's he gonna do next time? Slap me silly with a butter knife? The guy's stuck in the past. Not like we can't relate, you and me. But I think we're finally stepping out of the boots that have been stuck in that mud hole for years."

He nods in agreement.

"Sam's freakin' lucky I had just returned from the station and didn't have any weapons on me. Otherwise, I would've turned and stuck my blade in his head, no questions asked."

"Yeah?" he asks with an inquisitive look. "So you still want to kill him, even if he steps away? Even after what Jack said? You angry? Because after I ate breakfast with him yesterday, when he apologized and explained the bind he was in back then, he started reminding me of my dad, but then the fucker stabbed you and now I despise him again. I don't know what I'd do if I were in your position."

"I'm angry, of course." I see Jules ahead in a slim black dress that matches the rest of the women's. Her hair's up with a few strands framing the sides of her face.

She's talking to her mom, and as far as I can tell, Sam's not around. I wink when she turns our way and she winks back. "Let's just say the marching orders he was given last night hurt him more than anything I could've done, and we'll leave it at that."

"So you're through?"

"With what?"

"You know, the whole punishment, vigilante thing."

An enduring laugh yields my answer. I shake my head and pat his back, still the same man I've always been when it comes to defending my loved ones. Men are beasts and I'll put the guys who fuck with us in their place until the day I die.

The twins enter the room and Sophia motions for them to stand on the far end by the window, on the opposite side of the line of women.

"What's the deal? Aren't we supposed to be the ones up there waiting? This is backwards, Cove. Are you walking the aisle? Or is Soph? And I thought for sure she'd ask me to give her away."

My cell rings as he responds, "It's a second wedding so I'd say anything goes. We didn't practice, so it's whatever she wants, I guess. Besides, there's no aisle to walk down."

The call's from my lawyer—a guy that's worked for me for over a decade. I let it go to voicemail while Cove and I stand in the doorway, trying to figure out what the hell we're supposed to do.

Jack walks past, looks around, and leans against the

back wall, still texting. I shoot a short whistle to put the cell away, only to hear mine ring a second time. Lawyer again.

"You should turn that off," Cove says.

I gaze at the screen, wondering what's up. It's unusual for him to be calling. "I'm gonna take this, give me a sec."

"What? It's my wedding, you dipshit."

"Just hold on."

He walks ahead with a sigh, joining the women next to the window that overlooks the lake. Sophia takes his hand and the two of them stand together, watching me, waiting for me. Jules glares with her *get your ass over here* face. And Jack decides to take the position next to Cove. The line is set. They're ready.

I hold a finger in the air, answering the call.

"Hello?"

"Mark, it's Ron Mulligan, over at—"

"I know. What's up? I'm busy right now, so make it fast."

"Yes, okay." It sounds like papers are rustling on his desk before he continues. "I was calling about Paul's will."

"What? What about it?"

"First, I apologize for this slip up."

"What fucking slip up is that?"

"Again, let me start by saying my office apologizes for this. We were recently in the process of digitizing all of our older cases when one of my administrative assistants brought this to my attention. A video was never given to you. It's from Paul."

"What, like one of those, *if you're watching this, that means I'm already dead,* things? Is that what it is?" My heart starts racing.

"Yes. I can email you the file right now if you'd like. We've transferred the outdated DVD to our digital files and you'll be able to view it on your computer."

"You should've fucking given it to me over a decade ago. What the hell? How the fuck could you miss such a thing?" I try not to raise my voice, since the entire room is watching. Jules gestures that I need to get my ass moving while the minister checks his watch. Cove and Sophia are facing me, holding hands and waiting impatiently to begin. Even Jack's got his arms crossed, tapping his foot.

"Mark?" Ron says.

I stare at Sophia, watching a bouquet of Christmas lilies fluttering in her nervous hand. The movement resembles a heartbeat, pulsating as she waits. Her brown hair's in a bun and her chestnut brown eyes, the ones that are carbon copies of Paul's, are lively and bright. She's biting the corner of her bottom lip, trying to hold in her excitement.

"Mark, I'm emailing this to you now, okay?"

And Cove... his expression is confident, full of energy and spirit. I've never seen such a powerful stance from him before. Devotedly, he smiles at his wife and squeezes her hand in a loving gesture.

The email sounds and I end the call, hanging up on Ron to open the message. Fuck, I can't believe it's him.

"Mark. We're waiting," Jules pleads.

I tap the screen, seeing a still image of my dad sitting with a cigar in one hand and a glass of liquor in the other. A red play button covers his face—suggestive of blood from the spot where he was shot. My finger hovers over the screen...

"Mark," another plea.

My head lifts to Jules then to the rest of my family. Silver painted birch twigs strung with white lights form an arch above them... the arch... my strength and support, my beginning and end. My nephews kick red lily petals lying beneath their feet, sending the pieces shooting quickly into the air, and spiraling slowly to the floor... significant to Jules who's mentioned a sign of maturing love is fallen petals. Fucking amazing, the way she set the room so well, nothing too showy, keeping things simple and modest, placing the focus on family, the couple, and love. What could be more important than that?

I turn off my cell and say, "To hell with you," before joining everyone in the soft light of a winter afternoon.

"Sorry," I say, taking a place behind Cove.

He releases Sophia's hand and turns to me, whispering into my ear, "What the fuck was that? Way to hold up the ceremony."

"I guess it's not as bad as being late for my own wedding."

His mouth twitches, the corner lifts, and a smile grows. He steps behind me and Sophia and I are face-to-face. My sister giggles and moves behind Jules, handing her the bouquet.

"It *is* your wedding, dumbass," Cove says, pushing me forward.

Wait... what?

Jules blushes and says, "Hi."

"Hi." I flash a smile.

She steps closer, raising a hand for me to join her.

Dax and Xav let out screams of delight, kicking more petals in the air while saying, "We got you good Uncle Mark."

I gawk, in total disbelief. How the fuck did... and she... and they... damn, they suck. Fooled!

Her finger lifts my chin, helping me to remove my jaw from the floor.

"I take it you're surprised."

"No, I knew all along."

"Sure you did." She takes my arm and we turn to the minister. "I'm sure. You knew *all* along."

I can't hear a word the minister says, my senses ceasing to function... vision blurred... hearing reduced, and sounds muffled... but I can feel Jules' warm and comforting hand in mine. I'm stunned, in a daze until the minister gets to our vows and I watch Jules pass the bouquet to Sophia. She turns back and bumps my arm with a smile. How long was that? Five minutes? She nudges me again, guiding me back to the ceremony.

"... Bride and groom are here on this glorious day to marry one another. No one else's strength of will can create such a union. It is their words, their intentions, their vision that must define and shape this marriage. So I call upon them now to state their promise before this group—the pledges that will bind them together."

I take her hands in mine, about to speak, when I notice she opens her mouth to do the same.

"Go ahead," I say.

"No, sorry, you first."

"No, go. We said if we ever got married we'd say our own vows, so you start."

"No, you speak."

"Jules, you'll complain for the rest of our lives that you wanted to go first, so go."

"Mark, just do it!"

"I told you to."

"Say the vows so I can have some fucking wine," Jack mutters.

"You're not drinking where guests can see you," I say, still holding her hands and admiring her breathtaking features. "Say it," I whisper. "Tell me."

She inhales a deep breath and nods. "I-I Jules." Her nose wrinkles and she sniffs, trying not to cry. She looks down, blows a puff of air, and fans her face. "Okay. Okay. I can do this. Wow." She takes another deep breath and starts again. "I Jules, take you Mark, to be my husband." A single tear runs down her cheek. "To have and to hold from this day forward." She stops and takes another breath, filled with emotion. "Sorry."

"It's okay," I say tenderly, squeezing her hands.

She nods with a lick of her lips and continues. "For better or for worse, for richer or for poorer, in sickness and in health, I promise to love and cherish you… until I can't stand you anymore, at which point I'll have to kill you and feed you to the bears."

The group laughs, even her mom, who likely thinks she's kidding. I drop my shaking head, trying to regain composure. Fuck, I love her.

"Your turn." She shakes my hands.

I swallow hard before I begin. "I, Mark Jameson, take you, Julia Barringer—my Jules, to be my wife." Her face is beautiful under the lighted arch. I pull her closer and set my hand against her cheek, wiping the tear from her face. "I promise to always protect you, princess. I vow to kill any person who fucks with you. And I pledge to continue being the arrogant prick you love." She smiles and kicks my leg playfully. "For better or for worse, for richer or for poorer, in sickness and in health, I promise to love and cherish you… maybe."

"That was perfect," she says as Karina steps forward, handing us a pair of hammered, white gold rings. They look tough, the type of badass ring I enjoy wearing. "She made them," Jules whispers.

"No shit?" I guess everyone's in on this.

"No shit, Mark." Her mom smiles and gives us each a kiss on the cheek.

"Thank you," I say.

"Groom," the minister directs, "as you place this ring on—"

"We got it covered," I tell him, taking her hand. "Let's get this moving so we can get the after-party rolling." I place the ring on her finger... "Welcome to the family, princess. I love you. Now let's fuck."

And she places the ring on my finger... "You're mine. I love *you*. Now let's fuck."

The minister clears his throat and says, "Believe it or not, I've heard worse. Shall we end?"

We nod.

"It's my pleasure to now pronounce you husband and wife. You may kiss the—"

"Groom," she says, moving forward and taking control. Our lips meet and everyone drones, "aww." Our tongues swirl. They wait. We kiss. Everyone waits. We sign the register with Sophia and Cove, still kissing, scribbling our signatures with our arms out, but mouths glued together.

"Gross! Enough!" Jack complains.

Her legs wrap around my waist, making it easier to carry her out.

"Where are they going? I want cake," Xavier says.

"Yeah, I want some fucking cake," Dax adds.

"We'll be right back, don't you dare cut that cake!" Jules calls out. "Five minutes!"

"Don't embarrass me," I say.

"Ten minutes!"

"At least an hour," I shout.

We pass Sam standing by the door. He must've been hiding out back here, and he's damn lucky he behaved. "Hope you're happy," he says. Yeah, well, he *almost* behaved. We ignore him though, not giving a shit.

We rush to the second floor corridor, her taking off her heels while I remove my suit jacket and tie along the way.

"God, that's the type of wedding I've always wanted."

"It's not over yet. We have to go back for the cake and to hang out with everyone. Oh, and dance! What song did you pick? Please tell me."

"The Police, *Every Breath You Take.*"

"You remembered." She takes my hand. "That was the first song I played on your iPod the night you got dragged into the lake with Dayne's body. The night I wrapped you in the comforter to warm your body."

"Fuck, those were good times." I smirk.

"More to come."

"True." I open the door to the suite and we race upstairs. "Get that fucking dress off, quick." I slip out of my shoes, pants and shirt. "Bra and panties too. Everything. Take it all off!" I tug my boxers down and pull her into the bed.

"Hello, Mrs. Jameson. My wife."

"Hi." She smiles.

"Lucky number two." I nestle under her chin and nibble at her neck. "My life's been full of them, but this is the best one yet."

"Hmm?"

"We wed on the twenty-second day of the twelfth month at two in the afternoon—you did that for me. Twelve, twenty-two, at two. You're brilliant. I couldn't have asked for a better woman to spend the rest of my life with." I hover above her, running a hand down the length of her body. My head lowers... and I trace my tongue up the inside of her thigh, through the soft folds of her pussy, and to her tits.

"We're perfect together," she says, her palm resting over my heart.

She smiles... I blush... and my cock rubs over her lips, waiting to feel her wetness.

"Fuck, me." She opens her legs wider, inviting me in.

We stare at one another, my hips moving in slow circles, teasing her arousal.

"Fuck, me," she begs. "Please, fuck me."

I slide in—pouring every ounce of love I have for her into this moment, kissing her fiercely, and thankful that she's mine. Her hands are held high above her head and her body caressed with my lips.

"I love you so much."

My wife.

I spent my whole life fucking like a porn star, but I fuck Jules like I'm her man. Face-to-face so I can revel in her beauty, our lips joined, and her needs of the essence.

"Fuck." I dig into the sheets, my dick overcome with pleasure.

She arches her back and we move in perfect rhythm, maintaining the pace with each slide of my engorged cock. We breathe in gasps, our bodies on fire and sensitive to the increasing tightness of each other's muscles.

"I want you to lose control. Don't just make love to me, fuck me," she says.

My cock twitches and her tongue races into my mouth. I groan, deepening and lengthening my thrusts. Our entire bodies slide along the bed. Every inch of her is straining to stay in control as I deliver a passionate kiss to let go.

"Don't hold back. Cum for me and I'll bring you back to this feeling again later tonight."

She closes her eyes and lifts her hips, rocking into my cock.

"That's it, beautiful." My movements become slow and steady, guiding her to the start of her beating orgasm.

"Oh, Mark!" she cries. "Oh!"

My arms tremble as her pussy explodes around my shaft.

"Keep going, keep going. God, yes!" she shouts.

Her pulsations drive my dick wild, causing me to erupt. I grab her tits, grip at the bedpost, and fuck her madly.

"Yes!" she screams.

"I'm gonna cum," I say, in the last seconds before I explode. From the tip of my cock, down my legs, and up to my neck, my entire body stiffens. One... two... and, "Jules!" I clench and waves of heat surge through my paralyzed body. "Oh, fuck." My toes flare and legs shake as I collapse face down, panting in bliss.

"I love you so much, Mark."

Her soft hands rest on the back of my head, holding me to her chest. She strokes my hair while I move in short glides, staying inside her until the last drop of cum is released.

Our bodies descend into a restful state and I smile when she finger traces a heart onto my shoulder.

"Jesus." I sigh, pulling out and lying by her side. "What a dream. I can't believe you're my wife. Best wedding ever. Short, modest, plus a hot-blooded fuck."

"What now?"

"How about cake?"

"Cake. Then what?" she asks.

"Another fuck and more cake. Maybe a fuck with cake."

"And?"

"Sleep, work, and pussy."

"And?"

"Princess, I love you, but zip it."

"No, say it."

"What?"

"The saying. Your line."

I gaze at our reflections in the mirrored ceiling, placing her hand over my conquered heart. She looks up and waits...

"I'm Mark Jameson."

"Yes, and I'm Jules Jameson." She grins, wrapping her legs around mine.

We're one, and the final words will be spoken together...

"Welcome to *our* hotel."

EPILOGUE

Why the fuck would I watch that video?

I t's not like I don't already know what he'd say—that I was a bastard child, a pussy, and he hated me. An angry rant, exactly what I'd expect from Paul. Who needs to hear that shit again? I refuse to continue torturing myself when I have a beautiful wife and a kickass son to care for. Some things are more important than Paul Jameson.

But Jules watched it; the dominant control freak that she is. She needed to know, mostly because she never met him... and now she understands.

That's what she said after she viewed it too. "It's just him fucking with you and bitching about nothing. You're right; he was cracked in the head. What an abusive bastard. Now I understand."

And that's all that needed to be said. The video was deleted. End of story.

And none of it matters anymore because I won. We all did.

Cove, Soph, and me—we ended up in the perfect

relationships, are loyal to one another, own successful businesses, ones that are legal, plus we have remarkable kids.

And I got Jules.

Freakin' A, I'm the luckiest man alive.

What more could anyone ask for...

...well, I suppose some new sex toys wouldn't be bad... perhaps a leather cat hood for Jules... and I want to get her a Vesper vibrator necklace... oh, and she might like...

ABOUT THE AUTHOR

Aven Jayce was born in Buffalo, NY. She received her undergraduate degree from SUNY Fredonia and her graduate degree from the University of Colorado. Now in her mid-forties, she resigned her position as a college professor to enjoy life as an author, wife, optimistic introvert, and loving mama.

Books by Aven Jayce:

The NOVA Trilogy
Fallen Snow (Book One)
Desert Star (Book Two)
Sunset Rush (Book Three)
The Dark Scarlett (A continuation of NOVA)
Jameson Hotel Series
Long Shot Love Duet

www.facebook.com/AvenJayceAuthor

52269471R00217

Made in the USA
Columbia, SC
28 February 2019